"*Riley and the Great War* is a rollicking good historical novel that will keep the reader turning pages from start to finish. Jim O'Neal is a consummate novelist who knows both the craft and the art of good writing. Highly recommended."

— William C. Hammond,
author of the Cutler Family Chronicles series

See the back of this book for more information
on the Riley series of novels.

RILEY

AND THE

GREAT WAR

Linda,

Hope you
enjoy this —

Jim O'Neal

RILEY
AND THE
GREAT WAR

JAMES ANDERSON O'NEAL

Three Ocean Press
Vancouver, British Columbia

Copyright © 2018 by James Anderson O'Neal

Riley and the Great War is a work of fiction. Names, characters, places, and incidents are either the product of the author's imagination or used fictitiously. Beyond historical characters and events used for purposes of fiction, any resemblance to actual persons, living or dead, or to actual events or specific locales is entirely coincidental.

Library and Archives Canada Cataloguing in Publication

O'Neal, James, 1953-, author
     Riley and the Great War / James O'Neal.
(Tales of the American century)
Issued in print and electronic formats.

ISBN 978-1-988915-03-6 (softcover).--ISBN 978-1-988915-05-0 (ebook)

  I. Title.
PS3615.N42R55 2018   813'.6   C2018-901751-1
                               C2018-901752-X

Poems by Martha Fay Ormiston O'Neal

Copy Editor: Kyle Hawke
Proofreader: Carol Hamshaw
Cover Designer: Maddy Haigh
Book Designer: Patti Frazee
Cover Image: *The Great War* © 2018 Wade Edwards
Author Photo: Kristina Perkins

Three Ocean Press
8168 Riel Place
Vancouver, BC, V5S 4B3
778.321.0636
info@threeoceanpress.com
www.threeoceanpress.com

First publication, May 2018

Contents

For Riley

Prologue
The Columbus Raid

Cornelius

There is clarity in the desert. When the wind is down so the sand stays in place on the ground, everything carries farther than in other climates: sounds, sights, colors.

Watching from the rise overlooking the New Mexico border town of Columbus, Villa could see a great deal, even in the dark purple half-light just before dawn. He saw soldiers walking guard duty at the American fort, looking bored and sleepy. He saw three dogs, worrying at some piece of food he could not see. He saw a light burning in the hotel. On the slope below him, he saw men on horseback—his men, under the command of Pablo Lopez and Candelario Cervantes, ready to charge the fort, awaiting his order. He could even hear the occasional snort from their horses. To the north, in the far distance, he could see men led by Nicolas Fernandez. They were poised to charge the town. They, too, awaited his order.

Why did Villa hesitate? He was hardly musing about the clarity of the desert. That is a luxury for visitors to desert country, not for someone like Villa who had been born and raised with the desert sand and who knew little else. Nor was Villa, by nature, a hesitant man. He was driven by good instinct and bad devils, with hesitation not in his nature.

The Spaniard rode hard up the slope to Villa from the direction of Cervantes' men. His two Yaquis—primitive tribesmen from the north Mexico desert—followed behind. They reined in close to Villa, scattering the sycophants who always surrounded him. Their horses snorted and foamed and gleamed with sweat, for the Spaniard and his Yaquis did not care about their beasts. It was one of many things that made Villa uncomfortable with them and prevented him from trusting them. Yet it could not be denied that the Spaniard had done well since joining Villa. He was a deadly fighter and appeared to be a subtle, yet practical strategist. Still, Villa had learned not to put too much faith in appearances.

The Spaniard slipped off his big stallion and strode to his leader's side.

"All is ready, my commander," he said, in that accented Spanish that betrayed a childhood in Madrid. "Beltran, Fernandez, Cervantes, Lopez: all are in position. It only requires your order."

"And the fort?" Villa asked. "Signs of life? They are awake and alert?"

"They have guards posted, of course. As we knew they would. Nothing more. It is time."

Villa looked him up and down, as he had done many times since the Spaniard had appeared seemingly out of nowhere six months earlier. He was much taller than Villa, who was five-foot-nine and prone to flab around the middle. The Spaniard was well over six feet, muscled beneath his worn serape with a dark, handsome face gazing out from under his hat. He wore the crossed bandoliers affected by many Villista rebels, with a revolver at each hip, a rifle slung across his back, a machete and a club hanging from his belt. What one did not forget about the Spaniard was what Villa looked at now and sometimes saw in his dreams: the man's eyes. They were dead, yet not dead — dead to those warm desires and affections common to most of humanity, yet not fully dead, for deep behind the eyes were glints of amusement, a certain enjoyment of stimuli that Villa could only guess at. Something about those eyes made him not want to guess.

"Do you hesitate, General Villa?"

"It is a big moment, my Spaniard," Villa replied. "Attacking an American fort on American territory and raiding an American village, these are no small things."

Now the Spaniard hesitated. He knew that even at this critical moment, the idiot Villa might stand down. Too big a push, or too little, and he might order his men to fall back. The Spaniard considered his approach.

"No, they are not small things," he agreed. "And you are not a small man." The Spaniard squatted on his haunches, next to where Villa sat on a boulder, feeling the chill of the desert dawn. "There is no decision to make, not anymore, my leader. It was made when the whore Wilson recognized Carranza. It was made when his soldiers helped Obregón defeat you at Agua Prieta, you remember? Most of all, my commander, it was made when you stood up to the Americans as a man and spat on their shoes and told them that because they were not welcome in Mexico, you would not respect their safety."

Villa twitched with the memory.

"It is one thing to say they are not welcome and not safe in Mexico. It is another to cross the border and attack them here, in their country."

"Who says it is their country?" the Spaniard responded heatedly. "They stole it, as they stole what they call Texas and Arizona and California. Fuck the Americans. They must rot in hell. And all Mexico is rising to your banner, for you are the only one to stand up to them. You lost at Agua Prieta, yet our numbers grow. And why? Because you announced to the world that Mexico is for Mexicans and we will never be slaves to the Americans. That is what made you great, my commander. That is why you alone will rule Mexico."

Still, Villa stared vacantly into space, looking to the Spaniard like a cow ruminating dully on its cud. The sun would soon be up. The order must be given. Villa needed a further push, the Spaniard knew.

"It is not only what you have said, my leader. There is also what you have done."

Those words woke Villa from his reverie and caused him to jerk his head toward his lieutenant.

3

"What do you mean?"

"I am thinking of Santa Isabel, my leader," the Spaniard shrugged. "Lopez killed many Americans there. They will not forget."

Villa sprang to his feet, angry.

"Do not blame Pablo for that, Spaniard. You were there. From what I have been told, you started the killing. There was no reason for it, yet you killed those American miners and left them in the sun for the animals. That is why there is no turning back and I did not order that."

The Spaniard shrugged again.

"You seemed pleased at the time, my leader." That was a slight exaggeration, but it would serve. "You wouldn't give Lopez to the gringos, even though they asked for him. And then, you haven't forgotten San Pedro de la Vaca, surely?"

Villa started as though he'd been bitten. He remembered San Pedro de la Vaca. His men had slaughtered seventy-seven villagers whom Villa suspected of being Carranza sympathizers. Villa himself had been caught up with bloodlust. He had shot the head off a troublesome priest who knelt before him in the dirt. In the bloody slaughterhouse that was Mexico in the years of the revolution, this had not been a uniquely violent incident, nor did it seem to matter to most Mexican peasants in the north. Villa remained their hero. But it haunted Villa. It convinced him there was no turning back from the path of violent revolution and no possibility that America would support him over the American-hating Carranza or the quasi-communist Zapata. It also convinced Villa, anti-Catholic though he might be, that he would go to Hell.

"Give the order," the Spaniard said. "You have no alternative."

Villa glared at him and then wheeled around to again peer down the slope, toward the town laid out before him. After a moment, he pulled his pistols from his belt and waved them at the horsemen who sat, waiting for his signal to gallop to the soldiers in the field and pass them the order to attack.

Villa fired his pistols in the air.

"*Adelante!*"

The couriers spurred their beasts and rode down the hill, some veering to the right to the nearby troops of Lopez and Cervantes, others to the left for the longer ride to Fernandez and Beltran. The Spaniard lingered a moment to gaze admiringly at Villa, who stood breathing hard, staring at the scene below him. It was unfortunate, the Spaniard mused, that Villa had fired off his pistols. The shots had been unnecessary and they might have alerted the fort. Still, if that was what Villa required to find the courage to attack the United States, it was worth the indiscretion.

"I'm proud of you, my commander," said the Spaniard. "*Viva Villa!*"

He gracefully swung onto his stallion, gestured to his Yaquis, and the three of them galloped away. Villa realized he had no idea where they were going, as it had never occurred to him to give the Spaniard instructions on where to be during the battle. The Spaniard would do as he wished.

Villa sat back down on the rock, staring at the fort. Still no sign of activity. He waved away an old woman who offered him a drink of water. She did not offer tequila, as all knew that Villa did not drink spirits. Villa wondered idly what the next few hours would bring, but it hardly mattered. He was a bandit from Chihuahua, a desert rat, leading a troop of hungry and untrained peasants onto American soil in an attack on one of the greatest powers on earth. As the Spaniard said, he had no alternative. Alternatives must be for the rich, Villa thought. He felt he never had any alternatives at all.

Several hours later, Susan Moore was also looking down a slope, toward Columbus, just a few miles from where Villa sat. She was watching the town burn.

Susan had been a spinster in New York City. "Spinster" was a universally recognized, highly specific term in those days, one which defined and limited a person as much as a term like "whore" has always done. She had reached her late thirties without finding either religion or a man. In desperation, she'd left New York for El Paso, to find an old sweetheart named John Moore. John was nothing special as a man, but she had felt he was a man who might take her into his life. As it turned out, he had, and they'd married. But El Paso wasn't sufficiently godforsaken for John's taste, so they found themselves in Columbus, where they'd bought a dry goods store a few miles southwest of town, almost on the Mexican border. What in the name of God had possessed a couple from New York not only to move to a dusty hole in the universe like Columbus, but then to start up a store selling clothes and hardware—not even on the shithole main street of Columbus, but miles out into the desert on the Mexican border—was anyone's guess. Some blind faith in freedom and individualism and opportunity overtook the entire United States during the nineteenth century and there was no reasoning with it. People like the Moores were scattered all over the American West and their spirit lives in the hardscrabble, anti-intellectual, lower middle class of America today.

Susan and John had laid out their clothes carefully the night before, knowing that a Villa raid was anticipated by the entire town. They slept on the porch overlooking Columbus, but not that much sleeping was done.

Early in the morning, they heard the pistol shots, signaling the raid. They saw the Villistas charge the fort and the town, and they saw what little resistance there was in town quickly wiped out. The town was slaughtered. Because no soldiers had been posted to protect the village of Columbus, the Villistas rode through town shooting up the place and killing civilians at will. The soldiers in the fort, however, were able to fend off the invaders and mount a respectable counterattack. Or that was how it appeared to the Moores, sitting on the porch in their nightclothes.

John told Susan to get dressed. As they donned their clothes with the sun rising, the sounds of gunfire became more infrequent. They could see fires burning throughout the town, with the highest pillar of flame shooting up from the hotel. John held his shotgun in his arms and stood on the porch, waiting. In the distance, a Mexican appeared, his horse slowly plodding up the slope toward him. Then another Mexican appeared, and then another and another until there was a file of them. John didn't move. Susan stood behind him. She thanked God they had no children.

Out of the town, out of the smoke, rode more men. As they came closer, John could make out a bandit riding alongside two Indians. They did not look like they were from any of the local tribes. Susan, and even John, still had enough New York in them that their concepts of time and space were out of joint. It seemed that they watched the bandit and the Indians approach them for a very long time. Susan knew that was how it was in this country. Something or someone would appear on the horizon, you would watch and watch and watch, then suddenly whatever it was would arrive and, in a whirlwind, life would change forever. That was what was coming now.

The leader became more distinct as he drew near. He wore the crossed bandoliers of a bandit. Over them, a cape flapped backward in the wind. Rather than the classic Mexican sombrero, he wore a soft slouch hat an American cowboy might wear. Susan saw the bullwhip tucked under the horn of his saddle and, as he got closer, she saw the long and pointed mustache on his face and the beads of sweat on his horse. She didn't look much at the Indians. The bandit was enough.

At length, the three riders entered the yard and reined in at the porch. Everywhere, there was the stench of sweat and hot horse. John hadn't moved, didn't point his gun at them. In the near distance, more Villistas were coming up the slope.

"Good morning, my friend." The tall leader spoke Spanish with an accent Susan had never heard. "You are John Moore. I have heard of your store."

"We're not open," John replied gruffly, praying silently for courage.

"You will pardon my accent, I hope." The bandit smiled. "I am not Mexican, I am from Spain. You speak Spanish very well, señor. Or so I've been told."

Susan did not like the implication that this Spaniard had any interest in John, who shrugged.

"We have had a long morning already," the Spaniard said. "We have been only partly successful. Perhaps there is a little more to do."

By this time, the Spaniard and his Indians had been joined by five or six Villistas, men who had been driven back at the fort and were in a mood for trouble. The Spaniard sat back in the saddle and considered John Moore. A big man at six-foot-four, John was close to the Spaniard's height and probably twenty pounds heavier. He moved well and stood his ground, a man who knew his center of balance. The Spaniard was happy to see that John was no stranger to the art of fighting.

"Señor Moore, I have something to propose to you. I would like you to put down your shotgun and step off the porch so we can talk."

"I can hear you fine from here."

"Ah, but that was not my point." The Spaniard smiled and slid off his horse. "Mr. Moore, it is a bad morning for you. You look like a man who knows how to take care of himself, a man who knows how to use his hands. You are holding a shotgun, facing eight armed men. Behind you stands your wife, a fine-looking woman who, I can assure you, will be raped by each of these gentlemen behind me if I don't stop them. You may think you can kill me, though I assure you that will not happen. Even if you were to accomplish such a feat, you could not kill all these gentlemen behind me." The Spaniard took a few steps closer to Moore, holding his eyes. "There is one chance that you will survive and your wife will neither be raped nor killed in the next few minutes. Would you like to know what that chance is?"

John was trembling so much the gun was shaking in his hands. It was obvious to one and all that he would not be shooting anyone today. Susan held her breath, watching.

"I will give you this one chance," the Spaniard said smoothly. "While I was living in Madrid, I studied your sport of boxing. It is a sport more for Englishmen and gringos, of course, but I tried to learn. I found it enlightening."

Susan wondered what sort of bandit would so carefully distinguish Englishmen from gringos.

"And so, Mr. Moore, here is your one chance. Put down your shotgun and step off the porch. Put up your hands and fight with me, here in front of your home. If you win, I give you my word, my men will ride away and leave you and your wife at peace."

"And if you win?"

"I'm sure the answer is obvious to you, Mr. Moore. I will beat you to death and my men will have their way with your wife until she is dead. But that will happen anyway, if you refuse to fight me. Take your opportunity, Mr. Moore." He smiled. "It is the American way, is it not?"

Susan didn't tremble. She knew that if John fought this Spaniard, he would be killed. She knew that if he didn't fight the Spaniard, he would be killed. She knew the Spaniard knew it too. She wasn't sure what John knew. She didn't tremble. She couldn't even move.

John seemed similarly frozen, at first. Suddenly, he dropped the shotgun and leapt off the porch, landing on the Spaniard and pitching him backward until both lost their balance and rolled onto the ground. In an instant, the Spaniard pushed John away and jumped to his feet. John followed suit, his eyes wild. The Spaniard dropped his cape and hat and raised his fists, nodding at John to do the same. They circled each other. By now, the sun was well up in the sky. The Villistas dismounted and crowded around the fighters. Susan did not think to run.

Circle, circle, circle. John launched a roundhouse punch that the Spaniard easily avoided. Another. Circle, circle. The Spaniard skipped around and around John, waiting for his move. He was disappointed. The two punches John had thrown had exhausted the shopkeeper's imagination. This was not good sport. The Spaniard dropped his right shoulder, feinted with his right and jabbed with the left. Again. And again. Three jabs landed on Moore's chin and he went staggering back. The Spaniard nodded sadly, disappointed by the quick outcome. He nodded at one of the Yaquis, who tossed him a cloth bag with something heavy in it.

"Señor Moore, I fear boxing is not your sport." He reached into the cloth bag and pulled out something heavy, something made of iron. He tossed it to Moore. "Put this on, señor. I am curious to see how it works. They are a pair, but you will wear one and I the other."

He took the remaining weapon from the bag. It was a curious metal band, quite heavy, like a dog collar spiked with diamond-shaped points of iron. The Spaniard threw the bag back to his Yaqui and placed the device over his right hand. John, seeing what was coming, shook his head and threw away his matching weapon.

"As you wish," said the Spaniard.

The small crowd of onlookers drew closer in, some chuckling, all of them anticipating the kill. The Spaniard and John Moore again circled each other, feinting. Susan clutched the porch rail tighter, still unable to move.

One, two, three. The Spaniard ducked his head, threw a left and drove in with the right. The blades crashed into John's face. One blow and his brains lay splattered upon the metal knuckles. John was dead before he hit the ground. There was no surprise, no thrill, no emotion. Even Susan just stood there, numb. This was simply what was going to happen from the moment the Spaniard appeared.

The Spaniard moved first, gesturing to the Yaqui to toss him the bag. He wiped the blood and brains off his knuckle device while the Yaqui retrieved the other one. Back they both went into the now-bloody bag. The Spaniard mounted his horse. He looked at Susan, then at the men. He pointed at Susan.

"*Para ustedes*," he said, and he was gone.

They stared at her. It seemed at least a minute before one of the Villistas stepped forward.

"Señora," he said. "You have gold? Money?"

Susan took a moment. Her husband was dead. She was on the verge of rape and death no matter what she did. The Villistas slowly approached the porch while the Yaquis remained where they were, unsure of their entitlement to the white woman.

"Inside," she managed, pointing into the house. "What I have is inside."

Susan backed into her home, followed by the first Villista. The rest followed close behind. They were sufficiently intrigued by the prospect of Susan and her gold that they did not see the pistol lying flat on the table. Susan seized it and started firing, indiscriminately, until six shots had been discharged and the chamber clicked empty. Cursing, the Mexicans dove this way and that. Susan dropped the gun and ran out the back door, ran for her life into the desert. She had no thoughts, no plan, just the running. Shots flew past her ears and raised puffs of dirt at her feet. She felt a burn in her leg, another in her hip. No matter. She just kept running and she ran until her legs gave out and she collapsed onto the ground and rolled under a mesquite bush, where she waited to die. When the pain overwhelmed her, she slipped into unconsciousness.

Susan Moore was rescued by soldiers from the fort, out searching for Villistas. Years later, when a commission was established to allow American victims of the revolution to claim compensation from the Mexican government, Susan Moore was awarded $13,310. She received the award in 1938, twenty-two years after the Spaniard beat her husband to death.

Part One

Independence

1

The Notebooks of
Grandpa Jimmy

Jim

Riley was my grandfather on my mother's side. He was born on May 6, 1898. He died on October 18, 1993. Every day in between, he was a tough son of a bitch.

I hardly knew Riley while I was growing up. Maybe once a year, sometimes twice, we'd visit my mother's parents or they would visit us. Often, Riley wasn't even there, just his wife, my grandmother Marta. Riley was always a little bit of a mystery to us grandchildren. His presences were never explained, any more than his absences. He wouldn't be there, then he would, always smoking, usually holding a bourbon in his hands, never saying much. My parents called him "Daddo," which I guess is an Irish name for Grandpa. We never called him anything.

He wasn't anything like Grandpa Jimmy, even though everyone said they were best friends from long before Grandpa Jimmy's son (my father) married Riley's daughter (my mother). Grandpa Jimmy was James Cornelius O'Neal; Riley was Walter Ira Riley. Both men came from Independence, Missouri, just like Harry Truman. Grandpa Jimmy was fun, friendly, talkative, fascinating: everything you'd dream of in an

Irish grandpa. It wasn't that we grandkids were scared of Daddo, exactly. We could tell he "loved us," like grown-ups talked about, whatever that meant. But Grandpa Jimmy lit up any room he happened to be in, at least until he grew old and his mind began to slip. Riley just came and went, like a spell of weather, with no explanation.

I never really got to know Riley until Grandpa Jimmy's funeral in 1991. The family gathered for a memorial at Riley's house, even though Grandpa Jimmy was to be buried in his beloved New York. Grandmother Marta had died years earlier. The house, in a village in Mexico where Marta had grown up, smelled musty and old, just like Riley. He was still as I remembered him: short, lean, wiry, with a downturned mustache, deeply tanned skin, and a shock of white hair. Always the cigarette, always the bourbon, almost never talking.

I'm not much for funerals and I'm not much for family gatherings. I went to the funeral because it was Grandpa Jimmy and I have wonderful memories of him, and because since I live in Minnesota, a trip to Mexico in January makes a funeral sound like a vacation. We planned to stay on for a few days after the ceremony, baking the cold out of our bodies. There's something a bit surreal about going to a funeral on Sun Country Airlines, surrounded by tourists drinking tequila and cursing their children.

Riley lived at the Ortega hacienda, the long-time homestead of Marta's family. It was located outside of Chihuahua, south of Ciudad Juarez, the old homeland of Pancho Villa. That meant nothing to me except, first, it was damn hard to get to and, second, family lore said that Riley met Marta in 1916 when he was in Pershing's army, chasing Villa around the Mexican desert. Apparently Riley was luckier than Pershing, who never caught Villa.

We were all assembled in the large great room at the hacienda. As I remember it, there was my whole family: my wife Sally and my young children Anne, Jonathan, and Peter. My father, Grandpa Jimmy's son Walter Hal, and my mother, Riley and Marta's daughter Fern Arlys, were both there. And there were the expected assortment of relatives, not many, as Riley only had the one daughter and Grandpa Jimmy had just one son.

My father made a toast to his father, otherwise it was a pretty quiet affair. Food was laid out on the long table, but no one seemed very interested. Riley stood in the corner, smoking. I talked trivialities with my brother Mike.

"You'd have thought Grandpa Jimmy would have a bigger funeral," he said to me. "All those years out east, he knew everybody there was. You'd think they'd show up."

I knew better.

"He lived too long. You want a lot of people at your funeral, die young. Everybody comes then. If you're in your eighties or nineties, everyone you really knew is dead, so… Oh, hi, Daddo. How you holding up?"

Riley had appeared, silently, at my elbow. I only knew he was there from the cigarette smell.

"How you boys doing?"

"Good," I said. "I'll miss Grandpa Jimmy, though. I knew what he meant to you. It must be hard."

There was a long pause, one that I came to know and even expect during the next two years.

"Can you come with me for a minute?"

Mike, who was far more polite and more tolerant of old folks than I ever have been, moved as though to go with Riley.

"No, Mike," Riley said. "If you don't mind, I want to talk with Jimmy for a minute."

Christ, I've always hated being called Jimmy. My mother called me that when I was young, but otherwise it was just Riley and Grandpa Jimmy who did. Riley took my elbow and pulled me along into the room by the staircase that served as a sort of study.

I didn't know it then, but I was to come to know every square inch of that room. It was about eight by eleven. There was an old desk with a swivel chair, a worn leather sofa with an easy chair facing it. On the floor was a faded, but beautiful, rather ornate flowered rug that must have been a holdover from the glory days of the Ortega hacienda. Otherwise, the room was all Riley: spare, worn, redolent of tobacco and whiskey, sure of what it was and how it got that way, uninterested in frills. On the desk was a bottle of Jim Beam bourbon, a pack of cigarettes, a small globe, some papers, and an old ink blotter. A lovely portrait of Marta, looking wistful, hung on the wall behind the desk. On the outside walls, floor-to-ceiling windows looked out on the desert, where a dog was chasing tumbleweed like it might have been doing when Riley first came to Chihuahua.

Riley waved me to a seat on the leather sofa. He took a cigarette out of the pack and poured two glasses of bourbon, one of which he handed to me. He sat on the easy chair across from me and stared at me for at least two minutes. Then he spoke.

"Grandpa Jimmy and I went back a long way."

So that was it. He needed to unburden himself of some memories.

He got up and walked to his desk. Bending over, he slid a large, seemingly heavy box out from underneath and heaved it up onto the desktop.

"What's that, Daddo?"

"Don't call me that. Your grandmother told the family to call me that because she read it somewhere, but it never sounded right to me. If we're going to do this, you have to just call me Riley."

Not much to say to that except, "Do what?"

Riley shoved the box across the desk.

"Open it."

I opened the top. Inside were a number of large spiral-bound notebooks, the sort that I used in school before everyone got computers. With the number of single-spaced pages within, they could hold a lot of material. They didn't appear to be in very good shape.

"Look at them."

I opened the first notebook, a red one. A crabbed but legible handwriting filled every inch of white space. I read the first sentences:

> There is clarity in the desert. When the wind is down so the sand stays in place on the ground, everything carries farther than in other climates: sounds, sights, colors. Watching from the rise overlooking the New Mexico border town of Columbus, Villa could see a great deal, even in the dark purple half-light just before dawn.

I put the book back in the box.

"Sounds like Grandpa Jimmy. I think I remember him talking about the clarity of the desert."

"It's Grandpa Jimmy, all right. I called him Cornelius."

"I know."

Riley nodded and walked back to his chair.

"Are these Grandpa Jimmy's memoirs?" I asked him.

"I suppose," he said.

"You haven't read them?"

"Of course I've read them."

"So why are you just supposing?"

Riley took another drag. I sensed that he used his cigarette as a timing mechanism, but perhaps all smokers do.

"Sit down."

I sat back down on the leather sofa.

"Those notebooks contain a lot of things," Riley said. "A lot of things that Cornelius did, and mostly a lot of things that Cornelius and I did together. You know that both Cornelius and I, we were away from home a lot? I feel badly about that, but it had to be. Your grandmother, Grandmother Marta, she made it possible. She took care of the family, of both your parents, and that was the important thing. Never forget that."

There was another long pause, perhaps to let Grandmother Marta sink into my memory.

"Cornelius and I were travelers. We just couldn't seem to help it. We'd come back home, me to Independence, Cornelius to New York, but then something else would come up and we'd be off. Hard to have a family that way. Cornelius wound up with four wives over the years, just because he couldn't keep one. I was lucky with Marta."

As Riley paused, I was planning my exit, imagining my wife's poisonous thoughts about my absence.

"Now Cornelius is gone," he said abruptly. "And I'm past ninety and I'll be gone soon, too. That's okay. Without Marta and Cornelius, not much is left for me here. I'd have been happy leaving behind just the family, your parents and you and the rest. Cornelius wanted more. He wanted to leave a story, so he started writing and he didn't stop until he filled that box over there. He finished the last notebook just before we left for Berlin. Then he died."

Oh, yes, Berlin. The family went into a tizzy when Riley and Grandpa Jimmy, ninety-one and ninety respectively, took it into their heads to go to Berlin in the fall of 1989. Nobody knew about it until it was over. They just flew over, did God knows what, and came back. Some people at the funeral claimed that the trip took so much out of Grandpa Jimmy that it caused his premature death. I didn't see how anybody's death at the age of ninety-two could be considered "premature." Of course, we were aware that the fall of the Berlin Wall happened when they were over there. What the connection was, or if there was one, none of us knew.

"Cornelius wanted the chance to be remembered," Riley said, now looking me squarely in the eye. "I suppose it's my obligation to see that he is. That's where you come in."

I was clueless.

"Jimmy," he said, giving me a hard stare. "I've read every word Cornelius wrote in those notebooks. It's true, mostly, but he only knew his part. There were times he and I got separated, and there were times I saw things or knew things he didn't. So what we've got in that box is only part of the story. I think I owe it to Cornelius to tell the rest before I die."

He went into a coughing fit. After more than seventy years of constant smoking, he finally was starting to cough. His lungs didn't end up killing him, though. They were good to the end.

"You can write," he said to me after the coughing was done.

"I write for my job, law stuff," I said with a shrug. "Really I just edit now, I haven't written anything from scratch in years."

I didn't like the drift of this conversation.

"Doesn't matter, there's no one else. I need to tell you my side of things. Then I'm done. I'm reconciled to that."

Well, you can see where this went. There was no way that I could spend significant periods of time in Mexico, listening to my grandfather (and not even my favorite grandfather) drone on about his memories. But he had played the "reconciled to death" card and my family had already planned to spend a few days under the Mexican sun after the funeral before returning to frigid weather in my beloved home state. I supposed I could spend a couple of hours each of the next three or four days in the hacienda, listening to Daddo drone on, while the kids played in the pool and my wife read her book. I didn't golf, anyway.

Riley made me take the box of Grandpa Jimmy's manuscripts back to my room and told me to start reading at the beginning of the first notebook. So, that night, I did.

2

School Days in Independence

Cornelius

The Rileys and the O'Neals were both part of the wave of common folk that came over from the borders of the British Isles in the eighteenth century. Both families were Irish. By the time Riley and I arrived, the families had plenty of years to assimilate and they did so thoroughly, wholly adopting the accents, attitudes, and lives of what was then the West, now the Midwest. Both had landed in Charleston, South Carolina, traveled westward with the country, passed through the border states of Tennessee and Kentucky, and ended up in the plains of Indiana, Illinois, and Missouri. The process took about a century and had allowed us to lose completely the brogue of Ireland. We took on the drawl of the South, then the flat accents of mid-America that Riley still speaks in and that I can turn on or off at will. Of late, our people have turned Protestant and Republican, a process that took perhaps a century and a half. We remain stubborn, hard, practical, and insular. Good people to take to war, maybe not to take to a dance.

Not that the two families went through these processes together. My family, the O'Neals, had stayed in the South for several generations, mainly in Louisville. It was only when my father Jack took us west and settled us in the dusty streets of Independence, Missouri, that our two families merged. That was in 1910, when I was eleven. Riley's family went west long before that. They were already Protestants and Republicans when we met, while we'd become, thanks to Jack, atheists and communists.

I wish you could have known Jack O'Neal, for I can't describe him. He taught me German when I was six years old, specifically so I could read Goethe in the original language. That gives you some idea. Jack grew up in Louisville, Catholic and Irish but losing both fast. He was born too soon and in the wrong place. He would have been right at home in the Greenwich Village of the twenties, which I came to know, or in the New York of the fifties, which I also experienced. He was an intellectual in every sense, good and bad. He would sit in our front room, drinking cup after cup of coffee, smoking cigarette after cigarette, talking philosophy and history and literature and whatever came up. I've never been sure how much he really knew and understood, or how learned he really was, but I've never doubted his love of thought. It was equaled by his love of my mother and me. I was an only child with all the consequences. Aside from caffeine and nicotine, books and the family were Jack's great loves. He was useless when it came to money, business, or working with his hands. That would be a problem in any age, but in the plains of America at the start of the twentieth century, it was calamity.

I was born in Louisville. My parents had just moved there from New York. My father, born and raised in Louisville, left as soon as he could and fled to New York City, the American center of the intellectual life he loved. He enrolled at City College, where he puttered at philosophy and German literature, another true love. He became a socialist and a sort of communist, although all he ever did was read and talk about it. Later, he forced upon me the difficult and serious prose of Marx, Trotsky, and Luxemburg.

At college, he met fellow student Rose Cornelia Toolan, my mother, a quiet and intelligent Irish girl from Brooklyn. Together, they frequented the bars and coffee shops of the city, listening to poetry and politics, drinking and smoking and making love. It was a good time to be young, but when is it not? They married upon graduation, in the spring of 1897, and I came along a year or so later.

In her heart, Rose knew what she was signing up for. Jack would never be a leader of men, nor a plutocrat, nor a success in much of anything. He was a thinker and a reader, but he lacked brilliance. New York had no more patience for such men than any other place did.

Perhaps New York had less patience; it is a hard place for the gentle. So Rose did not object when Jack took her back to Louisville. A bookstore they opened there lasted a little more than a year, long enough for me to arrive. Then came a move west to Springfield, Illinois, where Jack tried selling what he called men's furnishings. The so-called "City of Lincoln" was no more hospitable to O'Neal the haberdasher than was Louisville to the bookseller. I believe it was two, but possibly three moves that followed, then we arrived in Independence to try the bookstore plan again.

The century was ten years old, I was eleven. In a number of ways, I expect, I was a thoroughly detestable child. For one thing, I was too smart for my own good. Worse, my intellect came out in an annoyingly articulate form. I spoke in complete, grammatical sentences at the age of four. Now, don't get me wrong: I am not bragging, for I actually regard this as something of a confession. I do not claim to have excellent judgment, nor true erudition, nor a special talent in writing or thinking or diplomacy. I don't believe I have any of those things. All I've ever had—and I've had them as long as I can remember—are a flair for words and the self-confidence to use it. It is remarkable how far such poor talents can take you in this life.

So I burst into Independence at the age of eleven, radiating my gifts. My father bought a vacant storefront in the middle of town and opened a bookstore that he called Open Minds. That the name of this Missouri bookstore was Open Minds tells you something about Jack O'Neal: it was like advertising pigs' feet in Tehran. I loved the store, though. It had two stories with one of those twisty staircases leading upward. Dark, but not too dark, and smelling that glorious smell of paper and ink. I was raised with that smell and never got away from it. The store was right on Maple Street in Independence, close to where Harry Truman later lived. Harry is how Independence is now known, mostly. Riley and I saw him around town, but he was older and we didn't get to know him until much later. I liked his sister.

Before Harry, Independence was primarily known as the gateway to the West, since it was the last outpost of stores and whores and laundered drawers before a party disappeared into the real wilderness. Kansas City didn't even exist when Independence was outfitting, screwing, and saying farewell to the poor bastards who settled the West. When the O'Neals arrived, though, those days were long gone. Independence was a sleepy little town consisting of a few blocks of commerce centered on Main Street and Maple Street, names as American as it is possible to imagine. Beyond that, in all directions, was "the country," mostly farmland where people raised grains and truck gardens and a lot of horses and Missouri mules. After Springfield, which at least was a capital city and still echoed with Lincoln's memory, Independence looked depressing and flat. Even the accents of the people there were flat.

But not me. I was round and active and up for any mischief that came my way. Since this was my fourth, or maybe fifth, home city, it wasn't a real big thing for me to walk as a stranger into a new school. I was just born confident, I guess. We moved at the beginning of August and I spent about a month helping my parents set up the store, not meeting any kids or doing much of anything, really. When school started, I was ready.

My parents had it set up so I started in the sixth grade, one grade higher than my age would have suggested. Back then, any child with a modicum of intelligence skipped a grade or two, sometimes more. I'd skipped two in my time, so sixth grade was actually a step backward. It was the most my parents could negotiate. By that time, I might add, I could speak German pretty well and read it perfectly, having learned from my father. I was very familiar with Goethe and Schiller and a lot of other German literature, I loved Shakespeare, and I was generally loaded for intellectual bear and about as repulsive a child as one could meet. I stormed into school that first day in Independence, certain to conquer whatever I encountered.

I joined my classmates in a schoolroom that included fourth, fifth, and sixth-graders. The teacher was a slovenly, dull fellow named Mr. Taft, which happened to be the name of the president at the time. I don't know where Mr. Taft came from or how he wound up as a teacher in Independence, Missouri in 1910. I do know he was dreadful at his job and didn't seem to care. In my experience, American public schools have a number of truly excellent and passionately inspired teachers and a number who are simply turds, with little in between. Mr. Taft was of the turd persuasion.

It quickly became apparent to me that the underground culture of the school consisted of an ongoing war between the Farm Kids and the Town Kids. Within those camps, of course, there were more subtle gradations. I was a Town Kid, as I lived within the borders of Independence and my father was a shopkeeper rather than a farmer. I was also a Smarty Pants, and therefore ineligible to join the clique of Town Kids who smoked, fought, and made trouble. The leader of those Town Kids, as I learned on my first day of school, was Tom Klapmeyer, who achieved his leadership status by virtue of being large for his age and having bad parents. The Farm Kids did not really have a leader. To the extent they did, it was Riley.

On that first day, I took my assigned seat in Mr. Taft's class. You could tell the boys who were Farm Kids by their overalls, dungarees that no Town Kid would consider wearing. It was harder with the girls, but also less important. With girls, what mattered was cute and not cute, which in my experience is true in most places.

Mr. Taft took attendance and immediately went into the first lesson. Mr. Taft was a thirtyish, heavyset man with a bad complexion, cheap-looking clothes, and bad breath. I'm sorry to be so hard on him, but a teacher in a grade-school classroom is imbued with great power, like the captain of a sailing ship in the British navy. Captain Bligh didn't get many breaks from Fletcher Christian, either.

The first lesson happened to be on American history. Mr. Taft said we would start with a discussion of the colonization of America. He said we would begin with the Pilgrims on Plymouth Rock. I raised my hand.

"What about Jamestown?" I asked.

Mr. Taft paused.

"What?"

"Jamestown was founded in 1607 and the Pilgrims didn't land in Plymouth until 1620. Shouldn't we start with Jamestown?"

I know, it was detestable.

Taft's smile was uncomfortable, but I think only because he passed through this world in a chronic state of discomfort. He actually spoke the old cliché, "Well, if the new boy thinks he knows so much, maybe he should teach the class." It was the opening I had hoped for. Of course, I immediately stepped to the front of the room where I began talking, a state of being I have always preferred to listening.

"It was the age of the Stuarts," I started, prepared to cover the entire seventeenth century as it had been explained to me by Jack O'Neal. I was working in a bit about the quarrels between Protestants and Catholics when Taft realized his maneuver hadn't worked and he thrust me back in my seat.

I glanced around the room, lacking the maturity to realize that the stares from the boys in the room—the girls didn't look at me at all—were not admiring but rather were expressions of sullen and dangerous hostility. It was only many years later, after I returned from much travel, that I came to realize that "sullen" and "dangerous" were adjectives that accurately described a great many of the Jacksonian masses of the mid-America from which I came. Not my mother and father, not me, not others, but a great many. Riley, for example, was often sullen and always dangerous.

I received my first lesson not long after my aborted lecture. At midday, we were sent outside to eat our lunches and work off some energy. We didn't call it "recess." We didn't call it anything, we just went outside, with no adults to supervise us. The "playground" was just a hard piece of ground, with spots of brown grass hanging onto life in inhospitable Missouri clay.

Over the years, I have watched in horror many times as sick and hostile cultures play out their rituals in godforsaken places, from African jungles to fascist beer halls to the Algonquin Round Table. In their way, schoolyard rituals rank with the worst of them. Children are quickly branded with the identities they will not escape in this life, at least in the minds of their classmates. They become The Fat Girl, or The Pretty One, or The Mean Tough, or The Athlete. Most are given the most common identity, the Nonentity. Naturally, based on my performance on my first day, I immediately became The Smarty Pants. Even if The Fat Girl becomes pretty or The Pretty One becomes fat, they retain their identities forever in the minds of their schoolmates. Even now, I am sure that if I returned to Independence and disinterred some ancient relic of a classmate, he would immediately remember me as The Smarty Pants. Damn right, too.

That day, though, I was too ignorant to notice the winds of peril swirling around me. I followed the crowd, all grades at the school, onto the playground. I was carrying a paper sack that contained the sandwich and apple that Jack had packed. No one looked at me. I sat on the ground, my back against an old oak tree, and ate. Looking around, I could immediately pick out the more obvious identities of my schoolmates, without being conscious of it. There was The Fat Girl, very tall as well as fat, her back to the schoolhouse wall, angrily mouthing off at some boys who were taunting her. I picked out The Retard peering through thick glasses at his piece of chicken and dribbling a little at the mouth. The Pretty One sat on a bench, surrounded by her female acolytes. Nonentities swarmed around, oddly difficult to focus on.

Given my morning performance, I should have been more watchful. Unbeknownst to me, Tom Klapmeyer and his crew of mean, poor white Town Kids had gathered around the corner of the schoolhouse. It was their usual spot to spend the lunch hour, spitting and bragging, usually planning devilment to visit upon weaker kids. Me, this time.

Tom Klapmeyer ached to be considered the Mean Tough of the school, but he wasn't. I was to learn that this distinction went to Kip Miller, generally an affable but quiet young hoodlum who beat the daylights out of another boy about once a month, apparently to work out his meanness and maintain his usual air of pleasant equanimity. When you saw a crowd of excited boys gathered in the lot across the street from the school, with dust flying upward from the center of their circle, you knew that Kip was again modulating his temperament. Kip was the undisputed Mean Tough because, though short in stature, he had big muscles and athletic quickness and, unlike any other boy in the school, he actually got in fights on a regular basis. Others mostly talked about fighting. Only one boy was known to have beaten Kip in a fight, and that was Riley, of course.

Tom Klapmeyer was just The Bully. Although big and strong for his age, considerably taller and heavier than either Kip or Riley, Tom was mostly talk and his victims were invariably smaller and weaker than himself. He was the leader of a group of five or six Town Kids who liked to see themselves as rowdies and toughs. They acted like lords of the playground because they pinched girls and played dangerous or humiliating tricks and occasionally, acting as a pack, beat up vulnerable boys. They stayed away from Kip and Riley. With the universally shared bully's instinct, they would have known to stay away from them even if Kip hadn't long ago revealed Tom's yellow streak to public view, and even if Riley hadn't mauled Kip in the most memorable fight in Independence playground annals, when both were nine years old.

Tom Klapmeyer, by the way, grew up and became a policeman, working for the Pendergast machine in Kansas City. I thought that was interesting.

Lost in thought, I sensed something to my right. Turning my head, I saw that a big boy was walking toward me with a sneer on his face, followed by a group of smaller boys who were similarly sneering at me. As they approached, Nonentities quietly headed toward me as well, not wanting to draw attention to themselves but not wanting to miss the excitement. The playground noise ebbed away to a dead silence. I felt a sudden hollowness in my stomach as I realized that I was at the center of whatever was about to happen.

Klapmeyer stopped just before his feet touched mine. He folded his arms and leered down at me. He was a beefy boy, with heavy arms and a piggy face and dirty chestnut hair. He wore a flannel shirt despite the September heat. From my vantage point on the ground, my back against the oak, I got a good look at the large clodhopper boots on his feet. Later, I heard a rumor that he tucked razor blades into his boots to use in fights. I saw no razor blades and suspect Tom spread the rumor himself.

"You think you're a smart ass, don't you?" Klapmeyer said through his sneer.

There didn't seem much to say to that.

"I think you need a beating," he said next.

I said no thank you and that roused him into giving me a vicious kick on my leg with his clodhopper.

"Get up." He kicked again. "Get up or show yellow right now."

My stomach was churning so much it was more of a distraction to me even than Klapmeyer. I am very familiar with fear. With me, it seems mostly a gastrointestinal condition. My stomach swirls and churns and I am incapacitated, at least momentarily, from doing anything at all. This is how I have been affected countless times, in countless situations on almost every continent of the world. That day on the playground was neither the first nor the worst time. It was just a time.

At such moments, I am temporarily incapacitated from action, but not from thought. Even when most afraid, I hear a voice in my head commenting on the situation from an outsider's point of view. At that moment, it told me to get up, so I did.

I am not sure what it means to be a brave man. If it means being someone like Riley, I am nowhere in the running. But while I am often afraid and while fear sometimes gets the better of me, the voice in my head generally tells me to stand up for myself because if I don't, the consequence will be worse than whatever my fear wants me to avoid. I usually listen. I did with Tom Klapmeyer.

On my feet, I thought to escape my predicament with words,

but I wasn't given the opportunity. Klapmeyer immediately pushed me, hard, back against the oak. When I bounced back, he shoved me again.

"Little shit," he said the first time he pushed me. "Fat boy," he said the second. This seemed unkind.

On my third bounce off the tree, I knocked away Klapmeyer's arms and began wildly windmilling my fists at him. My face was burning. I had never before been in a fight and had no idea how to keep my hands up for defense or throw my weight behind a punch. I simply churned my fists in front of me, backing Klapmeyer up and occasionally landing a body blow that accomplished nothing. At first startled, Klapmeyer then smiled as he kept backing up. We both knew that I could not keep up my frenetic punching very long and that when I stopped, I was done.

It seemed as though all the boys in the school had surrounded us. There were a few girls in the crowd, but mostly the girls hung back by the school, watching in amused disapproval. No sign of any adults. The voice in my head, which would not allow me to be a coward, was now telling me my arms were tired and I was about to be beat up, something I had never before experienced. "Beat up, beat up," it repeated to me. "He's going to beat you up." I must have looked silly and scared and out of control. I couldn't see myself, of course. But someone else did.

I slowed with fatigue. Seeing his moment, Klapmeyer gave me a backhanded slap.

"You pansy," he said, and he shoved me again, which he seemed to enjoy.

He was about to knock me down when a voice cut through the air and stopped him cold. It was the first time I heard Riley's voice or became aware of his existence in any way. The voice sounded much as it did when I spoke to Riley yesterday: flat, calm, quiet in the way that everybody can hear.

"Stop," he said simply.

Yet in the heat of the moment, with Tom Klapmeyer about to put his fist in my face in the presence of the entire student body, that one word demanded attention and obedience. Klapmeyer froze in the act of swinging, then turned to face a boy our age coming toward him from the edge of the crowd. I hadn't noticed this boy before. He had dark skin, short black hair, wore overalls like the other Farm Kids. He was short: never in his life did Riley exceed five feet, seven inches. He was thin, but *hard* thin. He looked as calm as if he were about to go to bed. He stepped to my side.

"This is my friend," he said.

Klapmeyer's reaction astonished me. I didn't yet know the history of Riley and Klapmeyer and Kip Miller. I didn't know that Riley rarely spoke, rarely played, rarely did much of anything to call attention to himself, yet was held in a sort of awe by all the kids and not a few adults. There has always been an aura around Riley. No one can sense it faster than a bully.

Tom Klapmeyer, for example. They had never tussled because Tom knew better. He had seen the Kip Miller fight. He knew Kip could wipe the walls of a room with bloody Klapmeyer any time he chose, yet Riley had matched Kip blow for blow until it was the great Kip Miller who cried uncle. Riley was not for him. And Tom was smart enough to know that if Riley publicly labeled anyone as his friend, even Smarty Pants Fat Boy, that friend was not for him, either.

Bullies in fiction are often depicted as slouching away. This is not surprising, for all bullies are cowards who are also show-offs. Their response, if they are in a public forum and meet adversity they know they cannot resist, is to twitch and sneer and ultimately take themselves off with a gait that is a sort of strutting retreat. That is what Tom Klapmeyer did when Riley cut him short. After a pause for twitching and sneering, he turned and slouched away.

Riley tossed back his head in a gesture of dismissal and the crowd, again to my astonishment, ambled away in silence. Riley looked me up and down.

"He won't bother you no more," he said.

I was both relieved and mortified. I didn't know if it was better for my all-important reputation at school for me to be rescued by this stranger or beaten to a pulp by The Bully. At the moment, neither option seemed attractive.

I just said, "I'm not your friend."

Riley got a little smile behind his eyes. His speech, whenever he broke his customary silence, always had a touch of formality, by the standards of his age and station.

"Well," he said. "It appears that you are, now."

3

The Riley Sisters

Cornelius

A few days later, I walked home with Riley after school.
I had sought, and received, permission from my parents to have
supper with the Riley family on the condition that Mr. Riley give me a
ride home in his buggy when the meal was finished. The Rileys farmed
eighty acres about ten miles east of town, across the Little Blue River,
but when the children got toward school age, they moved the family
to a house closer in, still in the country, but a more reasonable walking
distance to school.

Riley and I spent as much time together as we could after our
initial introduction and we hit it off wonderfully. Riley was a patient
and attentive listener, which is about all I can or need to ask for in a
companion. What I provided Riley is harder to figure, but perhaps
initially, I was a curiosity. On occasion, Riley would cock his head and
consider me, saying, "You sure can talk, can't you?"

We quickly sorted out the issue of our names, arriving at the
understanding we have employed in addressing each other ever since. I
asked Riley his name and he said he was Walter Riley. Even at that age,
I could never abide the name Walter.

"But what do people call you?"

Riley didn't seem to understand.

"They call me my name. They call me Walter."

"What do your friends call you?"

"Walter."

I snorted.

"Not very good friends, I'd say. What about your family? Do they call you Walter?"

"Of course. Sometimes Walter Ira, if I'm in trouble."

This was getting worse and worse.

"Your first name is Walter and your middle name is Ira? That's almost as bad as my middle name and my middle name is Cornelius."

So from then on, I called him Riley and he called me Cornelius and it seemed to serve.

The walk from school to the Riley home was about three miles, but we were boys and the distance didn't matter. I remember that walk through the heartland. The September day was warm. We turned off the playground and walked down a street between the oaks and the lindens and the elms. Colors were just starting to turn on a few trees. Mostly there were the usual greens and browns, but occasionally there would be yellows or even a flaming red on an early maple, like a lit matchstick in a family's yard. Later, I was to become very familiar with strolls along Unter den Linden in Berlin and Birdcage Walk in London, but they don't hold my mind like that peaceful walk through the gathering Independence twilight.

We saw boys playing and men walking home from work. Women poked their heads outside, calling for their schoolchildren to get inside. Couples sat on porches, rocking. People waved and we waved or nodded back, but we didn't know anyone to speak with, Riley being country and me being new. Before long, the houses and the trees thinned and we were out of town. On each side of the road, a berm sloped down into fields that stretched a long way. Not flat, like Iowa, but nicely curved and rolling, with apple trees calling to be picked. Whenever a tree was close enough to drop its fruit on the road, Riley or I would pick up an apple and chuck it as far as we could, just for the movement and to watch the arc of the throw.

I remember a yellow dog barking and running behind us a ways. I like dogs and tried to get it to come up so I could pet it. This dog seemed leery of my face or of Riley's reputation or something, for he froze where he stood, barked some more, and took off.

"Dogs don't have much sense," Riley said. "That dog barks at me every time I walk by him and I walk by on this road every day to and from school, so he barks at me pretty near every day except weekends. It's always me, just the same, not like it's dangerous or a new excitement or nothing. Why should he keep barking when it doesn't do good?"

"Dogs bark, Riley, that's what they do. They eat shit, too, who knows why they do that? They just do it."

"Like I said, they don't have much sense."

"Well, I find it comforting. Who knows, maybe the dog's talking to you? Maybe all this time he's been telling you where some buried treasure is hidden and he goes back to his friends every day and says that fool boy didn't listen to me again. Where do you live, anyway? This is an awful long walk if you do it every day."

"There."

Riley pointed ahead, in the distance. I could make out a house, about half a mile off. It looked like girls in dresses were in front of the house, playing at some game.

"You got sisters?" I asked.

Riley stopped his trudge and nodded his head.

"Oh, yeah." He pursed his lips and took a deep breath, like he was contemplating a dive into a lake or a jump off a cliff. "I got sisters."

Riley, it turned out, had five sisters: Bessie, Ann, Hazel, Fayette, and Gussie, whom I came to think of as "the famous Riley sisters." Truth be told, they were never famous, but there was a flamboyance to them that just came naturally and made them seem famous to me. They acted like I figured famous people would act, like everyone was all the time watching them and noticing and caring about their smallest word or deed. Riley was just the opposite: he was all deed and never cared what others looked at or thought.

Even in that passel of female personality, the oldest, Bessie, stood out. Short and stout, with barrels for bosoms and legs like stumps and a face like God's own wrath, she took your eye without opening her mouth. Then she'd speak and you'd know this was someone you would never forget, no matter how short your acquaintance. Her voice was deep like a man's, but when a woman's voice goes that low, she can resonate to your depths like no man could. And stronger than Bessie's looks or her voice were Bessie's opinions. The Lord having endowed Bessie with looks and a voice that made her unforgettable but, it must be said, not inclined to attract promiscuous affection, He apparently made up for it by granting Bessie instant and infallible judgment about each and every issue, person, and object that crossed her path, along with the unshakeable confidence to express that judgment loudly and often, with or without provocation.

She was in the process of so expressing herself when I first saw her on that September day and also on the last day I saw her many years later, biting the nurses in the old folks' home two days before she choked on her own vomit and met the Maker with whom she had always been on such knowing and familiar terms. No doubt her first words to the Lord were to correct Him in some shortcoming, confident of His chastened appreciation. I loved Bessie, the greatest foil for jokes I ever knew. When I first met her, she was fifteen.

"Walter Ira Riley, where have you been?" were the first words I heard spoken by her *basso profundo* instrument. We were just entering the grassy yard in front of the Riley house and I stopped where I stood, unsure if the vibrations I had just felt more than I heard could really have come from the five-foot, two-hundred-pound gargoyle in a sundress who faced us from the porch.

"And who is this?" she boomed before Riley could answer, pointing at me.

Riley ignored her, which I was to learn was his usual response to Bessie. Instead, he introduced me to all of them.

"Girls, this is my friend, Cornelius. He's staying to supper. Ma said."

Apparently Riley's mother hadn't seen fit to share the knowledge of the dinner arrangement with the girls.

The gargoyle stepped off the porch and approached me warily. She looked me up and down, clearly not liking the view.

"Are you baptized?" she asked.

I was too taken aback by the question to come up with a smart remark, which was most uncharacteristic of me. I allowed as how I'd been baptized in the Roman Catholic Church as a baby, to please my father's parents.

Bessie snorted.

"That was just a christening. To be baptized, you got to be dunked and you got to be old enough to make the decision yourself. Otherwise it ain't baptism."

"Well," I said, "maybe that's why it didn't take. Now I'm not Catholic and I'm not religious. In fact, I'm a socialist. Guess the water just washed off me."

The other girls looked politely curious.

"What's a socialist?" Hazel asked.

Bessie immediately turned to the house and roared "Ma!"

On cue, Ma Riley was at the door. I believe she'd been listening.

Ma Riley always reminded me of a turkey. Skinny legs supported a stout, strong body. Various parts of her hung down and flapped when she moved, including her breasts and large flabs of fat that hung below her meaty arms. She was always a little sweaty, a little out of breath, and her hair was always frizzy and wild. She had the best heart of anyone I ever knew, and was the only person alive who could silence Bessie with a look. Or with a double-ought twelve-gauge, for that matter, but I never knew Ma to need one. Ma's name being Fern Arlys Riley may be why everyone called her Ma.

"Bessie, I've told you not to bellow like that. It ain't feminine. You sound like a durn bull."

"I ain't feminine," said Bessie with perhaps a touch of understatement. "This boy says he's a socialist."

"What's a socialist?" This again, this time from Fayette, who was behind the times.

"Somebody who don't believe in the Lord," snapped Bessie. "Ma, this boy can't come in the house."

I was delighted at the fuss I was making.

"Well now, Bessie," I said, "socialists can believe in the Lord if they want. It just seems like most of us don't."

Ma was having none of it, not from Bessie and not from me.

"Bessie, hush up. Cornelius, in our house, you'll respect our beliefs and we'll respect yours. Fayette, a socialist is somebody who reads lots of books and has lots of ideas it's hard to understand, so

Cornelius is a smart boy, it's just that he's wrong. Now, everybody inside. Supper's ready."

Having summed up the state of play, Ma turned and stepped back inside without waiting for discussion. And there was none. We just went in silence to the supper table, Bessie scowling and me grinning.

I'll pass quickly over supper, for you can imagine it. John Riley, the patriarch, was a stolid man with large and tough-skinned hands. Ma had more than enough personality for the both of them, which John seemed to find comforting for he looked fondly at his wife as she dished out the potatoes and kept Bessie in check. Food kept on coming out of the kitchen in endless waves and, since I was just eleven, nothing could have been more welcome. It was good solid food, lots of meat and lots of mashed potatoes and lots of gravy poured over it all. Of course, the big meal had been the midday dinner, as this was a farm family.

Riley and his father said little, which was obviously their custom. Female voices dominated from the start, with Bessie pronouncing judgments, Hazel infallibly cheery, and Fayette and Gussie talking clothes. Ann was mostly quiet, like the men. Ma presided, joking and teasing and passing the food. I held my own, though, and probably talked more during that one meal than any male in the history of their table to that point. I remember telling stories about people in Springfield and trying to tell Fayette a little about socialism although Ma kept me from going too far, lest Bessie grow intolerable. Once in a while, I stole looks at the silent males at the table. Riley had his head down, eating, and didn't seem troubled by the female babble or his friend's peculiar talkativeness. John Riley had more of a dreamy look, I'd say. Anyone could tell by a glance that he was a farmer. His clothes, the dirt in the creases of his skin, everything about him bespoke that special calm that only seems to imbue those who are close to the land and the seasons. A farmer's time clock isn't on his wrist and that makes a deep difference in people.

John had married rather late in life and was probably around fifty when I met him. He could have been any age. He was a gentle man, quiet, at peace. He had worked this same land his whole life, as had his father before. He didn't read books, but he read newspapers and was sharper with the dollar than his son ever was. You have to be, being a farmer.

After supper, two of the girls helped Ma wash up while the rest of us helped John do some chores. The ride in the Riley cart back to my home was a quiet one. Fayette and Gussie wanted to come but weren't allowed, so it was just John, Riley, and me. Even I didn't say much as we rode. We just listened to the clop of the horse and took in the September evening. Eventually, we reached Maple Street in Independence and stopped in front of my door.

"Cornelius," John said. "Thank you for coming tonight. Walter and I need you to get a word in with all them females at the table."

Riley pulled his cap over his eyes.

"You don't need to worry about that," he said. "Cornelius can talk for all of us."

John smiled.

"That's a mighty big ambition for you, son. You do the talking for everybody on this Earth?"

"Yessir," I said. "That's just what I mean to do. I'll be the talker and Riley can be the doer. And we'll get along fine."

4

Tornado

Cornelius

From then on, through the next five years, I was frequently at the Riley homestead and farm, and Riley was frequently at the O'Neal bookshop. Jack and Rose took to Riley, pleased that their loud and pushy son finally had a friend. I like to think that John and Ma took to me. She was never bothered by my attitudes or philosophies and I think she and John saw through how superficial a hold I had on them. I was just a smart boy, taking in a lot of words fed me by my father and making out like I had real opinions about them. Mostly, though, I was just showing off.

It even got so I would help John Riley in the fields out on the east eighty, working alongside Riley and his sisters. Since Riley had no surviving brothers—the only other boy had died in childbirth, a common occurrence of the time—the girls were not exempt from field duty. We also worked with some Mexican migrant workers whom John employed: they stayed in a simple shelter constructed for them on the east eighty. This was a joy. Riley had learned Spanish from them at a young age and spoke it well enough to pass for a native. By diligently paying attention as the workers talked, I was also able to pick up the language to a considerable extent. By the time that Riley and I went off after Pancho Villa, we could pass for Mexicans as we chose.

The Mexicans taught us other things. We boys loved to pass summer evenings sitting with the Mexican families in the outbuilding in the fields that John gave them for their use while at the farm. It was there that Riley started smoking and I learned that I don't like smoking. I remember a young Mexican boy named Jesus: Bessie thought there was something vaguely improper about his very existence, with that name. Jesus smoked hemp and carried a knife, which he could toss with a flick of his wrist to leave it quivering in a tree trunk twenty feet away. He taught us the trick, though Riley was better at it than I.

I remember for two years in a row, there was a lovely Mexican family with the name Rodriguez. The mother of the family taught Riley and me to make tortillas, and this time I was better. I learned to make enchiladas and other good Mexican peasant food. The third year, that family didn't come back, but that was how it was with the migrants. I hope they found a better place to go.

One important thing that happened in those years was that Riley learned to box. Riley was born knowing how to fight—Kip Miller could tell you that—but boxing is something different. I never saw it as "science" the way that the boxing people say, but it is a definite art requiring speed, strength, and a certain kind of cunning and toughness, the kind that Riley had in spades. He was a natural, if ever there was one.

It happened this way. I had another set-to with Tom Klapmeyer, this time when I was fourteen. I suppose it had to happen. I got the idea from that first incident that my friendship with Riley made me invincible. At first, Tom and I didn't have much to do with each other. Even in a school as small as ours, there was little occasion for the members of one group to deal with the members of another if they didn't want to. Tom ran with the toughs of the school. Riley and I formed our own clique, with a few of the quieter boys as satellites. From time to time, though, Tom Klapmeyer would come to my attention for a stupid remark in school or crude bullying of another student and I started mouthing off to him. Only a little remark and a glower back at first, maybe once or twice at age thirteen, three or four times at fourteen. A day was coming when something was going to happen. Riley knew it and Tom knew it. I was the only ignorant one.

It happened during the summer. That was odd, because we rarely saw Tom and his type in the summer, being so busy at the Riley farm and following the Mexican workers around. I left the bookstore one afternoon on my way out to the farm. I don't think I was working in the fields that day, I was just going to see Riley. Klapmeyer and a knot of his friends were loafing down the sidewalk toward me. I never cared for meeting that crowd, but they hadn't bothered me for a long time and I didn't think much of it. Klapmeyer had taken to calling me "professor," sneering at my vocabulary and general cockiness, I suppose. Anyway, as he walked by, he suddenly said "Professor, are you afraid of squirrels?" When I said nothing, he said, "Then why do you keep your nuts in a sack?" and hit me in the groin.

I suppose I could be wrong, but I recall this as the first time in my life I was ever hit in the balls. I'd heard about it, of course, and my sense was that the experience lived up to its reputation. A sharp, irresistible pain blotted out my thinking and I sank to my knees. The pain wasn't even so much centered in my groin at first, but seemed to take over my whole body. The blow having been so sudden and unexpected, it was harder to recover. I simply knelt there on the sidewalk, stunned.

Klapmeyer and his buddies laughed and kept walking. I thought one of them might have swiped at my leg with his foot as he passed, but I wasn't sure. I just bent over, head near the concrete, and tried to breathe.

Of course, my first conscious action as the pain slowly subsided was to look around to see if anyone was watching my humiliation. I saw no one except the group of toughs disappearing around a corner. I considered for a moment the possibility of catching up to them and challenging Tom to some sort of fight, but somehow the idea seemed unreal and silly. Having been Riley's friend through a long and adventurous life, I've had plenty of occasion to consider whether I am a coward or a brave man and I don't think I'm particularly either. I can willingly take dangerous actions and have. I get scared, but don't necessarily give in to my fear. Mainly, actions that might be thought courageous simply seem to me improbable and it is hard to get myself started into action until the moment passes. Riley... well, I'll speak of Riley presently.

So I simply picked myself up and walked to the farm as planned. This doesn't mean that I accepted what had happened with equanimity. Far from it. My adolescent vanity was hurt in the extreme and I cursed myself for being a coward. I spent most of the walk agonizing over what

I should do next, but none of the options seemed like anything I could see myself doing.

Riley knew something had happened as soon as he saw me. I had the notion not to tell him, but I'm not very good at not telling things, especially with Riley. So the story came out and Riley had a simple prescription: I should learn to box. Whether I fought with Klapmeyer was irrelevant to Riley, but he thought it important that I be prepared to do so. Fighting was part of life, Riley figured, so I should learn it.

As it happened, Riley knew exactly where I should go for my instruction. He had taken to sharing a smoke at times with Kip Miller, his former rival for recognition as the toughest boy in Independence. Kip wasn't an easy friend to make, but he shared with Riley a gift for silence and a practical approach to the world. Kip had been taking boxing lessons for some time at a gymnasium in Kansas City and he had tried to interest Riley in joining him. Riley had never taken him up on it, figuring he fought as well as he had to and didn't want to make a habit of it, but he thought it would be just the ticket for his friend Cornelius.

Curious in spite of myself, I agreed. On the appointed day, we rode two of the Riley family's horses the long journey into Kansas City. Neither of our fathers was difficult to persuade. The crops were in and there was no work in the fields, so John Riley was indifferent to how his son chose to spend his free time. My father, I think, was bewildered but vaguely pleased that a son of his would actually try something as manly and physical as boxing. Our mothers maintained a wary, skeptical silence.

Riley seemed progressively more nervous as we rode the ten miles or so into town. He had only been to the big city a few times, despite its proximity to Independence and never without at least one of his parents. He grew even less talkative than usual. He brooded on the more urban images: a saloon being entered by a staggering, dirty fellow who looked like he should be going out rather than coming in; a copper who twirled his billy club and hitched up his pants as he looked us over; a dog pissing on the sidewalk. There were even automobiles, the horseless carriages that always drew a crowd when one passed through Independence. Only the well-to-do could think of owning one of these contraptions, Mr. Ford's Model T having only recently arrived on the scene. Yet the streets of Kansas City featured multiple automobiles as we clopped along, vehicles that roared and honked as they evaded horse manure and careless pedestrians. Between those two friends, Mr. Ford and Mr. Edison, life in Kansas City was on the cusp of some major changes and anyone who read the newspaper knew it. Even I did.

Kip Miller had given Riley crude directions and they served the purpose. We reined up at Skelly's, the ancient gym where I was supposed to learn to be a man. It was in the West Bottoms, an industrial area in the lowlands just west of downtown. The neighborhood was dominated by a giant stockyard that stank badly, but not as badly as it would in a few years when the whole place caught fire and seventeen thousand cows and pigs burned to death. We tied our horses to the still-omnipresent hitching posts, hoping the passing autos would steer clear and not frighten them to death. For a moment we stood at the door, both reluctant to go in, which you would understand had you seen the place.

Skelly's was in the middle of a shabby block on 13th Street right next to the John Deere Plow Company. It had a brick front over wood-frame construction, built perhaps around the time of the Civil War. The name "Skelly's" appeared in faded red paint over the chipped and dirty door, but was accompanied by no explanation to reveal whether this was a barber shop, a whorehouse, or a stable. Finally, I was the one who pushed open the door and strode inside.

We saw a large, open space with a dirt floor. It was very dimly lit by gas. Two boxing rings dominated the space, with some dilapidated training equipment placed seemingly at random wherever there was room. We saw barbells, dumbbells, some punching bags, and some heavy bags. Jump ropes lay scattered helter-skelter around the floor, looking like the hemp had seen far better days. What I saw was a dump. Riley, however, took one look and fell in love.

As our eyes adjusted to the darkness, we began to focus on the human beings (speaking broadly) who inhabited the gym. A few older, disreputable types lounged on benches along the wall. A well-muscled fellow who looked old enough to know better worked at a punching bag. A few boys who plainly had no idea what they were doing idly lifted a dumbbell or thumped a bag, while no one paid attention to them.

One ring was empty, but a sparring match was in full swing in the other. It dawned on me that one of the fighters was Kip Miller. I had seen him in action on the Independence playground just once, beating the snot out of a boy for no known reason other than to keep himself in shape and work out his aggressions. I never understood Kip Miller at all. Tom Klapmeyer was just an ignorant bully who enjoyed thrashing the weak and who feared the strong: nothing unusual about him. Kip, while driven to fight, seemed utterly lacking in animus toward anyone in particular. Maybe the world was his enemy. He had never met his father and his mother was a known whore: perhaps that had something to do with it.

In the ring, along with Kip and his opponent, was a bent old man who occasionally pushed the fighters apart and otherwise kept his own counsel. This was Skelly. He had been a fighter himself, of course, a good one. He was tall with a long reach, stooped over like a big gangly bird. His face was partly covered by a droopy, pure white mustache that made a striking contrast to his lined brown skin and his dirty brown hair flecked with gray. I wondered idly if he stooped so much when he was fighting.

I didn't know it at the time and I don't think Riley did, but Skelly was a particular favorite of the Pendergasts, both the late alderman Jim and his brother Tom. The Pendergasts *were* Kansas City in those days. Jim was a big, flamboyant politician who was a very powerful man in Kansas City. He died a few years before we walked into Skelly's and leadership of his organization had passed to his younger brother Tom. Riley got close to Tom Pendergast because of Skelly and that caused us no end of trouble later. That's another story, though.

For now, the point is that Riley was introduced to real boxing at Skelly's. Kip eventually noticed us watching and he raised his hands to signal that he wanted a break. Skelly stepped in to separate the fighters, but the other boy either didn't realize soon enough what was happening or he had a death wish, for he took one late swing at Kip. Our friend ducked the blow lazily, stepped in, and landed three quick body punches and a right cross, decking the boy as a lesson.

"You were done anyway," Skelly said to the prone fighter.

Kip waved us over.

"This is Riley," he told his trainer. "I told you about him. He fights pretty good."

"You mean he took you?"

"Sure," said Kip, unabashed. "But that was before I was coming here. Not sure what would happen now."

"I guess I ain't sure, either," Riley said. "Don't mean to find out." He elbowed me forward. "This is my friend, James Cornelius O'Neal. He'd like boxing lessons, Mr. Skelly, if you'd take him."

Skelly looked at me dubiously.

"He don't look like a boxer."

"I'm not a boxer," I said, taking charge. "I don't know that I want boxing lessons." Not if it meant sparring with Kip Miller, I didn't. "I just said I'd come here and watch."

Skelly had taken my measure and Riley's.

"All right, watch. You, Riley, get in here a minute."

He meant the ring. Riley stood his ground.

"This is for my friend. I thought it would do him good."

"I just want to check something. Come on, I won't hurt you."

Some of the loungers, obviously regulars and likely cronies of Skelly, ambled to the ring to watch. Left little alternative, Riley climbed through the ropes. I wasn't sure where this was going, but Skelly knew. He held out his hands.

"Put yours under mine," he told Riley.

This was a kid's game. Riley looked at him, unsure if there was some trick, but there wasn't. Skelly expected him simply to put his hands palm-to-palm to Skelly's, underneath them. He was to reverse his hands over Skelly's and try to clap them before Skelly could pull his hands away. A kid's game.

Clap!

The noise was not of Riley clapping hands with Skelly, but of Skelly's palms striking against his own chest. Riley was too slow.

Clap!

Again Riley tried, again he missed. It surprised me, as Riley had the quickest hands I ever saw. Until now.

They reversed roles.

Clap!

This time, the noise was of Skelly clapping his hands down on Riley's, before Riley could move. Skelly put out his hands again, but Riley stepped back.

"Don't need to keep doing it. Result won't be any different."

Skelly nodded and put out his hands, palms facing Riley this time.

"Get in a stance."

I thought Riley would leave, but he was hooked. He spread his feet with the left in front and raised his fists as he had seen Kip doing. The right protected his jaw. Skelly called cadence.

"Left! Left! Right cross! No, hit my right with your right when I call a cross. Right cross!"

After a few more blows, Skelly started backing around, working his feet. He kept his eyes on Riley's feet as he called the shots. Riley didn't always shift his weight correctly, but he didn't trip over his feet and made a nice smacking sound each time his fists hit Skelly's hands. This went on to where I was bored, then he had Riley skip rope. He even arm-wrestled him, holding him in place until he had gauged Riley's strength.

"You'll do," Skelly said. "If you're here tomorrow at noon, we'll start. You keep coming, you won't have to worry about Kip Miller."

Skelly turned, bent through the ropes and walked away, leaving Kip chagrined, Riley mesmerized, and me just standing there. I was clearly not the belle of this ball. Without a word, we headed home.

Riley came back the next day, and many a day after that he made the three-hour ride to Skelly's. He learned to box, all right.

It was August, 1914, not quite a year after we went to Skelly's. It was a memorable month for us, and of course, for the world.

While German armies raced through Belgium and killed Russians at Tannenberg, starting the Great War that nobody would know for years was only the First World War, Independence went on pretty much like always. It was a hot summer, I think, but Missouri summers were always hot. I was finally comfortable at the farm chores. Mr. Riley paid me to work with the migrants whenever I could. Riley was having a hard time keeping up with everything his father wanted done, what with Skelly's and time spent smoking and talking with me and Kip Miller and Jesus. We knew about the war, but I don't remember talking about it much. Riley and Kip talked boxing and Jesus talked women. I didn't have a lot to contribute on either subject, but I'm sure I talked anyway. I do that.

If nothing else, and there was plenty else, the hours would have kept me out of farming. I had to get up at five and drag myself to the Riley farm, not an easy feat for a town boy. Often, I would stay the night with the Rileys, just to get an extra few minutes of sleep.

One particular morning at the Riley house, I knew before I got out of bed that it was going to be a hot one. The air was dense and thick. Riley and I shared a narrow bed and both of us awoke soaked in sweat. We lay there, conscious that each of us was awake and neither wanted to move. We heard the voice of Riley's father call us from the front porch. I groaned, Riley rose silently. Another day.

We rode in the wagon to the east eighty. Given the heat, the day passed routinely. Bessie and Hazel served the midday meal under Ma's close eye. Riley and his father were repairing a fence at the far edge of their property. Three of the Mexicans and I were pulling weeds, one of the jobs I hated the most. Of course I hated all of them, but weeding was so hard on the back, I had to stop to stretch on just about every weed. The Mexicans were far more diligent, maybe more resigned. A pair of dogs scrapped with each other along the fence by the old cemetery across the road.

On one of my stretches, I suddenly had an odd feeling. The clouds were dark and dense. Jesus was pulling weeds a few feet from me.

"You notice something?" I asked him. "It feels funny."

Jesus kept working. "It's the weather. The sky is green."

So it was. Understand, this was before radio and the weather service and all those unctuous announcers who stand in front of maps and tell us if it's going to rain. Weather pretty much came as a surprise, especially to fifteen-year-old boys who don't pay attention.

There is something hellishly random about tornados. I've been in earthquakes, hurricanes, and floods—and don't misunderstand, I don't like them. But a tornado doesn't make any sense or show any justice. The sky turns green and the air gets dead, like inside a pyramid. Then a twister shows itself, bouncing up and down on its victims like some crazed animal. Then it's gone, leaving behind furrows of hideous damage adjacent to untouched land. You don't know until it's over if your number is up.

"Run!"

John Riley had seen the twister over the tops of the trees north of the farm. He and Riley dropped their tools and ran, straight toward us. My mouth fell open as I saw them come and slowly realized what was happening. Riley outdistanced his father, then hung back to let him catch up. The Mexicans ran and I followed. We were all heading for a ditch that ran along the south edge of the field. The tornado also came toward the ditch, gaining on us.

The Mexicans all got to the ditch ahead of us. Riley could easily have passed me, but he would have gone too far beyond his father. John waved us forward, on and on. I saw the twister behind him, chasing him like a monster from a ghost tale. I just ran, fast as I could, with no thought of waiting for my friend or his father. The noise grew and grew, thundering, shutting off all possibility of thought. The ditch ahead seemed never to be at my feet, then suddenly it was. I jumped, landed, and rolled. John Riley was right behind, with Riley at his side urging him on. The twister bounced up in the air over their heads, seemingly to pass over them and jump in our ditch. But it didn't.

It swooped down. It landed flush on John Riley and sucked him straight up, up and out of sight. I saw the bottoms of his boots as he flew into the maw of the monster. Riley landed in the ditch on top of me.

He never saw his father again.

5

Cornelius Is a Liar

Jim

When we were settled again in our seats in the study, Riley asked me, "Did you read the first chapter?"

"I read more than that," I said. "I read the one about Villa and then I read all the way to where your father got killed by the tornado."

Riley nodded.

"Well, then you know Cornelius is a liar."

I suspected as much, but it was still something of a disappointment. "Is any of it true?"

"Oh, it's all true, what he knew of it. What I mean is, when there's a hole in what he knows, Cornelius can't help but fill it in. That whole introduction. How would Cornelius know what the Spaniard was thinking, or when Villa fired his pistols, or any of that? He made it up."

"How about the Moores?"

"That was real enough. You can read about them in history books, without some of the details. Cornelius met Mrs. Moore years later and she told him the story. I just don't understand why writers think they can make things up when they don't know something. It's wrong."

That didn't seem worth arguing about to me. I looked out the picture window, watching my kids swim in the pool while my wife sat in a lounge chair and read a book. I still wasn't sure about this whole project.

"Did you ever meet your Aunt Bessie?" Riley asked me. "I forget."

"No, I never did."

"Cornelius was hard on her. You have to understand, Bessie was a brilliant woman. She was the first woman admitted to the Harvard Divinity School. Did you know that? Did real well until she was expelled. She and Cornelius would argue and argue and she held her own with him." He smiled. "Course if she didn't, she'd smack him in the kisser. Cornelius got that part right, Bessie was a firm-minded woman when it came to that. Ma was the only one who could handle her, and when Ma died... well, life and Bessie sort of fell out with each other."

Another pause. I asked Riley what he wanted to talk about today.

"Oh, I thought I'd fill in some details that Cornelius passed over. He doesn't explain about the Mexican Revolution and he just sort of passes over how we left Independence. You need to understand that part. If old Mr. Murray had been just a little quicker, we wouldn't be here talking."

6

Going After Villa

Riley

The Columbus raid was the talk of the country in early 1916. I heard about it at the drugstore in Independence, where I was picking up some sundries. Money was tight for everybody back then, but it was especially tight for us after Pa got sucked up by that twister. I tried, Lord, how I tried. I offered to quit school so I could work more at home, but Ma wouldn't hear it. She and the girls worked those fields like Mexicans to make up for Pa being gone and to let me stay in school. I even got to keep taking boxing lessons some, on account of Skelly being willing to meet me after dark. Those were hard times, though. Had to let some Mexicans go and had to grow less crop, which made the money problems worse. Just couldn't seem to keep that farm up like Pa could. My grades dropped and I fought with my sisters all the time, just one thing after another.

Anyway, I was at the counter with old man Clinton, figuring whether I had the money to pay for what I'd picked out, when Mr. O'Neal came in the store. His bookshop was just a few buildings down Maple Street from the drugstore. Clinton's was where Harry Truman had his first job as a boy. Didn't mean much to us then in March of 1916. Harry was just another young fellow from Independence, trying to work his dead father's farm like I was and not having much better luck. I was more impressed with Jack O'Neal, who seemed to me like the smartest and best-educated man I could ever imagine. He was good to me, too.

"Hello, Doc," he said to Mr. Clinton as the bell over the door tinkled to announce his arrival.

Mr. Clinton was no more a doctor than I was, but that's what you called druggists in those days, or at least we did.

"Hello, Walter," he said to me when he saw me standing there. "How are you? How's your family?"

"They're fine, Mr. O'Neal. We're making do."

"By the way, Jack," Mr. Clinton said, picking up a newspaper that had just been delivered to the store, "did you hear about Villa? What he's done now?" He handed Mr. O'Neal the newspaper. "The dumb greaser's gone and attacked the United States, near burned down the whole town of Columbus in New Mexico they say. Even Woodrow Wilson can't let that go."

I think Mr. Clinton was needling Jack, knowing his political views. For all I knew, Pancho Villa had been a regular subject between them. Visiting with Cornelius and his family, I'd heard Jack talk about the Mexican Revolution, along with the war in Europe and Wilson and Taft and Teddy Roosevelt and all the other issues of the day. Jack's sympathies were with the Mexicans, of course, but his problem was that the Mexicans kept killing Mexicans, so being sympathetic with them got a little complicated. I think Wilson was having the same problem.

For the last half of the nineteenth century, Mexico was run by a tyrant named Porfirio Diaz. Tyrants have their bad sides, Lord knows, but at least Diaz was one of those old-fashioned tyrants who knew their limitations. He didn't try to get rid of the church or control how people lived, like a lot of the twentieth-century tyrants after him who seemed to operate on ideologies and hatreds and just plain cussedness. Diaz didn't hate anybody and he didn't care what people believed, he just wanted money and power. You can tolerate a fellow like that. So Mexico was stable for a good long spell.

But Diaz got old. In 1910, when he was eighty, some little bitty radical kind of fellow named Madero ran against him and looked to win, so of course Diaz had him arrested. Madero escaped and the so-called Mexican Revolution started up and it didn't stop until the twenties. Some would say it never stopped and is going on to this day.

It wasn't an orderly revolution like ours, with a beginning, middle, and end. It was one big mess with all kinds of factions, one side coming to power and getting thrown out and coming back, leaders changing sides and making friends with old enemies and vice-versa and then back again. You try to read a book about it and you give up after a while because you don't much care anymore who did what to who. Madero came to power, then he was thrown out by a thug named General Huerta, then a politician named Carranza got up an army in the north while Zapata was sort of a communist peasant down in the south. And, most famous of all, up in the States, was Pancho Villa.

Villa was just a desert bandit at first, like generations of Mexicans from right around this place where we're sitting now. The border between the U.S. and Mexico has always been bandit country, where travelers get dry-gulched by Apaches or comancheros who know every inch of the desert and have a thousand hiding places to hole up in. Victorio and Geronimo roamed this land in their time. Villa joined the bandit tradition shortly after the reign of the great Apaches.

Villa was born in 1878, the bastard son of a sharecropper, on a hacienda not far from here in Chihuahua. Villa told us the old story that he became an outlaw as a teenager, when he shot a man who was trying to rape his sister. I don't believe it for a minute. Villa might have shot that fellow, but he was set to be an outlaw the minute he was born. You could tell by looking at him. He had bandit eyes and a bandit walk. Being born where he was and when he was, and being the man he was, he was a bandit for sure whether he had a sister or not.

Leaning up against the drugstore counter, Mr. O'Neal glanced up from the newspaper.

"This was a mistake. I understand Villa's feelings, but this was the wrong strategy."

"Goddam right it was the wrong strategy," Doc exploded. "Little greasers killed American women and children. They already murdered those engineers, now they're after our women and children. Well, they're gonna find out who they messed with. Finally."

I knew for a fact that Doc Clinton didn't care a hoot about the war in Europe and wanted us to stay out of it. He wasn't real interested in the Mexican Revolution either, until Villa's men shot some American engineers on the Santa Isabel River, which also isn't far from my hacienda. But now that Villa had crossed the border and killed women, far from the first women killed in the Mexican Revolution, Wilson just had to up and whip him. Didn't seem as peculiar to me then as it does now.

Jack O'Neal was another one whose opinions seemed to flip-flop for no logical reason, if I had thought about it back then, which I didn't. If I remember right—I didn't listen very hard— Jack's first thoughts on the Mexican Revolution were in favor of Madero, against Huerta, but he wanted Wilson to stay out of there and let the greasers decide their own fates. Then when Huerta took over, he got partial to Carranza, who hated America, and he wanted Wilson to stand up to Huerta, whatever that meant. Then he got mad at Wilson for sending troops to Veracruz and he started supporting Villa over Carranza. I guess anybody who was against the folks in power was pretty much all right with Jack O'Neal unless he was looking to bring back the old regime, like Huerta. 'Course, the problem with that philosophy is you got to keep changing horses once your horse is on top. Seems confusing. But Mr. O'Neal understood German and read big books and was known to be the smartest man in Independence at such things, so I guess he knew what he was talking about.

Jack and Doc Clinton fell to arguing, over nothing so far as I could tell. I was thinking and I walked out of that store with my brain racing. By the time I reached home, I knew what I was going to do. I was going to fight Pancho Villa.

"Are you crazy?" said Cornelius when I told him. "Why would we go and do a thing like that?"

"You don't have to if you don't want to," I said. "I just offered that you could go if you want to. Your father says President Wilson has to send troops in. They're going to find Villa in the Mexican desert and fight him 'cause he killed American women and children. So I figure I want to be there."

Cornelius thought about it. He'd talked endlessly, as Cornelius would, about leaving Independence, but now that the prospect was sitting on his doorstep, he wavered. Running off to the Mexican desert in hopes of hooking onto an army may not have been what he had in mind.

"So what's your plan? Just what would we do?"

"It's not like I got a plan, Cornelius. I gotta go. It's just that simple." These were probably the most words I'd said to my best friend since we met. "I'm not a farmer. The girls are better farmers than me. They and Ma and the Mexicans do the real work and keep it going and

I hate every minute of it. I have to get out of here or I'll live forever on that farm and never see what's out there in the world."

Cornelius nodded.

"What does Ma say?"

I snorted.

"Sweet Jesus, do you think I'd tell her? This just has to be done. I'll run off and leave a note so she knows I'm not dead and it's not her fault. If you don't want to go, I understand."

"You're gonna run all the way to Mexico?"

"Not for real, you dope. I'm hopping a train."

"You know how to hop a train?"

"No. But Kip Miller does."

This was sure true. I'd gotten to know Kip better from Skelly's gym. He told me how he'd disappear once in a while, just to get out of Independence and away from his mother who beat on him when she was drunk. One time, he rode the rails all the way to St. Louis and back. Said one day he wouldn't come back at all. I was always sort of waiting for that.

Cornelius knew about Kip Miller's trips because I'd told him. He grinned at me.

"You see, Riley? You do have a plan. Let's go see Kip."

Kip came with us. Once we told him what was up and what we were going to do, I suppose it was inevitable that he'd sign on. It was all right with me, as I thought Kip would be a good comrade in a fight.

I felt bad as it would soon be April and the fields took lots of working and I knew the girls would hate that I left, but Ma would handle it. She always did. I hoped she'd understand what was in me and why I had to take adventure where I could find it. I left her a note, but it wasn't a very good one. I'm sure that the one Cornelius wrote for his folks was much better.

It was March 15, 1916, less than a week after the Columbus raid and though we didn't know it, the very day General Pershing led five brigades into Mexico to hunt down Villa. We were living in a marvelous age, when word of the Columbus raid got to little Independence by telegraph just three days after it happened. President Wilson did like Doc Clinton said he would. He whistled up Jack Pershing, who'd been cooling his heels in San Antonio waiting for something to happen, and sent him into the desert to find Pancho Villa and kill him. If I'd known it at the time, I'd have been even more on fire to get there than I already was.

I rolled out of my bed at 1 a.m., being far quieter than I needed to be with everyone in the house sound asleep. I'd already packed a knapsack with some clothes and tools and provisions, and hidden it in the shed. The horse nickered when I saddled it up. I was sure the noise would wake Ma and maybe it did, but I didn't hear anything from the house. With a last look around, I set off to meet Cornelius and Kip at the railway yard, like we planned.

They were already there when I arrived. I hitched my horse where she'd be found. The Independence rail station was pretty simple back then. There was the station building, which was closed, a water tower, and the tracks. The night yardman, Mr. Murray, mostly slept in a little shed on what was called the platform, which was made of brick and not raised at all, more like our patio here at the house than a real railroad platform.

Everybody in town knew that Kip Miller rode the rails as he pleased and Mr. Murray could never catch him. I hoped Kip's luck would hold. I asked the boys what all they'd brought with them. Being young and stupid, we hadn't even talked about that until then.

Cornelius brought a change of clothes, five books, and an apple. Kip hadn't brought anything. He said you have to travel light.

I was only a little better fixed than my comrades. I brought two shirts besides what I was wearing, an extra pair of pants, socks and underwear, a loaf of bread, some sausage, a knife I'd bought from Jesus, a hammer, a screwdriver, and some nails. Not sure what I thought I was going to do with the hammer and screwdriver, but Pa had impressed upon me for years that a man needs his tools.

Our plan was simple, which probably isn't surprising. A freight train was due to stop in Independence at 4 a.m., making some small drops before pulling into Kansas City. We planned to crawl into a freight car while Mr. Murray was occupied helping unload the freight. We would then jump the train at Kansas City and find one going south, as far south as we could get. We would only get out when we had to eat and we wanted to keep those stops to a minimum. We were aiming for San Antonio, where we heard Pershing was stationed. Once we got there, we would figure a way to get ourselves in the army. Smart, weren't we?

Even Cornelius was silent as we waited for that freight train. I don't know what that night was like for a boy like Kip, but for Cornelius and me, it was momentous. We loved our families, we were good boys and well-thought-of in our small town, yet we were throwing all that away for an adventure in a Mexican desert. It made no sense, but I couldn't help it. I had to go. I guess Cornelius did, too.

We heard the train coming from a long ways off. We were skulking on the far side of the tracks from the station and Mr. Murray's shed, so the train would block anyone's view as we crept to a car. Mr. Murray must have been sleeping real soundly, because we saw no sign of him even when the engineer blew his whistle approaching the stop. Then the train pulled in, blocking our view of the station and, more importantly, Mr. Murray's view of us.

Kip had told us we wouldn't have much time, as the train wouldn't stay very long. He was going to go first and locate a car with a door he could open, which he said wouldn't be hard. Then he'd wave us up and we'd pull ourselves into the car and close the doors. Simple.

The engineer didn't even shut down the engine, so brief was the stop. Kip trotted over, bent at the waist, and started pulling at doors. He couldn't open either of the first two cars he tried, either because the doors were locked or he just couldn't get enough purchase. I could feel Cornelius tense up. Then the third door slid open, Kip waved to us, and he pulled himself into the car. We ran over, bent at the waist like Kip had been. I motioned Cornelius to go first, as I feared exactly what happened. Cornelius was never fat, and he certainly wasn't at seventeen, but he's always been on the fleshy side and not very athletic. The floor of the freight car was pretty high off the ground. Kip, who was maybe the best athlete of all us boys and who was experienced in the matter, got in with no trouble, but Cornelius was another story. He threw his knapsack into the car, grabbed the sill, and hoisted himself, but only got about six inches off the ground and hit his knee in the process. I tossed in my knapsack and cupped my hands for Cornelius to use as a step. Lord, he suddenly seemed heavy. I got him in, but in my concentration on the task I didn't hear what was coming up behind me.

It was Mr. Murray. As far as we could figure out later on, he'd seen us by the water tower and hid on our side of the tracks, waiting to catch the great Kip Miller in the act at last. Once I got Cornelius hoisted up, I was pulling myself up behind him when I felt a hand grab my left leg.

"Got you!" Mr. Murray shouted triumphantly. He pulled me back onto the ground and looked me in the eye. "Is that you, Walter Riley? What in thunder are you doing here?" He had me by one arm and was shaking me. "Your ma is going to shit fenceposts when she hears about this." I could hear the train shift gears. It was starting up. "Why are you hanging out with a lowlife like that Kip Miller? This town expects something of you." He was still shaking me.

The train started to move. I hit him.

He never saw the punch coming and I caught him right on the button, the point of the chin, like Skelly taught me. Mr. Murray was a shriveled-up little man maybe fifty years old and he reeled backward like they do in the movies before falling down. I had no time to see if he was all right. The train was picking up steam and I ran after it, toward the hands of the boys reaching out to me. Cornelius got hold of me first and heaved me toward him, with more strength than I knew he had. Then Kip took hold and the next thing I knew, I was lying on top of them in the car. That's when I was hit by the enormity of what I'd just done.

Everybody in Independence knew Mr. Murray and everybody in Independence knew me. Up until this moment, I'd been a good boy, son of an esteemed citizen, the boy who tragically lost his pa in a tornado. Now I was a runaway, not only the bad kid who abandoned his ma and sisters to run a farm all by themselves, but a thug who punched old Mr. Murray in the face, like near killing the man before running off in the middle of the night.

If it weren't for Mr. Murray, I think we might have given up and gone back to Independence long before we got to San Antonio. But we couldn't do that now. We were outlaws without a home.

It was a good clean punch, though. And I wasn't wrong about the effect of that night's events on my reputation in Independence. Many years later, in Washington, I finally met Harry Truman, who was then President of the United States. When he heard my name, he looked at me hard and said, "Aren't you the one who busted poor Mr. Murray in the snoot?"

"No," I said. "It was on the button."

Part Two

Mexico

7

Rematch

Cornelius

The death by tornado of John Riley understandably affected his son, my friend. He talked less than ever, if that was possible. He felt the weight of the farm and the family and his father's memory all come landing with a thud. Quite a load when you're sixteen.

Ma took it with so much strength that you wondered about her. Riley told me he never saw her cry. The girls bleated like sheep, even Bessie, but Ma never did more than look out the window silently for about a minute, after we told her. She kept working, like always. It made things worse that we never found the body. Almost like John could still be out there somewhere, fixing the fences. Life at that farm just wasn't the same.

Riley stuck it out for one full season in 1915. The farm did all right, but Riley always said it was because of Ma and the girls and the Mexicans, not him. Then, in March of 1916, Pancho Villa raided a New Mexico town called Columbus and the president sent General Pershing after him. My father came home from the store all excited about the raid, as he was passionate about current events and Mexico was high on his list of hot buttons that year, even more than the war in Europe.

I was shocked the next day when Riley told me we had to join the army and get in on the hunt for Pancho Villa.

"You've been saying for years you want to get out of this little town and see the world, Cornelius. This is our chance. I can't stay here anymore. I can't go to school, I can't work the farm, I can't walk down the street to your dad's bookstore one more time. It's choking me."

"We're not eighteen yet!"

"We will be, soon. I bet they don't check hard anyway."

"We graduate in two months, Riley. We can go then."

"Not and catch Villa, we can't. He'll be strung up in Texas by then and we'll have missed the only adventure we'll ever have." Riley looked ready to sob. "I can't stay here two more months, Cornelius. I have to go and I have to go *now*."

I said I'd think about it and I did. I didn't sleep that night. It was one thing to imagine myself leading a cavalry charge or strolling down Broadway. It was quite another thing to pull up and leave my parents, leave home, and head for a foreign country with no real idea of what was to come. But Riley was right. This was adventure and you don't turn that down.

We hooked up with Kip Miller, who was experienced in running away, and we rode the rails down to San Antonio, where Pershing's army was encamped, waiting for orders to march into Mexico. Or so we thought. Turns out that the very day we jumped a freight train, Pershing took five brigades of infantry and horse soldiers across the border. We spent the next ten days in boxcars, so we didn't hear.

It was a hard trip. Riley had to punch the station man when we pulled out of Independence, so we knew there would be cops waiting for us in Kansas City. The three of us jumped out while the train was slowing around a bend and we hiked into the city. Being careful, we were able to get all the way to Texas without getting caught by any railroad bulls, but it was hard traveling nonetheless. We didn't have much food and it was cold, still March, most of the way south. I got along because I had some good books: Jack London, Ambrose Bierce (who had been killed in Mexico a couple years before, writing about the revolution), and out of duty to my father, Rosa Luxemburg. I was slogging through her book, *The Accumulation of Capital*, which was as exciting as it sounds, but which Jack O'Neal thought was the best book on economics ever written. I think it was guilt over running away that made me stick to it, but I actually finished the thing while we were pulling into the station in Fort Worth.

Although we were heading into an unknown future, the relations among us three boys were complicated by the past. Riley and I continued to be perfectly synchronized, me talking and him listening, the shared cold and hunger and uncertainty only drawing us closer to each other. Kip, though, was a hardcase. I don't think he ever got over the fact that Riley licked him back when he was nine, and he brooded over what would happen if they went at it again, now that they both had been tutored by the great Skelly. Or maybe Kip just got tired of my yapping. Regardless, Kip grew more overtly unpleasant as we got further south.

I forgot about such things as we pulled into San Antonio. In those days, San Antonio was a bustling town full of soldiers. It sits in the Texas Hill Country, but hills aren't what you notice. The landscape seemed flat and dry to a Missouri boy. It was hot, but without Missouri humidity, that part was bearable. We boys were hungry and filthy, ready to start our new lives by joining the army. We rolled off the train, careful that no one was watching. Not knowing where to go, we left the station and turned toward what seemed to be the town, walking purposefully down the sidewalk like we had a specific destination in mind.

The town was sleepy and mostly Mexican, as far as we could see. I barely glanced at the Alamo as we passed it—there were none of the statues and such that you see today. I don't think Kip even knew what it was. A Mexican lady was selling tortillas on the street and I bought one for each of us, noting that the money I'd taken with me was nearly gone. The lady smiled at us and I tried out the Spanish I'd learned from Riley's Mexicans. It seemed to work.

"*Donde esta* General Pershing?" I asked in my innocence.

She waved us vaguely down the direction we'd been walking. If we'd been walking the other way, I suspected she'd have waved us down that way. Still, we walked on.

A young soldier came out of a doorway and practically bumped into Riley. He didn't look much older than we were. I swallowed the last bite of my tortilla and asked him where we could find General Pershing.

"Maybe a couple hundred miles south of here by now," he said. "He left two weeks ago to find Villa."

The soldier moved on, leaving us crestfallen. We'd missed him.

We asked around the town. Pershing had left San Antonio at the vanguard of a noble parade of infantry, cavalry, and artillery. There were even tanks, of a fashion, new to the army and the world. Most marvelous of all, rumor was that the government was giving Pershing airplanes to look for Villa and his bandits in the harsh desert terrain. This was indeed the epitome of modern warfare, showing that the United States was more than a match for the armies now stalemated in the trenches in France. We had missed it.

Sitting in a dusty cantina, we debated our next move. Kip, who was growing increasingly crabby, favored giving up on the army entirely and moving on. I was inclined toward going home, but Riley was determined to find Pershing. It wasn't enough for him to walk to the fort and sign up, for he figured the fight would be over by the time we went through training and were sent to join Pershing.

"What did Villa ever do to you?" I asked. "Why are you so anxious to kill him?"

But there was no reasoning with Riley. So we laid low in San Antonio a few days, doing odd jobs to pick up some money, and looked for a way south. We slept outside, which you could do in those days. We cleaned out an old lady's stable and she let us move into it. I finished the last of my books. Kip got more and more ornery, never talking but cussing and taking offense at the slightest thing. Riley and I both knew this was coming to a boil.

Just when I wasn't sure we could stick in San Antonio one more day, we found our way out. Making the rounds of the shops in town, I met an old peddler who traveled back and forth across the border in a wagon, selling baskets woven by peasant women in Chihuahua. He had sold his wares and was preparing to make the return trip, back to the center of the area where Pershing was headed when he set off. This being too good an opportunity to pass up, I charmed the old man with my Spanish and my smile and the prospect of three strong gringos to scare off the bandits and we were set. Another three weeks and we were in Chihuahua. Not a bandit did we see. Nor Pershing.

Chihuahua was a poor village, probably not much different than it had been at the time of the *conquistadores*. Being dumped there was only marginally worse than being dumped in San Antonio, especially since Riley and I spoke Spanish. Kip did not and his utter dependence on us to know what was being said by anyone we met only flustered him and fueled his discontent. His temper wasn't cooled by the fact that as far as we could tell, we were no closer to finding Pershing than when we'd started.

We learned in San Antonio that Pershing was going to march to Juarez, then turn south into Villa country, following what traces he could pick up of the Jaguar, as Villa was called. We thought that by catching a ride with the peddler, we would have a good chance of beating Pershing's army and meeting them when they arrived in Chihuahua. Trouble was, we didn't know if that was where Pershing was going and, as it turned out, neither did he. Pershing was wandering in the desert, to somewhat less purpose than the Israelites. A troop of his men had one major skirmish with Villa, south of Chihuahua. Unbeknownst to any of the Americans, Villa was badly wounded in the scrap and crawled off into a hole to heal. Pershing's army mostly chased its own tail around the desert, watched closely by the Villistas and even mildly harassed by the army of Carranza, the supposed ally of the United States.

Our first night in Chihuahua, we used what little money we had left from our odd jobs in San Antonio to get a room in a boarding house. We three shared one bed. Since I had finished reading my books, I decided to read parts of *The Accumulation of Capital* again, as I wasn't sure I had followed Luxemburg's argument. She claimed that capitalism is inherently doomed to fail because it depends on continued expansion into new markets. Once there are no more new markets, the cost of producing goods will inevitably outstrip the wages of the workers, meaning there will be no one able to pay for the goods and the system will fail in a series of catastrophic famines and rebellions. Communists were cheery, that way.

"Kip," I said, feeling the devil rise up in me. "This book claims the war in Europe is an inevitable result of our economic system. What do you think?"

God knows why I asked a show-off question like that to someone like Kip, but Kip had been annoying me with his sour moods and I was bored. When he just stared sullenly at me, I kept it up.

"Come on, Kip. You're a thinking man. Is socialism inevitable?"

Kip was fast, you had to say that for him. In one fluid motion,

63

he drew a knife from his pocket, leaped onto the bed where I lay, and held the knife to my throat.

"Think you're funny? Is *this* funny?"

Riley rose to his feet.

"Stop it, Kip."

His words caused Kip to bolt up and confront Riley nose-to-nose.

"What'll you do about it, Riley? You want to take this away from me? Try it. C'mon, you're the real tough guy. Try it."

Kip waved the knife under Riley's nose. Riley didn't move an inch, looking as cool and collected as if Kip were holding out a drink instead of a blade.

"It's hot and you're bored and Cornelius irritated you," he said. "Those are stupid reasons for anybody to fight and die."

"You whipped me once, Riley. Think you can do it again? You do, don't you?"

"That was when we were nine years old, Kip. It don't mean nothing now."

"It does to me," Kip said, throwing the knife onto the bed. "Neither of us knew how to box back then. Now we've learned. We need to find out who learned most."

"Don't matter, Kip. I don't ever want to fight you. No reason for it."

"Not for you, maybe. I got a reason. It's going to happen."

After another long moment of staring, Kip turned and left the room.

"You should've fought him," I said helpfully.

"Me! You're the one who riled him up."

"No, you're the one who riled him up, back when you were nine. What did you two fight about, anyway?"

"I don't remember. Sometimes you just have to fight."

Riley was right about that and we both knew the time was coming with Kip. He managed to find some tequila while he was walking the streets and the next day he plainly had the sort of hangover that Chihuahua tequila is likely to give you. That made him even more ornery. This was the day fated to see bout number two between Riley and Kip Miller.

It happened in a flat, dry field, not unlike the fighting field across from school back in Independence. We had spent the morning walking around town, talking to folks, trying to get a lead on Pershing. No one knew anything about his whereabouts, anyway not anything they'd say to some young gringos with no business being in town. It's good we weren't shot by Villistas, just for luck. The day got hotter and we got hungrier, with no obvious way to satisfy ourselves. We helped an old man unload peppers from his farm wagon and he gave us a few for our trouble. We sat on a little berm in a dusty field, munching on peppers and feeling sorry for ourselves. Little kids played in the street, getting filthy. Various country people lounged on sidewalks, looking like they had never had anything to do and never would. Women walked in and out of the market where we had unloaded the old man's peppers. We didn't have the least idea where Pershing was or what we would do next. We'd hit bottom.

I called over a scruffy-looking dog of no discernible breed. I scratched his ears and gave him a pepper. I threw another one for him to fetch, but when he ran after it, Kip suddenly flung a stone at him, hard as he could, catching the poor dog in the belly and driving him off. It looked like it wasn't the first time the dog had been hit with stones, and he knew not to hang around.

I was angered, but Riley reacted before I could do anything. He rose to his feet.

"All right, enough. You want to fight that bad, come on. You don't need to take it out on a dog."

Kip didn't need more of an invitation. Riley was bouncing on his feet, getting into boxing mode, but Kip had none of it. He simply barreled off the ground and onto Riley, savaging him with haymakers from both fists and no regard for defense. Riley evaded the blows with minuscule dips and dives of his head, occasionally catching Kip's fists with his open hands. From the start, this was a different fight than the boxing matches I'd seen Riley conduct at Skelly's. That was sport, with Riley dancing and dodging and emphasizing defense, often taking down an opponent without suffering a single hard blow himself. This fight was for blood.

After his initial wildness, Kip settled into a boxing stance and threw jabs from both left and right. Riley blocked them, but you could hear the weight of the blows on his arms. He got in an occasional counterpunch to the body after blocking a jab, so fast you barely saw it. Mostly, Kip pushed forward and Riley shuffled backward, reflecting their contrasting styles. Kip wore a look of pure hate, springing more from his nature and his life than from any feeling toward his opponent. Riley looked merely interested, watching Kip's moves and waiting for openings.

Passersby surrounded us, like the schoolchildren in Independence when Kip fought in the pasture. I could tell the men were surprised and impressed by the skill of the fighters. This was no ordinary brawl. I vaguely heard the sound of a motorcar screeching to a stop and the slamming of doors, then two more men joined the crowd. I paid them no attention.

In the beginning, I assumed this would be Riley's fight to win. In part, of course, this was because I had learned that Riley always succeeded in any endeavor he tried, but it was also because Kip started so aggressively, throwing so many wild punches that missed their mark, as I had against Tom Klapmeyer. I assumed he would tire and Riley's more efficient style would win the day. So it seemed at first, with Riley landing counterpunches and even knocking Kip back with a jab on the button that startled him. The jab taught Kip a lesson, though, and he fought more sparingly of himself for the next several minutes. The fighters weaved, ducked, punched, circled, punched again, covering the entire field with their movements. Onlookers yelled encouragement, some inevitably betting on the outcome. No one made the least move to break up the fight or said anything to suggest this should be done. The people were no doubt grateful for the unexpected entertainment.

I suppose the fight lasted maybe twenty minutes, a very long time in a hot Mexican sun when a skilled boxer is doing his best to beat the bejesus out of you. There were relatively few pauses for breath. Both boys were soaked in sweat; Riley was bleeding from a cut on his mouth and Kip's right eye was swollen half-shut. It seemed the fight would go on for hours when, in an instant, it was over. Kip lowered his head and lit into Riley's body, catching him in the gut and seeming to knock out his wind. Stepping into his advantage, Kip launched an uppercut right into Riley's groin, then caught Riley on the chin as he bent over. I heard a sharp American voice immediately behind me call "Foul!" which seemed incongruous. I started forward to launch myself on Kip and try to save my friend, but Riley needed no saving. Stepping backward from the blow to his face, he pivoted on his right foot and brought a hard left smashing into Kip's kidney. Then came a right cross before Kip could protect himself, two left jabs and another right. Kip was down. It was over.

Riley stood over his man long enough to see for sure he wasn't getting up. He then clutched his groin, limped away, and dry-heaved. I held him up, as I didn't think he could stand. The crowd slowly dispersed, except for the two men who had arrived in the motorcar. One of them walked up to us and I realized for the first time he was an American soldier. Indeed, he seemed the very image of an American soldier: young, tall, ramrod straight, with a handsome, hawkish face. His boots shone, his uniform was neat, and the soft ranger hat on his head was set just so. He actually carried a riding crop, whether to use on his motorcar or his driver being unclear. He wore a pistol on each hip. In that dusty field in that dirty Mexican village, he looked like he had stepped out of a boy's adventure book.

"I'm Lieutenant George Patton of the Punitive Expedition," he said. "That was some of the best damn fighting I've ever seen. Who are you boys?"

8

Lieutenant Patton

Cornelius

Thirty minutes later, we were bouncing along the Mexican desert in the back of Patton's motorcar, one of Pershing's small fleet of vehicles. We left Kip lying where Riley dropped him and I don't know what became of him. We'd have waited for him to recover, but Patton didn't have much interest in losers.

"Can you imagine living in this goddam country?" Patton asked rhetorically, gazing with disapproval on the dry wasteland through which we passed. "Nothing but dust and heat and eating beans all day. No wonder these greasers don't amount to anything."

"Where are you from, General?" I asked.

"California. I'm not a general, I told you, I'm a lieutenant. But I'm an aide to a general."

Still, I could tell he liked me calling him that, so I said, "You'll be a general soon enough, I suppose. So I'll just call you that, least until Riley and me are soldiers ourselves."

This time he just smiled, so "general" it was.

There was always something a little uncanny about George Patton, but it took us awhile to figure out what it was. He was one of those folks who live in two worlds at the same time, one being the real one and one being this fantasy story that was playing in his head. His family was pure military, especially his grandfather who Patton came to tell us was some sort of Confederate hero. Everything Patton saw and did went through this internal fantasy filter, in which George was a sort of military god, worshipped by the crowd for his courage and strength and skill. Not surprisingly, he was a master of the romantic weapons, a fine pistol shot and a champion swordsman. He could ride a horse with Pershing's best Indian guides. But he was also a true expert on military history and was an advocate of tanks and of the use of air power in war right from the beginning, which was partly why the Punitive Expedition was the first American military endeavor to feature both. In some ways, the foolish and unsuccessful Punitive Expedition was when the United States said goodbye to the old century and hello to the new one, the American one.

Patton was easier to understand and predict once you realized he had this film of himself running in his head. He was somewhat like Churchill in that way, but Winston had more self-awareness and more of a sense of humor about himself. George Patton was a little insane.

"Where we going, General?" I asked him.

"Hardly anybody in this man's army knows where he's going. We were sent to fight a bandit who won't fight and we can't even find him. Every greaser you see could find Villa for us if he wanted to, but we haven't had a sniff of him since we crossed the border. That right, Hiram?"

Hiram was the driver, Sergeant Hiram Wallace.

"Mostly, sir. Not sure every greaser knows where Villa is, but you can bet that Villa knows where we are, every minute."

"That's certain. A regular army's a hard thing to hide, especially in a desert full of spies for their own kind."

I wondered how Hiram felt about Patton's comments on Mexicans. Hiram looked Mexican himself, or anyway mestizo. Turned out he was a mixed breed of a Scottish trader and an Apache squaw. He was a handy companion because he knew the desert and could pass for a Mexican or an Indian if he wanted. Patton, a perceptive user of men, picked him out of a troop and persuaded Pershing to appoint Hiram his driver.

"But if you're asking where this automobile is going at this particular moment," Patton continued, "we're going to Juarez to sign you boys up. General Pershing is based there, waiting for one of his units in the field to find Villa's trail. There's a rumor Villa is wounded and is hiding out somewhere, but so far it's just a rumor. I'd surely like to find that son of a bitch."

"What would you do to him, General?"

Patton gave a wolfish grin and pulled out one of his revolvers, holding it up for me to see.

"I'd say 'Pancho, this is the West. Stand up and pull your weapon.' Then I'd shoot the stupid spic between the eyes. I could do it, too. Then maybe we could get out of this stinking desert and go fight in France where we belong. This place might serve as practice for the troops, but there's no real honor scraping around this desert. France is where we need to be. That General Ludendorff, now there's a man worth fighting."

I didn't know the name yet. Ludendorff was considered the master strategist behind some big German victories early in the war. Patton was a bore on the subject of getting into the European war and regularly cursed Woodrow Wilson for being too much of a pantywaist to join the fight.

As usual, Riley said nothing as we sped through the desert. Patton looked over at him curiously.

"You all right, boy?"

"Yessir."

"You're not saying much."

"He never does, sir," I cut in, playing my usual role. "Riley is a silent man. But you've seen he has other ways of communicating."

"Well, he can box, if that's what you mean. I boxed at West Point, so I know. Riley is your name? Why do you want to join the army, Riley?"

Riley shrugged.

"Had to get out of Independence. Not cut out to be a farmer, I guess."

Patton slapped his knee.

"Exactly! Let other men till the fields and keep the accounts. Some are born for better things, higher things. Some are born for adventure, for sacrifice, for spilling their blood on the altar of battle. That's why you're here, isn't it, Riley?"

"Well, actually, I was just a horseshit farmer."

Hiram snorted. At first Patton didn't know how to react, but then he slapped his knee again and let out a loud, forced bray of a laugh.

"You're all right, Riley. You're all right."

Even so, his eyes showed that he wondered.

Hiram proved his worth the next day. We bivouacked in a tent in the desert. The soldiers at least had fairly warm blankets, but Riley and I shivered in the chill, such a remarkable contrast to the heat of the day. Army rations for breakfast, then on the road for the push into Juarez. With perhaps two hours to go, Hiram slowed as we approached a stopped car in the middle of the road. I believe this was the first car we'd seen during the entire drive from Chihuahua. It was a Model T Ford and an old Mexican peasant stood gazing mournfully at it. It had apparently managed to stall in the middle of the narrow road, requiring us to drive on the desert sand if we wanted to get around it. Patton instructed Hiram to stop.

"I advise against it, sir," Hiram said. "Old ambush trick. Look at the arroyo over there." Hiram bobbed his head forward and to the right, where the tops of shrubs denoted a depression in the dirt, of indeterminate size and depth. "Could be big enough to hide some bandits. It's a good spot for bushwhackers."

Patton grunted.

"A little action would be just what we need. I've been bored to death driving around these gulches. Besides, I have an idea we might get some information out of this man. Stop the car."

We stopped. Hiram immediately gestured to me to hand him his rifle from the back, which I did. Patton turned to Riley.

"You really speak Spanish?"

Riley nodded.

"Then you come with me. We're going to take this old man's water and tell him he can either die in the dust out here or tell us how to find Villa. At least it will be something to do. Hiram, keep us covered if you like."

That was that. Patton stepped out of the vehicle and strode toward the old Mexican, not looking to see if Riley followed, which he did. I could see that Hiram was scanning the arroyo, watching for trouble.

"*Hola,* señor," said Patton. "Car trouble?"

The old man said nothing. Patton nodded to Riley, who translated and listened to the response.

"He says the car just stopped. It's done this many times before. The car is a son of a whore."

Patton chuckled.

"*Tiene agua?*" he asked the old man.

"*Sí.*"

"Tell him to bring it to us, Riley."

Riley hesitated. I could tell that he didn't much like Patton's plan. At that moment, Hiram tensed and fired his carbine toward the arroyo.

"Get down!"

Riley was quicker than Patton. There was no discernible time between Hiram's shout and Riley barreling into the lieutenant, not enough time to blink. It's not so easy to bring down a man that you're standing next to just by bumping him, especially when the man has a head of height and maybe twenty pounds on you, but Riley managed it. He brought his leg behind Patton's left knee, for one thing, an old trick from the playground in Independence. The noise of the shot came just as Riley knocked Patton down. Not sure where the bullet went, but it didn't hit Patton.

All hell seemed to break loose for the next thirty seconds or so. Hiram jammed the car into gear and pulled to level with the Mexican's vehicle, forming a V with its point facing the arroyo. Shots were hailing down on us, but only from that location. Patton pulled his revolvers. The Mexican dove toward his car. Riley told Patton to give him a gun. Patton threw him one of his revolvers and Riley without hesitation shot the old Mexican, the first man he ever killed. We had quite the little firefight for a short time. I even joined in, using another rifle in the back of the car. I fired into the arroyo with no idea what I was shooting at, just trying to hit the points where flashes of gunfire appeared. In a few seconds, we realized the shooting from the arroyo had stopped and the only gunshots were ours. We waited, breathing hard behind the shelter of the two vehicles. No more shots came. The bandits, or whoever they were, had gone.

Patton reloaded his pistols.

"Now that was invigorating," he said. "Too bad we only hit a scared old man."

Hiram walked to the Mexican's car and peered in.

"There a gun on the seat," he said. "If the old man had got hold of it, you'd be dead."

Patton didn't say anything to that. Later, in Pershing's camp, I asked Riley how he knew the old Mexican was going for a gun.

"Didn't," he said as he took a drag on his hand-rolled cigarette. "Didn't care to find out."

Patton was quiet as we continued our drive. I was to learn that Patton could change like that—expansive and loquacious one minute, then silent and depressed the next. Of course, war can do that to people. Occasionally, Patton looked askance at Riley, sizing him up. Very little was said by any of us the rest of that day. Around suppertime, we pulled into the army camp near Juarez.

I'd never seen an army encampment before and this was an unusual one to start with, a combination of the nineteenth and twentieth centuries. The principal modes of transport were still feet and horses, but Pershing also commanded a ragtag fleet of motorcars and trucks and, for the first time associated with a United States combat unit, airplanes. It was just over a decade since the Wright Brothers made their flight at Kitty Hawk, but already air power was part of military thinking. We drove past rows and rows of small tents with men in brown uniforms idling round them, hardly mindful of mounted officers clopping along the dirt paths we drove on. Then, as though we passed into a new world, we came upon a cleared, hard-baked field with six biplanes scattered around upon it. Scruffy-looking men, the pilots, bent over their plane engines with large tools, working on the newfangled innards of the flying machines. Other men lolled on the ground or tended campfires, exchanging stories of their hair-raising attempts to get these planes in the air and keep them there. Riley and I had never seen more than one plane at a time, and then at rare barnstorming appearances in fields near Independence. This seemed to presage the arrival of The Future. As I look back, the whole twentieth century seemed to be a long series of repeated arrivals of The Future.

Hiram kept on driving and Patton seemed uninterested in the surroundings. He was focused on finding Pershing and making his report. As we were soon to find out, he was also focused on his plans for us, particularly Riley.

Hiram stopped the car in front of a small wood-frame building that would have looked like a hunter's cabin had it not been sitting in the midst of a desert and surrounded by an army encampment. The cloud of dust that the car made as it stopped was nothing, as dust was everywhere. There was dust on the ground, in the air, on the faces and uniforms of the men, in our eyes and noses and mouths. As a man walked out the front door to greet us, slapping his sleeves with his gloves, I saw there was dust even on Black Jack Pershing.

"Hello, Lieutenant. Good to see you back."

Patton saluted and Pershing returned it. Pershing looked at Riley and me.

"Who are these boys? Recruits?"

"Not exactly, sir. You'll understand better when I make my report. If I could have a few minutes, sir?"

Pershing looked at us dubiously, but waved Patton inside and shut the door behind them. Riley and I were pretty raggedy and Pershing, despite the dust, was famously fastidious in his dress. He must have just come in from the field, as he kept himself very clean and orderly even in the roughest of conditions. It's remarkable, as I write this in 1982, that the man I was looking at made his reputation as a horse soldier, fighting Indians in the West. Pershing was known to the whole country as brave, tenacious, organized, disciplined, and the epitome of a fighting soldier. While not tall, he was trim and stood so straight that he could intimidate much bigger men by his physical presence alone. Patton had gazed at him with what looked like adoration and Pershing's smile when he first saw his junior officer suggested that those feelings were reciprocated. What I did not know at the time, but found out soon enough, was that Pershing was married to Patton's sister.

It was, in fact, quite a story. The general had a long and devoted marriage to his first wife, who died suddenly and tragically only about a year before the Villa expedition. To everyone's surprise, Pershing quickly found solace in the arms of George Patton's sister, a much younger woman who simultaneously brought joy to the middle-aged general and professional advancement to her ambitious brother. When Pershing got the Villa assignment, Patton harassed him mercilessly until he was given a position as Pershing's aide. Since then, while Pershing's troops wandered through the Mexican desert looking in vain for Pancho Villa, the restless Patton was sent from troop to troop, village to village, running errands, which as much as anything were intended to keep him occupied and distracted from complaining to his commander about the lack of combat.

All this, we learned from Hiram as he took us to the mess tent for the best meal we'd had in days: beans, hardtack, and coffee. Two other soldiers of Hiram's acquaintance joined us at the table. They were curious about us and I related a fair amount of our story since leaving Independence, not embellishing events more than courtesy required for the sake of the entertainment value. Riley's conquest of Kip Miller and his quick dispatch of the Mexican on the road drew curious looks from the men, especially when my account was confirmed by Hiram.

"Well, you made yourselves a good start in this army," said one of them, a tanned old veteran of a corporal who I noticed was missing the third finger on his left hand. "George Patton is the general's aide and also his brother-in-law. Saving his life made you two important friends."

Hiram was wiser, or perhaps knew Patton better.

"Don't count on that," he said. "I don't see Lieutenant Patton as the type to appreciate being saved. He wants to do all the saving there is to do himself. Besides, in my experience, if you want to make a man your enemy, your best course is to give him cause to be grateful to you."

"I've made the same observation," Riley said. "And he doesn't need to be grateful to me. I don't expect we'll even see him much, once we get assigned somewhere."

"Why in blazes did you want to join the army?" Hiram asked. "These boys and I have done it pretty much all our lives and don't know any better, but why did you come all the way from Missouri to chase after some greaser in this god-awful desert?"

Riley locked eyes with Hiram. I sensed that the two felt something in common as men of action, for Riley was almost forthcoming, by his usual reckoning.

"I'm eighteen. The life laid out for me is to work a farm with my mother and sisters. That ain't the life I want. So this expedition seemed like a chance to make a break, to do something so different from that life that nobody would ever expect me to go back there again."

Hiram nodded. He offered us his smokes and Riley took one, I did not.

"Well," Hiram said, "I expected it was something like that. Pretty much a common story. If you want adventure, though, you're in the wrong place. We haven't had a whiff of Villa yet, anywhere we look."

"We've gotten a good whiff of every other damn thing in this country," said the corporal. "Don't smell so good, ourselves."

The men suddenly got to their feet as they realized George Patton had entered the mess tent and was approaching our table. Riley and I joined them, figuring we were about to become soldiers and might as well act like it. I even saluted, though Patton didn't acknowledge it.

"All right, men, take your ease. Hiram, we're off again in the morning. Heading back to Chihuahua, got to see one of the señors. These boys are coming along."

Hiram started.

"Sir?"

"I said these boys are coming along. The general has made them my civilian aides. Boys, will you agree to follow my orders and be entirely at my command?"

This seemed odd.

"Are we joining the army, sir?" I asked.

"Well, no, not exactly," Patton said. "You see, the general believes you can be useful to me as I scout the country, given that you both speak Spanish, but the general did not feel it was appropriate to sign you on at this time. So that's the way it's going to be. I'll meet the three of you at the car at dawn. Be ready for a long drive."

Patton turned on his heel and strode out before we could respond or even grasp exactly what he had said.

Hiram could easily see what must have happened and he explained it to the table. Patton wanted the two of us on his expeditions, so Riley could fight and I could cook and talk with him and we could both act as interpreters. But General Pershing was no doubt painfully aware that he had suffered some criticism for making his brother-in-law his aide over the bids of more senior and more qualified men. He could hardly now give his aide an aide, certainly not two of them. So the compromise was that we remained civilians and Pershing simply looked the other way. Thus, our military service would wait.

We were disappointed, for we assumed this meant we would not see any fighting. As it turned out, this wasn't exactly the case. While Pershing's regular troops continued to wander lost in the desert and largely missed engaging with the enemy, our own very different Mexican adventure had just begun.

9

The Ortega Hacienda

Cornelius

We met Patton at dawn, as ordered. Soon we were again bumping along into the desert, just like the day before. We were even heading back to Chihuahua. On the way, Patton explained why we were going there.

It seemed a gentleman rancher named Ortega had been endlessly petitioning Pershing and officials in Washington to allow him to help mediate the political situation in Mexico, especially as regards Carranza and Villa. Pershing had little patience for such self-promoting blather and ignored him, but somehow Don Ortega rang the right bell in Washington and one of his connections intervened on his behalf. The Don had insisted that a courier be sent to him and that it be none other than George S. Patton. So Patton claimed anyway. He described our task as tedious and trivial, but we were ordered to be diplomatic with the rancher and hear him out, so we would.

The Dons were wealthy landowners in northern Mexico. They remained a significant power in the north, although their status was being threatened by the political upheavals and associated pillaging. They were neither as organized nor quite as rich as the large plantation owners in the south, whose particular nemesis was Emiliano Zapata. The Dons mostly kept to their haciendas, living well and lording it over the local peasantry in what essentially was a feudal system. They had existed in this fashion for centuries and fared especially well under Porfirio Diaz. Diaz had been perfectly content to leave the Dons to their estates as long as they paid the piper, but the current president, Carranza, was hostile toward them and therefore not at all to their liking. The growing popularity of Pancho Villa and his addiction to banditry and violence didn't help matters any, as far as the Dons were concerned.

Riley and I knew none of this as we rode along and we wouldn't have cared if we had. All we knew was that Mexico was damn hot and exceedingly boring and looked to remain that way for the foreseeable future. Even I didn't say much or ask Patton any questions as he laid out the mission to us. Riley looked like he might not say anything ever again because it would be too much trouble.

We arrived at Señor Ortega's estate at twilight. His ranch went well out into the desert, but the heart of his estate was situated in a more pleasant countryside that was gently hilly and featured enough water to allow some tree growth beyond the usual desert scrub. I remember it as looking more like the country you'd see around San Antonio than the barren north Mexico desert.

Ortega was obviously a lucky man. Cattle roamed near the road, tended by his *vaqueros*. As we approached his hacienda, we passed through a small village inhabited by the country people who worked Ortega's land and owed him their allegiance. I found it far more pleasant and orderly than other Mexican villages I had seen. There was a store and a bakery and a blacksmith shop, with a stable that I assumed contained the great man's own mounts. In the bakery, I saw an enormously fat woman rolling out tortillas while joking with a little girl who sat nearby and watched her toiling away. It all seemed quite idyllic, if you were a Mexican peasant.

We pulled up in front of adobe walls protected by a large iron gate. Two *vaqueros*, dressed in full cowboy garb and carrying large shotguns in addition to the sidearms at their belts, leaned against the wall. Not wishing to appear overwrought at the appearance of these armed gringos at the gate, they lazily looked at us under heavy-lidded eyes. After enough of a pause to demonstrate we did not impress them, one of these gentlemen asked if one of us was Lieutenant Patton. Hiram said that was the case. So assured, the sentry turned, unlocked the gate, and swung it open for us. We drove through the entrance into what seemed to me the most beautiful place I had ever seen.

We were surrounded by green, for one thing, whereas I'd looked at nothing but sand and rock since leaving Missouri. There were trees: not just Joshua trees but honest-to-god willow trees with their mossy cascades and even oaks towering over the scene. There was a pond, no doubt man-made, with water that pleasantly reflected the surrounding greenery. I don't suppose there was a unicorn dipping his neck to drink from the pool, but if there had been, he wouldn't have looked out of place.

All this beautiful, unexpected nature was simply to frame the hacienda, the centerpiece of the estate. It was just as it should have been: a large, rambling one-story structure of pink adobe with impressive wood beams, an inviting stone patio in front, and a peasant, perhaps a gardener, sleeping on a bench near the massive front door. Señor Ortega was indeed a lucky man. A life in this place would be worth living and worth fighting to keep if it were threatened.

It appeared that Señor Ortega did, in fact, think it was threatened. We saw additional heavily armed *vaqueros* posted at strategic points on each end of the house and spread out along the walls, pacing and smoking and looking like all fighters look on guard duty: mostly bored, but occasionally shaking themselves into vigilance to keep from nodding off.

As we pulled to a stop at the end of the drive, the front door of the house swung open and we were greeted by the man himself. Don Eduardo Antonio Ortega y Villanueva stepped onto the patio with a broad smile, his arms outstretched in welcome. He was a burly man with a bald dome and a heavy black beard. He was casually dressed, more like an American than a Mexican, with a white shirt opened to the breastbone, black pants, and riding boots. He limped rather badly, which we were to learn was the result of a withered leg, an affliction from birth.

"My friend, Lieutenant Patton," he boomed in a deep bass. "Welcome. You honor my home."

Patton returned the smile.

"The honor is ours, Don Eduardo. Your English is excellent."

"You are too kind," said the Don as he shook Patton's hand. "I have spent much time in the States. It has been necessary for my business, and it also has been my pleasure to get to know your beautiful country."

Well, wasn't this just chummy, though? Patton had given us the impression that this Don had the vapors, a claim that tended to be confirmed by the firepower patrolling around the grounds, but Ortega himself seemed happy as could be.

Apparently, being the help, we were beneath introductions. Patton didn't refer to Hiram, Riley, or me and Ortega didn't ask. He waved us in and said his servants would tend to our luggage.

"That's kind of you and we will gratefully accept your hospitality for tonight," said Patton. "But of course, we don't want to impose on you for long and we have our duties to attend to. So perhaps you and I should get down to the business that you wanted to discuss."

Ortega clapped his hands.

"I know you Americans. Always practical, always in a hurry to get right to business. It makes you so pleasant to do business with. But tonight, we need not discuss this. I am proud of my hacienda and insist that you take the evening to relax and enjoy our poor level of food and drink. There will be much time for business tomorrow."

Before Patton could protest, Ortega turned and walked energetically, despite the limp, through the foyer and down a hallway.

"My family is anxious to meet you," he called back to us.

Not having a choice, we hurried after him. A tall man I hadn't previously noticed fell in step behind us. He was dark-skinned and dressed in white, like a servant. I imagined he was Ortega's majordomo of some sort, but since he was help, he didn't get introduced either.

A girl and a young boy were standing in the hallway, looking respectful and dressed for company. The boy looked about ten and wore a Mexican suit and a bolo tie, despite the heat. He was sweating and looked very serious. It was the girl who drew the eye. She was a true beauty whom I pegged to be a year or so younger than Riley and me, who were eighteen at the time. She wore riding breeches, boots, a yellow blouse, and she held a *vaquero's* hat at her side, looking like she was about to go riding. The cowgirl outfit showed off her figure to advantage and it was worth the show. She was a short little thing, barely five feet tall, but her tits strained nicely at her blouse and her waist was trim and her bottom nicely rounded. Forgive an old man his memories.

Above the neck was even more of a treat. I've always been partial to Mexican girls, but this one would stand out at the most glamorous fiesta in Mexico City. She had unusually high cheekbones, lovely olive skin, and deep dark eyes that could flash with joy or anger, yet always conveyed a trace of sorrow. Her dark hair was pulled back, but I later saw that it was a suitable frame for that gorgeous face: jet black, lustrous, soft.

Not sure how much of this I took in at that first moment, of course. Possibly just the tits.

"Here is my family," Don Eduardo said proudly as he waved at them. "My son Miguel and my daughter Marta."

The boy bowed stiffly, while Marta inclined her head but gave little further acknowledgement of us. Don Eduardo introduced Patton and said we were American soldiers here on important business.

"They are our honored guests, and we must do all we can to be gracious hosts."

I have some suggestions along those lines that involve your daughter, I thought to myself.

Patton may have had the same idea, for he stepped forward and after elegantly bending over the lady's hand, kissed it and murmured *"Encantado."* Say what you will, Patton knew how to turn on the social skills. He may have grown up out west, but he graduated from West Point and came from a long line of Southern military brass. Those boys know how to charm.

Patton actually rubbed Miguel's head and said "Hello, youngster," which seemed to please his father more than it did Miguel.

I noticed that the boy held a cane; he had his father's withered leg, but with him it was more severe. The poor young fellow walked with such difficulty, he was painful to watch.

Don Eduardo gestured to the tall, dark fellow.

"Gentlemen, this is my man, Francisco. I would be lost without him. His family has served mine for generations. Francisco will show you to your rooms, where you can wash off the dust of the trail. Please join me for drinks when you are ready. Francisco will show you the way."

Francisco seemed a dour one and he didn't acknowledge us at all as he was introduced. He simply waved us toward the stairs and set off, leaving us to follow again, which Patton and I did. In a moment, I realized that Riley had not moved. He was watching Marta turn and walk away, bound for the stables no doubt. I went back and squeezed Riley's elbow, but he stayed rooted to where he was until Marta was no longer in view.

"Cornelius," he said, his eyes glued to the spot where she had disappeared, "I'm going to marry that girl."

10

"These Are My Jewels"

Jim

"That was another lie by Cornelius. I never said any such thing, I'd have felt a fool. It's the sort of lie Cornelius tells once in a while. Gives the story some pep, maybe."

Riley stabbed at the fire with a poker. It didn't seem cool enough for a fire, even in the evening, but then I wasn't Riley's age. Old men need their warmth.

"Is the rest of it true? Is that really how you met Grandmother?"

"Oh, that part's true enough. If you walked out that door, you'd see the exact spot in the hallway where I first met her. She was the most beautiful woman I ever saw. The most beautiful sight I ever saw, whether you're talking women or horses or art or buildings or anything that might be called beautiful." Riley sank back in his chair and picked up his drink. "That was your grandmother. She beat all."

I believed him. Grandmother Riley was very beautiful even as an old woman and I could tell she'd have been a knockout in her day. As a child, I was always scared of Riley. He seemed dark and mysterious, but Grandmother was wonderful. She didn't grab at us or talk down to us, like most adults do. She would actually listen to what I had to say and then react to it, like I was an interesting companion. She spoke in a very soft voice and its volume and Mexican accent combined to make me lean in and listen carefully, and somehow this made her all the more attractive. I had to work a little to have a conversation with Grandmother and it was always worth it. I remember when I was very little, sitting on the sofa at the hacienda with my sister and Grandmother. My sister reached out to touch the necklace she wore and said, "You've got pretty jewelry, Grandmother."

Grandmother put her arms around the two of us.

"These are my jewels," she said.

Well, it sounds trivial, but I've never forgotten what she said or how her voice made me feel when she said it. My sister was the same; she reminded me of the incident at Grandmother's funeral. Some people have a way about them, I guess.

"I was interested that Grandpa Jimmy mentioned her sadness, even then. There was always something about Grandmother that seemed sad to me. I never understood it. It made her... special, somehow."

Riley sat quiet for a long time.

"Your grandmother was sensitive. The world touched her in ways I could never understand. Like how a person can be sensitive in the skin and get a rash just from touching some pine needles. That's how your grandmother was about sad things that happened. They touched her more deeply than most folks. It made things hard, to be that way in the world she was born into. She was raised wealthy when she was a little girl and her mother took good care of her. She was kept pretty isolated. Then her mother died a few years before I met her and that bothered her. And Mexico had its troubles and they affected the hacienda and her father, with the armed guards and so on. And then later..."

Riley's voice drifted off. I wondered for a moment if he was asleep. Then he knocked back some bourbon, lit another cigarette, and resumed the story.

11

Sanctuary

Riley

Patton kept his composure pretty well at dinner that night. It couldn't have been easy, since he was anxious to finish what he saw as a useless errand and get back to the army. Patton wanted glory, and he didn't see much prospect for it in chatting up an old Don and his offspring.

Cornelius and I thought it was a fine dinner, though. Hiram was allowed to attend, so it was the four of us Americans and the Don and his two children. I thought Francisco would be serving, but he was nowhere in sight.

"Francisco had to leave us tonight," said the Don when Cornelius inquired about him. "He received word that his mother is ill. She lives in a village about a day's ride from here. I gave him permission to see to her, of course. It is all right, we will be well taken care of by Juanita here."

Cornelius had been eyeing Juanita from the start. She was a well-figured, sassy-looking servant girl who'd been bringing in the plates. She wore a blouse cut to show off her cleavage when she bent to serve us, which she seemed to do a bit more frequently than you'd expect. She had a look about her that invited eye contact and she let you know it was welcome. Cornelius didn't talk so much that meal, making it an unusual one in my experience. He was watching Juanita.

As I said, Patton was on good behavior. He smiled and nodded as the Don prosed on about his life and times. It was a useful account of the state of mind of the big landowners in the desert at that time, if you could keep your mind off the girls who were present.

"There are a number of us here in the north," the Don explained, "men of property with haciendas and estates. Ranchers, mostly, of course. We take our cattle across the border and the Texans drive them north, up the old trails to the stockyards in Omaha and Kansas City, and on to Chicago. It was a good business back then, in the days of Diaz."

Patton was swallowing wine and was late on his cue, but in a moment he asked, "And now?"

Don Eduardo smiled, but it was not a happy smile.

"These are the days of revolution, don't you know? It is hard to know which bandit is the worst: Carranza, Obregón, Zapata, Villa, or Huerta, God rot his soul. All of them thieves and fools."

Marta clucked her tongue.

"Papa, our guests. Calm yourself."

The Don smiled indulgently.

"Believe me, my daughter, I am calm. I am always calm. I have my beautiful daughter and my beautiful son and my beautiful hacienda. What have I to fear?"

Losing them, I thought. He didn't look calm to me.

Patton cut into his beefsteak, which was very good, by the way.

"Have the Villistas been a problem for you, Don Eduardo?"

Our host shrugged.

"Nothing that is serious, Lieutenant Patton. They have gotten drunk and made themselves obnoxious in the village and occasionally they steal some cattle. But I have plenty of cattle." He made a small gesture at Juanita. "More wine, *por favor*. Open more bottles."

The wine had been flowing freely and both Don Eduardo and Cornelius were starting to show the effects of it, although Patton and I drank sparingly. I've never been much for wine.

When Juanita went to fetch more wine, no servants were left in the room.

"Do you know why I say these revolutionaries are fools, Lieutenant, whichever side they are on?"

Patton shook his head.

"Because they play with fire. Mexico is a land of peasants, *campesinos*. Diaz ruled with an iron fist and all went well. That is what the peasants want, in their hearts, because they don't know how to act and need a strong man to think and act for them. In a small way, I am the strong man here, on my land, in my village. All I've ever asked is to play my part. What is good for me is good for my people. But these *revolutionaries*"—he spat the word—"pander to the peasants. They lie to them, make them think they can live like their betters. It will reap the whirlwind, Lieutenant. Here, or in your country, wherever men live, the strong must rule over the peasants. That is the way of the world. That is how the Earth is made. The fool who preaches to the contrary will wind up disemboweled with his own machete."

"Papa!" That was too much for Marta, in front of guests.

"I'm sorry, I'm sorry. That was not appropriate before my daughter and my guests, but it is true, señors. The sooner these revolutionaries are hung by their heels and order is returned to Mexico, the better."

Cornelius couldn't sit still for that, even drunk and lecherous as he was.

"Your pardon, sir, but my own father is a sort of revolutionary, you could say. He believes in the rights of the worker and the power of the masses and such."

Patton glared at him, but Don Eduardo smiled.

"What does your father do, young man?"

"He owns a bookstore, back home. In Missouri."

"Ah, but that is a good revolutionary, young man. He sells books and makes a profit and raises a fine young man to go into the army."

"Well, sir, many of his books are about the revolution and my father believes that revolution is coming in Europe and later to America."

"Where in Missouri is your father's store?"

"Independence."

Ortega's eyes twinkled.

"I shall watch with interest for news of the revolution in Independence, Missouri. It may be a while, so in the meantime, have more wine."

As soon as Juanita returned from the wine cellar, Cornelius lost interest in revolution. After dinner, as Marta and Miguel retired, Don Eduardo said that tomorrow Marta would show us the village. It sounded good to me, but Patton looked pained. As soon as the men were alone with their brandies, Patton asked Ortega to tell us what he wanted to say to Pershing.

Ortega shook his head.

"I'm sorry, Lieutenant, but I must request your indulgence. You gave me no word you were coming. There are certain arrangements that must be made."

"I don't understand," said Patton. "You've repeatedly sent word to General Pershing to have a courier come here. You said you had something critically important that could only be told in person. Here I am, ready to hear it. What arrangements need to be made?"

"Believe me, I would tell you if I could. I know it seems peculiar. All I can say now is that it will be worth your time. In fact, if you honor us by spending one more day and night in my hacienda, I can assure you of a gift that is your most urgent desire."

Cornelius snorted softly, the scoundrel. Patton scowled.

"Your pardon, Don Eduardo, but I did not come here to be given riddles. Or gifts. My most urgent desire right now is to get back to my mission, which is to find Pancho Villa."

"And that is my gift to you, Lieutenant Patton. There is no riddle. In two days, Pancho Villa will be yours. Now tell me, is that worth another day under my roof?"

With that, Patton lost all pretense of courtesy. He stomped his foot and threatened the forces of John Pershing to descend upon the hacienda, but he could not get Ortega to say more. It was stay the night and the next day or leave empty-handed. If we stayed, Don Eduardo said, then the day after the next would see the end of the bandit known as the Jaguar. Since Patton's most urgent desire was glory, there was certainly no chance in hell he would walk away from the chance that George Smith Patton, Jr. would become the man who caught or killed Pancho Villa.

So we stayed. We must have shifted back into being the help, for Hiram, Cornelius, and I bunked in the same room in the servants' quarters. My thoughts were on Marta, but Cornelius talked nonstop about Juanita. Her lips, her eyes, her body, how she kept flirting with him. Hiram finally had to throw a pillow at him to get him to shut up and go to sleep.

At breakfast, it became clear that Don Eduardo remembered that Patton had boasted over the dinner table about his horsemanship. The Don said that he and Patton would mount up and ride his estate, so they could get to know each other better. Patton enthusiastically agreed, probably thinking the Don would use the opportunity to explain how we were going to catch Pancho Villa.

"Don't worry for your men, Lieutenant Patton," said the Don. "Marta and Miguel will take them on a tour of our village and our grounds."

Miguel took this impassively, as seemed his nature. Marta looked demurely downward. I found myself hoping she was not displeased.

We gathered shortly after breakfast at the front door. Two beautiful horses were waiting. Patton truly was an excellent rider and cut an impressive figure when he hoisted himself into the saddle. Don Eduardo was far less dashing, but comfortable with his animal. They set off, accompanied by two armed *vaqueros*. We, too, had two armed guards walking with us, but what caused Cornelius the greatest joy was that Juanita also appeared, walking behind Marta. The servant girl was wrapped in a long headscarf, but her eyes still flashed and she looked even more of a lively goer than she had the evening before.

Young Miguel played the tour guide. He had his patter down pat, no doubt having shown other of his father's business associates around the grounds. It was a lovely day, cool, and the sights inside the hacienda grounds were a green, refreshing contrast to the desert that surrounded us. Miguel told us that Don Eduardo's grandfather built the hacienda and, in the years since, the Ortegas had held their estate against Indians, bandits, the Mexican government, drought, floods, and famine. While it was Miguel's voice, the words clearly came from Don Eduardo. We heard pride, arrogance, and determination, with an underlay of genuine worry over the revolution swirling around them.

At least, I did. Cornelius probably heard little, as he was lollygagging in back, walking next to Juanita. Hiram shot him occasional warning looks, but said nothing. Cornelius spoke softly to the girl in Spanish, asking about her family and complimenting her looks and last night's meal. She seemed amused by the attention. More of this, I thought, and Cornelius might spend the night in a different bedroom than ours. I hoped Don Eduardo was broadminded when it came to the virtue of his servants.

Marta veered left and led us to a small copse of trees in a corner of the grounds. There we saw a cross, marking the grave of her mother. Marta, Miguel, Juanita, and the guards all made the sign of the cross. Cornelius did too, for the wrong reason.

"My mother loved the hacienda," Marta said. "She loved the trees and the gardens. So my father decided to bury her here, rather than in the village cemetery where the other Ortegas are buried." She had no tears, just that sadness. "Someday Papa will rest here. And I."

Well, she was right about that.

We took a carriage ride into the village. Listening to Don Eduardo last evening back at the hacienda, it was easy to envision the place as a cozy Mexican version of a medieval town, full of contented peasants grateful to the lord of the manor. The reality, as was probably true of all medieval towns, was that the streets were dirty, the people were surly, and the atmosphere was tense with an undercurrent of hostility. As we passed by them, people looked down and knuckled their foreheads at Marta and Miguel as a form of salute, but there was no warmth or respect in the gesture. They stared sullenly at us gringos and, while I saw no one actually spit on our shadows, they may just as well have done.

Not that it bothered Cornelius, of course. As we looked in at the village church and listened to Miguel prattle on, Cornelius became ever more forward in his attentions to Juanita, who as a result became ever more inviting. I knew that Marta was keenly aware of it, for she was careful not to look their way.

When we arrived back at the hacienda, Hiram was the first to peel off and head back to our room, tired of the forced courtesies and of the flirting between Cornelius and Juanita. The servant girl looked boldly at Cornelius.

"The señor should get out of the sun," she said to him. "Perhaps he would care for a visit to the servants' quarters, to see how we who work at the hacienda live. We are very lucky here."

She smiled and nodded to Marta, but I noticed no affection between the two of them. I think she might have reprimanded the girl for her impudence, but Miguel grabbed my hand.

"Soldier, come with me. I will show you my horse!"

Miguel took my hand and led me toward the stable, leaving

Marta little choice but to follow. Lucky Cornelius, I thought, though I would not have traded with him.

Miguel certainly had a beautiful horse, a little bay with lots of spirit who nickered at me from his stall. Also in the stable was a bicycle, which surprised me, since it hardly seemed the place to find a new contraption of the modern age. Marta told me her father had ordered it on a whim for Miguel, but since no one on the ranch knew how to ride it, it sat unused.

This was my cue, of course. What faster way to win a lady than to teach her young brother how to ride his bicycle? It would create all sorts of opportunity for laughs and fun, while showing me to be a caring, affectionate man. Two problems: I wasn't really a caring or affectionate man and I'd never been able to ride a bicycle.

I did try, once. A boy back in Independence let me ride his bicycle. I figured since I could ride any horse put under me, a bicycle couldn't be too hard. Of course, the first time you do anything, it's hard. I made the mistake of taking my first ride with a group of girls from our school looking on and giggling. I drove the machine right into a tree and wound up underneath it on the ground. I can still hear the peals of laughter from the girls.

I knew better than to repeat that experience in front of Marta, so I walked the bicycle over to a flat space, put Miguel on it, and ran alongside him. I'll say this, he made a better show of it than I did. The first time, he looked frightened to death and he tipped over as soon as I let go of him, but that's common. He jumped right back on without needing any encouragement and, after two more tries, he was moving along and pedaling under his own power, gimpy leg and all. Marta clapped her hands and cheered: she did love that boy. It was the first real smile I saw from her. Your grandmother's smiles weren't frequent, but they were powerful. She had so many reasons to be sad that when you brought her joy, it brought you joy. You didn't forget it.

We finally went back into the house, leaving Miguel to practice. Marta seemed to relax with me now, as though laughter was so unexpected an event, it created a sort of intimacy between us. She poured us each a goblet of water and nodded me toward a chair in the great room.

"You seemed so stern at first," she said to me in that sweet voice of hers. "The quiet, rugged soldier. But with Miguel, you were so gentle and kind. What sort of man are you?"

"Well, I'm not a soldier. Cornelius and I are just sort of aides to Lieutenant Patton."

"Yes, this Cornelius, do you know him well?"

"Very well. Cornelius is my best friend. We came from Missouri together."

Marta made a charming little frown.

"Your best friend is a forward man. Heaven knows what he and my servant are doing at this very moment."

I doubted that Heaven had much to do with it, but I said nothing. She asked me what Missouri is like.

"Greener than here. Gets hot in summers, like here. I don't know."

"Not as hot as here. I'm sure our desert just seems hot and dry and ugly to you."

I shifted in my seat and looked her in the eye, I fear with a certain intensity.

"I'll tell you the truth, miss. I've never seen a place I liked as much as this hacienda. Something about it. The air, the grounds, I don't know, something. This is the first place I've ever been to in my life where I thought I could settle down and stay forever."

Embarrassed, I looked away. It was true, though.

Marta smiled again.

"I feel that way. I feel just that way." She paused, considering. "Wait."

She left the room. I sat, sipping my water and wondering if I'd made a mistake, feeling like I hadn't. She returned with a journal of some sort.

"I've never read from this to anyone before, except my mother. I don't know why I have it now, but something you said… I want to read something to you. I write poems."

You know your grandmother's poetry. She wrote poems all her life. Cornelius would make fun of them, but I thought they were beautiful, because they came from her. Your grandmother wasn't at ease with people outside the family. She put all her feelings into her poems, so I love them because they're hers.

"This is a poem I wrote," she said a little sheepishly. "Please don't laugh, but you made me think of it when you talked about our hacienda. It is called 'Sanctuary.' I wrote it soon after my mother died, and it's about our house and our ranch."

Years later, she translated all her early Spanish poems into

English. This is "Sanctuary," which she read to me that day in a clear, proud voice.

> A wind-tortured bird, on his course to keep
> Draws strength from his song, to dare;
> My soul, like a ship on a storm tossed deep,
> Strives too toward the harbor fair,
> A shrine where the mask is removed, serene,
> A haven from Earth's lone strife.
> So I've oriented a port wherein
> To rest from the storms of life.

I was silent a moment.

"It's the most beautiful poem I ever heard, Marta," I said.

I meant it, too. I was in love. At that moment, I wanted to live in this hacienda, with this woman, for the rest of my time on this Earth.

12

Juanita, Ortega, and the Spaniard

Cornelius

Riley indeed fell in love with the beautiful Marta on that visit to the Ortega ranch. It was true love, the truest love I ever have witnessed. It had to be, for him to put up with her damn poetry. Pure swill, but Riley lapped it up like it was bourbon. Or so he said.

But I'm getting ahead of myself.

Don Eduardo introduced us around and got us settled in. The most interesting feature of his hacienda that I noticed was this pert servant girl named Juanita who hovered around behind the big butler fellow as he led us to our rooms. She was just a little older than Riley and me, maybe twenty or twenty-one. A little plump and likely to become fat one day, but right then she was exactly what you'd have in mind if you ordered up a buxom, lively servant girl. Round bottom, blouse cut to show off nicely rounded tits, dark skin, black eyes that had a way of looking down and then up at you with a question in them—or a desire. Yes, Juanita was the whole package, even almost clean, which in that desert at that time was quite an accomplishment and more than we could say for ourselves. I watched her closely from the start. She seemed to look over each of the gringos and I thought for sure she landed on me, for after the first few minutes, I kept catching her watching me, whereupon she'd look away and smile. She didn't give the same attention to any of my companions. Sound judgment, that girl had.

The next day, while Patton and Don Eduardo went riding, Marta and her brother showed Riley, Hiram, and me around the village. It wasn't much. Juanita fortunately went along and I took plenty of opportunities to smile at her and show off my Spanish. She didn't say anything with the young master and mistress on hand, but she didn't back away, either. I was itching to get alone with her before Patton got back.

My chance came naturally, with no effort by me. When we got back to the hacienda, the youngster led Riley off to the stable to show him a horse. Juanita then offered to show me around the hacienda, including the servants' quarters, the daring little darling. I naturally nipped along at her heels and I don't think the rest of the party suspected a thing. The hacienda was a big, rambling place and I grew impatient when Juanita led me on a tour rather than making straight for her room.

"Here is the kitchen," she explained as if I couldn't tell. "And here is the dining room," as if we hadn't eaten there the previous evening.

"Are you from the village?" I asked, to make conversation.

She paused for a moment.

"Of course, señor. Peasants like me do not wander far."

"Please call me Cornelius, Juanita. What are your duties?"

"I attend to the señorita. I clean. I serve drinks and meals. Tell me, Cornelius, what are your duties?"

"Mine?"

"Yes. You and your friend travel with Señor Patton, yet you wear no uniform. You both speak the best Spanish I have heard from Americans. Are you Señor Patton's servants? Or are you important men, the sons of big men in Washington perhaps? Or are you maybe a special kind of soldier, one who wears no uniform because his work is secret and dangerous?"

"You ask surprising questions, Juanita. How do you think of such things?"

"We servants hear things," she answered coyly. "Not all of us are ignorant of the world."

"Well, if I were the son of a big man, I'd dress a lot better, I'll tell you that. And I'm not a servant. As for that other thing, well, maybe it's too secret and dangerous for me to tell you."

She looked me over, as if sizing me up.

"As I said, I am not ignorant of the world. You are wondering why we do not go to my room. If I were to tell you that I sleep in a big open room with three other girls, would you be less interested in my living quarters?" She stepped toward me, so we almost touched. "And what if I tell you that I have one special duty? That I am the only one with a key to the bedroom of the late señora, that Don Eduardo has kept her room locked and empty, just as it was, and he allows no one to enter except for the servant with the duty of cleaning it? What if I tell you that this is the most private room in the hacienda and that this is the key for it?"

She pulled a key from the pocket of her long, full skirt and showed it to me.

"If you tell me that, Juanita, I will ask you to show me the room."

She smiled.

"A good servant always obeys."

She wheeled and skipped away, leaving me to trot along behind.

On the surface, all was splendid. Inside of me, however, was turmoil. Fact was, I was still a virgin. Girls attracted me and astounded me and aroused me, but so far I'd not had much success at being romantic with them. Back home I'd kissed some girls and kept company with one for almost a year. We petted and came pretty close once or twice, but neither of us ever had the nerve to complete the act. Once it became clear that Juanita was game and we had the opportunity, my stomach started churning because I didn't know how I'd perform or what it would be like. I was, however, keen to find out.

The room where Marta's late mother had slept was at the end of a hallway of bedrooms. When we reached the door, Juanita unlocked it and motioned for me to stay outside. She went in, shut the door, and came back for me in a moment. She said she wanted to make sure no one was there. It was a feminine room, with frills and jewelry boxes and no sign of a male presence, so I gathered that Don Eduardo and his wife had slept separately.

Juanita closed the door and locked it behind us. Before she could turn, I had my arms around her from behind and I was planting kisses on her neck and her ears. She tolerated it for a moment, then broke away.

"Stop now," she said, holding me at arm's length. "Be honest with me. Have you been to bed with a woman before? Honestly, now."

I was nonplussed. She certainly asked damn fool questions. But I was honest.

"No. But I came close. This girl back home, we... came close." The Spanish term for "dry humped" eluded me.

Juanita cradled my chin in her hand.

"You are such a boy, Cornelius. Come."

She took my hand and led me to the bed.

"Sit," she said, so I sat.

She stood in front of me.

"Will you do as I say? Even though I am a servant?"

I nodded.

She kicked off her shoes. Hooking her thumbs in the waistband of her skirt, she dropped it to the floor. She wore no underwear. She crossed her arms in front of her and pulled her blouse over her head. Standing naked before me, she was the most beautiful sight I had ever seen.

"I will be your teacher," she said.

Well, it was the most useful class I ever took. Juanita stripped me slowly and had me lie still while she explored my body. Over and again she'd bring me to a hard boil, then call me back and insist that I relax and return her favors. Interval training, I think they call it now. She guided my hand and told me what she wanted from me and how I should do it. I was young and naïve enough to forget my pride and let her lead. She taught me how to watch your partner, and react to her, and make the whole experience a shared one. I was never wealthy, I'm not especially good-looking, and I tend to run to fat, but on the asset side of the ledger, I'm a good cook and I'm a slow and tender lover, the way Juanita taught me to be. As a result, I've never lacked for female companionship. These are acquired skills that I highly recommend to my young readership.

When we ended in a wild, passionate climax that I know at least one of us did not fake, we dozed off together. While the sleep was welcome, it was foolish, for I knew that Patton and Don Eduardo would return soon and wonder where I was. I don't know exactly how long I slept. I wasn't sleeping too deeply, for I awoke from a jostling of the bed caused by Juanita rolling over. When I opened my eyes, I saw that she was reaching over the side of the bed, as though picking up something from the floor.

"What time is it?" I asked, in a sudden panic that perhaps the others were searching for us.

That concern lost priority for me when Juanita turned to face me. She was still naked, but the erotic effect was lessened by the revolver she had taken from under the mattress and now was pointing at my chest.

"I'm sorry, my pretty American boy. I hope this will not make you think less of women, but I must kill you now."

The world was spinning. This could not be happening. I just made incredibly tender and enticing love to this woman and now she was threatening to kill me? I couldn't even get out a sentence. I just stared into Juanita's eyes. I think I still had drool at the corner of my mouth from sleep. What was happening?

"It is my fault," she said sadly, but the muzzle of the gun did not waver. "You see, I said something I shouldn't. Don't worry, my *chico*, I cannot miss at this range and there will only be pain for a moment. "

"But they'll hear!" I sputtered.

"I will say you raped me, lover. Whether they believe me or not will make no difference. They will take time to decide. And time is what they do not have, for they will join you in death tonight. *Adios, chico.*"

She lifted the gun to my head. I drew a sharp breath and snapped my head back slightly, just slightly, as if I'd heard something. Her eyes shifted, just for an instant. Old tricks can still work.

It was enough. My left hand pushed the gun aside and my right fist drove into her face. The gun went off, but the bullet missed me. I snatched the pistol away and Juanita slumped off the bed and onto the floor.

Here is another lesson for the young: Don't get too sentimental after sex.

The pounding on the door began seconds after the gunshot. The locked door gave me time to throw on my clothes and to toss Juanita's clothes to her so she could do the same before the household intruded. I learned that it's a tricky thing to dress while training a revolver on a dangerous Mexican whore, but I managed it and opened the door.

The furies burst in. Leading the pack were Patton and the Don, who had returned from their ride. Behind them was a passel of servants. Riley and Hiram arrived a bit later, guns drawn. Fortunately, Riley had thought to tell Marta to stay put and keep Miguel in his room, so they were spared the sight of Juanita in *déshabillés*.

Patton and the Don began to bellow questions as soon as they saw that no one was pointing guns at them. I bellowed back, but I fear I was a trifle incoherent. The lovely Juanita was screaming "rape" at the top of her lungs. Patton assured the Don sternly that the United States of America would reimburse him for the damage to his wall caused by the gunshot, which seemed at the time a bit off the point. Finally, the Don gathered up both Juanita and myself and hauled us to the living room, where the board of inquiry commenced in earnest.

I poured out my story. I had time to concoct a lie, but none occurred to me that was better than the truth, so that's what I told.

"I admit, I trifled with the girl—"

"In my wife's bed!" Don Eduardo said in a strangled tone of voice, rising to his feet.

This appeared rather an obvious point to me by now, but it seemed to rankle him. He looked like he was about to leap on me and throw me on the floor and I don't expect Patton would have interfered. But I was able to complete my account.

When Juanita was given her chance, she was ready. She said she was showing me the hacienda and had taken me to the señora's room. I suddenly pulled a weapon—the very gun that had discharged—and ordered her to service me sexually. She did, but was so outraged by this violation that at the first opportunity she seized my pistol and attempted to shoot me, which I was able to deflect by slapping her hand away.

"And what do you say to that?" Patton asked me.

"That she's a lying little bitch."

Riley had a somewhat more helpful response.

"I've traveled with Cornelius day and night since we left Independence and I've never seen that gun. It's not his."

Patton looked thoughtfully down at the gun, which he was holding in his hand.

"It's German-made. Don't know if that matters, but it's German-made." He turned to Don Eduardo. "How long have you known this girl?"

"Just a week. Francisco brought her to help after another servant left us. She's his cousin from Veracruz."

Light was beginning to dawn.

"Wait a minute," I said. "She told me she was from this village. She told me she grew up here."

"Maybe that's why she had to kill him," Riley added. "He'd have caught her in a lie."

"But why lie about something like that?" Patton asked. "And who in tarnation is she?" Patton turned to Hiram. "Get her out of here," he said. "If she tries to run, shoot her."

Hiram took Juanita's elbow and led her out of the room.

The Don was pouring himself a drink. He seemed shaken, broken, nowhere near the masterful squire we had met. Perhaps he still suffered from the loss of his wife. In any event, he seemed at this moment more fragile than any man in his position could afford to be.

Patton now became master of the situation.

"Don Eduardo, does Juanita work for the Villistas?"

"Perhaps. Or for Carranza, I don't know."

Patton slammed his fist on a table.

"Or for Obregón, or for Zapata, or for any tin-pot *bandito* you've got in this crazy country." A glint came into the lieutenant's eye. "Or for you, Don Eduardo."

"For me?" Don Eduardo almost spilled his liquor. "What do you mean?"

"I think you'd better answer the question I've been asking you for twenty-four hours now. How is it you think you can bring us Villa?"

The Don took two more swallows and sweated like a field hand in summer before he answered.

"I will bring you to Villa, not Villa to you."

"How?"

Don Eduardo sat back down. He gestured Patton and Riley toward the sofa facing him.

"Sit, my friends."

They sat with their backs to the large picture window. I remained standing, unsure of my position at the moment, although it appeared the rape charges were forgotten.

The Don needed another swallow, draining his glass before replying.

"You are right, it is time to tell you. I only kept you in the dark because things could still go wrong. But Francisco will return soon and it is time."

"Francisco? Your servant? The one who's seeing his sick mother?"

"You are correct, Lieutenant Patton. I took a slight liberty with the truth there. The fact is, Francisco went to make final arrangements for the delivery of Villa into your hands. He will return, at any moment, with the Villista rebels whom we have convinced to turn their coats. They will this night give you the Jaguar and you will be famous men."

"Who are these men? Why are they betraying Villa?"

I glanced at Riley while Patton grilled the Don. This stank to high heaven.

"You must understand, I don't have all the details," Don Eduardo said. "Francisco is my most loyal servant. He has been with me from birth. He hates the Villistas because they are my enemies. He would die for this hacienda. He has many relatives, all through rebel country. He has built a relationship with a henchman of Villa, a man they call the Spaniard. Tonight he will bring the Spaniard who will take you to Villa to arrest him and take him back to your General Pershing. Arrangements have been made. Villa is wounded and lies abed, with scarcely any guard save the Spaniard and his men. You will take him easily. Then you will have glory and you can return to your country, and I... I will get back my life, here on this hacienda."

He lurched over to the sideboard and poured himself another stiff drink. He offered us none, although I wished he had. I could have used it.

Patton weighed the situation.

"This seems dangerous," he said, stating the blindingly obvious. "What guarantees do we have?"

The Don laughed out loud at this.

"Guarantees? Señor, this is Mexico! What guarantees exist?"

Crash!

A gunshot rang out and the large picture window behind the

sofa shattered. Riley and Patton, being men of action, hit the floor before the bullet had a chance to reach the opposite wall. Acting as one, they upturned the sofa and took their places behind it. My own reactions were slower. Before I hit the floor and joined them behind the upturned sofa, more lead poured through the shattered window and I saw the Don's head explode.

Riley fired through the window at no target that I could see. Patton had both his pistols out and blazing away. Hiram appeared at the door, apparently having abandoned his charge.

"Get out of here," Patton snapped at him from behind the sofa. "See if they're coming at us from another direction."

Hiram disappeared. Patton dropped down to reload.

"I'll cover you," he said. "Hit the door and see if you can find a way out. I'll follow."

Without waiting to see if we understood, Patton rose back up and began firing both his guns out the window. I rose and went through the door, Riley right behind me. We drew up sharp at what we saw in the hall.

Hiram lay dead on the floor, blood oozing from his head. Near the door was a tableau: Marta and Miguel, flanked by Francisco on one side and Juanita on the other, holding guns on them. Francisco nodded at Riley to drop his weapon and he did. Patton came racing from the room and stopped as abruptly as we had. He took a moment longer than Riley, but he dropped his guns as well. Francisco opened the front door and shouted out to cease fire. The shooting stopped.

In a moment, the front door swung wide open. Standing in it was a remarkable man. Six-foot-five if an inch. Improbably broad shoulders tapering to an impossibly narrow waist. A serape, a wide-brimmed felt hat, a drooping mustache, crossed bullet belts on his chest, a rifle in his hands. A bandit of your nightmares. He spoke Spanish, but with an accent I had never heard before.

"*Buenas noche*s, Lieutenant Patton," he said. "I cannot tell you how pleased I am to find you here and in good health."

And thus we fell into the hands of the Spaniard.

13

The Master of Love

Jim

R iley poked the fire.

"How far have you gotten?"

"You've just fallen into the hands of the Spaniard. Really, is any of this true?"

"Stop asking me that," Riley said. "Your Grandpa Jimmy and I will tell you what happened and you can believe us or not."

He poured more bourbon and sat down.

"I don't like it when you have to read the racy parts that Cornelius put in. Must be hard to read that about your grandfather."

Actually, I thought the bit with Juanita was the most interesting part so far. We always knew Grandpa Jimmy had a wandering eye and had never settled down with one woman, the way Riley had. Good for him, as far as I was concerned.

"I must admit, I couldn't sit still when I read the part about Juanita," said Riley. "Slow and tender love, he says. I calculated it out. We got back from the village about four and that gunshot sounded by six. What with the tour of the hacienda and the nap afterward, Cornelius couldn't have been at work for fifteen minutes, at the most. He makes himself sound like some sort of Don Juan. Juanita probably jerked back on his reins once or twice and suddenly he's the master of love."

I said nothing. Plainly this had touched a nerve with Riley.

"Well, Cornelius was always a fool with women. Fact is, this bout with Juanita pretty much summed up his luck. He'd blunder in and find some woman willing to go to bed with him and, next thing you know, she's got a gun on his chest and I've got to pull him out of it. Happened time and time again. Oh, well."

Minutes passed. Finally, I asked him what happened with the Spaniard. His dark eyes flashed at me.

"Let Cornelius tell you," he said. "That was a bad time."

14

To the Spaniard's Cave

Cornelius

We rode all night. It was Riley and me, Patton, Marta, and Miguel, with our hands tied, sitting our beasts as best we could. We were surrounded by maybe six or seven bandits, plus the traitorous Francisco and Juanita, all riding through the desert quietly. In front rode the Spaniard, never looking back at us, never saying a word. It seemed a bad dream.

The worst of it, perhaps, were the two Indians riding next to the Spaniard. I noticed them when I was being trussed and thrown on my horse. They stank, had evil faces and filthy clothes, and their eyes were the stuff of nightmares. I should know: I've had nightmares of them going on seventy years now.

I'm surprised I was able to stay on my horse, for the night passed in a slow daze, like a fever dream. It grew cold. There was a full moon that lit the desert eerily, bathing it with a sort of green. Marta looked ready to roll off her saddle with fatigue, as I'm sure I did. Patton, Riley, and Miguel all sat straight, ready for action, looking for an opening. Young Miguel was game, no question about that.

By the time we reached our destination, I was too strung out to care. We clopped into a small village, looking like every other goddam piss-poor Mexican village I had seen on this journey. Making no effort at secrecy—though, granted, it was five in the morning—the Spaniard led us to a home on the outskirts of town where we dismounted. I could barely stand and my companions weren't much better.

We were hustled into the small adobe residence. The Yaquis—for that was the tribe of the two Indians, I later learned—led the horses away. The Spaniard, all energy, clapped his large hands.

"Awake, awake! We have guests from America!" he called to the empty parlor.

A groggy voice from the adjoining bedroom said, "*Silencio!* Cannot a wounded man sleep?"

The Spaniard laughed.

"Your Excellency will not want to sleep when you see what I have brought you."

Moments passed. Then a hand appeared around the curtain that divided the next room from where we were standing. Slowly, the curtain was thrown back and a man appeared. It was him. The Jaguar. Pancho Villa.

"So," he said, yawning. "Who are these guests who disturb my sleep?"

Villa was far from an imposing figure. He wore long underwear, and nothing else, at this historic and previously unrecorded meeting with George Patton. He was on the short side, about Riley's height. He had the required drooping mustache and a slight paunch protruding at his midsection. His right leg was heavily bandaged at the knee and he could barely limp about. His eyes were slow to come into focus, but when they did and he gazed at us, those eyes became alive and piercing. I've known many formidable men and, for my money, you can spot them by their eyes. Villa had the eyes of a great man, the eyes you do not forget, even in his underwear, even at dawn in an adobe hut, even dribbling fluid from around the bandages on his right knee. I still can see those eyes.

"I want to sleep," he said.

The Spaniard ignored him.

"Your Excellency, let me introduce to you Lieutenant George S. Patton, aide to General John Pershing, as well as being his brother-in-law and closest confidant."

Villa winced. His wound was obviously serious and hurt him badly. The morning sun entered the room, making him squint.

"And what am I to do with this prize you have brought me?" he asked.

The Spaniard smiled.

"Well, perhaps we can make him tell us General Pershing's plans?"

That drew a hearty laugh from the Jaguar, wound and all.

"Pershing has no plans! He wanders the desert hoping to find me, but he cannot. When he is done wandering, he will leave. My Spaniard, I told you. This expedition is the most foolish thing I have ever heard of. Pershing has no hope of finding us and no mission beyond that. Carranza and Obregón, they are our targets. The Americans are irrelevant. I have explained this to you."

Villa walked slowly into the room and sank into a chair. A lackey appeared to attend to him. His face was pale as a desert Mexican's could be. Plainly the wound was as serious as we had heard.

"The Americans anger me, Your Excellency," said the Spaniard. "They are arrogant. You rule the desert, you speak for the desert people, yet they treat you as a bandit."

Villa waved his hand dismissively.

"I *am* a bandit. I was a bandit long before I was a politician and I find that my first job was the more honorable one." Villa looked again at us. "Do any of these Americans speak Spanish?"

"The young ones do. So I'm told."

Villa painfully rose from his chair and walked toward us. He stopped before Marta and Miguel.

"Señorita Ortega, I must apologize for the situation in which you find yourself. I am told your father was killed. I regret it, but your father conspired against me. When you dabble in politics, you must be prepared for the consequences. Did any of my men hurt you or your brother?"

Marta shook her head.

"Good. I am pleased to hear it. You will be safe in my care."

Villa nodded to one of his underlings, instructing him to take Marta and Miguel to another room and to keep them safe. I could sense Riley twitching until they were out of sight. The Yaquis joined us, having secured the horses.

"Sit, gentlemen, sit," said Villa.

There were just enough benches and chairs for Villa, Patton,

Riley, and me. The Spaniard and the other henchmen stood. Villa settled himself painfully in a chair, then nodded at a young Mexican woman in the corner, dressed in black.

"Let me introduce Señorita Rodriguez. This is her home. Like Señorita Ortega, she has recently lost her father. He was a brave fighting man, one of my best. He died in battle with the Carrancistas. He will be avenged, I have promised her that. Please, señorita, leave us now and let us be alone to speak. Thank you."

The Rodriguez woman took her leave.

"Spaniard, did you see any of the Americans on your way here? No? Well, you just missed them. A troop went through town in the middle of the night, I watched them from my window." Villa grinned. "It was quite amusing. These stern-faced gringo soldiers riding through the village, looking for the great and terrible Pancho Villa. It was all I could do to keep from throwing open the door in my underwear and shouting 'Here I am!'"

Villa laughed infectiously. Even under the circumstances, I found myself smiling with him.

Patton was not amused, though of course he didn't understand what Villa was saying. He asked me to translate and I asked Villa for permission, which he granted. Patton now had Villa's full attention.

"So, you are Lieutenant Patton. I have heard of you. My people talk of Pershing's young, handsome assistant who rides the desert with just one other soldier, bringing messages and doing errands. They say he carries pistols on both hips, like a *bandito*, and he must fear nothing to go so far with so few to guard him. Of course, that did not work out so well for you on this trip."

I translated.

"*Quizas*," said Patton, knowing that much Spanish.

"Who are these boys with you? Them, I have not heard of. No, do not translate, boy, you tell me. Who are you, who speaks my language so well?"

I told Patton what Villa had asked me, to be polite, then I answered in Spanish.

"We're nobody in particular, Mr. Villa. My friend Riley and me, we're just boys from Independence, Missouri. We came to see the country and hooked up with Lieutenant Patton here."

"You are not soldiers?"

"No, sir. Not exactly. We just work for him, I guess."

God, it sounded lame, as truth often does. When it came down to it, I had no idea why we were there. It seemed improbable to me, too.

Villa turned to Riley.

"You speak Spanish too, boy?"

"*Sí.*"

"Ask Lieutenant Patton why he came to the hacienda of Don Ortega."

When Riley translated the question, Patton straightened his shoulders.

"I will tell you nothing."

Villa tried to look stern a moment, then again burst out laughing.

"You see, Spaniard, the brave Lieutenant Patton will die before he tells us. He will undergo torture, even at the hands of your Yaquis, before he tells us. And it is so amusing, of course, because we already know!" Villa and the Spaniard shared a chuckle. "Lieutenant, I knew what would happen to you on this journey before you left General Pershing. I've had my eye on this young lady's father for a long time. His man Francisco has long been on our side. He told us how Don Eduardo was frightened to death that his precious hacienda would fall to the evil Villistas or to the cursed Carranza. The Don pretended friendship to Carranza, even to us, but we knew it was a fraud. We would have known it even if we did not have Francisco to tell us so. The Dons, the landowners, they care nothing for the revolution, nothing for their country or their countrymen. They care only for their wealth and their land and their cattle. They disgust me."

Villa clapped his hand on the Spaniard's shoulder.

"The idea was my Spaniard's, Lieutenant Patton."

Riley was silent, so I took over the translating duties again.

"He also told me that you are not only Pershing's right-hand man, you are brother to Pershing's wife. You must be precious to him. Yet you ride almost alone, here and there across our desert. If we could lay hands on you, surely the general would pay a handsome ransom to get you back.

"Revolution is expensive, Lieutenant," Villa went on. "Do you know how I spend most of my time? Not fighting, not riding through the desert, not blowing up trains. Señor Patton, most of my time is spent raising money and worrying about how to spend it. We collect tithes from *los campesinos*—not too much, just what we need to keep body and soul together. Much time is spent on this because some of the people are reluctant and must be watched and reminded so they pay their fair share. The revolution is for them, so they must help pay for it. Then I must watch my men to see they do not steal or take too much. And there are the many decisions. Where to buy guns? How much dynamite will we need for this raid? How can the men of Pedro Lopez eat so much, are they wasteful? You must know all about this sort of thing. You, too, are a soldier."

Patton grunted at my translation.

"Command is hell," he said through his teeth.

An odd thing then happened. The Spaniard snatched up a camera and insisted that he take a picture of Pancho Villa with his captives. Apparently Villa liked to be photographed, for Patton, Riley, and I were instructed to seat ourselves around him and have a group photograph taken. I wonder, sometimes, whatever became of that photo.

Señorita Rodriguez brought Villa a steaming bowl of menudo and then passed bowls to the rest of us. I was ravenous and thought the soup was the best thing I'd ever tasted. I've been partial to menudo ever since.

Once his translator pulled his face out of the bowl of menudo, hoping in vain to be offered another, Villa resumed.

"Well, Lieutenant Patton, you can understand how the prospect of a big ransom would be attractive to a working soldier, especially the leader of a revolution who has not a pot to piss in, as you gringos like to say. But how to find you out there in our great desert? Again, my Spaniard had the idea. He arranged for Francisco to whisper into the ear of his employer, Don Eduardo. He told the Don that the Spaniard who works for Villa is a traitor and will betray the Jaguar for enough money. He says the Americans would pay much if they could take Pancho Villa alive and that, for money, the Spaniard will deliver Villa to the Americans. And the Americans will be forever grateful to Don Eduardo if he is the one to make this happen."

Villa smiled and waved his hand.

"I know, it sounds foolish. Don Eduardo should never have believed it, but a frightened man grabs at shadows. He believed it because he wanted to believe it, because it gave him a way to save his precious land from the Villistas and to earn the gratitude of the Americans. He gave money to Francisco to pass to the Spaniard and Francisco told him to send to Pershing for an envoy. We knew it would be you. Who else would he send? And here you are."

"The United States does not pay ransoms," Patton said, through me.

"Well, that would be most unfortunate for us all," said Villa. "But they will. We will even return these boys for free. We are reasonable men, are we not, Spaniard?" Villa handed his empty bowl to his henchman and shouted to the kitchen. "Delores! Your menudo is the best! Better even than—"

"*Cuidado!*"

The hissed word through the window by a watchman outside froze the room for a moment, before the bandits sprang into action. Delores hurried in and swept the bowls back into the kitchen. The Yaquis pushed aside the sofa and the Spaniard opened a trapdoor that led into some sort of cellar. The wounded Villa, cursing, limped to the trap and climbed down the ladder into darkness. The Villistas bundled Marta and Miguel behind him, then Riley, then Patton. The Spaniard stood at the open door and looked down, with only the Yaquis and me left above.

"There is no room," he said. "Hide."

He pointed to the bedroom. The Spaniard disappeared down into the cellar and pulled the door shut above him. The Yaquis pushed me into the bedroom, just as there came a pounding on the front door. A deep voice called for the door to be opened, in Spanish but with a distinctly American accent. One of the Yaquis dove beneath the bed. The other pulled out a wicked-looking Bowie knife, wrapped one arm around my shoulders and pulled me against him, back against the wall beside the door so that we were hidden from the front room. He held his knife tightly against my throat, piercing the skin and constricting my breath so that I could only inhale through quick gasps, as quietly as I could. God, he reeked.

I heard Delores Rodriguez open the door.

"Señora, I am Lieutenant Summer Williams of the U.S. Army. Stand aside."

Boots stepped into the front room.

I suppose, if I were Riley, I'd have done something heroic. I'd have sacrificed myself by calling out, even though the Yaqui would have immediately slit my throat. Or better, I'd have flipped the Yaqui over my shoulder with some sort of wrestling maneuver and led the rescue myself. But I was me, and I've always been a trifle indecisive, especially with a knife held at my throat. So I stood silently, trying to breathe, while my blood trickled across the blade of the Bowie knife.

Delores Rodriguez saved lives at that moment, possibly Villa's but more likely those of the American soldiers. It turned out there were just three of them. An American troop led by a Major Howze had come through the village in the middle of the night, just a few hours before we arrived. They were camped not far away. A scout had seen the Yaquis when they were tying up the horses and these three were sent to investigate. It was known that Villa was sometimes accompanied by Yaquis.

Delores made the most of her mourning dress. She excoriated the soldiers for bothering her, saying she knew nothing of any Yaquis, her father had just died and she did not wish her mourning to be disturbed. As a very nice touch, she said he died of influenza in his bed and pointed to the room where we were hiding. While the Spanish flu epidemic was still two years away, even in 1916 no one wanted to risk contact with influenza. The soldiers pardoned themselves, asked Delores to watch for suspicious-looking Indians, and left. It was a full two minutes before the Yaqui loosed the knife at my throat and Delores opened the cellar door.

Even Villa seemed chastened by the good fortune of his escape. The Spaniard was livid.

"You see! You have been here too long! This is how revolutions end, their leaders stay too long in a place and are killed. Your wound is better, it is time to go."

"Easy for you to say my wound is better," Villa groused. "My leg hurts like fire. I will never walk as before, I know it." Turns out, he was right about that; history tells us the wound left Villa with one leg shorter than the other and a permanent limp. "But you speak the truth. I should move from here. Where to next?"

The Spaniard didn't hesitate.

"I have the place, Jaguar. There is a cave, in the desert near Parral. We can rest there, no one will find it. I have used this cave before, for my own purposes. I even have supplies there."

Villa sighed.

"A long ride with my bad leg."

"It is necessary," said the Spaniard. "We cannot lose you and you will be safe there. We can arrange for the ransom while you rest. And think of your legend, Jaguar." The Spaniard knew his man. "The wounded Jaguar retires to a cave in his beloved mountains, from which he emerges stronger than ever and leads the revolution to its glorious end."

Villa nodded.

"It is a good story, isn't it? Today we rest, with double the watch. Tonight we ride."

We slept the day away at the Rodriguez home, knowing we faced our second night in a row in the saddle. Marta and Miguel seemed in shock. While they had endured the death of their mother, that had been from illness. This was sudden shock and violence: the murder of their father, the forced ride through the desert, languishing in the hands of stinking villains. Nothing in their lives at the Ortega hacienda had prepared them for the last twenty-four hours. God, less than twenty-four hours ago I had been in bed with Juanita... Where was she, I wondered.

Juanita and Francisco had disappeared when we arrived at the Rodriguez house, but when it came time to ride that evening, there they were with the rest of the bandits. A party of about thirty of us set out for Parral as the sun went down, Villa saying a fond farewell to Delores and cursing under his breath from the pain in his bandaged leg, which stuck rigidly out to the side as he rode. Every bounce must have been agony.

The ride for the rest of us was not as bad as it could have been, in part because of Villa's wound. We stopped often and I will have to say they fed us well. Pancho Villa liked his food. I can't vouch for his famous fondness for ice cream, though, as we lacked refrigeration facilities.

We rode all night and camped for much of the next day. Another night's ride brought us near the village of Parral where, unbeknownst to us, a scrap had just occurred among a Villista mob, an American army troop led by Major Frank Tompkins, and some Carrancista soldiers of the regular Mexican army, to the extent there was such a thing. It was apparently a total botch-up that had diplomatic repercussions and required Pershing to retreat north. We knew nothing of it, as we bypassed Parral completely to find the Spaniard's cave in the mountains south of town.

We arrived at the foot of those mountains in the early morning of April 13, 1916, the day after the Parral fight. Villa groaned and swore from his aching leg. Looking up, I saw that our horses were plodding upward now, approaching a red dirt mountain as the rising sun was just cresting the horizon. To encourage Villa, the Spaniard directed his gaze to the middle of the slope, where gaped a dark slash of a mouth, the entrance to the Spaniard's cave.

"There it is, Jaguar," he said. "A few minutes of steep riding and we will be in a great warm cavern. We shall build a fire and have our meal and you can rest your leg to your heart's content. We will be safe there."

Some of us, perhaps, I thought. There was something uncanny about that ride up the nearly vertical trail to the cave. It was chilly. The horses stumbled and snorted on the trail, which was narrow and difficult to follow. A fall would have been serious, as the horse would break its leg for sure. We rode single file, with young Miguel immediately ahead of me. A fine rider, the boy still swayed dangerously in his saddle, no doubt falling prey to extreme distress and exhaustion. As we passed the last switchback and reached the entrance to the cave, an armadillo appeared on the trail with a dead snake in its mouth. I saw one of the Mexicans cross himself at the sight. I did not want to go in that cave, which looked to my tired and fanciful eyes like the entrance to Hell. Or perhaps my memory is tricking me and I only believe I thought of Hell because Hell is what we found there.

The Spaniard, comfortable with dark places, did not hesitate. While the rest of us waited outside the mouth of the cave, he and one of his Yaquis dismounted and walked inside. Soon flames flickered from the darkness and the Spaniard emerged, holding up a burning torch.

"We are honored to welcome you to your place of rest," he said formally.

Villa shuddered and seemed dubious, but he painfully dismounted and limped forward. The rest of us followed suit and soon all of us, horses included, were standing inside a very large, very empty rock chamber.

The Yaqui already had a fire going and by its light we looked around. The cavern seemed roughly in the shape of a wedge of pie, with the wide crust at the mouth where we stood and the walls narrowing into the darkness before us. There were three cots lining one wall, giving the impression that the Spaniard and his two Yaquis slept here from time to time. That impression was further confirmed when I noticed the fire was burning in a small depression that had been hollowed out of the dirt and the fire itself was nicely laid in a way that suggested it was already in place, waiting for us.

The Spaniard waved his torch over a corner near the cots.

"You see? We have water, food, blankets, even tequila. There is some hay for the horses, but we will get more. There is room for them here, the cavern is so large. There will be smells, but I'm sure the horses won't mind."

The Spaniard smiled, enjoying himself immensely.

"For God's sake," said Villa, "keep the horses outside."

"Unwise, my general. They may be seen and lead our enemies here. Don't worry. Only a small number of us need remain with you. The others can camp elsewhere and live off the country as they will."

So that's how it happened. Juanita, Francisco, and the bulk of the Villistas were directed to melt into the desert and assemble when they received word. Staying with Villa were the Spaniard and his Yaquis and a personal guard of eight men. And us prisoners, of course. I couldn't help but steal a glance at Juanita as she rode away. I can't say she did the same for me, not that I noticed. I never saw her again, which is just as well. The sex was good, but the waking up, less so.

If I was told that day that we would stay in that cave for almost two months, I would have thought seriously of shooting myself. Looking back, the two months don't seem so much in the span of my long life and I got to know two historical figures, Pancho Villa and George Patton, in a way that never would have happened otherwise. Given the choice, of course, I'd have passed on that opportunity.

Like always when people are shut up in a certain place, we developed routines. Marta and Miguel kept to their blankets off in the corner of the big cavern. Marta tried to entertain Miguel with games and songs as best she could, but otherwise stayed very much to herself. After the first few days, Riley took to hanging by the two of them, telling the boy stories of Independence. I'd make up yarns for Miguel from the fund of books Jack O'Neal had made me read. That was my favorite part of the captivity, as I could see I was able to get Miguel lost in the stories of Jim Hawkins on *Treasure Island* or Allan Quatermain in *King Solomon's Mines*. I could even get a little lost myself, when it was going well. Marta was grateful to both Riley and me for tending to her brother.

I must say, Villa was overall a preferable companion to Patton. Patton tried to befriend Miguel, mimicking Riley and me, but children can spot phonies and Patton was never quite a genuine person. He was always an actor in his own play. He'd be courtly and try to impress Marta and Miguel, but he spent most of his time brooding on his blanket as the chance for glory seemed to be passing him by. In fairness, we were all as bored as you would expect of people spending weeks in a cave.

Villa was bored too and sometimes would erupt in anger at one of his Mexicans over petty failings. On the whole, though, he was actually charming and Riley and I cautiously warmed to him. He would sleep late every day and awake grumbling over his wound. One of the Mexicans, Felipe, knew a little desert doctoring and would clean the wound and replace the bandages while another in the band, Jose, made his leader a breakfast of tortillas and beans. We prisoners ate the same as the rest, but Villa always ate later in the morning. Villa would then walk back and forth across the cavern to strengthen his leg. Over the weeks, he got so he could walk pretty well.

Come afternoon, Villa would turn expansive and begin to talk. The Mexicans would sit quietly, but plainly their interest was feigned at best. Patton, Marta, and Miguel avoided the talks out of principle, so Riley and I were his only attentive audience. That seemed to endear us to the bandit.

We'd been there a few days when Villa decided to tell us the story of how he became a bandit. The Spaniard was gone, trying to arrange our ransom, but he'd left the Yaquis to watch us. Villa planted himself on his cot and waved Riley and me over to him. Then, unexpectedly, he turned to Marta and Miguel.

"Come, come. I want to tell you something about myself, how I became what I am."

Marta regarded him coldly.

"I can hear you from here."

Villa shrugged, grinning.

"She can hear me, she says. I am Pancho Villa, the Jaguar, the scourge of the desert, and I am shown disrespect by a woman in a cave. Oh, if Carranza should hear..."

His grin expanded and his men laughed. He was playing to them. His charm was lost on Patton, who snarled as I translated.

"Maybe if you hadn't murdered her father, she'd be friendlier."

The Mexicans stirred, but Villa waved at them to be still.

"Señor Patton, we do not know how long we will be here together. I must heal my leg and you must wait until General Pershing gets our money together. If we are pleasant with each other, the time will pass more quickly.

"Now," said Villa, settling in. "I will tell you how I became a bandit. I am not ashamed of that word. They say I am a bandit and it is true, that is one of the things Pancho Villa is, a bandit. A very good bandit, the best bandit to come from Durango, which has produced many very fine bandits. Is it so?"

His men nodded. It was so.

"Señorita, I did not have your advantages. My father did not own a hacienda, he worked on a hacienda. We all worked in the fields for Don Lopez Negrete. The hacienda was El Rancho de la Loyotada, the grandest in Durango, grander even than yours, señorita, but we were poor as dirt. I could not go to school like you and Miguel. We children worked as soon as we could walk and, when my father died, I supported my mother and sisters by working.

"Boys like me, we knew only two ways. I could be like my father, scrabbling in the dust for Lopez Negrete until I died a young man, or I could become a bandit. We heard stories of the great bandits of the desert, Bernal and Parra and Alvarado. Sometimes we saw them come to the village for fiestas: lean, dangerous men with big mustaches and bandoliers crossed over their chests. These men did not fear anyone, not the Dons or the soldiers or God or the devil. Somehow, as far back as I remember, I knew that I would be one of them. Not just one of them, but the greatest of them all. I knew this as a certainty." Villa nodded in wonder at himself. "How could this be? How could I have known?"

Patton, who had told us similar stories about his destiny as a soldier, was annoyed.

"All boys think that way. It doesn't mean anything."

A strange remark, coming from Patton.

"Perhaps," allowed Villa, in a magnanimous mood. "But it felt very strong to me. As it happened, though, I became a bandit sooner than I meant to. This, señorita, is what I wanted you to hear."

No sale. Marta kept looking down, avoiding Villa's gaze. But she was silent, so she couldn't help but hear him.

"I was sixteen. I worked at another ranch owned by the family, El Gorgojito, but I still worked with my mother and sisters at the main ranch too. One of my sisters was named Marta too, like you, señorita. And she was pretty, like you. We called her Martina because she was such a little, delicate girl. She was fourteen and like all of us, she worked in the fields as best she could.

"It was not always a blessing for a peasant girl to be pretty. Martina was very pretty, the prettiest girl we knew, and smart and kind, but delicate, not meant for the rough life God had given her. Being pretty, she came to the notice of the *hacendado's* son, a pig of a man who was the foreman at El Gorgojito. We could see this man's eyes on Martina and we warned her and tried to keep her away from him, but he found reasons to come by our little home or to be waiting when Martina went walking. Whenever he looked at her, I would feel my blood flow hot in my veins. That is an expression, but I believe it to be true. When I feel something deeply, I feel it in my blood. I knew that if this man touched Martina, I would kill him. This was the reason I stole my first gun, taking it from a herder in the village when he was drunk.

"So the day came and, praise God, I was ready. I came home from the fields to find my mother and sisters crying and wailing: Negrete had taken Martina, just barged into our home and dragged her off, knowing I was away. I took my gun and went to the big house, pushed past the servants, found Negrete in his room with Martina, having his way. So," Villa shrugged, "I shot him."

Marta tightened her lips in disapproval. Miguel, however, was fascinated.

"Did you kill him?" I asked.

"It was actually quite funny," Villa said. "I had never shot a man and the gun was not a good one, so my aim was terrible. My first shot hit him in the foot and my second shot missed completely. He was coming for me and almost had me in his grip when my third shot went through his stomach. Yes, I killed him. And I was lucky not to kill Martina or myself."

"Was your sister all right?" Marta asked, perhaps in spite of herself.

"It depends on how you mean, señorita. She lived and she went home. She lives still at the Lopez Negrete ranch. But she was raped. Rape is a bad thing, señorita. It is always part of a revolution, but I forbid it of my men, as much as I am able. It can kill the soul of a woman and I think that's what it did to Martina. She is not the same. Of course, it was then that I took up the life of a bandit."

Marta shivered and pulled Miguel close to her, covering his ears. Riley saw how she was affected and he growled at Villa to change the subject.

That suited Villa, whose stories were usually more lighthearted and exciting. Day after day, he told us of raids on trains, facing down the Dons, rustling cattle, narrow escapes, midnight rides, all with great showmanship, as though these were tales from a boy's adventure book and not the dirty, dangerous events they really were. It's too bad Villa never met Churchill. They'd have hit it off famously.

Patton had some of their romanticism, but lacked their humor. He spent his time moping and plotting escapes, but it was hopeless. There were too many Mexicans with their eyes always on us. Even worse were the Yaquis. It seemed that day and night, at least one of the two always eyed us silently, giving us no chance at flight. Even when we'd step out of the cave to piss, a Yaqui was at our elbow. If we woke up in the middle of the night and looked around, we'd see a Yaqui glaring back at us. They were silent, dirty bastards and they smelled like rotting flesh when they came close. Faces as cruel as I've seen. Well, they proved their expressions were justified before too long. One we called Scar, for the jagged knife scar that marred his left cheek. The other we called No Scar.

Speaking of waking in the middle of the night, I remember once when I rolled off my blanket while asleep and awoke with a sharp pebble beneath me. Pulling it out and looking at it in the dark, I could see that it was not a pebble but a human tooth. In the morning, I showed it to Riley. He nodded over at the Yaquis, as though they seemed just the sort to collect human teeth.

The Spaniard came and left again. He said he had put out the word that they had the lieutenant and that Pershing would need to pay a ransom to get him back. After a few more days, he was off, checking in on Villa's scattered forces and on the status of the ransom demand. It was fine with me when he was gone. There was something not canny about that man. He smiled often, but as though it was a learned skill and not a natural act. Once I caught him looking at the fire when he didn't realize he was being watched. The look on his face stopped my breath. His eyes were fixed and glaring at something only he could see. His mouth was twisted in a leer. The overall impression was more of a primitive mask than a human face, yet that expression disappeared instantly when Villa called his name. Something inside that big man was very badly broken.

Another conversation with Villa occurred shortly after the Spaniard had left for the second time. We had been in the cave nearly two weeks. Villa was still trying unsuccessfully to draw Patton into conversation, with translation by Riley or me. The closest he came to it was when he started analyzing the American character.

"You must understand, Lieutenant Patton, I have nothing against Americans. I admire them, in fact. They are very rich and very smart. They have these cameras that don't just take pictures, but actually show movement of people so you see events as they are happening. It is wonderful. Mexicans could never invent such a thing, it is not our way. I tried for many years to be a friend to the Americans, Lieutenant. Why would not your President Wilson accept me as a friend?"

Patton snorted at my translation.

"You're a bandit, Señor Villa, that's all you are. The president of the United States does not make friends with bandits."

This tickled Villa.

"I read your newspapers, Lieutenant. It seems like presidents have no friends except bandits!" He laughed and looked around at the rest of us for approval. "You know the difference between a bandit and a big shot, Lieutenant? It is only how much money they have. If Wilson thinks Carranza will be his friend, he has bet on the wrong bandit."

Well, that certainly proved correct, although it's far from clear there was any right bandit in that revolution. Mexico was a mess and if Woodrow Wilson had half of Villa's common sense, he'd not have touched the place with a bargepole. But Wilson was a college professor and showing common sense was not in his repertoire, so Pershing was blundering around blindly in a desert he didn't know, looking for a man who knew it intimately, while yours truly was in the clutches of a murderous bandit and his massive henchman who gave every sign of criminal insanity. It was almost enough to turn me Republican.

The Spaniard returned after a few days, alone and with news. He and Villa talked softly with each other for several minutes at the entrance to the cave, while we captives watched apprehensively.

I did not have great confidence that the Americans would pay a ransom for us. If the decision got to Wilson's level, he was just the sort of ass who would refuse to treat with a bandit on principle. Even if Pershing made the decision on his own, it has not been my experience that there is a seller's market for brothers-in-law. So I was apprehensive when Villa came to us, but the news was good.

"I am happy to inform you that General Pershing has seen reason and agreed to our very reasonable ransom request. My Spaniard is making the arrangements and we do not expect you will require our poor hospitality much longer."

Patton spat contemptuously, apparently so that history would record his distaste for making deals with kidnappers. Me? I was all for it.

"I must say my farewells now, however, as business awaits. The Spaniard and some of my men will stay with you until you are delivered back to the American army. I have given instructions that you are not to be harmed." Villa stepped close to Marta. "Señorita, you may not credit it, but I regret what you and your brother have suffered. I regret much in this world, but it is the world we are given. Go with God."

It did not take long for Villa and his men to ready themselves and mount for whatever their destination might be. As he was heading for the cave mouth, Villa tossed some last words in our direction.

"Tell the lieutenant he need not have been so closed-mouthed," he said. "I would have enjoyed his conversation. And you boys, go home to Missouri. Leave the wandering life to bandits, like me."

He flashed us a last grin and rode off. Many years later, my grandson would watch a children's television show called *The Cisco Kid*, where at the end of each episode, the hero and his sidekick Pancho would ride off into the sunset, dust kicking off their horses' hooves. That always reminded me of my last sight of Villa, the Jaguar, riding off to his bandit destiny. Oh, Pancho.

None of us liked being left in the care of the Spaniard and his Yaquis, who stayed in the cave along with five of Villa's Mexican followers. I consoled myself with the thoughts that Villa had told them not to harm us and that they would hardly offer us violence since they were waiting for Pershing's ransom money. It did not take long for me to be disabused of this notion.

While the Yaquis watched us closely, pistols at the ready, the Spaniard led the Mexicans a little way outside the cave and spoke to them in a hushed voice. Several times, one or the other of the bandits stole a glance at us. They nodded in agreement when the Spaniard finished speaking. The lot of them then walked back toward us, the Spaniard in the lead.

"You will be happy to know," he said, "that the time set for the payment of the ransom is almost here. I'm afraid I must beg your indulgence one last time, as we will need to bind your hands before we can bring you to the exchange site. I am glad to say this will not be necessary for the señorita or the young boy, but we simply cannot take the risk that such a formidable officer as the lieutenant might find a way to harm us, even at this last moment."

Well, this stank. Patton's brow furrowed as Riley translated the Spaniard's statements and I could follow his thoughts as though he had spoken them. If we were shortly to be released, and since they would have guns trained on us anyway, why must our hands be bound? But there wasn't much point in arguing, as all they needed to do was point their weapons at Marta and Miguel and we would have to comply. So we did, meekly. The Yaqui whom Riley and I called Scar tied our hands behind our backs, efficiently and tightly. No Scar tied Patton's hands. Only when he was finished did the Spaniard tell us we would also need to be blindfolded.

"Again, please offer the lieutenant my apologies, but this cave is a secret place. We cannot let you lead the soldiers to it, as it is too useful a refuge for us."

He was smooth, that one. His explanation was obviously bullshit since we had not been blindfolded when we came to the cave, but he kept chatting as he tied the blindfolds around our heads, which left us little time to think or react. Just before the blindfold covered my eyes, I noted that the Mexicans were edging closer to Marta, while the Yaqui we called No Scar placed his hand on Miguel's little shoulder. Something was clearly wrong, but what could we do? With our hands bound and our eyes covered, and with the massive Spaniard immediately behind us and his heavily armed Yaquis and Mexicans surrounding us, we were at something of a disadvantage.

There was a pause. The Spaniard must have given some sort of non-verbal command, for we heard a rustle of movement and then Marta screamed. Miguel shouted "No!" and his voice was quickly muffled. I felt the gun barrel leave my head and heard struggling to my left, as though someone was grappling with Patton and Riley. I was yanking furiously at my bonds and turned toward the sounds of struggle, but instantly the Spaniard's voice barked at me to remain still. I nearly disobeyed him, as every inch of my body wanted to run, even blindly, away from the unseen violence to a place where I could at least work the blindfold off. The thought of the Spaniard firing a bullet through my gut the moment I took a step held me in place, swaying in agonized uncertainty while the sounds of struggle died down.

The Spaniard's voice came from behind me right next to my ear, nearly knocking me over with the start. He was breathing a trifle hard, but his voice was calm and steady.

"Now, Señor O'Neal, your turn has come."

I smelled something chemical, oddly medicinal. Then a hand covered my nose and mouth with a soaked and stinking rag, just as the Spaniard wrapped an arm around my torso from behind and held me firmly. This was death, I thought. I struggled, but the Spaniard was far too strong for me. My thrashing grew weaker and weaker, then the blackness came.

15
Hell

Cornelius

It was one of the strangest awakenings of my life and certainly one of the least pleasant. I remember hearing voices that called me reluctantly back to consciousness. My first perception was of a piercing headache, with a disgusting taste in my mouth to go with it. I had clearly been drugged into a stupor by whatever substance was in the Spaniard's rag. My next perception was that I was utterly unable to move. It wasn't just that my arms and legs were bound and immobile. Something was holding my head rigidly fixed: I could not turn it, raise it, or lower it. I was vertical, on my feet, with my back against a hard and uneven wall.

My blindfold was gone. As disconcerting as were the feelings with which I woke up, worse was what I now saw. I was in some sort of cavern, but not the same one in which we had spent the previous weeks. This was smaller and darker, with no visible exit. The light came from torches that were hung on the walls and from a fire burning in the middle of the cavern.

No Scar was throwing more branches onto the fire as I awoke. Next to him, on the ground, poor young Miguel lay tightly wrapped with ropes, his eyes open wide and staring vacantly. Scar, the other Yaqui, stood against the opposite wall, whetting the blade of a curved knife that looked like a sickle for cutting grain. The Spaniard sat cross-legged by the fire, smoking and staring in my direction with that fixed and intense glare that had so unsettled me before. In the farthest corner of my peripheral vision, I saw that Riley and Patton were beside me, similarly bound, their backs against the cave wall. I did not see Marta.

I took all this in with my first glance around. As I began to digest more detail, my stomach lurched. Piled near the fire were grim instruments of torture: knives, whips, canes, and a wicked-looking bulbous purple club, along with some mysterious devices whose function I could not even guess. Here and there around the cave were bones, human bones, including a skull that was missing its lower jawbone. Directly in front of me, not six feet from where I stood, was a wooden bench supported at each end by a metal H-frame that extended upward by three feet or so above the bench.

"Good, now two of you are awake," said the Spaniard. "As soon as the lieutenant joins us again, we can begin."

I was so disoriented and preoccupied that at first I did not notice it. He spoke in English! And not just English, but plain Midwestern American English, with no foreign accent. Could this be a nightmare induced by the Spaniard's drug?

The Spaniard tossed his cigarette into the fire and strode over to my left. I heard him slap his hand against flesh.

"Come, Lieutenant. Wake up now. We must begin our festivities."

Patton must have responded, for the Spaniard grunted approvingly and stepped back.

"You will forgive me for not speaking your language to you before this, gentlemen. It was important to me that my colleagues remain unaware of certain things about me. But now we are here, all tucked away in my little retreat, and we need have no secrets between us anymore."

I heard Patton's voice beside me croak, "Who the hell are you?"

The Spaniard smiled and gave a quick little bow of his head.

"My name is Otto von Kleist, Lieutenant Patton. I have the honor to be in the secret service of Kaiser Wilhelm the Second. You see, we are both military men, in our way."

This was far too much. A dark-skinned, six-foot-five Mexican bandit stands before us, complete with serape and bandoliers, and tells us in perfect Yankee English that he is a German secret agent. You have to admit, it was a poser.

"Where is Señorita Ortega?" Riley demanded.

"Not far," said von Kleist, or whoever he was. "She is just on the other side of that wall, in the cavern where we left her. I'm certain she is still entertaining the Villistas. I believe three of them had already had her every which way by the time I got the last of you into this room. But she is young and I'm sure she will last at least three complete rounds with them all before the men tire of her and let her die."

I knew that Riley was bound as tightly as I was since I heard no sound from him. If he could move, his hands would have been at von Kleist's throat, no matter the cost.

"Is there anything more you would like to know?" von Kleist asked. "I am happy to talk. I find that it gives me even more pleasure from what we are about to do. The more fear you have, the more delight I receive from your torture."

When no one replied, he said, "Surely you would be interested in my mission? You see, the Kaiser realizes that you Americans are close to entering the war. You rightly see that when the Kaiser beats the English and the French and the Russians, there will be no limits to what he can do. Your country wants to be a world power, but how can it accomplish that if Germany dominates Europe?" He shrugged. "Honestly, it does not matter a great deal to me. I find the affairs of nations boring, and not very relevant to my particular interests and talents. You, the one called Cornelius, is it true you speak German? I heard you claim that to the Jaguar."

When I said yes, von Kleist rattled off some phrases in German and I responded enough to confirm that I spoke the language well. It was eerie, hearing him speak all three of the languages that I spoke, and in each he seemed a native.

He reverted to English for the benefit of Patton and Riley.

"Your countrymen will all want to speak German soon enough, I think. The war had a very good start for us, but now all is bogged down in trench warfare in the mud. Such a waste, but the Germans will inevitably win. In Ludendorff, we actually have a general who understands modern warfare and our enemies have no one like him. The only thing that might stop them would be if America throws its full weight against them quickly, before England and France are defeated. That is why I am in Mexico. This so-called revolution here is ridiculous, of course, packs of ignorant bandits fighting over spoils, but it may prove useful to German victory in the war."

This was all a mystery to Riley and me, but I suppose Patton may not have been surprised. We later learned that it was suspected that Germany had an interest in provoking bad blood between America and Mexico so that Wilson would send troops south and be that much less likely to join the combat in Europe.

"It took me months," von Kleist went on, "but I was able to rise in Villa's ranks until I became his chief advisor. I counseled the raid on Columbus and I made sure Americans were executed at Santa Isabel. So you see, it really is by my handiwork that your General Pershing brought you here. And now, thanks to you, my efforts will be rewarded. Do you know how?"

I could hear Riley spit, softly. We remained silent.

"I will make very sure that General Pershing finds this cave. And he will find his brother-in-law and aide, and two other fine strapping young Americans, hanging by your own flayed skin at the mouth of this cavern. He will see that you have been raped, tortured, skinned, subjected to damnable violations beyond the most haunting nightmares of the American public. There will be photos, pictures of your corpses, and that of poor Miguel here, circulated across America, along with the picture I took at the Rodriguez home of you with Pancho Villa. It will become widely known that flaying and the *bastinado* with which you will be beaten are signs of the Yaquis and that Villa was supported by Yaquis. When all this is publicized, the rage of America will know no bounds. Your president will have no choice but to throw the entire weight of his armed forces into the hunt for Pancho Villa, which will only enflame the passions of Carranza and Zapata and the rest, and a war which is now localized will become general and widespread. Do you not feel honored, gentlemen? Your fate will keep America out of Europe long enough for the Kaiser to prevail there and then there will be no stopping German destiny."

None of this was accompanied by maniacal laughter or even particular zeal. Von Kleist spoke flatly, as though reciting a lesson, not showing emotion or much interest in it. At the mention of German destiny, he actually yawned.

"So you understand your role. I would estimate we have a good ten to twelve hours to achieve your torture and eventual death. My friends the Yaquis have special skills in this area to be sure, but with all due modesty, I am the master here. Wherever I have lived—in Prussia, in Spain, in Paris—I have always found private chambers such as this cave in which to perform my work. Over the years, I have developed particular mastery in torture, which is truly an art. It involves deep consideration of the mind as well as the body if maximum pleasure is to be derived from the pain and humiliation of another human being. We benefit from centuries of hard work and experimentation to develop ingenious and practical methods of intensifying and prolonging that most precious of manifestations: human agony. For example, consider the *bastinado*."

Von Kleist picked up from the floor the long purple club, which rippled with an obscene flexibility, as though it were an impossibly long but living organism, a giant worm or slug.

"You may have heard of this from your time in the desert," he said, coiling the hellish thing in his hands. "It is a bull's penis, dried in the sun and worked endlessly by the hands of the Yaquis into the whip you see before you. Think of the imagination and patience it took to recognize the potential of the penis of a bull as an instrument of torture. You would think a rawhide whip would be sufficient, yet this has a strength and supple power that no rawhide can match. Observe."

Suddenly he lashed the device backward and snapped it forward, flogging my abdomen. I screamed with pain so immediate and overwhelming I gagged and lost my breath, sucking in gulps of air.

"My Yaquis tell me they have seen a man take more than a hundred strokes like that before dying. Perhaps one of you will die that way, although I prefer even more creative techniques."

Von Kleist stepped close to me.

"You note that you are unable to move your heads. This is due to an insight I gained only through practical experience. I enjoyed making one victim watch the abuse of another, but it became difficult as they kept turning their heads or shutting their eyes when it was important to my pleasure that they observe every detail of their companion's suffering. Indeed, I enjoyed watching the effect on the bound victim even more than I enjoyed the actual physical torture. I found it more exciting and arousing. So I developed the technique of affixing the heads of my victims between two boards, so they are unable to look away, just as your heads are affixed right now. And there is one more item."

Von Kleist removed from his pocket a small device that looked like a tiny mousetrap, with jaws that opened and closed on a spring.

"Even the boards did not stop my victims from closing their eyes. So I investigated and found that eye doctors sometimes use these small traps to hold open the eyes of their patients. *Et voilà*, my problem was solved."

He put the device up to my right eye and propped it open so that I could not close my eyelids. Instantly I wanted to blink, but the little trap prevented it. Quickly, he fixed up my left eye, then did the same for Riley and Patton. All three of us were now utterly helpless and in his domination, not only unable to move but unable to look away from whatever he chose to show us.

"Now," said von Kleist to his Yaquis. "Bring me Miguel."

It took me years, decades even, but I was able eventually to piece together the story of Otto von Kleist. His family was and is one of the oldest and most prominent of the Prussian dynasties. He had an ancestor who was a famous poet and a cousin who became one of Hitler's top field marshals. Within his family had long been a strong streak of genius and a noticeable streak of eccentricity. And Otto was an eccentric child.

He had been born in 1889—the same year as Adolf Hitler, interestingly—on the ancient family estate in Pomerania, in that strange country between Germany and what is now Poland. His first name came from Bismarck, of course: "Otto" had been a popular name in Germany in 1889. He'd been a beautiful boy right from the beginning, tall and strong and well-formed and handsome in a blonde Teutonic way. He'd also shown every sign of having inherited the von Kleist genius. He spoke five languages, with a particular fluency in Spanish because he'd spent two years as a teenager at a military academy in Madrid. Gifted in mathematics, he also played the violin beautifully and dominated in all sports where size and strength were an advantage. In Spain he'd become an excellent swordsman and, later in his youth, he'd even taken up the English sport of boxing. He'd grown to a height of six feet, five inches by the age of eighteen. Those who casually observed the boy had found him reserved but confident, seemingly shy but sophisticated beyond his years.

Those who'd observed him more intimately noted other things.

I received much of my information about von Kleist's youth by buying an endless succession of beers in the basement bar of a Frankfurt hotel and sharing them with a man who had been a servant in the von Kleist household. I met him in the late 1930s, much of which I spent in Germany. I'd taken to devoting time on nights and weekends to trying to learn something of Otto von Kleist and good fortune led me to Manfred, who as a young man had worked in the kitchen at the von Kleist estate. He remembered Otto well, but didn't much like to talk about him.

Otto had been a solitary sort of boy. He would shut himself in his room for hours, even days, listening to German music on the newfangled gramophone. He'd kept volumes and volumes of journals, and one day he told Manfred to look at one. Manfred gulped his beer as he described to me what he saw.

"Pages and pages of drawings," he said. "Horrible drawings. Naked girls, naked boys, demons, pigs, rats, donkeys, rapes, worship of the devil. I never imagined such thoughts. I never imagined people even *had* such thoughts. And there were poems, about rape and torture and eating hearts. He had this belief that if you kill someone, you acquire that person's soul and it makes you powerful. Once I saw what was in those journals, I wanted to stop, but he told me to keep reading. He paged through it with me, showing me his favorite parts. I still have nightmares…"

"Why would he show you those journals?" I asked.

He shrugged.

"He knew I couldn't tell anyone. This was Prussia. The von Kleists are a great Prussian family, perhaps the greatest. Servants of such families could disappear easily, it happened often. So it was safe for him to show me. And I think… I think he wanted to watch my face while I read them."

There had been signs that young Otto did not restrict his interests to drawings and poems. Manfred was convinced that Otto had masturbated regularly over his journals. The servants had found small animals—squirrels and rabbits and whatnot—that had been burned or decapitated. Vandalism had been found in a local churchyard, with tombstones knocked down or defaced with the sorts of obscene drawings that filled his journals. Then, when Otto reached the age of fifteen or so, children and young girls began to disappear in the surrounding villages, never to be found. Otto had become more and more withdrawn, often disappearing for days and returning without explanation. His size and manner had discouraged even his parents from pressing him.

There is no doubt that the disturbing aura around Otto led to his being shipped off to military school in Madrid, while his cousins and peers had been attending universities or military schools in Germany. In Madrid, Otto's proclivities had become more pronounced, insofar as I was able to reconstruct. He used those years to master Spanish, boxing, and fencing, as well as his special skills. I learned that he'd taken a suite of rooms in one of Madrid's more dangerous neighborhoods and that the city experienced an epidemic of missing children similar to what had happened in Pomerania.

Like all aristocracies, the Prussian nobility was insular and prone to gossip. Word of Otto's talents and interests had circulated, eventually reaching the young Kaiser Wilhelm and his military advisors. Men like Otto are rare. His gift for languages, mastery of martial arts, and flexible attitudes toward the welfare of his fellow man made him an irresistible choice for the German secret service. He had been approached in Madrid by an experienced handler, after the idea was cleared with the von Kleist family. They had been honored to serve, of course, and particularly pleased that Otto would be taken off their hands and given a useful trade before he butchered his grandparents or did something equally embarrassing.

Truth to tell, Otto was far from the dashing, witty villain of *The Prisoner of Zenda*. He was actually rather dull. He was a sociopath and sexual sadist, creatures which doctors tell me lack both humor and empathy, however gifted they may be otherwise. Otto was also a practical man who knew himself. He quickly grasped that the secret service, especially when the nation was ruled by someone like Wilhelm, would give him the best possible scope to pursue his desires without fear of reprisals. So Otto became a secret agent of the German government in 1912, as Wilhelm was hatching the schemes that would erupt in world war two years later.

In 1915, when Wilhelm and his plotters were looking for ways to keep the United States out of the war, Spanish-speaking Otto had been the natural candidate to send to Mexico to make sure Woodrow Wilson was dragged against his will into the Mexican Revolution. Otto had first traveled to Sonora. He had heard of the Yaqui tribe and their particular talents for torture and he wanted to learn from them. This was where he'd taken Scar and No Scar into his service. They'd taught him the art of the *bastinado* and how to flay the skin from a human being without killing him. He'd taught them many of the techniques he had developed in his suite in Madrid while working on the little children he snatched from the streets. The Yaquis had become devoted to him, recognizing a true master in their field.

When he had secured his acolytes and his skin was sufficiently browned by the Sonoran sun, von Kleist had traveled to Chihuahua to join Pancho Villa. His mission had been to gain Villa's confidence and lead him to commit outrages against Americans that would force Wilson to send troops to Mexico. At the time, Villa's followers had included a fierce killer named Rodolfo Fierro, a cruel man who was hated by foe and friend alike. Von Kleist had immediately decided to set himself up against Fierro and to displace him as Villa's pet mad dog. On October 14, 1915, von Kleist's Yaquis had guided a troop led by Fierro into a bog filled with quicksand. Von Kleist had made sure the other men did not follow Fierro as he rode straight into the bog and became entrapped. The bandits had been delighted at the sight of this hated bastard sinking from sight into the mud. They'd mocked him and laughed as he disappeared. They were to learn that von Kleist was an even more murderous thug, though he was careful to remain popular with Villa's men.

From then on, Villa had learned to respect and rely on his Spaniard, but he always found something mysterious about the man. It had been von Kleist who made sure the Villistas had murdered Americans at Santa Isabel and who talked Villa into the raid at Columbus that inspired the Pershing Punitive Expedition.

What von Kleist now intended was a masterstroke, an outrage that would certainly divert the full wrath of the United States and preoccupy them with Mexico for years to come. The torture, rape, and murder of George S. Patton, General Pershing's own brother-in-law and the flower of the American military: you had to admit, the idea had a certain style to it. And it would work, not that this would much matter to Riley or me, or to Patton, of course.

Miguel was brought forward. He was a brave boy and didn't struggle with the Yaquis. Von Kleist spoke to him in Spanish.

"Relax, young one. It won't be long now. I want to speak a moment to the lieutenant and then we shall have our time together."

Von Kleist walked up to Patton, putting his face within inches of him. I could not turn my head, but from my peripheral vision I could see what was happening. Like me, Patton was tightly bound so that he could not move a muscle of his body, could not even close his eyes due to the hellish braces that von Kleist had inserted. The German let his hand wander over Patton's chest, downward across his stomach, and onto his groin.

"You know, Lieutenant Patton, there is great pleasure to be taken from pain. When I torture someone, I like to watch his eyes, or the eyes of other victims who I make watch. It has never failed to arouse me. When I see a particular look, a look of horror, a look of recognition that there is no hope, that the pain and humiliation they suffer will go on and on and there is nothing to be done, no way for them to end my dominion of them... And then there is sometimes a look of resignation, as though they are past caring, but I find a way to make them care again... It is very exciting to me, exciting in a sexual way. It does not matter if they are men, women, boys, or girls... It is far more special. I take their bodies, but what truly excites me is the taking of their souls."

Patton spat in his face, as best he could. Von Kleist smiled and rubbed the spittle lasciviously around his mouth. He opened Patton's breeches, pulled out his manhood, and started playing with it. Then he took a knife from his belt and rubbed it slowly on Patton's penis. Although Patton's eyes were propped wide open, his expression conveyed disgust and horror. Groans unwillingly escaped from his mouth. His penis became hard in von Kleist's hand, obviously pleasing the German. Von Kleist bent over and took it in his mouth.

There was nothing that Riley or I could do to relieve the horror of our situation. We could not look away, could not close our eyes, could not even vomit or cry out. All we could do was stand motionless, backed against a cave wall, eyes forced open, while unimaginable deeds occurred in front of us.

In a few moments, von Kleist left Patton and returned to Miguel. On a nod from their master, the Yaquis laid Miguel on the bench and No Scar tied his hands to the posts behind his head. Von Kleist gently stripped him and began by making small cuts on Miguel's face, feet, and chest. He reveled in smearing Miguel's blood on himself. For nearly an hour, von Kleist had his way with the poor boy, in ways I will not describe but had to watch. I believe von Kleist ejaculated at least three times, the last time after Miguel lay dead.

In the end, von Kleist danced naked before us, dangling Miguel's severed head for us to kiss. Now I ask, how could God make such a man? Then, I did not ask. I could not think. There was only horror.

The reaction set in quickly. Von Kleist, who had been dancing with manic energy before us, suddenly grew exhausted and collapsed wordlessly into sleep. Scar removed the braces from our eyes, perhaps not wanting us to become blind before our turns came. The Yaquis began to skin Miguel's tortured corpse. I may have fainted with the shock. In any event, my memory fades for a time.

The next I recall, the voice of one of Villa's bandits was shouting for the Spaniard. I must indeed have lost consciousness for a time, as von Kleist was dressed and awake. Cursing loudly, he walked toward the dark wall opposite where we were bound and pushed aside a large boulder, revealing a narrow passage back to the cave mouth. He was only gone a moment.

"Gentlemen, I regret there has been a slight change of plan," he said. "We received word that the Jaguar is engaged in battle somewhere on the other side of Parral. I must go to him to make sure the fool doesn't get himself killed. If we are to blame Pancho Villa for your deaths, Pancho Villa must be alive to attract the United States."

He walked up to Patton.

"I must leave you, I fear," he said. "I did enjoy you. Do not worry, my Yaquis will see that the plan goes forward in full. I have had my fill for now, in any event. Go with God, Lieutenant Patton."

And he kissed the lieutenant on the lips quickly, before Patton could bite at him.

Von Kleist gave the Yaquis his last instructions, in Spanish.

"Do what else you may wish with them, but skin them and leave them all hanging for the gringos to find. We shall meet in Parral."

Then he was gone.

The Yaquis looked at each other and shrugged. Both wore knives in their belts, but these were not designed for flaying. Instead, Scar lifted the big skinning knife they had used on Miguel. The wooden handle and the large wicked blade were curved, fitting nicely into the hand and offering the blade edge at the perfect angle for lifting thin layers of skin off an animal's flesh. Scar ostentatiously whetted the blade against a stone, sharpening it, while both Yaquis grinned at us. Lord, not only did they stink, they were ugly. They seemed creatures from pre-history, cave-dwellers who ate vermin and took savage pleasure in the torture of human beings. Well, of course, that's what they were.

After sharpening it, Scar held the blade in the fire. He then started toward us, focused on Patton.

Then, suddenly, Riley started talking.

I've emphasized that my friend Riley was a silent man who spoke in fragments and rarely uttered two sentences at a time. Well, he made up for it in that cave. He cussed the Yaquis in Spanish, mocking their manhood, their mothers, their ugliness, all he could think of.

"You dogs, you help your master to suck cocks? You are women! You don't dare to fight, you cut up bound men, and then you crawl to your caves and fuck each other!"

And so on.

This seemed imprudent under the circumstances. It certainly drew their attention to Riley and made him their first choice for a victim. Scar pulled a revolver and stuck it in Riley's mouth, holding the flaying knife at his belly. No Scar quickly loosened Riley's bonds and together they pulled and pushed my friend on his back onto the bench before us, with No Scar tying his hands over his head. Soon Riley was trussed and ready on the bench in the same position as Miguel, whose mangled and decapitated body now lay a few feet away.

Plainly, the Yaquis had experience skinning men on this bench. They knew exactly what to do. Scar straddled Riley's belly, facing him. No Scar placed himself behind Riley's head and held the table steady. I could now close my eyes, but I watched, looking for any chance to help my friend. Scar took the skinning knife and, to demonstrate the sharpness of the blade, he pricked the skin on Riley's throat, drawing blood. Riley just looked at him. The bench was placed with Riley's head to my right, his feet to my left. I could not see his right hand very well.

I started shouting in Spanish, telling them to stop. They did not. Scar carefully set the knife at the top of Riley's rib cage, just below his neck. Riley kept looking at him steadily. I saw blood spurt from around the blade. Now Patton was yelling, too, threatening the Yaquis and promising retribution. That blade was indeed sharp. Scar brought it down Riley's chest, peeling the skin like cheese. More blood seeped out. I could see exposed red flesh, the muscles on Riley's wiry frame twitching and bleeding. When Scar brought the blade all the way down to Riley's navel, Riley finally cried out. Scar held the ribbon of skin in front of Riley's eyes, making sure he knew what it was. I believe he even took a bite out of it. No Scar was taking in the proceedings avidly, leaning forward closer and closer over Riley's head, mocking him and letting his drool fall on Riley's face.

Scar began another peel. Riley was breathing hard, emitting grunts, and cursing softly. No Scar leaned further forward, practically nose-to-nose with Riley now, gloating in some incomprehensible tongue. I wondered how many peels Riley could stand.

And then I saw something amazing. It was Riley's right hand. It came loose from its bonds. While the Yaquis were focused intently on Riley's bleeding flesh, Riley's hand moved as if on its own accord toward No Scar's belt. Patton and I both saw it and stopped shouting. Riley's hand softly grasped the wicked hunting knife in No Scar's belt. Quick as light, before the Yaquis knew what was happening, Riley stabbed upward and behind his head and put the knife into No Scar's belly. Scar looked up. At that same moment, Riley yanked the knife from No Scar's gut and instantly drove the blade upward into Scar's chin, all the way to his brain.

Scar slumped dead to the ground. Riley, still bound to the bench by his left hand, rolled sideways and found his feet, the bench swinging from his arm. No Scar staggered but recovered and came at Riley, who somehow had managed to hold onto the knife. Riley brained No Scar with the bench, knocking him to the floor of the cave. Then he straddled No Scar and sliced open his jugular vein. The entire fight couldn't have lasted twenty seconds.

Patton and I were dumbstruck, but Riley didn't pause, for he still had work to do. He shook off the bench from his left hand and used the skinning knife to cut loose the two of us, telling us to keep quiet and nodding toward the cave entry to remind us that Marta still needed rescuing. With his shirt off and blood oozing from the streaks of bare red muscle on his chest, Riley looked like a vision from the fiery pits. He lifted the revolvers off the Yaquis' bodies and checked to confirm they were fully loaded. Patton reached out his hand for one, but Riley ignored him. We followed him to the cave entry, pushed the boulder quietly aside and peered out.

The Mexicans had a fire going in a large cavern. By its light, we saw what Marta had been subjected to. Four Mexican bandits were lying randomly around the cave floor, pulling at a bottle of tequila and making sarcastic remarks to their comrade, the fifth bandit, who was raping a limp, nude form that we knew was the daughter of Eduardo Ortega. We saw the Mexican's naked ass as he pumped and pumped into Marta's listless body. We heard him urge her on, order her to move, while his fellows laughed and encouraged him to beat her again.

Shocked and abused as he was, Patton was a leader of men. He motioned again to be handed a gun and whispered to Riley to circle to the left while Patton and I would circle to the right.

Riley had none of it. He simply stood up, a gun in each hand, and calmly walked forward. Patton and I watched, open-mouthed. It took a long time for the Mexicans to notice him, though Riley was in plain sight in the middle of the cavern and made no effort to be silent. When he was only perhaps twenty or twenty-five feet away, a bandit finally did notice him and shouted out in alarm. Then, like roaches when the light is turned on, all the Villistas rolled and scampered and reached for their guns. Still Riley walked on. A Mexican found his gun and raised his arm. *Bam!* Riley shot him dead. *Bam! Bam!* Firing the pistol in his other hand, he brought another down. *Bam! Bam! Bam!* He alternated, shooting first with one gun, then the other. The last to die was the fifth bandit, who had to roll off Marta and scramble naked for his pistol. Riley took very deliberate aim and fired a bullet clean through his skull. The cave stank of cordite. Five Mexican bandits lay dead. Not one had gotten off a shot.

Riley kicked the bodies to make sure they were, in fact, dead. He then looked around, picked up a blanket from the floor, and covered Marta, who was quietly weeping. With the same precision and deliberation with which he had killed the bandits, he took stock of the food and water. Patton and I stared at him and at each other, not knowing what to do.

Riley divided the bandits' supplies roughly in two and put half into saddle bags. He walked out to the horses and threw saddles and the saddle bags onto two of them. It seems odd to me now, but neither Patton nor I said a word as we watched. We didn't go to Marta, we didn't ask Riley what he was doing or where he was planning to go. We just watched him work.

Riley grimaced as he put on a shirt that he took from one of the dead Mexicans. Then he scooped Marta up in his arms, naked in her blanket. He settled her on one of the horses and mounted the other himself.

"Parral is just down the way. You can see the lights from the cave mouth," he said to us. "Watch out for Villa and the Spaniard. Don't try to follow us."

He took the reins from Marta's horse and they rode out the cave mouth and down the trail. I saw now that the sun was just rising. I could see the lights of Parral, just as Riley said.

I think we might have tried to follow them, or stop them, but we were not in a state to do much of anything. Patton seemed lost, confused. He was plainly suffering from the trauma of what the Spaniard, von Kleist, had done to him and from the knowledge of what would have happened had it not been for Riley. Later, he made sure to implore me not to tell anyone of the sexual act von Kleist had performed on him. Patton is long dead and his fame is secure, so it can't hurt now.

I watched my friend and his woman as they clopped down the trail, away from the cave. I was vaguely realizing something that has ever since been an important fact in my life, something I've had to find a way to reconcile and live with. My friend Riley was not only a loyal friend, a fine boxer, and a tough nut, he was also a cold and efficient killer of men. Seven bodies lay in that cave in the Mexican desert to prove it. I didn't know, at the time, just what to think of that.

I didn't see Riley again for six months.

16

The Incompetence of No Scar

Jim

I was packing. We really couldn't stay at Riley's house any longer. Sally was bored and anxious to get back and I had a job waiting for me. I'd just finished the section of Grandpa Jimmy's notebook that covered the Mexican Revolution and it seemed a good time to go.

My wife had already packed for herself and the kids, and I was in our bedroom throwing clothes in my bag. The smell of tobacco and bourbon told me that Riley had entered the room and stood behind me. I hadn't talked with him since I read what happened in the cave.

"I won't ask you this time if it's true," I said. "It must have been hell."

Riley shrugged. Our son Jonathan, age six, entered the room to tell me something. Seeing Riley, he turned and left.

"So now I understand why Grandmother always seemed sad."

Riley shook his head.

"That wasn't it, not entirely. She had that air of sadness when I first saw her. Her mother had died, but I don't know if that was it either. Your grandmother was just a sensitive woman. This was a hard . world for her, but she never let it destroy her."

"It must have come close, after the cave."

"Maybe. That was the worst time, it's true."

"How did you get your hand loose?"

Riley looked out a window at the pool.

"I watched No Scar when he tied Miguel's hands during his torture. He couldn't tie a knot to save his soul. Scar was good at knots, but I knew I could get loose if No Scar was doing the tying. So I mocked them to make sure I went first. Just lucky that No Scar tied the knots."

Lucky.

"What did you and Grandmother do next?"

Riley took a drag on his cigarette.

"We didn't stop in Parral, too much danger of running into Villa. We rode until we found a house out in the desert that looked like nobody came around much. The woman there was kind. She felt for Marta and took care of us, fed us both. We stayed a long time. Marta didn't talk at first, but the woman and I nursed her and gentled her along. All the time I knew I needed to get her home. I knew that my mother and sisters would help her and be the best medicine she could have and that's what happened."

I closed my suitcase and sat on the bed. I looked at the box of notebooks.

"There's still a lot to read," I said.

"Take it all with you. I don't need it now. Take the box and read it all, if you've a mind. Let me know what you think."

"I will."

I was oddly disturbed. Somehow my talks with Riley as I read the story had become part of the experience. I didn't think it would be the same, just reading the notebooks cold. Riley read my thoughts.

"I might come up your way," he said. "I want to make sure Cornelius doesn't get away with some of his stories. He always needs me to balance him off." Riley looked uncomfortable, wanting to ask me something but not sure of the answer. "Would it be all right if I came to Minnesota for a while, so we can talk about the notebooks?"

"Yes," I said. "That would be all right."

Part Three

France

17

Good Days and Bad Days

Cornelius

The trench was dark and wet. I looked across it and watched a slug oozing out from under Riley's collar and wriggling slowly across his face. I was too spent and disinterested to reach across and flick it away. Apparently so was Riley, for he allowed the slug to complete its progress across his chin and make its way under the collar on the other side of Riley's neck. Neither of us moved.

"You suppose this is what it's always like?" Sid Crew asked. "What it's been like for the Frenchies and the Brits all these years? Jesus."

"Fuck," said George Keller.

"Don't worry, boys," I said, appointing myself morale officer. "The Americans are here, now. We'll clean this mess up and get back to Paris, and then you'll see some real action."

"Fuck," said George Keller.

The lantern in the trench sputtered and went out, leaving us in darkness. No one moved. There was some artillery fire far off: French 75s, it sounded like. Didn't know if it was ours or theirs, didn't care. With the darkness, rats scurried closer to where we were sitting. Lord, they were fat. God knows what they ate in those trenches that made them so fat, but it wasn't something I cared to dwell on.

Sid wasn't satisfied.

"I thought we come here to charge the Krauts. They told us the Germans was comin' and beatin' the Brits and the Frenchies, and we was gonna charge in and save their sorry hides and save Paree and all that. But here we are, sittin' with rats in the mud."

"Now, Sid, you know what they told us. Germans stopped coming when the Brits beat 'em over on some river and now it looks like they're not trying for Paris anymore. So we're sitting here, waiting for the next plan."

"Well, shit, Jimmy, we could be sittin' here another four years, like these Europeans been doin'."

"Have some patience, Sid. We just got here."

And the night passed.

We were in France, privates in the 28th Regiment of the First Infantry Division. It was late April of 1918, almost two years after the events in the Spaniard's cave. Insofar as we had experienced, France was a world of gray and brown mud. We swallowed mud, slept in mud, struggled to walk through mud, spent our waking hours trying to keep mud out of our rifles. We looked like mud-men, swamp figures caked with brown, with haunted eyes staring through the crust.

We were told that we were dug in near a town called Cantigny, which we had never seen. We gathered that we were to die for Paris, which we had also never seen. That was all right. Men had long died for concepts, like religion and freedom and justice and revenge, and you can't see those things either. Perhaps it's easier that way. When you see the details, you see the flaws.

I'll pass quickly over the two intervening years, at least for now. Riley made it home to Independence with Marta and Ma immediately took her in on the farm, as Riley knew she would. By the time I got back to Missouri, she was well-settled and part of the family. Against all odds, Marta got along with the Riley sisters, even Bessie to the extent that was possible for anyone. I was best man at their wedding, on March 24, 1917. Marta astonished us all by asking Bessie to be her maid of honor. From that day on, she was the only person on Earth about whom Bessie would not utter a hard word, which rendered Bessie pretty silent on the subject of Marta. Understand, even Jesus

Christ did not escape hard words from Bessie. She thought him weak on temperance.

I will also pass over another adventure that Riley and I shared. We volunteered to serve in a reserve unit that was sent to put down a race riot in St. Louis. Since this is about the Great War, with its ridiculous prelude in Mexico and its deadly postlude in Germany, St. Louis doesn't fit in the story. Perhaps I'll tell it some other day.

Why did we enlist? Especially, why did Riley enlist when he had just gotten married to the love of his life? The war in Europe, of course. It had been an unseen presence in our lives from when we were boys of sixteen and now we were men of almost twenty. We had envied those boys in France and England who got the chance for adventure, right there at their doorsteps. They could fight and shoot people and risk death. They were battle-tested, certain of their manhood and their places in the world. By contrast, they made us feel callow, unproven, held back. Truth be told, I was bored and Riley was more bored. It is a central fact of our lives together that while Riley loved Marta deeply and always told himself that he missed life in Independence, the truth was that he was an incompetent farmer, his sisters annoyed him, and he could never be back home a day without eyeing the horizon and wondering what lay beyond. I was the same way, but at least I admitted it. It's why I spent most of my life in New York: living there is like forever living in an adventure.

But after the tour in St. Louis, where we tried somewhat unsuccessfully to keep the locals from killing colored people, we landed back in Independence. Our reserve unit was released from duty, told we'd be called up when our good president finally got off his dainty Princeton ass and sent troops to Europe. We'd been at war with Germany for months, but the only troops actually earmarked for Europe were a group called the First Expeditionary Division that was organized out in New York, mostly from veterans of the Mexican fracas. That bunch was finally starting to be sent over to France, where our old friends Pershing and Patton were disporting themselves. Pershing, of course, had been put in command of the American forces that were charged with saving Europe's bacon, but exactly what he was doing over there wasn't clear to the eager young men cooling their heels in the heartland. Nothing, as far as we could tell.

It came to a head for us one evening when Riley and I were

having some drinks at Tom Everett's bar in Independence. Riley should have been working all day in the fields and then staying home with the missus, but instead he left the afternoon's fieldwork to the Mexicans and worked out at Skelly's, keeping up his boxing form. It was early October, I think, 1917. I was ordering us another round of beers when I looked up and saw Johnny Ball walking into the place, in full uniform.

"Johnny Ball, look at you," I said. Johnny was an old schoolmate of ours and he'd gone off to join the war a while back.

"Riley. Jimmy."

"So what's the story, Johnny? What happened to you and what are you doing here, all dressed up fancy like that?"

"My Ma died. I'm on leave."

"Shoot. Sorry, Johnny. I didn't know that."

"Sorry, Johnny."

"S'all right. Gimme a Pabst, Tom."

"Should be on the house, Tom. This man is serving his country."

"Shut up, Jimmy."

"So tell the story, Johnny. How'd you get in the army? What's goin' on?"

Johnny took his beer and sat down with us.

"Gettin' in the army ain't hard, boys. But once you're in, it ain't necessarily what you expect."

"What did you expect?"

Johnny stared into his beer.

"I don't know, that we'd be doin' something exciting, I guess. We did training and that was pretty much what I expected, 'cept we learned new kinds of stuff I didn't think about, like gas masks and how they're fighting out of trenches over there. You know how many times I've had to crawl up out of a hole in the ground and go running like a fool pointing a bayonet and yelling some crazy thing they tell us to yell?"

We didn't know.

"Anyway," Johnny finished, "we're still training, going over stuff we've already learned. But some of the forces have finally started getting on boats and heading off to France, so I guess the day is coming."

Then the conversation drifted off to schoolmates. I learned that perennial dumbass Tom Klapmeyer was in jail for robbing a store in Kansas City.

Anyhow, that was the last we saw of Johnny. But I think we both knew this conversation meant something to us. My girlfriend of the day was weighing on me, wanting more from me than I was ready to give and Riley was itching to get off the farm, however much he denied it. It wasn't a month later, after the crops were in, that we got on a train to New York to join the First Expeditionary Division.

It was a good day. Everybody who'd been in the hole with us that morning was there again that night. The days consisted of looking over the edge of the trench, watching for the enemy to venture into the No Man's Land that divided our trenches. Sometimes we'd creep out of the trench to observe the enemy positions or just because our officers were bored. The nights mostly consisted of sitting or lying in the trench, but not peering over the edge of it.

"How long do you suppose we'll sit here?" Sid Crew asked.

"Stop talking about it, for Christ's sake," said George Keller, a natural-born pessimist. "Just shut up and let the time go. You talk about it day and night, it seems longer."

"I just want to know," Sid sniveled. "We just sit here looking at 'em, this war could take forever."

"Then let it. I ain't so anxious to stick my head up and get it blown off. Something'll happen sooner or later, trust me."

I should talk a little about the trenches. After four years of fighting, northern France was scarred everywhere with long deep ditches filled with warring soldiers. There were generally three trenches for each side, about ten feet or so deep. They were dug zig-zag, so no one could shoot machine gun fire all the way down the length of the trench. Troops would rotate between the frontline trench, the support trench behind it, and the reserve trench behind that one. In my memory, though, it seems like we were always in the frontline.

Wood shoring supported the walls of the trench and there were duckboards to walk on. Sandbags piled at the forward lip of the trench were there to stop bullets. There was no ceiling or cover overhead, so the rain—and there was plenty that spring—just came in on you. Cubbyholes dug here and there in the walls of the trench allowed you to snuggle in there when it rained, to get some kind of cover over you. Got you closer to the rats, though.

Everybody who was in our war talks about those rats. Big as cats, fat, used to people. Hungry enough to bite you when you were sleeping. There was special urgency to securing our dead quickly, for if you didn't, the rats would strip them to the bones. Every soldier in the trenches could show you rat bites on his body, not to mention the insects and some varmints that I couldn't identify. It was dark in the trenches even in daylight, so it was hard to see the vermin as they bit at you.

About half a mile north of us, close enough to be easy to see when there was light and the smoke and gas weren't hanging low, were the German trenches. As far as we could tell, they were just like ours: long narrow gaps cut in the dirt, probably with the same wood-slat floors and the same lanterns and the same rats.

What happened, of course, was that about four years earlier, in August of 1914, the German army had come charging like demons through Belgium and into France toward Paris. There was a pincer movement from the west and the east and if the pincers had closed on Paris, the war would have been over in a month. But the Frenchies dug in and got some support from the Brits and the Belgians sacrificed a generation to stop the German offensive cold in northern France. Nobody had thought what to do beyond this point and, during the next four years, nobody came up with a good game plan. The two sides just sat in their trenches, getting eaten by rats and staring at each other, with an occasional charge or burst of mustard gas to release the tension. Hell of a war.

Each side was looking for a trump card to tip the balance in their favor and each side thought it had one. Lenin and his Bolsheviks took over Russia in 1917 and, a few months later, entered into a treaty with Germany that took Russia out of the war. The Kaiser pulled his troops from the Eastern Front and marched them into France, supporting a series of new offensives aimed southward to take Paris at last.

The Allies had the Americans. Foolish German aggression against American shipping finally forced movement out of our constipated Princeton president and we declared war, sending General Pershing to save the day. But Pershing was sitting in Paris, refusing to put Americans under the command of Europeans and insisting that he wouldn't be ready until 1919 to put an American force in the field. Meanwhile, the reinforced German armies were mounting offensive after offensive, all pushing toward Paris and seeking the endgame before the Americans could bring its full military might into play. It was a critical time.

In April 1918, after a browbeating by Clemenceau and Lloyd George that could only be called embarrassing, Wilson directly ordered Pershing to put some American troops in the field to aid the French and British troops trying to save Paris. That's why we got in the trench near Cantigny. We were moved up from a training camp in the south of France and led into our hole in the ground where we were going to beat back the latest German offensive, Operation Georgette, which the Germans called "the Peace Offensive" because it was supposed to end the war. But General Haig of the Brits issued a Special Order of the Day to "fight to the end," and by God they did. The Brits beat the pants off the Germans at the Lys River on April 29, 1918 and that ended Georgette. Both sides sank back into the mud, including our little American regiment at Cantigny. I have to admit, that trench chilled my soul, however much I tried to cheer up the platoon. The last time that Riley and I went underground, things hadn't gone so well.

Sid Crew was a little guy from New Jersey, gangly, with a very loud voice. He wore what looked like a dog collar around his neck. I don't know how he got away with it, but he did. When anybody asked him why he wore it, he just shrugged. He always seemed to rile Stan Becker, who was usually pretty grouchy anyway. These guys, like most of the fellows in our platoon, had seen service in Mexico and looked to be staying with the army as long as it would feed them. Riley and I kept quiet about our own time in Mexico. It would have been hard to explain.

The sergeant of our platoon was named Pete Bickel. He was the dumbest one in the trench, so he was in command. He told us to call him Sergeant Pickle if we wanted—which we didn't.

"Jesus, my gun is full of mud," Sid said one day as he worked away at the barrel. "I don't know how it gets this way. Every damn night, I have to do this."

Stan Becker glared at him from across the trench. George Keller suggested that if Sid kept the mouth of his barrel out of the mud, things might improve.

"I dropped it when Tommy got hit. He was right next to me, for God's sake. Lucky I didn't shit my pants. Forget about the gun."

"You never forget about your gun," Keller said coolly. "Nobody in this trench gives a goddam if you shit your pants, but you hold onto that gun and you shoot it if you get the chance. At a German, not us."

It had been a bad day. We were out of the trench, hauling in some supplies, when a shell had gotten lucky and landed right in the middle of us. Tommy Hill, from Wisconsin, got splattered all over the rest of the platoon. I was looking at a Tommy stain on my trouser leg when Keller was speaking.

"I care if he shits his pants," Riley said. "Might improve the smell around here."

Riley making a joke was enough to lighten the atmosphere, which was what he intended. I would have joined in, but the Tommy Hill stain weighed on me.

Sergeant Bickel lit a cigarette and took a deep drag.

"What'd you think of those airplanes today? What were they doing?"

A handful of German biplanes had circled over our lines before flying back.

"I've never seen one of them planes do anything," Stan Becker said. "They just fly around, 'less they crash. It's foolishness."

"What I hear, some of these pilots the Germans got are real good," the sergeant commented. "That Red Baron and his crowd."

"Red Baron, shit. I'll believe it when I see it. I think this whole airplane thing is foolishness. I seen an airplane back home in a field, puttin' on a show. Didn't mean nothin'. Don't scare me. Don't impress me."

And those comments, courtesy of Stan Becker, pretty well summarized the whole twentieth century. In my time, I've heard similar disparagement of automobiles, radios, televisions, the atom bomb, and computers. In one man's lifetime. Of course, some things deserve to be disparaged. If what we now call World War I was the first truly technological war, you can keep it. I was there.

We were now well into May, still sitting in the trench. There were good days and bad days. The worst, we lost five men from the platoon in six hours, all from lucky shots by the Germans. George Keller was one of them. He died cursing. Lots of men do, in my experience.

Pete Bickel died without saying anything at all. An order had come down that our platoon was to move out during the night and dig a line of foxholes about a hundred yards into No Man's Land, closer to the German lines. Why that patch of mud was so much more desirable than the one we were sitting in wasn't clear to us, but it was something to pass the time. At midnight, an artillery barrage from behind us lit up, battering the German lines and throwing shells all the way into the outskirts of Cantigny. Must have been French artillery, since Pershing still hadn't moved up the heavy American guns. After an hour of fireworks, Sergeant Bickel waved us up and over the top and we ran as quickly as we could, laden as we were, toward the Germans. Their artillery was aimed over our heads, but once we appeared, they opened up with rifle fire and found some targets among us. I became separated from Riley, who was off somewhere to my right. Some of the men were firing toward the Germans, but I saw no point, as I saw nothing to hit. I zigged and zagged and kept an eye on Bickel for the hand signal to stop.

He gave it. Per orders, I slid to the ground, pulled out my entrenchment tool and started digging into the mud like an animal, praying I'd cover myself before a German bullet found me. Bickel and a few others were working with me. I couldn't see Riley, but figured he was with a knot of men from our platoon about twenty yards away, digging as we were.

We almost made it. We got the hole dug, about eight feet long and five feet deep, like a big grave. Four of us rolled down into it: me, Dick Miller, Stan Becker, Rollie somebody. Bickel, facing our lines, took one in the back just as he was about to throw himself in after us. He died without a word, his face hanging over the lip of the hole, staring down at us. I pushed him back so as not to have to look at him.

We lay on top of each other, breathing hard, with all hell breaking loose above our hole in the earth. I developed a great need to piss, which is a tricky thing when you're crammed in a tiny mudhole with three other men and with shells and bullets screaming over your head. I finally just opened my pants, rolled over halfway, and wet the dirt. We waited.

Eventually the shooting died down, as it always does. Sleep was out of the question. The four of us got out our entrenching tools again, digging around to give ourselves more room. We ate the dry rations we had carried with us. Our orders had been to hold our position until further word, but we didn't know when further word would arrive. I poked my head above the top a few times and saw that our men had dug themselves into similar holes up and down a line that stretched well into No Man's Land. Once, I was rewarded by the sight of Riley, who poked up his head from a hole to my right at the same moment I did. We waved and smiled at each other. It was good to see him.

Further word came after almost an hour. A courier, with a job I didn't envy, came running to our hole and told us that, two minutes after he moved on, one of us was to run back to the trench we had just abandoned for further orders. Being the wordy one in the foxhole, I was chosen. I scurried back the way we had come, this time with no gunfire and no sound at all, except that of men running from their holes as I was, to receive our next orders. Riley passed me just as we reached the trench and jogged downward into the dark ground.

The trench was crowded, but one man dominated the trench just by standing in it. We all fell silent when we saw him. It was Colonel Ely, commander of the 28th.

Hanson Ely was fifty years old. He made me think of what Patton would be like when he was fifty. Ramrod straight, eyes of a hawk, you'd know he was a soldier no matter what he wore. Colonel Ely had deep sunken eyes, maybe the deepest I've ever seen, so deep his eyes disappeared entirely in the shadows of the trench. His posture made him seem much taller than he was. A brush mustache, thick eyebrows, hooked nose. He was of the officer elite, the class into which Patton was born. Ely mistimed his birth, arriving in the world shortly after the Civil War and fifty years before America entered the Great War in Europe. As a result, he lived a long life, fought valiantly and died a respected man, but no one today remembers him. Patton, who died in a car accident when he was sixty and is known today by all, better timed his birth and wouldn't have traded his fate with Ely's for any amount of money. Ely suffered from an oversupply of peace during his lifetime or at least from wars that no one cared much about. Peace to soldiers is like warm winters to ski resorts: bad for business.

Shortly after Riley and I arrived, the aides surrounding the colonel called for silence. Colonel Ely stepped onto a stool in the dark, smelly trench. He was lighted from below by kerosene lamps, which threw an eerie glow onto his face from the underside, like when boys try to look like monsters. The trench grew silent.

"Today, the 28th Regiment of the First Division of the United States Army is being given the greatest honor in its history," Ely said in a high-pitched, pinched voice. This was bad news: in combat, you only want honors retrospectively and only when you're alive. "We have been selected to perform the first American-only offensive operation in this war. Gentlemen, we are going to take Cantigny."

Well, Sid Crew will be happy, I thought. No resting in mudholes today.

"Some of you have been here awhile," the colonel continued, "and you have risked your lives to move forward to a new position without knowing the reason. Others of you have just come forward to this frontline trench. Now you know why: Cantigny is a critical town, set on a hill that overlooks all Picardy, the gateway to Paris. The Huns can't take Paris if they don't hold Cantigny. And we're going to take it from them before the sun goes down tomorrow."

Even then, this seemed like an exaggeration, and it was. Historians now say that Cantigny had little strategic significance, but American troops needed a win after their embarrassing loss at an earlier engagement at Saint-Mihiel. I suppose that would not have sounded well as the send-off message to the men.

Ely hitched his thumbs in his belt, as though to seem less formal.

"General Bullard gave me the orders directly, in the company of Lieutenant Colonel Patton, a courier from General Pershing himself."

Well, well. Robert Lee Bullard commanded the First Division, but what struck me was Patton's new rank. Georgie Patton was moving up in the world, but was still running errands for his brother-in-law Black Jack, even though Patton was now in charge of a newfangled tank unit. I wondered what Patton would think if he ran into Riley and me on the fields of Picardy. I figured he would look like someone had stepped on his grave.

"General Bullard reminded me that our men haven't seen much fighting yet," Ely informed us. "When they did fight the Huns in what the Germans called Operation Georgette, they met with some bad luck."

This was well-known and quite an understatement. While the

Brits covered themselves with glory and pushed back Georgette at the River Lys, badly trained Americans were thrown to the wolves at Saint-Mihiel by their French commanders and they ran before the German infantry. Speculation was that Clemenceau hounded Pershing unmercifully about it, which Riley and I later discovered to be true.

"So today, we right the balance and show the world what American troops are made of," Ely continued. "We ordered some of you forward to take position closer to the enemy and to make room for more of our troops here. Now, you know why. These officers will give you your orders. Those of you from the foxholes will return to them and relay the orders you receive. Men, today you will make this the American Century. God bless you."

I swear to God, that's what he said. I wasn't to hear the twentieth referred to as the American Century again for many years thereafter, after Henry Luce used the phrase, but Hanson Ely said it just like that, in a filthy trench in Picardy. And if you ever have to pick a single day when America established its dominance in the world, which would last the rest of my long lifetime, May 28th of 1918 is as good a day as any. And it was done by us, the men they came to call the Black Lions of Cantigny.

18

The Battle of Cantigny

Cornelius

As far as I recall, Riley and I didn't exchange any hugs or meaningful last words when we separated to return to our respective foxholes, nor do I recall making a joke or any sort of lighthearted remark. I just dropped into the earth when I reached my foxhole and Riley kept going. We had a lot on our minds.

We'd received many orders and by then it was getting close to dawn. I did my best to remember everything I had to impart to the small crew in my hole. The nut of it was that we were to lie still the rest of the night. At about four in the morning, a hellish artillery barrage would be unleashed upon Cantigny. It would last two hours, during which we were to stay put and stay sane and not get ourselves killed. When it stopped around dawn, we would see a flare that was the signal for us to advance. We were then to charge over the top of our foxhole and run like hell for the town of Cantigny, shooting anyone who was in front of us. As the frontline of the advance, we were to run all the way through the village, stopping for nothing until we reached an abandoned trench line on the other side of town. We were then to entrench there, making ourselves the new frontline, with Cantigny now behind us and to the south, rather than ahead of us and to the north.

All quite simple, really. Unless you consider that we were human beings made of very frail material like gristle, guts, and blood; that we were already exhausted and tense to the edge of breaking; that we were now to lie sleepless in the mud while Hell's ungodly chorus burst over our heads; that we would have to summon the grit to go over the top and run hell for leather across a hundred yards of barbed wire and entrenchments carrying a rifle, a gas mask, and three days of rations, while nasty German soldiers shot bullets and artillery shells and hurled gas grenades at us. Coupled, of course, with the fact that none of us had even a vague notion of how the town of Cantigny was laid out and no one in the briefing had chosen to enlighten us. Well, we thought, it's not that big a place, after all. Go north, that's all. How difficult can it be? God help the working doughboy.

"What's the story, Jimmy?" asked one of them in my foxhole.

"What took you so long?" asked another.

"Are we moving?" inquired the third. "What's happening?"

I tried to put a bold face on my answers.

"We're attacking, boys. I got the orders from Colonel Ely himself. Come dawn, we take Cantigny."

I wish I could say I was met with cheers and huzzahs, but there was nothing like that. The men looked doubtful, sullen, unhappy—what I could see of them in the infernal dark of the foxhole. But not one of them balked. It's really quite a remarkable thing. These were free Americans, out on their own in No Man's Land with no real officer watching them, just a fast-talking private relaying supposed orders for them to go running into what, for some of them at least, would be certain death. There were no threats, no mutiny, no running away. The boys just swallowed their doubts and lay back down in the mud, waiting for dawn and thinking their private thoughts. I'll never understand humanity.

And me? I didn't run either. I *thought* about it. I also thought about just burrowing deep into the mud of the foxhole and staying there, covering myself up and waiting until the noise of battle stopped and I could melt away in whatever direction looked most promising. I knew I wouldn't do it. I knew I'd do just what they said, clamber over the damn lip of the damn foxhole at dawn and run full-speed toward whatever fate awaited me that day. I would not do this for the capitalist system, since I was a communist at the time. Nor for courage, since I was shaking so badly I couldn't light a cigarette. I think it was just because the other men around me were all going to do it, so I had to do it. I guess that's why wars can happen: soldiers do what they're told, even when no sane person would consider it.

"Jimmy. Jimmy, you awake?"

There was an insistent whisper at my elbow, asking a question that struck me as idiotic, since who could sleep in that hole on that night, knowing dawn would come?

It was Stan Becker. Sid Crew was in Riley's foxhole and his absence made Stan a bit easier to live with, but that night we were all on edge.

"'Course I'm awake. Who the fuck could sleep tonight?"

Stan rolled onto his back and blew smoke upward.

"What are you thinking about?"

I snorted.

"You're asking damn fool questions tonight, Stan Becker. You think I'm thinking about philosophy? I'm thinking about getting my ass shot off tomorrow. That's what I'm thinking about. What the hell are you thinking about?"

"Same thing," he acknowledged. "I just don't want to die here. Not here and not yet. I need to tell you something."

"I don't want to hear it."

"No, I need to tell you. I got to tell you, Jimmy. This is pretty much the most important thing in the world."

I raised up on my elbows.

"Stan Becker, there's only one important thing in the world right now for you and for me. That's how the hell to keep from getting our asses blown off before sundown tomorrow. Unless you got a magic potion that lets us do that, I don't want to hear what else you got on your mind."

That seemed to sum it up, pretty much. We fell silent, each left with his own thoughts.

Silence didn't last long. It was broken by the first of endless blasts from the artillery to our rear, throwing shells over our heads and into the battered buildings of Cantigny. The Germans responded in kind, though they lacked our firepower. We were the furthest forward of any of the Americans, so the shells from both sides went over our positions without harming us. It was a long and very loud night.

Dawn was different in the trenches of Picardy than I ever remembered experiencing in Missouri or Mexico. The sky was always covered with lowering gray clouds. The sun never showed itself. Instead, dawn was a feeling, an impression that gradually took hold of you because of a trick of the light that you really didn't experience in any but a primal way, below the consciousness and below the senses. You knew it was dawn, but it was hard to say how or why.

Dawn came that way that morning at Cantigny. I poked my head up just enough to take a look over the lip of our foxhole. The artillery had died away in seeming anticipation of an assault by infantry. Yet no order came: no flares, no bugles, nothing. Smoke and fog obscured vision. I looked to my left and saw a line of foxholes similar to mine, with helmeted heads similar to mine poking up here and there down the field. I glanced to the right. At first, no one was visible in Riley's foxhole, dug in maybe thirty yards away. I wondered if Riley had given the order to stay down and if I should do the same.

Suddenly, two hands appeared. Then a helmet and a shadowed face, looking first toward Cantigny, then toward me and back and forth. When he pushed himself upward and I saw his scrawny body, I knew it was Sid Crew. No one else had that short, narrow torso, the jerky movements, the legs splayed here and there like a newborn colt. What the hell was he doing, I wondered. He actually pulled himself up and out of the foxhole and crouched for a moment, looking warily ahead toward the Germans. Did I miss an order to advance? Yet no one else appeared.

As though at a signal, Sid burst from his crouch and ran straight toward me, rifle held in front of him, head down, feet churning through the mud. This was madness. I yelled and waved him back. No message, no urgency could justify exposing himself this way in the growing light.

"Sid, go back!" I shouted. Or I think I did.

Gunfire. The Germans in the frontlines of Cantigny could easily see Sid as he ran. He made five steps, ten, crouching and dodging. Then he was hit, as I knew he would be. He fell instantly, dropping to the ground as though it had opened beneath him. I stayed where I was. Riley didn't.

Behind Sid, I saw Riley jump up from his foxhole, screaming something terrible. He ran forward, just as Sid had done but with no rifle in hand. Bullets flying around him, he scooped up Sid at a dead run, flung him over his shoulder and kept running, somehow not being hit, all the way to our foxhole, where he fell in and rolled end over end, tangled in a gray and brown ball with Sid's body.

The men in my foxhole surrounded them, me at the forefront. When they landed, Riley lay at the bottom, cradling Sid. Sid was dead. He'd been hit at least three times, one lucky shot right through his forehead. Riley looked like a wild man, staring at Sid with an intensity beyond anything I had seen in him, even that night in the cave.

"Riley," I said as I grabbed his shoulder to shake him out of it. "Riley, are you hit? What happened?"

Riley stared at me, eyes crazed, not like Riley at all. Then a new barrage came, the Germans throwing mortar shells at us to stop the anticipated charge that now everyone knew was coming. There was one loud hit, louder than anything we'd heard, closer than anything we'd experienced. Riley was the first of us to leap up to see. I was right behind him. The Germans had scored a direct hit on Riley's foxhole. We could see blood and body parts raining down. If Riley hadn't run to rescue Sid, he'd have been one of the dead. He screamed again.

By now, I was beyond consciousness, beyond action. I looked at the bloody rain, at Riley, at Sid's body. There were no words, no thoughts, no orders. Riley also looked wildly around, but then I saw resolve creep into his eyes. Here we go, I thought.

And we did. Riley grabbed Sid's rifle, put his hands on the top of the foxhole and heaved himself up. "Go!" was as much as he could bring himself to shout. He ran straight at the Germans, straight at Cantigny, all alone. I followed. Then the men in our foxhole screamed and followed. While Riley ran ahead of me, never looking back, I glanced around enough to see others pouring out of foxholes, running with us. The orders, the flares, they never came, but the Black Lions followed Riley into Cantigny.

You need to picture this, if you can. Cantigny was just a small French village, old, nothing special about it except it was on a point of land overlooking a great part of the county of Picardy, gateway from the north to Paris. The first ranks of Germans had placed themselves across the line of ramshackle buildings that constituted the southern border of the town. The Germans had placed mortars and other small artillery in the alleyways. In the windows of the houses that lined the street on which we ran, we could see rifle barrels and glints from German helmets. There were perhaps four blocks of such houses, long vacated by civilian personnel as a result of the battles back and forth over this insignificant little town that had raged now for four years.

Into the maw of this trap ran Riley at top speed, followed by the 28th Regiment. Shells landed around him, around all of us. Rifle fire scarred the ground. Men fell, many men, but not Riley and not me. Something seemed bent on protecting us at Cantigny.

We burst into a mortar emplacement located in the center of the German frontline. My bayonet was fixed. I saw Riley shoot a German who had a rifle pointed at him, then leap over a pile of sandbags and disappear from view. By now, several men had caught up to me. We hit the sandbags in unison, spearing the defenders with our bayonets as we'd been taught. A big man reared in front of me: I shoved the bayonet forward with all my strength and skewered his belly with the blade. He was still alive but helpless and flopping—for the life of me, I couldn't get my blade out of him. While all around me, men were shooting and dying and screaming and hiding and grappling, I was swinging the body of this German back and forth, trying to get purchase with my foot so I could free my weapon. It was a bizarre dance.

Finally, I freed my bayonet. I heard a voice ahead of me, calling. "Come on!"

It was Riley. He had fought his way through the emplacement and was heading onward. Those of us left alive and able followed him into town, seeking out the enemy, shooting them. We turned left down a larger street. Now the shooting slowed. We walked, warily, watching the windows and doors. A gun was fired from the upper windows of a livestock barn. Riley and I, with two companions, burst through the door of the barn. Nothing there but a few cows and the smell of manure. Then a boy in a German uniform, he couldn't have been more than fifteen, appeared in the loft above and fired at us. We cut him down instantly, cleared the building, and moved on.

So it went, the battle of Cantigny. Down one street, into a building, shoot some Germans, lose some men. On to the next block, the next building, clear it out. On and on.

I don't know how long it took for us to reach the far side of town. Probably it wasn't that long, but in a fight like that, time takes on a different dimension. At the end, you only remember images. I remember driving my bayonet into the belly of the big German by the mortar, how flowers of blood bloomed around my blade. I remember that the boy we shot in the barn had just a little growth of beard, probably all he could manage no matter how long he went without shaving. I remember Riley pulling two Lugers off dead Germans and kicking down the door of a shop, killing the enemy one after the other with a gun barking from each hand. I don't remember much in between.

Orders hadn't meant much or been much in our mind during that fight, but when we reached the field on the far side of town, we remembered we were supposed to entrench to repel the likely counterattacks. We found a line of trenches running along the north side of town, just as our old line had run along the south side. We took them over, using our entrenching tools to enlarge and stabilize them. I wondered how many soldiers had used the very trench Riley and I found ourselves in: Germans, English, French, Belgians perhaps? All in all, it had been a hell of a war for the doughboys.

We were exhausted and lay down next to each other, the shooting over and the work done for the moment. Remember, we were boys. Two boys from Missouri who had seen and caused more death than ever we could have imagined. We looked at each other. Riley seemed different to me. Even the rape of Marta, the tortures of von Kleist and the Yaquis, these had left Riley's essence untouched. Somehow, Cantigny was different. Riley had changed in some fundamental way. He became sadder, more cynical, deadlier. I don't know why. Perhaps the things that truly move human hearts are impossible to predict, since they are fundamentally chaotic. So Oppenheimer told us, much later, at Los Alamos. He spoke of changes in the space and time continuum, but it may apply to changes in the soul as well.

We slept, awakening to the sound of the first counterattack—a German artillery barrage from not far away, to our north. This wasn't a bad one. But there followed another, and another, and another. Gas attacks drove us to the hated masks: fortunately, both Riley and I had kept the cursed contraptions. When you wear a gas mask, you can't see to shoot. As a result, many men disdained them and wound up inhaling the mustard gas, dying in agony in the mud. One after the other, the counterattacks came.

I don't know that I've ever been so exhausted as at Cantigny. In the end, the Germans came back at us seven times, trying to take back that damn little burg. We held. When they gassed us, we wore our masks. When they charged us, we fixed bayonets and threw them back. When they shelled us, we hid our heads, prayed, and lived. After seven tries, the Germans gave up. After three days of hell on this earth, we held the town. The coat of arms for Picardy featured black lions, and ever since that battle, the 28th Regiment has called itself the Black Lions of Cantigny. I've only gone to one reunion and Riley never went to any. I remember that at my one reunion I saw Stan Becker, who also lived through that fight and many that followed. He'd become an insurance salesman in Peoria. I asked him once what it was that he so wanted to tell me that night in the trench, waiting to charge into Cantigny.

Stan scrunched up his face, deep in thought, but he was never able to remember what he had wanted to tell me. Guess it wasn't so important after all.

At the end of the seven counterattacks, I dropped where I stood and so did every man in the trench, Riley included. The Germans could have walked through us, shooting us as they wished. I think I slept for hours, only waking when a sharp and highly polished boot started kicking me in the hindquarters.

I tried to swat it away but it kept kicking. Angered, I rose up from the mud and looked into the handsome, hawk-nosed, ax-blade face of George S. Patton.

"Get up, now," he said. "Von Kleist is in Paris. And you boys are going to help me kill him."

19

The White Cloud

Jim

Riley had checked into a Residence Inn in Eden Prairie, a suburb southwest of Minneapolis. The motel was within an easy drive of both the airport and my home, which was in the next suburb to the north. I looked around his room. It was a typical layout, one that business travelers could easily navigate in pitch darkness due to their familiarity with it. The only homey touches were a bottle of Jim Beam bourbon on the kitchen counter and a brand-new expensive coffeemaker to replace the cheap motel version. It seemed that Riley meant to stay awhile.

"What have you read?"

"The first chapters in the France section."

Riley nodded. He took in smoke and blew it out.

"Notice anything? Like anything missing?"

"Not sure what you mean," I lied. I knew exactly what he meant.

"Did you notice the dates of the events in those chapters? Like the date of the Cantigny fight?"

"Around the end of May, I think."

"May twenty-eighth. Then there were three days of counterattacks. I figure Patton found us around the first of June. What happened in the summer of 1918 that's relevant to your life?"

I was right.

"My parents were born. They were both born in August of 1918. And I remember hearing about how you got a letter when you were in training in France, telling you that Grandmother was pregnant. I think I remember seeing a picture of my mother as a baby that Grandmother said she sent you when you were in a hospital over there."

"This one."

Riley pulled the photo out of his breast pocket and handed it to me. It was one of those old-fashioned black-and-white shots. Grandmother Marta was a beautiful dark-haired, dark-eyed young woman lying in bed, cradling my mother in her arms. Marta named her Fern, after Ma. Fern Arlys Riley, who grew up to marry Grandpa Jimmy's son Walter Hal O'Neal, my father. Mom was a good-looking baby and became a good-looking woman, much more like Marta than Riley.

"So what you're saying is missing from what I've read so far is any mention of the pregnancies. Did Grandpa Jimmy even know by then that he'd gotten his girlfriend pregnant?"

Fay Anderson was the name of my paternal grandmother. She never married Grandpa Jimmy. We grandchildren didn't get the real story until we were adults and not much of the story even then. They'd had a fling and consummated it shortly before the boys went off to war. She and Marta didn't know it but they were both pregnant when the troop ship left New York. Fay was poor and from not much of a family. Ma took in both the young mothers and, when they arrived, the babies. Quite a household, what with Ma and all the Riley sisters (minus Bessie, who was off to Harvard) fussing around the babies. Word was that Fay ran off and wasn't heard from for years. I've only met her once. She wasn't very interested and neither was I.

"Cornelius knew. He got a letter, same as me. His was a lot shorter. He showed it to me. Fay just wrote she was pregnant but didn't expect anything from him.

"We were in training down south of the fighting. The letters came the same day and we read them together, first one, then we traded and read the other guy's. Cornelius didn't say a word. Just walked off. Not like him."

"We knew Grandpa Jimmy never spent much time with family,"

I said. "I don't know that my father ever lived with him more than a year or two at a time."

"I guess neither of us were much as fathers. Traveled too much. That's just how it was."

We had one of our pauses. We sipped our bourbons and listened to a truck in the parking lot outside the window. We could hear the muffled blare of a television in the next room, but I couldn't identify the program. We were both uncomfortable because we were on the verge of talking about family stuff.

I thought I'd switch to an easier subject.

"What was the deal with Sid Crew?" I asked.

Riley's dark mood didn't lighten.

"Sid Crew?"

"Why was he running from your foxhole over to Grandpa Jimmy's? You were all dug in waiting for the order to advance and suddenly he bursts out of cover and gets himself killed."

Riley walked into the kitchen and poured another round of bourbon.

"He was ordered to do that."

"By who?"

"By me."

And it came out. Riley said he was scared, sitting in that foxhole, waiting to charge. Not scared of getting himself killed, but scared he'd mess up, scared he'd make a wrong move or give a wrong order and get everybody else killed. The men in his foxhole, by unanimous consent, had put him in charge after Bickel's death. His stomach was tight. His nerves jumped with every shot from either line. He hadn't asked to be in charge and he didn't like it. This didn't sound like the Riley I knew, certainly not like the Riley of Grandpa Jimmy's prose, but this is what he said.

He said he finally couldn't stand sitting still one more second, so he told Sid to run over to the other foxhole and see if they were ready in there.

"Sid looked back at me like I was crazy," Riley said. "I *was* crazy. It was just stupid fear and impatience that made me do it. But I told him to go and Sid didn't argue. Next thing, he'd pulled himself over the top and took off running.

"Soon as he did, I knew I'd done wrong. I didn't know if I should yell to stop him or if that would make it worse. Then the shots came, just ripping him apart. I ran over and scooped up his body and fell into the other foxhole, no thought at all except praying he was alive. You know what happened. The worst of it, a shell hit my own foxhole, where I'd just been, and killed everybody in there. Everybody I was supposed to watch over was dead and I was alive, only because of my own cowardice and stupidity.

"So I fell down onto the ground in that foxhole. My mind wasn't making words, didn't need to. It was one of those moments when you know, you know right away that your life won't ever be the same. This moment will stay with you, hound you no matter where you go or what you do. There won't be a single day for the rest of your life when you don't think of this moment. And there hasn't been.

"I lay there on my back in that hole, looking up at the sky. The sun was just coming up. It was the first time in months that the clouds were starting to break up. I watched them—maybe it was only a few seconds like Cornelius says, but it seemed a long time. Most of the clouds were gray, like always. But I remember the sun was just coming up over the horizon and it was throwing rays onto one little white cloud off to the west. I watched that cloud. Sunrise, sunset, they always remind me of that day at Cantigny, how I failed my men. And then I just shut out thinking and ran to kill somebody. Don't remember if I knew anybody was following me, and I didn't care.

"It was a bad day."

20

The Most Important Man in France

Cornelius

It reminded me of our first drive with Patton, from Chihuahua to Pershing's encampment, except instead of the sunny, scorched Mexican desert, we drove through the muddy, cloud-covered French countryside. If the sun existed at all in 1918, you couldn't have proved it by us. Gray and brown were still all we saw.

Just like on that first drive, Patton sat in the passenger seat up front, while Riley and I bounced along in the back. The driver wasn't Hiram, of course. I never got his name. Patton talked all the way, with an edge to his voice he didn't have before. Von Kleist can do that to a man.

"He should be in Paris by now," Patton said. "He left Berlin three days ago. We don't know exactly where he'll turn up, but we're watching all the known German sympathizers in the city." Patton looked back at us. "Might interest you to know, I've been keeping an eye on you boys, too."

We said nothing. Patton wasn't the sort who needed encouragement from his audience.

"Your families are well, last I knew. Everybody's still at your farm, Riley. Thought you'd want to know. It's hard to get word out here."

Patton was showing off, bragging about his sources, but I took the bait.

"How do you know what's happening back home, sir?"

"Same way I know about von Kleist. The army lives on intelligence, boys, don't forget that. The infantry is the heart and soul of the army, but without spies, the bravest men in the world can come to grief. I've learned that."

"So, sir," I said, "you've got spies out in Independence at Riley's farm?"

Patton gazed down his formidable nose at me, then laughed.

"Well, I'll allow that my mission in Independence doesn't utilize official channels." He pulled an envelope from his pocket and handed it to Riley. "From your wife. I had everything addressed to you boys come to me. Congratulations on having babies coming, both of you. Nice to have children."

Neither of us asked if Patton had children, though he seemed to invite it.

"Why are you so interested in us, sir?"

Riley stuck his letter in his pocket unread, out of pride, I suppose. Patton looked to the road ahead.

"Didn't want to lose track of you boys. We went through something together, back in Mexico. I don't know about you, but I haven't forgotten. I mean to kill that son-of-a-bitch von Kleist and I figured you might want to help me."

Patton turned to the driver.

"Now, son, you just turn off your ears for a little bit. What we're talking about doesn't concern you."

"Yessir," said the driver, who looked ten years older than the officer who'd just called him "son."

Patton swung back to us again, this time with an intensity that nailed us in place.

"The Brits have a man placed close to the Kaiser. He's been feeding them intelligence since the war started, not that they've made much out of it, but he's a good man. The Brits know their spies, I'll say that for them."

He was right there. Riley and I came to know that up close in the years ahead.

"Von Kleist was pulled out of Mexico and sent to the Eastern

Front, gathering intelligence for Ludendorff. Von Kleist just goes wherever the Kaiser has devil's work to be done and there's always plenty of that in Russia. Next we heard of him was just last week. Britain's man spotted him at a bar in Berlin, of all places. Got him drinking and asked him where he was going. Von Kleist must have been drunk. Said he was going to Paris, to kill the most important man in France." Patton looked at me. "Know who that is?"

It was obvious, so I nodded.

"Clemenceau."

The Tiger. Georges Clemenceau. Many thought Clemenceau's iron will and talent for bluster were the only things keeping France alive. A physician, a rabble-rousing journalist, and a radical socialist for his whole career, he became prime minister of France for the second time in November 1917, when all seemed lost and the smart boys in France were positioning to negotiate the best peace possible. After Brest-Litovsk, where the newly installed Bolsheviks cut their deal with the Kaiser, the Eastern Front was a nullity and the Germans could consolidate all their forces for a last push to take Paris before the Americans could take the field. But Clemenceau spat in their eye, defying the odds, heartening the populace, and jailing his former colleagues in the press who got in his way. He regularly visited the front, hobnobbing with the French infantry, the *poilus*, in their rat-infested trenches without a thought for the German guns a hundred yards away. "War until the end," he preached, in speeches young Mr. Churchill would remember and emulate in years to come. Clemenceau's visage had come to symbolize France: florid face, drooping white mustache, portly bearing, fierce as the tiger for which he was named. No question, if von Kleist could stick a knife in Clemenceau's back, just as Operation Blücher came pouring through Picardy and most of Pershing's doughboys still had their pants around their ankles, well, it would be goodnight Pierre and no mistake.

"Clemenceau," Patton confirmed. "The very man General Pershing has been closeted in meetings with for the last month. Seems the Prime Minister and Mr. Fancy Pants Foch"—the recently appointed supreme commander of all Allied forces—"don't believe that Pershing is getting men up to the front fast enough. So getting near Mr. Clemenceau won't be a problem for us, boys. General Pershing's been more concerned with getting away from him once in a while."

Riley looked troubled.

"Sure about that intelligence, sir? Hard for an assassin to get to the prime minister of France, surely. And why would von Kleist be blabbing about such a thing in bars?"

Patton gave him a hard look.

"Riley, you're a killing gentleman, I won't deny that, but I'm not aware of your intelligence qualifications. Britain's man is highly placed and never steered them wrong, they tell us. No, von Kleist is on his way. Given the role Clemenceau plays, propping up the French with just his personality, it's the obvious move. You send your best killer after the man you most need killed. But Herr von Kleist isn't expecting our welcoming committee."

Looking back on it, the thing seems as queer as Uncle Fred's nappies, but we were still recovering from the Cantigny fight and here a very superior officer was telling us what was what and it wasn't our place to argue further. Especially since Patton kept saying the name "von Kleist," a name that had a hold on us like no other.

"Much as they want one, no one in Britain's secret service or ours has a picture of von Kleist. We three are the only ones on the side of the angels who've seen him. So General Pershing agreed to let me come get you as soon as we heard about von Kleist's mission. We're going to stick to the good Monsieur Clemenceau like a spot of Côtes du Rhone on his foulard. And when von Kleist shows his crazy face, we're going to kill him."

Patton lowered his voice, though I'm sure the driver could still hear him. His eyes had a menacing look.

"Combat's a tricky thing and I know there are no guarantees, but one thing, boys. If it can be done, I want you to make sure that I'm the one who gets to kill him. I mean to shoot that pervert right between the eyes.

"And one other thing," he said after a pause. "If somehow it looks like he's going to gain the upper hand, you need to kill me. I'm not going to be in that man's power again."

Patton turned away and didn't say a word for the rest of the drive. We, too, were silent, contemplating what Patton had just said. We'd been through a lot already, but after all, neither of us had yet seen our twenty-first birthday.

21

Clemenceau, Churchill, and Pershing

Cornelius

To the greater world, Paris means a few square miles of splendid history and high culture divided by the Seine, running perhaps to Montmartre and Sacré-Coeur on the right bank and the Luxembourg Gardens on the left. But to greater Paris, that is merely a sliver embedded in the center of a large and sprawling metropolis, street after street of slums and businesses and empty lots that could just as well be in Warsaw or Pittsburgh or any other modern city.

Our car passed through these streets and they were empty, void of all the life and charm that Paris represents to the rest of us who don't live there. The war had taken its toll, as had the imminent advance of the Germans in Operation Blücher. Pedestrians looked over their shoulders, hurrying from doorway to doorway. Lights were extinguished almost as soon as they appeared. The City of Lights was a dark and dreary place, even in the middle of the afternoon when we arrived.

Still, neither fear nor hunger nor the gloom of pending disaster could entirely make Paris into something it wasn't. I recall that we were driving generally south down a narrow street, more like an alleyway, deserted and overhung with despair. We went by two very large railroad stations, which looked like the fanciest places around. Suddenly we turned and a panorama opened up and we saw what people are talking about when they talk about Paris.

The Seine was flowing peacefully between banks of beautiful, serene buildings. Near to hand we saw the back of Notre Dame, its gargoyles staring back at us. In the distance we could see the Eiffel Tower, that unmistakable monument to engineering that stands like nothing else in the world.

Here, despite the war, despite the impending invasion of the enemy, Parisians walked the streets, sat at the cafés, perused the shops. They seemed an entirely different species from the good people of Independence. I remember a skinny old guy, in black pants with a black jacket over a black shirt, scanning the oranges at a fruit stand as if it were the most important task in the world, one that might take all afternoon. A portly middle-aged man stood in a *pissoir*, calmly reading a newspaper and peeing noisily while nicely dressed ladies strolled by unconcerned. Handsome young couples, and others not so handsome and not so young, held hands. The grace and beauty of the surrounding architecture seemed to make Parisians graceful and beautiful. This is civilization, I thought. This is what I want. The notion that it might all be destroyed in the next few days by invasion or that these people might be driven off these streets by conquerors who cared nothing for them was suddenly more than I could bear.

Our car rumbled over an old bridge—the bridge was beautiful, too—and passed onto what I later learned was the Left Bank. A short distance ahead, we came to massive stone walls that enclosed an area that obviously encompassed acres of very valuable city land. The gate was barred and patrolled by French soldiers, but we were quickly waved through. It appeared that Patton had already made his face well-known in the city, for the guards saluted him with a knowing air.

Once the gate was opened to us, we saw the Luxembourg Palace. It took my breath away. Remember, we were still just boys. Until that day, our knowledge of great cities was limited to a view of New York from the training station at Governors Island, for we'd never been allowed to get off that island and go into Manhattan. Here in front of us loomed a huge, nicely symmetric European palace, built at the height of French glory and converted into legislative chambers to house the French National Assembly. I remember vast grounds nicely manicured, an obelisk in the center court, as we drove along a half-circle up to the massive grand entrance. We got out of Patton's car with our mouths agape, I can tell you.

Patton wasted no time. He hustled us inside, up a marble staircase, down long hallways into what must once have been a servant's bedroom far in the back of the palace. There were two cots, a washbasin, not much else.

"Wash up, boys. You're about to meet with the brass."

Ignoring our raised eyebrows and quizzical looks, he turned and disappeared, shutting the door crisply behind him.

Palaces are fine to look at, but aren't much to live in. The few inches of cold water sloshing in the washbasin hardly sufficed to clean months of mud and stink off two young men.

"Do you suppose he's going to bring us new clothes?" I asked Riley. We'd been living in these uniforms for days and had fought the battle of Cantigny in them.

Riley didn't know, of course, and he said nothing. As best we could, we splashed some water in our faces and sloshed it in our mouths. Then we took off our boots and hit the cots, hoping in vain to catch some more sleep. In what seemed less than half an hour, Patton was at the door, hustling us up and out.

"We still stink, General," I said, knowing Patton still wouldn't mind being called a general.

"It's an honorable stink, boys," he said, a glint in his eye. "You're heroes from Cantigny, the first American offensive in this man's war. Stink smells good on you right now."

We hurried to keep up as Patton led us down miles of corridors, fancy ones once we left the servants' quarters. Great portraits of effeminately dressed noblemen glared down at us in disapproval. I swear that one of them looked just like Skelly, but with shoulder-length hair and a goatee.

Patton led us to a large wooden door, in front of which was a small table, behind which sat an officious looking Frenchman in a black swallowtail suit. His cheeks were remarkably sallow and his hands trembled over a pile of papers in front of him. Behind and flanking him were armed soldiers: four French, but also two Americans and two

Brits. Patton ducked his head insolently to the sallow swallowtail, who glowered and nodded back silently.

Patton turned to one of the Americans and said, "It's them," probably unnecessarily. The American, followed by one of the French soldiers, knocked and went through the door. In a moment, he was back and waved us in. This was obviously an important room and no doubt contained important men, but Patton strolled in as always, like he either owned the place or didn't give a damn who did.

We entered what proved to be a long narrow room dominated by a conference table. Over Patton's shoulder, we could see three men seated at the table, each of them with aides seated directly behind him. I recognized two of the three men instantly. I had seen one of them before and both were famous around the world. Seated with his back to us, turned to look at his brother-in-law, was Black Jack Pershing, appearing just as he had in Mexico, although perhaps a bit less dusty. Across from him was an overweight fellow, aged forty or so, whom I did not recognize. His face was round and pink, his head was balding, and he wore a heavy old-fashioned frock coat with a vest. The real force in the room, though, sat at the end of the table. He was the most famous man in the world, after the Kaiser, and the only man who could stop the Germans from seizing Europe. Clemenceau. The Tiger.

At the moment we entered, he was living up to his nickname for we had caught him in mid-rant. Clemenceau's English was good, since as a young man, he had lived in New York and married an American. He hunched at the table, pounding his right fist into his left palm. His bald head was sweating, his black eyes were ablaze, and his white mustache bristled, giving him the appearance of an enraged Gallic walrus. His eyes slid briefly to us as we entered, but he never lost focus on the object of his rage, the unfortunate General Pershing, who sat ramrod straight and took it.

"When will you listen, General?" Clemenceau fairly shouted. "When the Kaiser has taken Paris? When I am hanged from a lamppost at the Place du Concorde? What will induce you Americans to move?"

The pink-faced fellow shifted in his seat and spoke up, perhaps to forestall an undiplomatic remark from the American. His surprisingly deep voice spoke with an upper-class British accent.

"To be fair, Mr. Prime Minister," he said, "the Americans have advanced quite far, all the way across the Atlantic, in fact. I know

General Pershing is aware of how appreciative we are that he and Mr. Wilson have come to our assistance, the New World riding to the aid of the Old, as it were. But, General Pershing, I think you can understand our frustration. We British have been fighting side-by-side with our French allies since 1914 and we are approaching our limit. The Germans are in Picardy, at the threshold of Paris. We need your men. There is no more time."

Pershing was unmoved. His flat Missouri accent was a startling flash of home.

"Gentlemen, we know your position. We have discussed it at length and you know the position of the United States. We will move into the field in force when we have overwhelming superiority and when our men are adequately trained. We are nearly at full force now in the south of France and we will be ready. We will defeat the Kaiser as planned, but we will not move prematurely—"

"Prematurely?" Clemenceau cried out, unable to contain himself. "Paris will not survive the month without reinforcement! You know that right now, our codebreakers are trying to ascertain when the attack will come. It will not come in weeks, or months, it will come in days. We need those men now, *mon général*, if France is to survive."

I was astonished on several levels. First, astonished that these men blithely carried on this discussion in the presence of two filthy American privates. Second, that Pershing would think France could wait. Based on what I was seeing, Paris was on the edge of the abyss and one more push would shove her into it.

Black Jack calmly returned Clemenceau's icy stare.

"As we have discussed, Mr. Prime Minister, I am sensitive to the difficult situation facing the noble French people. But in my judgment, the best way that the American army can help them is to wait until we are fully trained and capable of fielding overwhelming force—"

Clemenceau's big fist slammed onto the table.

"'Overwhelming force!' And what if the noble French people have been overwhelmed already? Is that your plan, General Pershing, to let the European powers exhaust themselves so America can sweep up the winnings?"

I had no experience in diplomacy, but this didn't sound good. The Englishman thought so, too, for once again he intervened.

"We are allies here, surely. We are all seeking the most effective and efficient way to realize our common goal of defeating Kaiser Wilhelm and ending German militarism. Am I not correct? General Pershing, what is your latest estimate for when your forces will be ready to take the field?"

"1919, 1919!" Clemenceau was practically squawking. "That is the only date this general knows!"

Pershing seized the moment to deflect the conversation.

"Actually, Mr. Churchill," he said, rising to his feet, "my forces are already in the field. The evidence is in this room and I think we should take this moment to acknowledge them." Pershing strode to our side and gestured toward Riley and me. "Gentlemen, these are two of the Black Lions of Cantigny."

I looked over at Pershing like he was crazy, for it was the first time I'd heard the phrase. Even in 1918, the military's public relations machine worked fast. Cantigny was being touted by the army as the first American offensive of the war and the first American victory. Given the widespread criticism of Pershing's lethargy and the embarrassing showing made by the Americans in our first fight at Saint-Mihiel, Cantigny was just the ticket. As Charles Lindbergh would later tell me, timing is everything to a hero.

This explained why we'd been trooped in our muddy outfits into the presence of greatness, far more than did our mission to protect Clemenceau. I expect Pershing was tired of the Tiger's tongue-lashings and he felt that a couple of exhibits of American heroism would go a long way.

To our shock, Pershing stepped between Riley and me and put his arms around our shoulders. They felt like a yoke.

"Mr. Prime Minister, these boys are from Missouri, the state where I was born. Just two days ago, they were in foxholes, facing shot and shell for the liberty of the French people you so nobly serve. Two days before that, they charged into the town of Cantigny, into the teeth of a well-entrenched German brigade, and took one of the most strategically critical points in the entire German line. Afterward, their regiment held the town against seven consecutive counterattacks attempting to take it back. I cannot tell you how proud I am of these boys."

This sounded all right. Military scholars have since pointed out that Cantigny wasn't really that strategically significant: it was a high point on a hill, in a region full of hills. But who listens to military scholars? When heroes are needed, they are found.

Even Clemenceau had to accept our convenient heroism. After shooting Pershing a venomous glance, he composed himself, pushed up from the table, walked over to Riley and me, and kissed our cheeks, each in turn. We really were in France.

"Gentlemen," he said to us, "you must forgive an old man if I seemed ungrateful as I spoke to your general. There is no man alive who more values your presence in our country and your service here than do I. It breaks my heart to see the sacrifices made by all the young men whom we old men send out to fight this war. The world would be a better place if it were the politicians and the generals who were sent out to fight in war, but how would we fit our bellies into the foxholes?"

For emphasis, Clemenceau patted his ample girth.

Everyone laughed and it was genuine laughter, for Clemenceau seemed so genuine in uttering those words. We could easily understand why the *poilus* loved him. Clemenceau would indeed be a huge loss to the French, to all the Allies, and so he was a very suitable target for a killer like von Kleist.

Then came the crowning astonishment.

"Which is Riley?" the prime minister asked.

After Patton pointed him out, Clemenceau reached out his hand and one of his officials placed in it a small box. Clemenceau removed from the box a red and green ribbon, to which was attached a small metal cross on crossed swords.

"Private Riley," he intoned. "Having been mentioned in dispatches by your commander at the great U.S. victory at Cantigny, having displayed courage and resourcefulness in the face of enemy fire, having led the advance from the foxholes and been the first man into the town of Cantigny, having contributed fearlessly to the taking of the town and subsequently having held the ground through seven enemy counterattacks, the nation of France is pleased to award you at this time the Croix de Guerre."

Again he kissed Riley on both cheeks, rather making a habit of it.

It was a remarkable moment in a room full of remarkable men. Pershing and Patton were grinning. The eyes of the one Pershing had called Churchill were positively brimming over—I was to learn in years ahead that Winston was a sucker for this sort of thing. Then Clemenceau grasped Riley's hand and gazed intensely into his eyes.

"*Merci*, Monsieur Riley. For my country, *merci*."

Riley stood there, looking sick.

Pershing took the opportunity to lay it on a little thicker.

"Seven counterattacks in two days. After an advance into withering fire. Mortars, howitzers, a gas attack. It's a wonder these men didn't go out of their minds."

"Ah, but General," I said, "Riley and me, we never go out of our minds. They're small minds, but we stay inside them."

Pershing's eyes narrowed disapprovingly and Patton kicked my shin. Clemenceau had already turned back to his papers, paying us no further mind, but the Englishman let out a phlegmy cackle, immediately suppressed. His eyes twinkled. This was the moment I learned that Winston had a keen sense of humor.

Clemenceau was back to business, looking hard at Pershing.

"I need you to double the Americans under French and British command immediately. Anything less and Paris falls within the fortnight."

"What is the latest from your man, Mr. Painvin?" Churchill asked.

"There is no latest," Clemenceau barked. He was certainly a moody fellow. "I have codebreakers who can't break codes and allies who won't fight, but still I will win."

Churchill ignored the slights.

"It is important to know when and where the enemy will move on Paris. If Monsieur Painvin can break the code—"

Again Clemenceau pounded his fist on the table.

"I know that. The man is our best and he has worked without sleep since the message arrived. Have you talked to these codebreakers? I cannot understand anything they say. They talk of numbers and letters and patterns and it is all a jumble in my head. But this I do understand," he said, turning to Pershing. "Without the Americans, Paris is lost. Even if the Kaiser himself knocked on my door and told me which bridge the German army would use to cross into the city, I could not stop them without men."

Pershing was brave, I'll say that, to look the Tiger in the eye and deny him.

"You will have three million American men, Mr. Prime Minister, and they will save France because they will be a unified and trained fighting force. In 1919."

The only question was whether Clemenceau would strangle the man or expire from apoplexy on the spot. Patton seized the moment.

"Mr. Prime Minister, these two soldiers are here for another reason. You will remember our discussion of the German assassin."

Clemenceau was dismissive.

"Every German in France wants to kill me. For that matter, it has seemed like a good share of Frenchmen have wanted to kill me for as long as I remember. I don't see what is so special about this one man."

Lucky Mr. Clemenceau, I thought. Three of us in the room knew what was special about von Kleist.

"Mr. Prime Minister," Patton persisted, "we believe this man is the top secret agent in the Kaiser's employ. He is a master of all forms of weapons, speaks several languages perfectly, and has an aptitude for disguise. The U.S. government knows of only three men who have seen him in person and they are myself and these two soldiers. If this man is in Paris to kill you, sir, and we believe he is, it will be a great advantage to you if one of the three of us is with you at all times."

"You insult my own security forces."

"Your own security forces have approved the idea, sir."

Patton gestured to one of the French officials, who nodded.

"We've been over this, Mr. Prime Minister," said Pershing. "I thought you had agreed."

"And I thought you were here to fight, General Pershing. However, I shall take your brother-in-law as my nanny. Come along then, I have a speech to give." As he strode to the door, Clemenceau again glared at Pershing. "Do not mistake me, General. Whether or not you fight, France will fight. I will fight. I will fight before Paris, I will fight in Paris, I will fight behind Paris. And *la belle France* will triumph."

Having delivered his well-practiced exit line, he strode from the room. The Tiger's belligerence was worth an extra army to France, just as Winston's would be to England twenty years later. Clemenceau had to be saved, plainly.

A number of the French officials hurried after their leader. Patton told us to get some sleep and be in our rooms by midnight, ready to relieve his watch. Then he followed. Pershing, too, left the room, without a glance at us. We were left at sixes and sevens, with a pair of remaining Frenchmen and the man called Churchill.

One of the Frenchmen seemed on good terms with Churchill, for he smiled.

"Still more than an hour before your dinner with Le Colibri," he said. "How I envy you."

These fellows seemed friendly enough, so I ventured to ask about Le Colibri.

"Everyone in France knows Le Colibri," the French official said. "He is the repository of all knowledge of French cuisine. His name means 'The Hummingbird,' and like a hummingbird he flits from restaurant to restaurant, dining here and there, writing reviews that mean the life or death of a chef. Every restaurant in town leaves open a table for Le Colibri every night, for he never announces in advance where he will dine. He simply appears, *voilà*, and suddenly the chef knows he must make the greatest meal of his life. He is the guardian of the great French traditions, apostle of how we dine, which means how we live." The Frenchman, plainly enjoying himself, lowered his voice. "To dine with Le Colibri is a high honor, an honor denied even the Tiger himself. It is said that Georges Clemenceau once disagreed with Le Colibri over a particular sauce and he has never been allowed in the man's presence again."

Churchill seemed amused, but impatient.

"As you say, we have some time. May I be permitted to speak with Monsieur Painvin? I would like to be able to report in some detail to my government."

The Frenchmen remained agreeable.

"If you like. As the prime minister said, I find these codebreaking fellows utterly incomprehensible. I will see if the time is convenient. Please wait here."

The next moment, Riley and I were alone in the big conference room with Winston Churchill. He was then forty-three and the Minister of Munitions for Great Britain. He was often in Paris at the time, planning the munitions needs for late 1918 and early 1919. The younger son of an eccentric peer and an American adventuress, Winston had already been a fighting soldier, a journalist, a published author, a member of the House of Commons, and the First Lord of the Admiralty, infamous for losing the Battle of Gallipoli a few years earlier, the most brutal British defeat of the war. Despite his celebrity, Riley and I had never heard of him. Over the years, Winston was to stir up lots of trouble for the two of us. Well, if I tell you that in the fullness of time, Winston assigned Riley to kill Michael Collins and used me as his personal spy in Hitler's Berlin, that gives you some idea. He also became our most loyal friend, next to each other.

Winston pulled out a long cigar and lit it. He gazed at us through the clouds of smoke.

"May I ask, where are you gentlemen from?"

"Missouri."

"Oh, yes, so General Pershing said. My mother was an American. I have always had a great fondness for your country. In many ways, you represent the future of the English-speaking peoples."

Something of a conversation-stopper, that. Winston turned to my friend.

"I haven't yet heard your voice, Mr. Riley. Do you speak?"

"I do," said Riley, "but with Cornelius around, there is rarely the need or the opportunity."

Churchill smiled.

"I fear some say the same about me. With some validity. Where did you meet Mr. von Kleist?"

Riley spoke before I could answer.

"Better ask Lieutenant Colonel Patton, sir. Not sure we're free to speak."

Churchill frowned so I spoke right up, to lighten the mood.

"This Le Colibri, sir? The Hummingbird? How did you get invited to dinner with him?"

My diversion worked, for Churchill was a greedy man when it came to the pleasures of the table.

"It should be quite interesting. You see, there is a French chef at a famous hotel in London called the Carlton—"

"I know," I said. "You mean Escoffier."

This set him back a peg or two.

"How on Earth do you know of Escoffier?"

"Some Americans appreciate fine food," I said coolly.

As it happened, I did have some interest in high-class food even then, maybe from learning to cook Mexican from Riley's farmhands. I read somewhere about Escoffier, who had re-invented French cuisine in London at the Carlton, and before that the Savoy, with daring new dishes like peaches melba and *suprêmes de volailles*, whatever that was.

"Very good, Cornelius," Churchill enthused, patting my arm. "Excellent. Well, Le Colibri is no fan of Mr. Escoffier, who he believes has betrayed the French traditions with his lighter sauces and modern techniques. I dine quite regularly at the Carlton and find Escoffier's dishes to be sublime. So I have for years challenged The Hummingbird to allow me to dine with him. I will be served the food of a chef of his choosing who will represent the traditional styles so that I can decide the controversy for myself. I promised to write up the result for the London and Paris papers. And tonight, after years of entreaties, he has accepted the challenge."

"Why now, do you think? The city is a wreck and the Germans are knocking on the door."

"Perhaps that is why, because it may be the last opportunity for quite some time. Or perhaps Le Colibri is patriotic and wishes to thank the British for our victory at Saint-Mihiel. Whatever it is, I am grateful, for I mean to have the meal of my life."

Winston positively glowed.

The affable French official returned, followed by the most nervous and exhausted-looking person I had ever seen in this life. He was a young man, extremely thin, whose clothes hung from him as though he'd lost 30 pounds since he'd changed them, which indeed proved to be the case. The man sucked spasmodically on a cigarette, hands shaking, eyes streaked in red with puffy gray beneath. His hair seemed to be falling out in clumps.

"Gentlemen," said the French official, "allow me to present to you Georges Painvin. He is the hope of Paris."

As Churchill reached for the codebreaker's hand, Painvin collapsed to the floor in a heap.

22

The Codebreaker and
the Hummingbird

Cornelius

"Good Lord, what's the matter with the fellow?" Churchill demanded.

The French official knelt beside Painvin, gently massaging his wrist and slapping his cheek.

"It happens," he said. "He has been working without stop for days, ever since the cipher came into our hands. We try to make him rest but he is obsessed."

He looked it. As he snapped his head forward off the floor, having been out for only an instant, Painvin clutched at the official bending over him. He blurted something over and over in French, which Winston later told me meant, "It's longer."

The official soothed him, telling him yes, it was longer, and he must calm down. He helped Painvin back to his feet, switched to English, and pointed out Churchill.

"This is Mr. Winston Churchill, a great official of the British government. He asked to meet you."

Painvin just gazed at him like a beaten dog, quivering and murmuring to himself. Churchill clapped his hand on Painvin's shoulder and essayed his warmest smile. He spoke gently and reassuringly to him, in French, but Painvin, following the French official's lead, responded in stuttered English.

"Forgive me, sir. I have not slept in five days. I feel the weight of Paris on my shoulders, but I cannot break the code. I cannot! I had it in my hands, I was reading their traffic like a great sign on the roadway, but now, they have changed the code and I cannot. I am so close."

His voice died away and I feared he might faint again. Churchill took his arm and walked him to a chair, willing the codebreaker to sit. He pulled up a chair for himself and gazed into Painvin's troubled eyes.

"I will help you if I can. Tell me."

I was to learn that Winston, who knew no more about breaking codes than your grandmother's cat, had supreme confidence in his own ability to master any subject and surpass the experts in it. In fairness, he often did just that. Setting aside the incident at Gallipoli, and his thickheaded approaches to Ireland, India, and Mrs. Simpson, Churchill generally succeeded more than most and in a wide variety of fields. He saved the world, after all. How many people can say that?

They reverted to French and lost me, but I've reconstructed the gist based on what Winston later told me and by thumbing over historical literature on codebreaking, which makes much of Georges Painvin.

A mere lieutenant and only in his early thirties when we met, Painvin was a prodigy at the arcane art of breaking ciphers. Before the war, he had been a schoolteacher whose subject was paleontology, of all things. Taken into the French intelligence service called the Bureau du Chiffre at the start of the war, he proved naturally adept at the painstaking, hand-done calculations that were then state-of-the-art on both sides for deciphering enemy messages. Painvin's great success occurred just two months before our meeting, when he broke the so-called ADFGX code used by the Germans. The French didn't think the enemy had yet realized that their code was broken and their messages were being freely translated by the French. Nevertheless, as Operation Blücher pounded its way toward Paris, the transpositions changed and Painvin's work became useless. Why? Because "it was longer."

For those who give a damn, the letters ADFGX refer to the letters running along the top and side of a square, like so:

```
    A  D  F  G  X
A
D
F
G
X
```

The letters of a message were transposed and spread across the resulting table, impenetrable to anyone who lacked the key. Painvin solved this after hours of intense calculations, with no electronic assistance, finding probable patterns of word beginnings and letter placement until the letters were unscrambled into messages that made sense.

But, as Operation Blücher approached Paris, Ludendorff's own code wizards changed the pattern. Now, instead of a five-by-five grid, it was a longer six-by-six grid. While this doesn't sound like much of a change, it destroyed the Allies' ability to read the enemy messages at the most crucial time in the war, with just days before the rape of Paris. With no way to know where and when the principal blow would fall, the Allies could not concentrate their forces but had to spread them thinly across too broad a front. Coupled with Pershing's refusal to provide substantial American reinforcements, the result looked to be a disaster. No wonder Clemenceau was short with Pershing and Painvin looked like dog's vomit.

Painvin's French babble died away again, leaving him counting on his fingers as though running endless calculations through his fevered mind. Churchill looked troubled. Suddenly, a quiet voice spoke in a plummy, high-class English accent.

"Sir, if I might have a word."

I swear, I absolutely had no idea the man had entered the room. At the open door loomed a tall, well-put-together gentleman wearing the sort of comfortable wool suit that one associates with hunting parties in the English countryside. He was well over six feet, slightly balding, with a trim mustache and an air of impeccable discretion. It was Hutton.

One way or another, I came to know many of the great spies of the twentieth century, from von Kleist to Klaus Fuchs to James Jesus Angleton. They were a mixed bag, mostly loony. Bill Donovan might as well have entered a room playing a trombone for all the attention he drew to himself. I only knew two spooks who truly had the gift of invisibility when they wanted to exercise it. One was Angleton. Hutton was the other.

I wasn't to know it then, but Hutton was from the English secret service and was assigned the unenviable task of shadowing the British Minister of Munitions as he flitted around the scenes of battle. With a subtle turn of his head, he beckoned Winston to him. They conferred briefly, quietly, and Churchill nodded. Winston turned to face the room.

"My friend Mr. Hutton has had an excellent idea. Plainly, Mr. Painvin is overworked. There are times when rest and relaxation are essential to the human spirit. Without them, we cannot function as we should, as we must. Fortunately, we have the answer."

He then reverted to French, speaking directly to Painvin, but I knew what he was saying. He invited him to dine with Le Colibri.

Painvin's eyes grew in diameter by a factor of three.

"Le Colibri?"

Plainly the name was magic to the codebreaking little paleontologist. Scratch a Frenchman and you will draw clarified butter, for they are all gourmets by birthright. Painvin gabbled for five minutes, with me understanding nothing but "Le Colibri," which he must have mumbled seven times. Only the French official seemed less than enthused.

"But Mr. Churchill, it is impossible," he said. "The war is at the crisis, Paris may fall tomorrow. This man must work—"

"The war has been at the crisis since it began," said Churchill. "If this man does not relax his mind, he will never solve his puzzle."

"There's wisdom in that," chimed in Mr. Hutton. "I recall cramming for my exams, sir. Couldn't catch on to trigonometry to save my soul. Finally I chucked it, went to a pub, and had a few and, *snap*, it came clear in my mind."

The Frenchman was unimpressed.

"But security?"

"Security will be impeccable," Churchill assured him. "Mr. Hutton will never leave Monsieur Painvin's side and he will also be accompanied by these two American heroes who led the charge at Cantigny. I was a Sandhurst man myself," Winston added, puffing up at his military school background. "Monsieur Painvin will be safe as houses and we will have him back in three hours, better than new and in all likelihood with the solution in hand."

Better men than this French official have succumbed to Winston Churchill's oratory. It took a few more minutes, but before long everything was settled.

Not for Riley, though. He begged off by insisting he had to get some sleep before his turn to watch Clemenceau arrived. I was disgusted, but not surprised. Riley was never interested in food and the prospect of an evening with such as Le Colibri would not have charmed him. On the other hand, I was delighted and wanted nothing more in life.

I never found out who that French official was, but he must have been highly placed, for when Churchill wore down his reluctance, he authorized the unusual outing without seeking higher approval. Next thing you know, four of us—Churchill, Hutton, Painvin, and I—were riding into the Paris evening in a government car. Riley quietly melted away, apparently to seek some shuteye. He was due to relieve Patton at midnight, whereupon he would presumably be assigned to peer under Clemenceau's bed to make sure von Kleist wasn't hiding there.

In turn, I was to relieve Riley in the morning and knew it would come soon, but I didn't care. The idea of stuffing down the best of French food, hand-selected by a famous gourmet, had me dribbling at the mouth. The fact that it was going on nine in the evening and I had last eaten a quick lunch of army rations at noon didn't dampen my anticipation. By the time we reached our destination, I'd have eaten Winston's cigar if he hadn't held it close to him.

Paris was beautiful that night, war be damned. I know the Palais du Luxembourg was where we started and is on the Left Bank, but beyond that, I have no idea of our route or the location of the restaurant where we were being taken. I remember snapshots only. Streets lit by gaslight or not at all. A little boy running down the sidewalk with a baguette taller than himself. A violin player cadging for coins. Churchill and I talking food while Painvin clutched his stomach, head in his lap, endlessly counting over on his fingers. Hutton in front, eyes constantly watching for trouble.

Churchill told me more about Le Colibri.

"There are two truly great men in Paris today, perhaps three if you include Marshall Foch, but I believe he has yet to prove his merit. I refer to Clemenceau, of course, and then Le Colibri. Together, they represent all that is great in the French people."

I thought this a bit much.

"Clemenceau, sure, but a gourmet? What exactly does he do besides eat?"

I saw Hutton smile. Even Painvin looked up for a brief moment to roll his eyes.

"What is more French, Cornelius?" said Churchill. "To a Frenchman, eating is far more than it is to anyone else. It is art, it is life, it is what makes life worth living. That is why Le Colibri is France! At age fourteen, he ran away from home to come to Paris, where he worked as a kitchen boy at La Tour d'Argent. He rose through the ranks and was a promising sous-chef by the age of nineteen. But then he ate a meal by some great chef or other and was so taken away that he said he knew he could never match such perfection. He has never cooked again, from that day to this."

"Sounds a tad impulsive."

"Not a bit! You don't understand Le Colibri. Every move is calculated, just as he can take one taste and immediately break down the components of a sauce. His taste is so calibrated, so exact, that he simply was stating a fact. He could never be the greatest chef, but he could exercise the primary talent he was given. His palate."

Still a Missouri boy, I wasn't sure what Winston was talking about. All I understood about palates was that they had something to do with my cousin Ian's harelip. Painvin caught the drift, even with his poor grasp of English.

"You are right, you are right," he said. "Le Colibri, he is a wonder! You read his account of a meal, of a dish, and you taste it yourself... He is so exact... *C'est merveilleux...*"

"And his name means The Hummingbird? Why do they call him that?"

Churchill smiled.

"Perhaps you will know when you see him. For here we are."

The driver pulled to a stop in front of a small café located beside a broad boulevard. There was no sign of any sort in front. The front wall of the first story was almost entirely taken up by a large picture window through which you could see the dining room dimly lit with candles on the tables and the softest of gas lighting. Inside were impeccable white tables, a small blaze in a stone fireplace, and neatly dressed waiters snapping to attention. There was not a customer in the place, but it looked very welcoming, as though it were all displayed just for us—as indeed it was. Soft Gallic music played, though perhaps I only imagined it because of the charm of the setting.

The *maître d'hôtel* opened the door and made us welcome. We entered and were shown to a table toward the rear of the small dining room, near the fire. Churchill immediately grabbed the seat nearest the head of the table, leaving the place of honor for Le Colibri and pulling Painvin into the seat on his right. I stepped around the end of the table and seated myself opposite Winston, hoping to catch Le Colibri's pearls of wisdom as he dropped them. Hutton made a wry face, which I surmised was to reflect his unhappiness at having to sit with his back to the kitchen door. Since the alternative was to sit with his back to the front door, he accepted the inevitable and sat immediately to my left.

Churchill displayed his eagerness by asking after Le Colibri. The headwaiter, a kind-faced middle-aged man you'd want for your father, shrugged and smiled.

"With Le Colibri, who knows? It is rare that we know in advance he is coming, even rarer that he does not dine alone. He comes when he comes."

"Like the dysentery," I ventured.

"Hush, Cornelius," Winston admonished. "Tonight, you must be respectful. In return, you will be astonished."

I noted, for the first time, that Winston Churchill called me Cornelius, as though we were old friends. To him, we were always Cornelius and Riley, from that day until the last day we saw him, a few days before his death. Indeed, I already felt him a friend, not yet knowing he was a great man. One cannot really be friends with the great, but with Winston you could come close. He possessed a quality that is one of the least compatible with greatness in any human being: he was a good egg.

We ordered drinks while we waited. Winston had a scotch whiskey, so I joined him. Looking back, it seems strange that Winston would so overwhelm his senses of taste and smell with whiskey and a cigar immediately before a meal that he had looked forward to for so long. But Winston was not an ordinary man and not one to behave as though he were. I, too, had both whiskey and a cigar, but I knew no better. Painvin and Hutton sensibly abstained.

"Well, Cornelius," said Winston, leaning back in his chair and exhaling upward, "what shall we talk about?"

What a night! Surrounded by the horrors of war, me just a day removed from rats and mortar fire and mustard gas, yet here I was about to dine on the world's greatest food, drinking and puffing away with the man I consider the greatest conversationalist of the twentieth century beyond myself. Winston started the bidding by asking about Cantigny. He let me get off some brief remarks on the battle in a manner that reflected well on Riley and me, but soon it became apparent that when Winston invited conversation, he was actually inviting listeners.

Winston followed my discussion of the trenches outside Cantigny with a discourse on the horrors of the war, then of all wars, touching on his own adventures in the British cavalry and as a prisoner of war in South Africa. He spoke of his enemies in that war, the Boers, and transitioned from those cranky Dutch Afrikaners to the even crankier German nation currently marching toward the collapse of Paris.

"The Germans, of course, are a great people," Winston conceded quickly. "Of all the great nations, only the Germans hold war as the fundamental value, the great goal, the sole true purpose to which a great people must dedicate themselves. The British will fight when they must, the French will fight when they must, but of the great peoples of the world, only the Germans will always fight, because fighting is the central ideal of their race."

"Germans do more than that," I pointed out. "My father had me reading Goethe as a boy and there's Beethoven and—"

"Of course, of course," Churchill said, waving his hand dismissively. "There is no question that historically the Germans have contributed as much to human culture as anyone. All great nations produce great artists. Even their great artists have seen the horror lying at the heart of the German: Goethe wrote of it eloquently. Their art feeds their bloodlust. Listen to *The Valkyries*, read even their children's tales. The German must make war and these days, with airplanes and poison gas and all the other modern instruments of death, war cannot be abided. That, trust me, will be the great conundrum of this century."

From the horse's mouth, that. Looking back, of course, we had seen nothing yet. Years later, I stood at Oppenheimer's elbow as we watched the first mushroom cloud sweep over the Jornada del Muerto. It was certainly a hell of a century.

I don't recollect how, but the conversation turned from the Germans to their leader, Kaiser Wilhelm. Winston grew more animated, leaning forward in his chair and gesturing across the table at me.

"Put yourself in his place, Cornelius. Imagine you are not particularly intelligent, though not dense. You are neither an outstanding student nor a masterful warrior. Nevertheless, from the day you are born, everyone surrounding you impresses upon you that you are the most important man in the world, chosen by God to rule absolutely over the greatest warrior race in existence. All other mortals are your inferiors, they should be subservient to you, and the race which you have been chosen to lead should dominate all other peoples of the world by natural right. This is not a hypothesis or a topic for discussion, this is the most fundamental truth in the world and it is hammered into your brain every day of your life with no one to question it. The only justification for your exalted existence, the only purpose behind it all, is for you to build your people into the great fighting force they were meant to be and to lead that force in the greatest conflict the world has ever seen. Only by doing that can you and your descendants fulfill their chosen destiny. If this were how you were raised, Cornelius, might it not turn your head? Just a little?"

I puffed thoughtfully on my cigar.

"Can't say. The issue didn't come up a lot back in Independence, as I recollect."

"Well, it has been the Kaiser's entire existence."

The door to the kitchen opened and the *maître d'* slipped in.

"He is here," he said quietly, signaling his staff to make ready.

I looked out the front window and saw that a large black limousine had pulled to a stop at the door. The *maître d'* and several of the waiters hurried out and surrounded the rear passenger door. Slowly, the man inside slid his bulk off the seat, pushed to his feet, and with several arms supporting him, plodded to the door of the restaurant, where he stood momentarily framed in the entryway. He was, without question, the fattest man I ever saw. He stood at only middling height, but his great gut extended his overcoat in front of him by three feet. His jowls were rolls of fat, framing a face stolen from a cornice at Notre Dame down the street. He looked unwashed, as though washing such

197

a massive edifice would have taken too much effort. His black eyes in his great square head stared balefully ahead, not approving what he saw.

We rose immediately. I knew how he had gotten his nickname. Out of all humanity, no one looked less like a hummingbird.

Churchill bowed low to him.

"Le Colibri, we are honored."

The famous gourmet responded by making a noise, something like "Faugh." I wondered if we were hearing the remnants of last night's fabulous meal.

Le Colibri allowed the staff to remove his coat. He was wearing some sort of chocolate soldier's uniform, maroon with gold braid on the shoulders and big brass buttons. I wondered what the hell army he was in.

He stepped to the head of the table, shaking off the staff's help and barely acknowledging Churchill. He turned to the headwaiter.

"Tonight we must speak in English, for our guests. All is ready?" he asked, *basso profundo*.

"It is, Le Colibri," responded the *maître d'*.

"Malraux?"

"He is here. He came as soon as your man called. We all did."

Le Colibri grunted. He settled himself in his chair and waved to the rest of us to resume our seats. Then he nodded at the *maître d'*.

"Bring him."

The *maître d'* opened the door to the kitchen and waved. A tall man with a mustache, wearing the classic white uniform and hat of a chef, entered and gazed raptly at Le Colibri.

"Monsieur Malraux. You are ready for us?"

"*Oui.*"

"These gentlemen require your best work. They are guests of our country. Except for this little one here, who is obviously a Frenchman and looks a wreck."

Indeed, Painvin wasn't improving in appearance as the evening wore on. He was now sweating in the warmth of the fire and he continued to count endlessly on his fingers. It did not appear that his night off was having much effect.

"I see that our guests have begun the evening by ruining their palates." Le Colibri sniffed at our empty glasses and the butts of our cigars. "However, that is for them to repent. We shall begin with our aperitifs."

The staff snapped into action. The chef, an up-and-comer named Henri Malraux, disappeared into his kitchen. The waiters blended into the walls, standing ready. The *maître d'* stood where he was, yet seemed to disappear entirely. That evening was my first experience of expert Parisian table service, which is to say the best table service in the world. The restaurant was supposed to be closed that night, but all hands turned up for the honor of impressing Le Colibri and his guests.

If you have never been served at a great Paris restaurant, you must seek out the experience. For the food, of course, and also for the experience of finding yourself in the hands of true experts in the art of waiting tables. Several waiters are assigned to you and you immediately expect them to be intrusive and the whole experience to be embarrassing. Instead, they are a marvel. They seem not even to be there, yet you never want for a thing throughout the long evening. Courses come and go, plates are replaced, glasses refilled, but you never need to ask for anything because the waiters think for you. They operate as an extension of your will. Even with our company, with my Yankee accent and Painvin's obvious neurosis, the waiters were as respectful and friendly to us as to Churchill or to Le Colibri himself. I've read that Apaches knew how to make themselves invisible and I've already commented on the talents of Hutton and Angleton. I'd say a trained French waiter could equal any of them.

Over soup, Churchill said we had been talking about Kaiser Wilhelm and the German people. Le Colibri scoffed.

"Do you know what Bavarians eat? Meat, meat, and more meat. They are full of hate and aggression because they are full of animal flesh. They can make a good boar sausage, though."

Winston saw history as vividly and personally as did Patton, but whereas Patton imagined an endless series of combats with himself as the victor, Winston saw the complex interplay of the world's "great peoples," each of which he spoke of as an individual with specific characteristics. Thus, attributing a nation's foreign policy to its collective digestive system perfectly suited Winston's manner of thinking.

He sought to involve me in the conversation.

"Some think America is the next great world power, Le Colibri. Are you familiar with American cuisine?"

Le Colibri made a face, or perhaps he just looked like that.

"There was a man, whom they called a chef, who came from America to cook for me. It was the last time ever, until tonight, that I agreed to dine on someone else's terms. I prefer to dine alone, choosing my tables where I please and when I please to concentrate on the senses without the blather of conversation." Cheerful fellow. "The American made what was supposed to be the peak of their cuisine and what was it? A turkey."

"Surely there was more than that," I said, standing up for the home team.

"Nothing worthy of the table. My impression of American food? Plain. Plain, plain, and more plain. So while they will not contribute anything meaningful to culture, I expect it is true that they will dominate the world."

"Why?"

"They are a simple people who make simple food. They will not be troubled with subtlety or nuance. They will simply take what they want and justify what they do with a childish morality. Thought is the enemy of worldly greatness, so Americans should become great indeed. If ever you taste American food and find it to be adequately seasoned, you will know they are in decline."

I would have demurred, but I was too absorbed in my bisque. Never had I experienced taste like this. The Mexican food I'd had with the migrants was wonderful, but far from subtle: when you bit into a jalapeño, you knew what you had done. The lobster bisque we were eating sidled up to you. At a perfect temperature, pleasing to look at, rich but not heavy, redolent with an aroma that told you how delicious it was before you tasted it—this was food on an entirely different level of reality than I had ever experienced. I was content to savor it, leaving the conversation to Winston, who was certainly game.

He asked for trouble.

"And what of the British, Le Colibri? What would you say of our island race?"

"Nothing that has not been already said. Everyone knows that British food is foul, perhaps the worst in the world."

"Come, sir, you are simply airing your prejudices. Come with me to Simpson's and have our simple roast beef and see what you say then."

"I dined at Simpson's as a young man. It was execrable. Mushy vegetables, heavy sauces, nothing of grace or distinction. Contrast that with this…"

He gestured toward the waiters, coming forward with our fish. To this day I don't know what kind of fish it was, but it was poached and it was sublime. After Hutton had gently and silently corrected my choice of fork, I placed a bite in my mouth and was unable to restrain myself from shoveling in the rest as fast as I could. Winston allowed that the fish was outstanding.

"You see, Mr. Churchill," said Le Colibri, "when you speak of the great peoples of the world, you use different criteria than I. You care about armies, economies, factories. I have developed and refined myself so that I have one great interest and one alone: satisfaction of self through the smell and taste and texture of food. For this, there are but two great peoples. There are the French and the Chinese. We and we alone have devoted ourselves to the art. We have realized its potential by creating the sauces, perfecting the techniques, and mastering the nuanced experience that makes dining the one truly civilized occupation."

No one loves food more than I do, but even I was wondering if perhaps Le Colibri should take up a hobby.

With the meat course, the talk turned to Escoffier. Le Colibri used Malraux's handling of the *tournedos de boeuf* as an exhibit demonstrating not only the laughable inferiority of Simpson's, but also the superficiality and empty showmanship of Escoffier's innovations, which he regarded as pandering to wealthy but tasteless British. This triggered a sharp rejoinder from Winston, whose normal parliamentary debating technique (insert blade in kidney and rip) was blunted somewhat by his status as guest. Neither Painvin nor Hutton said a word throughout the meal. Painvin sat with his eyes closed, fingers still twiddling, murmuring to himself, although he did manage to eat every morsel on his plate.

As we awaited dessert, Winston looked torn. On the one hand, we'd had the meal of a lifetime. On the other, his most vigorous arguments had failed to make a dent in Le Colibri's contempt for the British in general and Escoffier in particular. Of course, Le Colibri was a sensualist. Over the years, I came to observe that great sensualists frequently develop contempt for the world, because they begin with contempt for themselves.

Winston allowed a bit of his frustration with the gourmet to show.

"I fear I have not changed your opinion of Mr. Escoffier."

"If you came with the notion of changing my opinion, you were misinformed. Le Colibri does not change his opinion."

Churchill shook his head.

"I came for your company and for a wonderful meal, both of which I have obtained and I am grateful. But tell me, why did you agree to join me?"

There was a long pause. Le Colibri rubbed his massive belly, belched softly, and pulled on his nose.

"I came because of your mother, Mr. Churchill."

That was a poser for Winston, clearly.

"You knew my mother?"

Le Colibri nodded.

"We met once. It was an occasion rather like this. Your parents were in Paris and asked me to dine with them. I was younger then and not so particular. We dined. Your father was a horrible bore. He babbled on of your politics with no thought for the food on the table before him. But your mother, she was beautiful. She just sat while her husband prattled and from time to time she looked at me. When we bid farewell, she smiled. Your mother, sir, had a smile as complex and subtle and satisfying as the sauce on tonight's fish. I can pay no higher compliment."

It was poetic in its own way, I suppose. Winston, who was devoted to the memory of both his parents, was absolutely at a loss for words, a position to which he was unaccustomed. It was Hutton who sensed the danger.

There was a strange sound coming from the kitchen, like an intake of breath suddenly cut off. I was sated with the meal and didn't respond at all, while Winston merely frowned. Hutton's hand quickly moved inside his jacket for his pistol. He'd eaten as heartily as any of us, but his training kicked in.

Fast, but not fast enough. Simultaneously, the kitchen door behind me and the street door before me each sprang open. Two men entered from each door, brandishing revolvers. Hutton stood, but then his hand emerged empty from his jacket. The corpse of Henri Malraux was flung through the kitchen door and fell at my feet. Behind it strode Otto von Kleist.

23

An Eventful Evening Out

Cornelius

He looked different than he did in the Mexican desert. His mustache was gone, his hair and skin were lighter, and he had added some weight. Although a homicidal sexual sadist, he was always a handsome fellow.

His eyes gave him away. As he kicked open the kitchen door and walked into the room, they were gleaming with mischief and bloodlust. He carelessly held a gigantic butcher's cleaver, dripping the blood of our unfortunate chef. Hutton stood motionless, the rest of us sat frozen in place. Even Painvin stopped his relentless fingering.

Von Kleist looked us over.

"*Bonsoir, messieurs*," he began, smiling broadly. Then he noted me and switched back to his perfect, unaccented American English. "Good God. You. Cornelius. Where in this Earth did you come from?"

My heart was pounding at my chest wall. Visions of horror in a Mexican cave almost unmanned me. I'd come to Paris to find this monster, but not to have him spring from the kitchen between cheese and dessert. How the devil had he found us? Treachery was afoot somewhere, plainly.

Von Kleist stepped to within a foot of my face and pointed his cleaver at my uniform.

"A real soldier now, it appears. You and Mr. Patton deprived me of two useful friends back in Mexico. Someday I must hear how you did it. Ah, ah!"

He turned his cleaver to Hutton, who was sidling away, likely planning some sort of heroics, although what he could do with four guns and that maniac's cleaver pointed at us was unclear to me.

"I don't know who you are, but you look like some sort of bodyguard. You're doing your job well so far, aren't you?"

Hutton allowed himself the trace of a smile, one professional to another.

"No harm to this point," he said evenly.

"You are somewhat lackadaisical concerning our poor chef here. Perhaps his sauces were lacking."

Even von Kleist jumped as Le Colibri pounded the table.

"How dare you? You have murdered the most promising chef in Paris! Get out immediately!"

All of us, I think, were shocked at the man's audacity in the face of such firepower. One of von Kleist's sidekicks pointed his gun directly at Le Colibri's enormous skull, but von Kleist motioned for him to stand down.

"I do apologize," he said, shaking his head, "but I could not leave without making the acquaintance of the most important man in France. And I believe, sir, that man is you."

As he said that, he turned to Painvin.

So all of us were wrong. Von Kleist's target was not Clemenceau, but Painvin. The man who topped the Kaiser's death list this week was the Frenchman who had broken the ADFGX code, the only man who might break the enhanced code that held the key to Operation Blücher. And somehow, likely through the treachery of that French official who surprisingly acquiesced to Painvin's presence at this dinner, we had delivered that very man into the hands of the Kaiser's most deadly assassin. Not to mention Sir Winston Churchill, your humble servant, and a very fat French gourmet.

A gourmet who would not be ignored.

"You shit!" Le Colibri shouted. "To despoil a house of cuisine? You are German, I suppose, though you speak like an American. Go fuck yourself!"

Von Kleist threw his arms wide, still wielding the cleaver and with a pistol tucked in his belt.

"I am to fuck myself? Can you be specific, my friend? Is it to be up the arsehole?" He stepped toward Le Colibri, smiling gaily. "I have long wished to accomplish such a thing, but alas I lack the flexibility. Perhaps you will demonstrate for us. Perhaps I can assist you."

He stopped immediately behind the Frenchman's seat at the head of the table. Wrapping his right arm around Le Colibri's midsection, he placed the cleaver beneath his enormous belly. The other four agents kept a gun trained on each of us, rendering us helpless to assist him. My gaze was taken by a sudden flash of headlights coming alight in the street across from the restaurant.

Von Kleist's gaze was focused on Churchill, although he did not relax his hold of the cleaver against the Hummingbird's gut.

"You, Mr. Churchill, are an unexpected bonus for me. The Kaiser will be so pleased. Yet in my own view of things, it might be best to let you live. By all accounts, you have been a uniquely inept minister for your government. I convey Kaiser Wilhelm's eternal gratitude for your colossal blunders at Gallipoli, by the way."

Winston flushed red, but said nothing. The suggestion that Winston was inept was bosh, of course, but Gallipoli was still a raw wound.

"Take your hands off me," snarled Le Colibri, unafraid.

Oddly, the car outside was turning to face directly at the front wall of the restaurant. I saw that it was a taxicab. Painvin slapped himself in the face.

Von Kleist bent low to whisper intimately into Le Colibri's ear.

"It will be my pleasure to release you, fat one. After such a big meal, you will no doubt want to loosen your waistband."

With the cleaver held firmly in his right hand, he cut into and across the man's huge belly, slicing a long and bloody gash through Colibri's shirt, deep into skin and fat. Von Kleist jerked his victim upward and held him steady, so that a stream of blood and globs of entrails sloshed across the table. First it came as a surge, then a flood, for opening The Hummingbird released a torrent of great meals past and present, covering us all in purple viscera.

"My God!" Churchill screamed.

"I have it!" Painvin screamed.

"Riley!" I screamed, for I saw the face of the taxicab's passenger just as the car came smashing through the front window and skidded to a stop in the middle of the dining room.

In the chaos, the best men kept their heads. Hutton tipped over the table, away from us and toward Churchill and Painvin, giving protection to the most valuable men in the room. The taxi's passenger door sprang open and Riley's lithe form somersaulted out, coming to rest in kneeling position with his gun arm outstretched. Trust Riley to know whom to shoot. Von Kleist still had only a cleaver in play, so Riley rapped off two shots that went through the throats of two of the German agents. Hutton was winged reaching for his revolver, but was able to draw it and knock down a third.

Von Kleist reached out his long arm. His enormous hand closed around the back of my neck and he pulled me to him, using me as a shield. Riley was occupied by the fourth agent, who had taken refuge behind an overturned table of his own. Von Kleist lifted me bodily— Lord, that man was strong—and carried me under his arm back through the kitchen and into an alley in back, where a car waited.

I was incapacitated with fear. I knew what it was to be a prisoner of von Kleist. The notion of repeating the experience completely overwhelmed me, making me helpless in his hands. He flung me against the car. When I rebounded, his fist came crashing into my face, for all the world like a battering ram into plywood. Stars flew, my knees buckled, I sank back into the rear seat of the car.

Then, nothing.

24

Jim Is Dubious

Jim

"This really happened? You drove a taxicab into a restaurant? Really?"

I'd been late arriving because a deposition had gone into the early evening. Riley and I met at a diner on the Bloomington strip to discuss the latest chapter. Minnesota restaurants don't allow smoking, so we took a number of breaks while he went out to the parking lot.

"You didn't pay attention. I wasn't driving, I was the passenger."

"That's nitpicking. What happened?"

Riley stared into his coffee. He wasn't eating, God knew if he ever ate anything.

"The whole thing seemed off to me. Something about them taking Painvin to dinner with some famous eater while Paris was under threat, it just didn't sit right. So I didn't go. Then I thought more about it and realized what was chewing at me. That Frenchman said Painvin was the hope of Paris. That was close to being the most important man in France, I figured. So I thought I should stick close to them."

Riley sipped his coffee.

25

American Gas

Riley

I slipped out of the palace and found a taxicab. I was running in luck because the driver spoke a little English. He was an old fellow named André, all het up over the Germans about to take Paris. Turned out he and his taxi were one of those that brought the French soldiers to the frontlines back in 1914 when Paris was threatened the first time in this war. French taxicabs were loaded up with soldiers and driven into battle because there weren't enough trucks available. I saw bulletholes in the door of the cab from that day. When I told André I was an American and needed his help to protect some important people, he was raring to go.

We followed Cornelius and the rest to the restaurant. You'd have thought André had secret service training, he was so good at this. I remember him saying, "They dine with Le Colibri? Then they are lucky men. If they die tonight, they die happy."

We parked on the street across from the restaurant, where we could watch through the picture window. The streets of Paris were empty that night, the city being under a sort of siege. I didn't know just what I was looking for, but I figured I'd know trouble when I saw it.

We sat there a long time. André talked about his children and his dog. His wife was dead but he talked about her, too. I didn't know anybody could take so long just to have supper.

The men came out from around the corner to my left. Two of them, dark clothes, hands in their jackets, plainly ill-intentioned. Before I could get my gun out, they'd opened the door and rushed in. I saw their buddies come in from the back of the dining room, too. Then I saw a big man enter. Von Kleist.

André was a game one. I didn't need to tell him what needed to be done. With so many guns trained on our side, the only way to save them was to make a major entrance. André started the car, lined it up, and slammed on the gas pedal. I was ready.

We smashed the glass and skidded into the restaurant. I was shaken for a moment but since I knew it was coming, I was able to recover faster than the men inside. I flung open the door, rolled out, came up shooting. The rest you pretty much know, from what Cornelius wrote.

That blasted fourth agent took Hutton and me too long to kill. After we got him, we rushed into the kitchen after Cornelius, but he was gone. No car, no men, nothing. The dining room was a sight. Dead men all over, blood and guts, Churchill and Painvin hugging under the overturned table. Sure enough, the fright somehow jolted the solution to the code into Painvin. He was whisked back and identified the exact date and location of the German advance. Some smart fellows afterward claimed what he did wasn't that important, but I was there and everyone defending Paris thought it was important. The city didn't fall, you know. Not that time.

I was a wild man, knowing von Kleist had Cornelius and I could do nothing about it. Winston soothed me, but it did no good. After everyone was satisfied I'd told what I knew, I was left to cool my heels back in the Luxembourg, occasionally looked in on by George Patton.

I don't know that they ever did find out for sure who leaked to von Kleist the location of Churchill's dinner with Le Colibri. The German agents were all dead, so there was no one for Clemenceau's bullyboys to work over. As the days passed and it grew certain that Cornelius was dead, probably tortured to death, none of that seemed too important to me.

I was inactive in the Luxembourg Palace while the great battle for Paris was fought. Thanks to Painvin, the French launched an assault just before the Germans attacked. It was a near thing, but Paris held, as Clemenceau swore that it would. Ludendorff halted Operation Blücher in mid-June. He knew the game was up and now he was fighting, not to win, but to position Germany for the peace negotiations. Nevertheless, a lot of men still had to die. Pershing finally loosened his hold on American reinforcements, putting 170,000 Americans into the line in June and 120,000 more in July. I was one of them. I returned anonymously to my regiment and promptly plunged into heavy fighting at Château-Thierry.

It was back to the trenches for me, but there was no more boredom, no more quiet waiting and watching on the western front. All sides smelled the end at last and, as always seems to happen when men sense that peace and safety may be near, the fighting became continuous and more savage than ever. More than half the American Marine Brigade were killed or wounded at Belleau Wood. The Germans made a last desperate attempt to cross the Marne, but the Allies held fast in the end, in large part because of the ferocity of the fresh American troops. A new enemy, the Spanish flu epidemic, appeared from nowhere and sapped the numbers and the morale of both sides.

I missed the final horror, in the Argonne Forest. This was thanks to a rickety old steam engine pulling a line of tank cars that showed up in our camp one morning in July. Pershing was repelled by gas warfare, so American gas companies had worked closely with the British army to develop a new delivery method. The tank cars filled with mustard gas rolled up on a narrow gauge railroad to our lines, then the tanks were off-loaded onto wagons pulled by horses. As we infantrymen moved into position, the cylinders were lined up and connected in series, so that they could be "pooped"—that was the term, don't ask me why—simultaneously. We waited and waited for the atmospheric conditions to be judged propitious. A little before two in the morning, the gas was released and great gray clouds enveloped the enemy lines ahead of us. "Give 'em hell!" was the command, and so we charged.

Unfortunately, there was a change of wind. In what seemed only a few seconds, the gas clouds (our gas, American gas) enveloped us rather than the enemy. I struggled to get my gas mask off my belt and onto my face, but in the confusion I didn't get it placed properly and soon it was gone completely in the fighting. We were at the bayonet, hand to hand. I managed to plunge my blade into the gut of a teenaged

German boy who first looked scared to death and then dead. I paused to take a deep breath and realized that I was in very deep trouble.

We had been warned. Mustard gas has a sharp smell, like garlic, but you quickly become used to it. It is easy not to realize how much you are breathing in, especially when you are killing people and trying to avoid being killed yourself. As I rested from killing the young German, I realized that my eyes were watering badly and I was having trouble breathing. I remembered the training lecture. I knew that blisters were forming already in my nose and throat, that if they grew large enough, they would stop my breathing entirely. I didn't know where to run, but I ran. Ran until I choked, ran until I tripped and rolled on the ground, coughing my lungs out. I knew, from my training, that the worst was still to come.

I was lucky. Somebody picked me up and slung me on an ambulance cart, so I found my way to a hospital bed in the field. With mustard gas, the worst is two to three days after exposure. That was when I was blinded and didn't know if I would see again. That was when the blisters closed my airways, when every breath was a dagger in my chest with no air involved. I had it bad, I guess.

Those two months are a blur to me. I knew I was in a hospital of some sort, but nothing more than that. Slowly my sight returned, slowly I could breathe without agony. I was moved about with the troops and by the time of the Armistice in November, I was in a hospital in northern France, near my regiment in the Argonne Forest. I was able to understand it when the news of the end of the war reached us, but the loss of Cornelius and my own incapacity kept me from enjoying the news the way those around me seemed to enjoy it. As everyone knows, the Armistice became official on the 11th hour of the 11th day of the 11th month, 1918. I wondered how many men died at ten that morning to please someone's idea of symmetry.

Letters from home caught up to me. The babies were born in August. My little daughter's every mood was described in letters from Marta and from Ma. I questioned Marta's insistence on naming the girl Fern Arlys, after Ma, but I was in no position to quarrel. Hal was reported to be a fine son for Cornelius. His mother was staying at the farm with him, with frequent visits from the O'Neals.

As November turned into December, more news of the world reached our hospital. Two million Londoners died of Spanish flu.

Wilson went to Paris for the peace talks and the damned fool declined to review the troops, causing no end of talk back home and in the army. The Kaiser was in exile and Germany was nominally governed by, of all things, a socialist government.

The nurses were putting up Christmas decorations when I had a visitor. It was Matt Gately from the 28th, who was passing through and somehow heard I was stuck there. Matt had been the sergeant of a platoon near us in line and we knew him a little. Enough for him to seek me out on his way back from Germany, where he'd temporarily been part of the occupation.

"You look great, Riley," he said to me. "Really, really great. Mustard gas must agree with you."

I tried to smile.

"I've been lucky," Matt said. "Stayed out of hospitals. They give me the willies."

"Not so bad. Rats are smaller."

Now it was his turn to try to smile.

Gately parked himself on my bed, making me slide my legs over.

"I'm almost afraid to ask," I said, "but what's happening with the old outfit? I haven't heard much since July. Shouldn't you be shipping home?"

"Oh, who knows? We think the orders are coming and then they don't. The guys are going crazy. So. What's the story with Jimmy? Did I tell you I saw him?"

It took me a moment to realize he was talking about Cornelius. The room got very quiet.

"What did you say?"

"Jimmy O'Neal. Wasn't he a buddy of yours?

"He's dead."

"I heard that, too, but it's a crock. I spent a weekend in Berlin, kind of being a tourist since there wasn't anything to do at camp anyway. Saw the Brandenburg Gate, big palace where Frederick the Great lived, lots of stuff. Lo and behold, I'm walking down the street and there's this big crowd, so I sidle up to listen awhile. Turns out it's all German and I can't understand a word, but from the signs and the pictures of the hammer and sickle, I could tell it was the communists. Berlin is crazy now, all these rallies. If it's not the communists, it's the Freikorps. Now those bastards are *really* crazy."

I considered killing him, but I needed him to get to the point. He did.

"Anyway, I'm looking up at the stage and this little tiny woman is ranting away, really putting it to the crowd. I'm about to lam it, when I see that right next to the little woman is a young guy who looks familiar, real familiar. I'm telling you, Riley, it was Jimmy."

"Jimmy?"

"Absolutely. What happened when you two went off with Patton? That was all over the trench."

"You saw my friend Jimmy, the one I called Cornelius?"

"If I'm lying, I'm dying."

"And when was this?"

"Just last week. My hand to God."

That night I went AWOL. In two days, I was in Berlin.

Part Four

Berlin

26

Cornelius Goes to Prison

Cornelius

We raced through the dark streets of Paris, no headlights, brakes screaming on the turns. Von Kleist was in front, urging on the driver. I was in back, a gun barrel held under my chin by the thug sitting next to me, who was flung into my lap each time the driver spun the wheel. My teeth were chattering from terror, not of the driving but of the man in the front passenger seat.

Confident no one was pursuing us, von Kleist ordered the driver to slow down and turn on his headlights. We heard sirens, but saw no evidence that we were being followed. Von Kleist turned to face me.

"Mr. O'Neal," he said in that smooth American English that sounded so uncanny coming from a cruel-looking face I associated with Satan. "Once again, you manage to surprise me. I left you and your companions trussed up like pigs, in the hands of my Yaquis, yet you escape and they are killed. Whose work was that? Was it Lieutenant Patton's?"

I just stared, petrified.

"No, not Patton. Certainly not you. It was Mr. Riley who did the deed, wasn't it? And Riley again tonight. He seems to be a talented man."

I said nothing. Terrified as I was, I didn't care much for that "certainly not you" remark.

Von Kleist barked to the driver in German that he should head for what was apparently their safehouse in Paris. He reverted again to English for me.

"I feel I will meet Mr. Riley again. He interests me. No one else has bested me twice. I must be sure there is not a third time."

Von Kleist sank into a brooding silence for the rest of the trip. My imagination raced through images of burning, cutting, twisting, capped with horrific memories of Miguel's severed head. We reached a dark house somewhere on the outskirts of the city and I was marched inside. I was expecting chains, racks, perhaps the odd Yaqui or two for company. Instead, we entered a featureless French living room occupied by an elderly Gallic-looking householder in a bathrobe. Von Kleist told me to sit and I did. He spoke to the driver.

"Take this man to Berlin," he said, pointing at me. "Take him to Pabst. Tell Pabst to hold him for me."

The driver nodded and von Kleist leaned close to me.

"Because I have work to do, I do not have time to deal with you at the moment. While I am curious to know how you came to be in that restaurant tonight, I am in no hurry to hear your story. I will take you to my hideaway in Berlin. It is far more advanced and suited to my purposes than that cave in Mexico. Think of that as you wait for me."

And he strode from the room.

I thought of it, all right. I thought of it as I was driven in the back of a truck all the way to Berlin. I thought a lot about it when I was ordered out of the truck and hustled into the back of a large institutional building that I thought Germans were uniquely skilled at building until later when I visited Russia. Those Bolsheviks took the worst of German bureaucratic architecture, doubled its size, and squeezed out the last vestige of humanity. I was relieved when no one paid me much attention. I was hurried into a small cell, the door was locked behind me, and there I sat.

I was in that small cell for three months. My only human contact came twice a day, when food was delivered and my slops from the waste bucket removed. No one spoke to me, except to grunt in response to my inquiries. I heard no other inmates in the cells next to me. I had no books, no writing implements, no window, nothing. I kept only vague track of the passage of time. This was my first prolonged experience with solitary confinement. Things were worse in von Kleist's torture cave, of course, and later in the Bataan death march and even in an Alabama jail. The food wasn't so bad, it was just insufficient, and no one was interrogating me, violently or otherwise. No one seemed to recall I was there. Thus I spent the summer of 1918, while unbeknownst to me, the Germans were being driven across France and toward a final showdown in the deep green Argonne Forest.

I lost weight and did not quite lose my mind. It was a sadly depleted Cornelius who was roused from a troubled sleep one day in September 1918 and ordered to follow the guard who'd thrown open my cell door. It took me a few moments to realize this summons was real and not one of my fevered dreams. Impatient, the guard grabbed my arm and pulled me from my cot. I managed to stand and followed on shaky legs as he led me down bureaucratic corridors which, in three months of residence, I had never seen. I was stumbling, filthy, still not entirely sure I was awake. The guard flung open another door, not a cell, and pushed me inside. It was a seedy office with a desk behind which sat my nightmare, von Kleist.

He sat with his feet on the desk, hands folded comfortably across his belly. His uniform, unlike everyone else's in these last days of the Great War, was clean and crisply starched. His officer's cap was tilted rakishly over his eyes. All in all, he looked every bit the Maniac Who Broke the Bank at Monte Carlo. In stark contrast, I stood before him a smelly, filthy wretch. Once my escort closed the door, I was alone with the monster. He smiled at me.

"At last, Cornelius. At last, here we are." He nodded to the chair before the desk. "Have a seat. You look like you need it."

I didn't argue. I just collapsed in the chair.

"I apologize that it's taken me so long to come to you. You don't look your best, Cornelius. I fear our hospitality has been wanting. But then, we are at war, you know."

I let that pass. He would tell me soon enough where this line of dialogue was going and I didn't have the energy to spar with him. The bastard just terrified me.

"Perhaps you recall our last conversation. About my hideaway in Berlin, where I have subjected many people to the sort of treatment that we offered to you in the cave. You remember that, surely? You recall being affixed to the wall, with planks holding your head in place and clips, specially designed clips, holding open your eyes? I'm quite proud of that design. It was here in Berlin that I perfected it, after much experiment."

Von Kleist snapped to his feet, warming to his subject. He paced around the desk and behind me, hands on my shoulders, speaking softly into my ear.

"You see, it is not enough simply to inflict physical pain. Any brute can do that, there is no enjoyment in it for someone of my… predilection. For me, the experience all hinges on the victim's psyche, the victim's mental and emotional response to what is happening, what I am doing. It is quite an intimate experience, actually."

At this point, he was positively rubbing my shoulders as though he were giving me a massage.

"What I found frustrating was that as I tortured them, my victims would decompensate to the point that there was no real intimacy, no communication between the torturer and the tortured. They screamed and they drooled and they pleaded until they could no longer speak, but something was missing." Now he was whispering. "Do you follow me?"

I may have nodded, I don't know. I couldn't stop shaking.

Von Kleist walked around to the front of the desk and sat on the desktop, looking down at me.

"Then as I experimented, I found that I got more stimulation, more enjoyment, when I had more than just one victim. If I could take two friends, or lovers, or a parent and child, and subject one to torture while the other watched, the pleasure multiplied. I could bring myself to climax over and over again just watching the eyes of the one not being tortured while I inflicted pain on the other. And I discovered that the two victims didn't even need a relationship with each other to create this pleasurable effect. Do you know why?"

Still I said nothing.

"Because it is not concern for the victim that is at the heart of their fear. It is because they know they are next. All of them—the mothers, the lovers—are in their souls screaming, 'Not me! Do it to him, do it to her, just don't do it to me!' And I can see, in their eyes, the moment they reach that level of fear and hysteria, the moment they realize what they are capable of. It is truly a moving moment, the only thing that really excites me anymore."

He sighed and fell silent a moment. He was one sick fucker.

"As I worked with more and more victims, I realized that

something was getting in the way of our maximum intimacy, my maximum enjoyment. No matter how tightly I bound the watcher, he would turn his head, shut his eyes, find some way to shut out what was happening." Von Kleist looked into my eyes. "That was not acceptable. It would distract me and it was undignified, I kept rolling the person's head back toward me, holding his eyes open... Oh, you understand I am saying 'he,' but those watching the torture were both men and women. Some of my most intimate moments involved mothers and their children, women and their lovers. You understand."

"I don't understand anything about you," I managed to mumble.

He flashed a smile that would have been quite charming but for the cruelty in his eyes.

"I thought and thought and finally concluded that there were two movements that had to be controlled: the turning of the head and the closing of the eyes. The first was relatively easy in concept, a board tightly fixed on each side of the head, but the details were difficult! It was perhaps easy to affix the boards to other boards nailed on the wall of my apartment here in Berlin, but my Yaquis and I had a devil of a time trying to do it on a rough rock wall in a dark cave. You'd have laughed to see us, really! And think about it: what is the proper width to separate them? And the height? The width for a big, strapping man like Lieutenant Patton is very different from the width for a young mother whose child I am about to rape. Do you know, when we were in the outer cavern with all of you and that blowhard Villa, listening to his endless stories, my Yaquis and I would creep away to the inner cave to build two more devices, since we knew we'd have the three Americans there at some point. It was amusing, really. And of course, the clips for the eyes. They took much more delicate work, getting the springs correct, making them adjustable for size. You simply cannot take too much care, don't you agree? Cornelius, you may be wondering... what does all this mean for you, now?"

I almost threw up. That was exactly what I was stewing about, of course, with an occasional break to ask God how he could make such an ungodly piece of shit. I was a communist and an atheist, of course, but cultural habits are hard to break.

"My message to you, Cornelius, is that it is all in your hands. It is in your control to say whether you will die in my Berlin sanctuary, tortured for hours upon hours, developing the same intimate relationship with me that young Miguel achieved. Or..."

"I'll take the 'or.'"

Von Kleist smiled at that.

"That is what I am hoping, Cornelius, sincerely, although I would greatly enjoy the first option as well."

"What do I have to do?"

Von Kleist clapped his hands, startling me.

"To business! But surely you would like something—coffee, tea?"

I asked for coffee. This was very strange.

Von Kleist bounded to the door, stuck out his head, and demanded coffee. Two, in fact, suggesting we were pals now, as long as I said nothing that would induce him to torture me to death. He sat down again and stared straight into my eyes, willing me to listen.

"Forgive me, but I must give you some background of what is happening in our peculiar country. There is now no question, Cornelius, that Germany will lose the war."

News to me, since I had been shut up in a hole since June. As it happened, it would have been news to Pershing, too, but Ludendorff had been secretly demanding that the German government surrender since August, before the Allied advance reached German soil.

"What my friends and I wish to ensure is that we win the peace. What do I mean by that? Germany will not dissolve into nothing as a consequence of surrendering. There will still be a nation, a government, an economy. We, my friends and I, must remain at the top of that nation. But that will require some effort. You see, the loss of the war is encouraging factions that we cannot and will not approve of. There are socialists and there are communists. For the most part, they are fools and inconsequential. But they opposed the war from the start, and since the war is lost, they may have some temporary cachet with the German people. And there is one leader of the communists, in particular, who gives us concern. A woman, in fact. Have you ever heard of Rosa Luxemburg?"

I started. Rosa Luxemburg was my father's hero and the mention of her name by a monster like von Kleist was bizarre, to put it mildly.

Von Kleist snickered.

"I know you have. I recall your talk of her to Villa in the cave. You know of Rosa Luxemburg, you've read her books, you admire her. Good for you, Cornelius! I am impressed, for one so young. I find all those books about political theory and economics so tedious."

Our coffee came and there was a break. Von Kleist took cream, in case you're wondering. When the flunky had poured the coffee and left the room, von Kleist continued.

"You must have a grasp of the political situation, Cornelius. There are socialists, so-called, many of them in rump groups all over Germany. The most influential in Berlin is a man named Ebert, Friedrich Ebert, and we have our eyes on him. We think he may be useful to us as a pawn, someone who can unknowingly take the blame for what is to happen over the next months and keep his seat warm for someone of our choosing. But there are others who are more radical and who we are not comfortable with. There is a man named Liebknecht, for example, who would not be so malleable. At the top of our enemy list is this woman Luxemburg. She has brains and she can touch the hearts of working people. She will never rule Germany because she is a woman, but she could put Liebknecht into a position to annoy us. We do not like to be annoyed."

"I thought Rosa was in prison."

This comment drew another sharp laugh.

"Of course she is in prison. Liebknecht is in prison, too, it's a badge of honor for their kind. But she won't be there long. The war will end and she will be released. All of them will be released. We want them to be. The socialists and the communists, they must be released so we can blame them for what is about to happen. But we know that, prison or no, these people have plans. They are just like us—they know the war is ending and they are anticipating what will happen next. And here, Cornelius, at long last, here is where you fit in."

I was lost.

"You will be placed in the prison where Luxemburg is kept," von Kleist explained. "You will be given opportunities to be alone with her, to speak to her. You are a young American soldier, not good-looking perhaps, but better-looking than a creature like Luxemburg. You know her work, you can tell her what a genius she is. She will believe you. If you are not in her pants within a week of meeting her, I will be surprised. And then, Cornelius, you will report to me or to my delegates everything she tells you. Her plans. Whether she sees Liebknecht or someone else as the future of Germany. Her relationships with the workers' councils that are spreading like a pestilence throughout the country. Everything."

I thought for a moment. It repelled me to spy on Rosa Luxemburg and the cause my father believed in, but it repelled me considerably more to be tortured to death by a maniac like von Kleist and I hadn't the slightest doubt that would be my fate if I didn't agree. Plus, once I was placed next to Rosa Luxemburg, who knew what might happen?

"I'll do it," I said. "Whatever you want."

Von Kleist clucked his tongue and shook his head.

"Cornelius, Cornelius. You are thinking, I will promise him anything. It doesn't matter, much can happen, how will they know if I give them reliable information? This sort of thinking is not helpful, Cornelius."

A chill ran down my spine.

"I will know. I always know. If you withhold information, I will know. If you mislead me, I will know. And if you do those things, I will put you in my apartment and we will have our intimacy. You can rely on that promise. Do you understand?"

I leaned forward.

"I don't give a flying fuck about Rosa Luxemburg or Germany or anything else you talked about. I don't want to be tortured. If giving you whatever this woman tells me helps me avoid that, that's what I'll do."

And so it was set.

It was the very next day that I was transferred to Wansee Prison in Breslau, east of Berlin. It was apparent the authorities knew I was a special case and I was treated quite well from the beginning. I was given excellent meals to build back my strength. My American uniform was cleaned and pressed so that I looked my best. Considering von Kleist's charge, this was obviously part of the plan.

Two days of good food and kind treatment made a world of difference to me. I felt refreshed, energetic. I was in this mood when a kindly guard informed me that I was given library privileges. Plainly, I was expected to take advantage of them, though I would have done so anyway. Excited and wondering what awaited, I followed the guard to the prison library, which was surprisingly well-equipped. A woman sat at a desk, books piled in front of her as she scribbled away on a notepad.

I knew, of course, that it was Rosa.

27

Red Rosa

Cornelius

Oh, Rosa. Red Rosa. Brilliant, funny, incisive, warm. She rebuked Lenin at his zenith and he respected her for it. She exposed the hypocrisy of Europe's leaders and, for that, they hated and feared her. She was communism in its infancy, at its best, before it became organized into Communism with a capital "C," before Lenin's fanaticism and Stalin's brutishness made it a joke and a horror. She came to personify for me the best ideals behind Marx's doctrine and I came to love her during the short time we shared together.

The woman who peered curiously at me as she looked up from her writing was not what I expected from the masculinity of her prose. She was petite, spectacled, and dainty-looking. At age forty-seven, she should have looked like an old lady to my young eyes, but she had a girlishness about her, a glint in her eyes and a cock of her head that belied her age. She wore her brown hair tied back. Her eyes had the slight squint of a scholar, but they glowed with humor and a certain impishness. She had a well-shaped, slightly prominent nose over bow lips and fine white teeth that flashed when she smiled. As she was doing now—a wide grin that had me grinning along with her. This was an earthy woman whose innate humanity had survived a long hard imprisonment. I was smitten.

"What is this?" she asked, grinning. "An American uniform? A handsome young soldier come to rescue me? Gregor! Gregor, do you see? A handsome American soldier has come to save me. You must surrender immediately, for he cannot be resisted."

She was speaking to an elderly German in uniform dozing in the corner, obviously a guard of some sort. He seemed smitten with Rosa, too. He smiled and shook his head.

"Oh, Rosa, do not get excited. There is no rescue for you. Americans like communists even less than they like Germans."

Rosa laughed happily.

"Gregor, you have not been attending my lessons! When the workers triumph, it is you and members of your class who will benefit the most. But I forgive you, Gregor, for you bring me pen and paper and you smell so nicely of schnapps the way my papa did."

Gregor smiled and nodded off again.

This was the moment von Kleist had warned me about, my first exchange with her. She had been a fighter since her teens, he told me, and she could smell any trap set for her. Suddenly being granted access to the library, combined with the mysterious appearance of an American soldier, would likely set off alarm bells that could only be quieted by the prompt application of charm and a credible cover story, the one he'd given me. At the moment, none of this was on my mind. I was lost in Rosa's smile and the way she'd called me handsome.

"Pardon me. Did he say your name is Rosa?"

Rosa's eyes narrowed.

"You speak German, American boy?"

"I speak German. My father back in Missouri owned a bookstore and was a great enthusiast for German culture and also for German politics. He taught me the language and we read Schiller together."

"Schiller!" Her eyes lit up. "Then your father was a wise man who did you a great favor, for Schiller is the greatest of German writers. Greater even than Goethe, whatever they say."

"But your name? It's Rosa?"

"Yes, my name is Rosa. What is that to you?"

I sat across the table from her.

"I have heard that the great communist Rosa Luxemburg is imprisoned here. Can that be you?"

Rosa's expression fell.

"I have heard the same thing. And I hear that she is a horrible beast of a woman who would overturn the government and give the country to the Jews. I hear that she is ugly and smells foul and has a long nose and is bow-legged and short as a dwarf. Do you hear those things?"

I shook my head.

"You misjudge her. Rosa Luxemburg is a great woman. She's the preeminent intellectual in the communist movement and Germany's best hope for a revolution like the one in Russia. Do you know her history?"

Rosa shook her head, so I recited her own history back to her. Fortunately, Jack O'Neal was a Rosa enthusiast and I had the story down pat. How she was a revolutionary even in her teens, born to an affluent Jewish family that lived in Poland on the Russian border. How she suffered a hip disease in childhood that still caused her to limp. How by age five, she was fully literate and teaching the local serfs to read. As a student, she became a leader in the movement to protect Polish culture against Russian oppression and that led her to communism and total commitment to a worldwide workers' revolution. She'd founded the Polish Workers League and later escaped imprisonment by being smuggled into Switzerland in a hay wagon. A star student at the University of Zurich, she'd written crucial analyses of the workers' movements in Poland and Russia and the need for revolution based on economic reform, not nationalism. She'd consulted with Lenin and Trotsky before, during, and after the revolution of December 1917. She'd moved to Berlin, founded a journal, and been the intellectual leader of the left wing of the German Socialist Party until she was placed in "protective custody" in the summer of 1916, where to Germany's shame she remained.

"Stop, stop," Rosa said, waving her hand. "She is far too wonderful, you make me feel wholly inadequate by comparison. But is not Gregor correct? Americans hate communists, do they not?"

I offered her a cigarette, another gift from von Kleist, which she accepted greedily.

"Not all Americans," I said lighting her cigarette. "My father taught me Marx, the oppression of the masses, the economic forces behind it all. But it seemed unreal to me, a lot of jargon and abstractions, until I read Rosa Luxemburg. I felt her passion in what she wrote, a sensitivity for oppressed people that I couldn't find in Marx or Lenin. She made me think communism might be just what it says it is: the answer for the workers of the world. You made me think that, Miss Luxemburg."

There was no point continuing to pretend I didn't know who she was. If I had, she would have thought me foolish. I could tell from the way her eyes bore into me that my soft soap hadn't put her off-guard.

"Who are you?" she asked sharply. "What are you doing here?"

Time for the von Kleist cover story. It wasn't bad, but I knew instantly that I couldn't just spill it out or she'd never believe it. I had to let out the line slowly and deliberately.

"My name is O'Neal, James Cornelius O'Neal," I said softly. "Call me Cornelius, if you like, it's what my best friend calls me. I can't tell you more than that, I'm afraid. You're better off not knowing about me. In fact, you'd be better off not having met me. I am a great admirer, Miss Luxemburg, and I wish we could get to know each other, but believe me, for your sake, it's better that I leave."

And following my instincts, I rose, turned, and walked out of the library, leaving a surprised and disconcerted revolutionary behind to mull over our encounter.

I played my cards cautiously, for I knew that the guards were instructed to create occasions when Rosa and I would be together. The first two or three times I saw her, I made a visible effort to stay away and avoid contact with her. You'll say it was my imagination, but I felt that she was very interested in the young American soldier who had entered her life. When we ate in the same cafeteria, I felt her eyes on me even while she spoke to other prisoners, with whom she seemed very popular. In the library, I caught her looking at me over the top of her book, only to drop her gaze whenever I looked back. We were like schoolchildren playing a mind game. Prison can do that to a person.

My opening came during an exercise period in the prison yard. Rosa, an inveterate teacher and preacher of the Word According to Karl, had gathered a group of prisoners around her and was speaking on the economic imperatives of worldwide revolution. I sat at the edge of the crowd to listen.

"Marx tells us not only that the world must change," she was saying. "He tells us why it must change and how it must change. Like a good doctor, he does not stop with his diagnosis of the illness, he makes the proper prescription to cure the patient. You, the workers, are the patient. Your illness is the oppression and economic servitude that has been your lot under kings and barons and parliaments and today in Germany in a war in which your sons die to protect the very system that oppresses you. And when the war ends, will you be free? No, you will not. You will remain under the yoke of the powerful—it doesn't matter what nation they come from, for all class relationships are alike, everywhere, at every time. The change will only come when the means of production are controlled by the workers, by you, all of you. The day is coming. It has already come in Russia and it is now coming in Germany."

A prisoner eyed me, nervously.

"Hush, Rosa," a prisoner called out. "Not everyone is your friend here."

Rosa laughed.

"I say nothing I have not written, nothing I would not say to the Kaiser if he were listening. As for this American, I do not know his story for he will not tell it to me. Are you a spy for the Kaiser, American? Why will you not tell me your story? You know so much of mine."

Her audience was looking at me suspiciously. I smiled at them.

"My story is far less interesting than yours. But I have a question, one that is far more important than my own story. It concerns Marx."

Rosa smiled and nodded.

"You tout the Russian Revolution as though it fulfills the teaching of Marx. Yet you yourself have criticized Lenin. You say he is playing on national sentiments and failing to apply the internationalism that is the consequence of a truly Marxist view of the world. Are you not being inconsistent?"

Rosa's smile lit up the somber prison yard. She sensed a challenge and nothing sparked her more.

"'Inconsistent,' he asks. Does he threaten me, does he intimidate me, with such a word? Intellectuals fear inconsistency like drunkards fear sobriety. Shall I, a mere woman, recoil in horror from the accusation? My friends, it is a poor revolutionary, only an intellectual revolutionary, who worries about being 'inconsistent.' Such a revolutionary could not ignite his own penis to grow hard if his wife sucked it, much less ignite a worldwide workers' revolt!"

Well, this delighted the crowd, who laughed uproariously at my expense.

"But wait," cried Rosa. "The American asked a question and deserves an answer."

She stepped close to me and looked up into my face. The top of her head barely reached my chin, and I am not a tall man.

"I did tell Lenin that he is playing a dangerous game when he seeks to stir Russians against Poles and Lithuanians. I reminded him that if we are to be true apostles of Marx, we must speak for all workers of the world. Oppression follows the same economic laws in all countries and so the remedy is the same in all countries as well. But Lenin is a great man. He has done more to bring the blessings of communism to the real world than any of us. He faces struggles the rest of us can so far only imagine. So I am consistent, I think. What say you, my friends?"

Amid a chorus of cheers, a tough-looking working man made his voice heard.

"Aye, but will your penis grow, Rosa?"

She laughed along with the rest. A whistle blew to signal the end of the exercise period. As the group sauntered off, I grabbed Rosa by the elbow and pulled her close.

"If you want to know my story, find a way to come to my cell tonight," I whispered. "I'll watch for you. I'll tell you everything."

I released her elbow and walked off before she could speak. This I knew: between her relationship with Gregor and von Kleist's orders that the guards help me get close to Rosa, she could get to me if she wished. The question was, did she wish to?

Von Kleist had arranged for me to be alone in my cell, with no other prisoners in the entire cellblock. That night, I lay on my cot not knowing what to expect. Lights were turned off at eleven. I must have lain in the darkness until two or three in the morning, wondering if I had played my hand correctly, if Rosa was mocking me or truly had an interest in her young American.

All prisons have routines and prisoners become so accustomed to the routine that any variation is instantly noticed. I noticed that night that the usual prison guards did not appear in the doorway to the cellblock, to make sure I was present and not causing trouble. I was left completely alone. Then, when I had about decided the lady wasn't coming, I heard the cellblock door open softly. The light of an electric torch lit the floor in front of two people who were quietly walking toward my cell door. I recognized Gregor by his labored breathing. He opened the door to my cell.

"You have ninety minutes," he said to Rosa. "I must have you back in your cell then. I will be relieved as guard and you must be gone before my replacement comes."

Rosa nodded and walked into my cell. Gregor locked the door behind her and disappeared, shaking his head.

I sat up in bed. I wore an undershirt and my uniform pants; I had not undressed further in expectation of her. Rosa sat primly on the unoccupied cot across from me, her hands folded in her lap.

"I am here. I found a way. Tell me your story."

I made a show of looking around, although I knew we were quite alone in the dark.

"I work for the American Secret Service," I informed her. "I was sent to Berlin to impersonate a German worker and send back information about German forces and plans. I was caught and arrested just a week ago."

She looked skeptical.

"Why are you in uniform? Why weren't you shot?"

"I thought I would be. But I was taken before one of their secret service men, a man named Otto von Kleist. He told me that the Kaiser, along with everyone in government and the armed forces, realize the war is lost. He said he will need someone to talk to the Americans for him when they take over. He said he would treat me well, put me here where the prisoners are treated decently, and let me out as soon as the war ends. He said he just wants me to speak a good word for him when the time comes. He said he'd save me from being executed and then I could do the same for him. 'Brothers of the secret service,' he called us."

It sounded lame as I said it. I wasn't sure she was buying it.

"Why didn't you tell me this earlier?" she asked.

"Von Kleist was acting on his own. He got me a uniform to make me look more like a regular prisoner of war and he falsified my records. But if the army found out I was a spy out of uniform, I'd be executed as a spy. It didn't seem like a good idea for either of us to get you involved."

Rosa considered this.

"And now?"

My cue. I looked down, away, anywhere but at her.

"I admired your work. That part about my father was all true."

"I could tell it was."

"Then I saw you." I raised my head and looked her in the eye. "And I've seen you since, at the cafeteria, in the library, in the yard. I just had to know you. If the price was that I had to tell you the truth about me… well, that's just how it would have to be."

She shook her head.

"But you are young, handsome. I am old, dried up—"

"Don't say that!" I took her by the shoulders and knelt in front of her. Lord, she was small. "I would've known you even if Gregor hadn't said your name. I would've known who I was looking at from your smile and your humor and the way you challenge me when you toss your head. You're Rosa, my Rosa, the Rosa I've always dreamed of."

And I kissed her with all the passion I could.

You had to be there, is all I can say. Yes, she was nearing fifty while I hadn't reached my twenty-first birthday. She had a prominent nose and her eyes were scrunched from so much reading and writing and she walked with a limp from her childhood disease and the profile of her face could not be called pretty. But no one saw her that way. When she smiled, her eyes danced and her dimples flashed and she made happy the coldest of comrades in the tightest of circumstances. When she fought, she showed the toughness and spunk of a leopard, laying her foes before her and walking across their bodies with grace. When she wept, she plumbed the depth of a woman's heart. As we kissed, I lifted her from the floor and held her pressed to my body, of no more weight than a child. She returned my kiss with ardor and soon our hands were fondling each other, removing clothing, exploring the secret places. I laid her on my cot and entered her and we made love. I'd experienced both Juanita's skilled professionalism and the naïve virginity of the girls back home, but Rosa was different. Rosa showed me a woman's passion, avidly taking me in, holding me, seeking to enjoy each moment, each caress, as though it might be her last. Red Rosa. I love her still.

28

A Visit from a Giant

Cornelius

It was a glorious October, considering we were imprisoned in a country about to lose a war. The food was skimpy, but so it was for all Germans after the economy collapsed. Gregor was an understanding and sympathetic guard and, because of von Kleist's influence, we were given free access to the library and to each other's cells, which were both kept isolated from others. We made love every night. I had the ardor of youth, while Rosa was of a passionate nature when it came to the senses as well as the intellect. She would give herself to me completely, surrendering her whole self, avid to touch, to taste, to experience every pleasure of sex as though it would be her last chance, which it was likely to be. Oddly, neither of us were ever bothered by the idea that we were making love in a prison, with no control over who might suddenly appear. The sex was all-consuming and there was simply no room for other thoughts.

Those who have seen photographs of Rosa and remember our age difference might wonder at this. Rosa was hardly a conventional beauty. The fact that we did not wear prison uniforms did not really matter, as Rosa wore white blouses and long skirts that hid her figure. She had large breasts for a woman her size, a narrow waist, and rounded hips. What does not come across in photographs is Rosa's humor and passion. Her eyes clearly expressed her moods, whether they were silly, sentimental, passionately idealistic, or deeply sorrowful. You won't know it from her pictures, but Rosa was a beautiful woman. As for the age difference, all young men should get the chance to make love to older women. Juanita taught me some techniques, but Rosa taught me life.

I know I go on, but it's important to understand about Rosa and me to understand what followed. I remember one morning, just before dawn, we were lazing naked together in my narrow cot. We risked not being dressed should Gregor show up prematurely to return Rosa to her cell, but we both felt too comfortable and intimate to break the moment. Rosa was propped on an elbow, rubbing her hand over my chest.

"My pretty American boy. You are so perfect, such a gift to me. Do you know I have been in this prison for more than a year? And before that, other prisons, worse prisons. Do you know my crime?"

I did, but said nothing. Von Kleist had told me.

"I wondered about that. I wasn't sure communists needed to commit a crime to go to jail."

"The American is exactly right," Rosa laughed. "This is 'protective custody.' I have been in prison almost three years so I will be protected, from what I don't know. The only people I need protection from are the people who imprisoned me. Do you like when I do this?"

I nodded.

"And this?"

I nodded.

"And this?"

She'd been rubbing my chest, then moved down to my belly to my erect male member, which she gathered in her hand. She held it gently, but I wasn't sure of her intent.

"You are so perfect, Cornelius. I am given library privileges, I am allowed to walk outside, I am allowed to come here and make love to you. You speak German perfectly, you believe in Marx, you even say you've read my work."

Now she was idly tickling my scrotum.

"Are you too perfect, my American boy? The old women in my village would say you are an angel from heaven, but angels don't come to the likes of Rosa Luxemburg."

I didn't like where this was headed. I took her hand and wrapped it in both of mine, to forestall the tickling changing to a savage twist.

"I don't know what you mean, darling. What are you saying?"

She was far too smart not to have suspected that I was a spy for German authorities.

"I don't know what I'm saying, Cornelius. I don't know."

"Do you think somehow that you don't deserve happiness? That would be a very bourgeois notion, coming from you."

"It's not that."

She avoided my eyes.

"Then what could be the matter? How could anything be too perfect… unless…" I gradually allowed the light to dawn. "You don't think this was all arranged, do you? That I'm some sort of spy for your enemies?"

I let go of her hand and drew myself up indignantly, not an easy task when you're naked. Her mood shifted instantly into abject apology.

"Sweetheart, sweetheart, forgive me," she begged. "I am an old fool. I've been shut away too long. I don't deserve you."

I allowed her to soften my anger.

"Darling, you are too hard on yourself. You are beautiful, I am the one who is lucky to have found you. I read the other Marxist books because my father made me read them, but yours, yours were different. Your spirit shone in every word and now I find that you are tender and funny and passionate and everything a woman should be!"

I held her and kissed her, hard, making sure to rub my chest against her breasts. She responded, her mouth opened, and her hands again ran all over my torso. Still not satisfied, I pulled away and again studied her closely.

"One thing, darling. Never tell me your secrets. If you have any doubt, any worry at all, never tell me anything you don't want known. I don't need your secrets, I have you."

We stared at each other a moment, eyes locked together. Suddenly she threw back her head and laughed uproariously.

"Secrets! I have no secrets! Our movement has fallen apart, Liebknecht and I are in prisons, we have no plans that a three-year-old would worry about, and everything I believe I publish daily in the articles I smuggle out of here. Spy? There is nothing for you to spy on! I am just a silly old woman."

"We'll see how silly you are!"

And I laid her back and made love to her one more time, just to seal the deal. We were still under the covers recovering when Gregor came for Rosa, but it was worth it. She never suspected me again.

To this point, any suspicion would have been unjustified. In our first two weeks together, I didn't get a sniff of von Kleist. I didn't report anything to anyone and had nothing to report. Our conversations at first only lightly touched on current events. Instead, Rosa instructed me on communist doctrine and recounted her enthusiasm for children (she had no children, but was very close to the children of several of her revolutionary friends), animals (especially birds), and nature, the separation from which weighed heavily on her in prison. I told her about America and she asked endless questions about it. In the beginning, we spent more time plotting revolutions in Chicago than Berlin. She was very knowledgeable about the labor movement there and deplored management-induced violence. Workers' councils must be established in the meatpacking yards, we agreed.

Of course, she was especially charmed by my stories of Jack O'Neal, her bookselling admirer in Independence. She insisted that he come to Germany so she could thank him properly for liking her work and for creating such a beautiful American boy. I told her that Jack would like nothing better.

In my innocence, I began to forget about von Kleist. If I thought of him at all, I simply hoped he was off somewhere busy with the war, preferably being blown to pieces by American gunfire. As it turned out, I didn't see von Kleist while I was in prison, but I heard from him.

I was in my cell one mid-October morning, napping after an intensive night of communist theory and vigorous intercourse. Sometimes, by the way, Rosa would talk dialectics to me breathlessly while astride my middle, riding me like a jockey. Showing off, I suppose. Anyway, I didn't even open my eyes when I heard my cell door creak open. It wasn't Gregor. His footfall as he walked toward my cot told me that. It sounded more like the tread of the giant who tore down Jack's beanstalk.

It was indeed a giant, in a guard's uniform, almost as tall as von Kleist, with arms like trees, a vast belly, and rolls of fat framing a porcine face. A few months later, in Munich, I was to see many of these sausage-eating, beer-swigging, Jew-hating thugs. He barked at me to get up. I was still not fully awake and trying to take in this sudden apparition, so I didn't respond immediately. The brute thereupon reached down, grasped the bottom of my cot, and flipped it over, throwing me to the floor.

"I said get up!" He grabbed me under the arms and pushed me against the wall. "I am from Herr von Kleist. You understand?"

"You are from Herr von Kleist," I gurgled.

He had his forearm pressed against my throat.

"What do you have for me?"

"What?"

The pressure on my throat increased.

"What do you have for me?"

"Antipathy?"

This fellow was a bruiser, but not in von Kleist's category when it came to silencing me with terror.

He flung me to the floor.

"You are here to get information from that Jew whore. It is the only reason you are alive. What do you have for me?"

"Listen, I'm working on it." I stood up, not wanting to be kicked. "Tell von Kleist it's going well. I don't want to make her suspicious. I have to take it slow to gain her confidence."

"Which means you're fucking her," the goon spat at me. "You disgust me. I've heard of men so degraded that they fuck cripples, I've heard of men who fuck Bolsheviks, I've even heard of men who fuck Jews. But a man who fucks someone who is all three?" He shoved me. "You belong in the gutter. There is a pig farm near here, perhaps I should get the ugliest, fattest, filthiest pig I can find and you can fuck her."

"That would be nice, but perhaps your mother can't take the time."

That pretty much ended the civilities. He drove an enormous fist into my belly, doubling me over and taking away my wind. He followed up with a punch to the kidneys. There followed a pretty good beating, with the blows always landing where they would leave the fewest visible bruises. Perhaps Riley could have found a way to take this beast, but I was helpless from the start. What saved me was that von Kleist still hoped to make use of me.

"I left you your face, Jew-lover, so you can still fuck that whore," he scowled at me when he finished. "I will be back, soon. You better have something useful for me when I get back. If you don't, next time you won't have to worry about me, you will be visiting Herr von Kleist in Berlin. You know what that means?"

I nodded. There were no wisecracks left in me, nor any breath. With a last kick to my side, the ogre strode from my cell, leaving me alone and with much to think about.

29

Rosa Released

Cornelius

To hell with them, I thought. In my mind's eye, I saw Rosa with her smile and her passion and her dead-serious dedication to the cause of the lower classes, and I knew I couldn't betray her. Von Kleist had said the war was lost for the Germans. If so, maybe we would soon be released. I'd take my chances, I decided.

Considering how much the beating had hurt me, I was surprised how quickly I recovered. That same day, I was able to get to the library without difficulty or signs of injury. That was what the brute had wanted to accomplish, of course, but he had more skill at it than I would have given him credit for.

Rosa was seated in the library, with Gregor handing her a stack of books and talking softly to her. As usual, the three of us were alone. Apparently the other inmates weren't much for reading or perhaps we were the only ones allowed to use the library, I was never sure which.

Rosa smiled delightedly when she saw me.

"Cornelius, you must hear this! It is starting!"

Gregor threw up a hand in protest.

"Wait, Rosa, wait, I cannot hear this. I must leave. I cannot hear such talk from you, Rosa."

Gregor shuffled out to the sound of Rosa's laughter. He was a kindly old duffer.

I had two outfits in prison, my uniform and a plain set of German civilian clothes that von Kleist had given me. Rosa had three outfits, but all were the same: a white or gray peasant blouse with a gray or black skirt. This day, she wore her hair tied back and in a scarf.

"Sit down, Cornelius, we must talk. I have much to tell you to bring you up to date. I think we will be out of here soon, Cornelius."

As I sat, I noticed her slide a sheaf of folded papers out of one of the books in front of her and place it at the bottom of the stack.

"I will admit, I have not kept you informed about what is happening outside these walls. You must forgive me. I am so infatuated with my pretty American boy that I didn't want you to think of anything but me."

And you worried that I might be a spy after all, I thought. That was all right. If the war ended and we were given our freedom, none of it would matter. Needless to say, I was starved for news.

"The Germans are defeated. The Kaiser has fled. He appointed Max von Baden to lead a temporary coalition government and that so-called socialist, Ebert, is cooperating with it. You know of Friedrich Ebert? He is a socialist but bourgeois, a traitor to the cause who pretends to favor the workers but says he hates revolution. Ludendorff, too, has fled. But best of all, by far the best of all, Cornelius, is that the revolution has begun in Germany!" Her eyes blazed as she spoke. "Karl Liebknecht has been released and is back in Berlin! That would never have happened if Ebert didn't know the war was lost and he will have to recognize the Spartacists!" The radicals that she and Liebknecht led were called the Spartacists, after the rebellious slave. "Karl and Leo Jogiches are organizing the labor councils, publicizing the truth, and publishing my work from prison! There is more! It is happening as I predicted: the German military now sees that it has been played for fools in a war to benefit the upper class and they are in active revolt."

I had seen enough German soldiers to wonder if they would truly subscribe to the ideals of Karl Marx and Rosa Luxemburg, but Rosa was in full flow and nothing could stem her enthusiasm.

"Even with the war lost," she gushed, "some foolish admirals ordered a naval attack in the English Channel to cause more senseless slaughter. And the sailors rebelled! They refused orders to sail and the crews of two ships mutinied. When their leaders were arrested, Germans everywhere rebelled! The slogan is 'Peace and Bread.' All is ready for the Spartacists to lead a *true* people's revolution. The December Revolution will be purified and Germany will be the first nation to exemplify Marx's doctrines in full!"

She was transfigured, all right.

"Well, that all sounds wonderful, darling, but you're in here."

She rapped the table impatiently.

"Not for long. Surely not for long. If they released Liebknecht, they will release me. Then… and then, my pretty American, you will see what your Rosa is really capable of doing!"

I believed her. And she proved right, at least the part about seeing her true character put to the test. The rest of it, not so much.

"I hope you're right, Rosa. It's tragic for you to be stuck in here when the world is on fire out there. How do you know all this?"

She looked down, avoiding my eyes.

"I have ways, Cornelius. You know that I've been publishing despite being cooped up in prison. Obviously I have friends who stay in contact with me."

What you have is a little bird named Gregor, I thought. Not that I gave a damn. I asked her what the date was and she said November 4. We couldn't know it at the time, but the Great War had exactly one more week to go. Rosa told me that just before fleeing to Sweden, the German commander Ludendorff had reversed his demands for surrender and was publicly urging Germany to fight on. This made me think of von Kleist, who had told me that the German High Command wanted to avoid responsibility for a surrender they had been the first to advocate. For Ludendorff to flee the country and publicly demand that Germany keep fighting, after he had engineered a surrender that would preserve the country's resources, fit the plan precisely. By this time, there was no doubt that surrender was coming. It looked like the game of winning the war was over and the game of winning the peace was underway, with Ludendorff, the Kaiser, von Kleist, Ebert, Liebknecht, and Red Rosa all disputing the spoils.

A moment of silence ensued, during which Rosa's eyes became misty. She took my hand.

"What will you do, Cornelius? I will understand if you wish to return to America. You are a soldier, perhaps you have to go back."

241

"What do you want me to do, Rosa?"

"Darling, don't ask. I am selfish—I want you with me always. I especially want you with me when the revolution comes."

"That's what I hoped you'd say. I will be with you, Rosa. We will fight the revolution together."

I believed it at the time. All of it. I loved Rosa. I thought Germany was ripe for a revolution the same way Russia had been. I was transfixed by the thought of leading the revolution hand in hand with the woman I loved. Hard to believe, looking back, but I believed it. Even von Kleist seemed a problem that would be swept away in the whirlwind. Our love-making that night was especially intense, especially sweet.

In a way, news of the pending surrender made it much harder to wait. A day passed, then two, a third day began, and still we rotted in our cells. Rosa became quiet, tense, snappish. So did I, I suppose. How could Liebknecht be released and not Luxemburg? When would the surrender come?

Late in the morning of November 7, when I was contemplating that question as I lay in my cot, I again heard the heavy tread of my brutish visitor. I thought that thugs like him would give up with the German army, but I misjudged them. The giant, whose name I never learned, entered the cell and planted himself on the lone stool.

"What do you have for me?"

"Really? We really have to do this? I've heard that the war is over. Let's just call it a day and wait in peace until we can go home."

"What do you have for me?" he repeated in no uncertain terms.

He was starting to spook me.

"Listen, I have nothing for you. I will never have anything for you. Von Kleist is insane and the war is over. Go home and leave us alone."

"I don't like you, Jew-lover," he sneered, "which is why I am happy you have nothing for me. Do you think I will hit you? Do you think I will beat you more than last time? No, Jew-lover, you get no more chances." He pulled his stool closer to the cot so he could put his ugly face right up to mine. "You will go to Berlin and you will see Herr von Kleist. I will take you myself. Do you have any idea what that means?"

I could feel the shivers coming, the shivers that only von Kleist and the memory of a Mexican cave could induce. I clenched my jaw to restrain them, but there was no restraining those shivers.

"I see that you do. Herr von Kleist told me something of your history with him. What happened to that boy in the cave was nothing. In Berlin, he has tools and he has ways to prolong the pain that he has developed over many years. And he has time. You will pray for death every minute, on and on, even when you have no lips, no eyelids, no schlong to fuck your Jews with. Herr von Kleist tells me the stories, sometimes, when I have done well and he wants to reward me. I cannot wait to hear your stories, Jew-lover. Come!"

He grabbed the front of my shirt and pulled me from the bed. I was half-dragged, half-pushed down the halls, out a door and toward a truck. It was a gray, bone-chilling November day, but that wasn't why I was shivering. I could barely walk, I was so terrified. I saw the Yaquis, saw Patton being violated, saw Miguel's severed head. Most of all, I saw von Kleist, heard his soft voice, felt his breath. I couldn't do this. I couldn't succumb to him again. I braced my foot against the side of the truck to keep from being thrown inside.

"Stop! I'll give you something. I will. I'll give you something."

He took me by the scruff of the neck and spun me around.

"What do you have for me?"

I spilled what I had, whatever I could think of, which wasn't much. I told him that Rosa knew Liebknecht had been released and was working with the labor councils to undermine the transitional government. I also told him that she would join the movement as soon as we were released and that she wanted me to be with her. He asked how she knew what was happening in the outside world and I told him that Gregor was her courier. It was pathetically little and unimportant. When I was drained dry, he stared silently at me and I was sure it hadn't been enough.

But it was. Wordlessly, he shut the truck door and led me back to my cell.

"You will be released tomorrow," he said, shoving me inside. "Along with the Jew. You will stay with her, go to Berlin, keep fucking her, learn all that she and the Jew communists plan. Another messenger will come for you in Berlin. The war is not ending, you fool. The German army was stabbed in the back by the Jews and the Bolsheviks, but they will not win. Germany will be for Germans again, and we will rebuild and rearm and the world will fear us again. Stay close to the Jew."

And he was gone.

We were indeed released the next day, November 8, 1918. Rosa had been in prison for the better part of the last three years. A knot of guards took me from my cell, then did the same for Rosa. I left my uniform behind, not wanting anything to stir up awkward questions about desertion. As it happens, I needn't have worried: after Paris, the American command did not think I was AWOL, it thought I was dead. We were led to the prison gate, where a big tough-looking customer was waiting at the head of a crowd of happy, cheering supporters of the cause. Rosa ran to the tall tough guy and embraced him warmly. She introduced him to me as Leo Jogiches, her best friend. He stared at me like he wanted to knock me to the ground.

I didn't care. Rosa apparently hadn't noticed that Gregor was not among the guards who released us.

But I noticed.

30

Nobody's Brave Every Time

Jim

The next time I went to see Riley at the motel was after I read in the notebooks that Cornelius and Rosa Luxemburg had been released from prison. We were nursing bourbons, as always.

"He shouldn't have ratted on Gregor," I said.

Riley nodded.

"You're right, he shouldn't have. People do things they shouldn't. You never met von Kleist. He was a motivator."

"Did you ever do anything you shouldn't? You always seem to be the hero."

"You forget Cantigny. You forget Sid Crew. Anyway, no point talking about it now. It was a long time ago. I saw Cornelius be brave many times. Nobody's brave every time."

"You think it bothered him, about Gregor? He doesn't really say."

Riley considered that.

"Well, Cornelius had his blind spots. Sometimes he just didn't see things the way you or I might. Some things he could just put out of his head."

"Like my father?"

Riley said nothing. That night, I went home early.

·

31

The Red Flag

Cornelius

Barring the occasional times I saw Rosa teach Marxist dogma to other prisoners, I pretty much had her to myself up to this point. Our release changed that. I don't know how, but word had gotten to Leo in Berlin the day before that we were going to be released. As a result, he led a band of Spartacists to Breslau, eager to greet their heroine. In addition to the twenty or so who came from Berlin, they'd brought along perhaps twice their number from the nearby town, ordinary folks who were hungry and angry and also anxious to see the infamous Red Rosa. We marched from the prison to the town square, where Rosa mounted a staircase to address the crowd.

"My friends, my friends. So good to see my friends. Though I have been locked away, we have been together. Together in our enslavement, together in our hunger, together in our servitude to a government and a system that ties the working man in bonds as strong as the bonds that held me in Wansee Prison."

Wild applause.

"I will not speak at length now. My friends here will know that it is a rare thing that I do not speak at length, so you should be happy!"

Laughter.

"There will be time for speeches in the days to come, but what is important is that there be action! The war is over and the revolution is here. This need not be a bloody revolution. We all know there has been too much bloodshed. But let there be no mistake: the time has come. The hour of the working man has come. The revolution has come and woe to those who deny it!"

Pandemonium.

A neat little speech, coming from a newly released political prisoner. I hoped it wouldn't get us killed.

We retired to the home of a local supporter with whom Leo was staying. He whisked us into the living room, shooed out the camp followers, including the people who owned the house, and we were alone.

Rosa and I sank into chairs, still a little disoriented from the sudden release from prison. I studied Leo Jogiches. I hadn't heard of him other than a few random mentions from Rosa, but I should have. He was a brawling dockworker from Poland who had devoted his life to a revolution that Marx claimed was inevitable. Neither an intellectual like Rosa nor an organizer like Liebknecht, Leo led by force of personality and a willingness to do absolutely anything to advance the cause. He had a long face like a horse, dark whiskers, huge fists, and a voluble way of speaking that sprayed spit and words with equal rapidity and range. I knew that he and Rosa went way back and were close friends. Still, standing in that living room, he did not look happy despite his friend's release.

"Tell me everything, Leo. I am starved for news," said Rosa.

"You received the letter from Karl a few days ago? Yes? Then you know almost everything."

"And what is the 'almost' that I don't know?"

Leo looked miserable, like a boy about to be reprimanded by his teacher.

"You have to understand, Rosa, things are moving very fast in Berlin. The Freikorps is strong and getting stronger by the day. The labor councils are demanding food and better working conditions. Demonstrations in support of the sailors are erupting all over Germany and the Freikorps is putting them down. The government is doing nothing because it has no power. It is all Karl can do to keep up with events."

Rosa looked concerned, trying to read Leo's thoughts.

"What are you telling me, Leo? What is wrong?"

Leo laughed.

"You have not been to Berlin, Rosa. The very concept of calling some events 'right' and some 'wrong' has gone by the wayside. The world is mad. But I will tell you," he said, waving off her impatient interjection, "Karl has made a decision. He will declare a new government of the labor councils. He may have done so already."

Rosa practically squawked.

"What? Is he prepared? Do we have the resources, the weapons, the support of the people? What is he doing?"

"Rosa, I knew you would react this way. No, we are not ready. Karl has just gotten out of prison himself, but events in Berlin are getting beyond control. Karl is being pressured by Barth and the labor councils—"

"Barth!" Rosa spat scornfully. "Of course it is Barth! Karl could never stand up to that man."

"Emil Barth is a true revolutionary, Rosa."

"I agree he is a true revolutionary, but he cannot control himself! He has no sense, no judgment, he would lead us off a cliff out of spite and not know there was a problem until he lay crushed on the ground!"

"Who is Barth?" I asked, not wanting to be too far out of the loop.

"He is a steward of the revolution," said Rosa. "He heads the labor council of the metalworkers. Leo is right, he is a believer, but he doesn't have the sense that God... he doesn't have the sense of a goose."

"You were going to say the sense that God gave geese, Rosa. That's what people say in America, too. It's all right. Sometimes even we communists slip up and employ a phrase of the bourgeois."

I grinned at her and she grinned back.

"You see, Leo, how my American boy keeps me on my toes. You must be his friend. Please say you will be his friend. Say it, say it."

She was hanging on his arm playfully and he finally nodded, his hangdog face not betraying a trace of sincerity. Rosa returned to business.

"When can we get to Berlin? We must get there as soon as we can."

"We take the train tomorrow, but remember, Germany is still at war and it is losing. The trains are not reliable. They go when they go. We will be in Berlin as soon as we can."

Well, that had to do. Others were allowed back into the room. The homeowner opened bottles of wine, an unimaginable luxury. The conversation flowed—of politics, revolution, and old friends. At one point during the evening, I stepped out of the water closet to find Leo waiting for me. He was looking at me angrily.

"Who are you? Why are you here?"

"Rosa told you. I'm an American and her friend."

"Not good enough, boy." He poked my chest, which always irritates me. "That woman is important to me and she is important to the cause. I know you are lovers. That makes you important, too."

"How is that any of your business?"

"Rosa is my business and the cause is my business, make no mistake. Has she told you that we were lovers once? You might as well hear that now rather than later. Don't worry, we haven't been together that way for many years. But we are comrades and I would die for Rosa, never doubt it. If you betray her, if you hurt her in any way, you will answer to me and it will not be pleasant. You understand?"

I'd had about enough of this sort of threat. Still, Leo was a head taller than me and looked like he could eat me for breakfast and enjoy the burp afterward, so I simply nodded. Leo gave me a last probing stare and went into the water closet himself. The evening was about over, to my relief.

No one was surprised when the train was late the next day. Very late. It was early evening before we pulled into the Tiergarten station and hurried to the office of the Spartacist Bund, where Rosa hoped to forestall Karl Liebknecht from prematurely declaring a revolutionary government. But when we arrived, we were too late. The farce had already occurred.

Liebknecht had decided to go ahead and declare a new government, but word had leaked to the von Baden government and an official named Philipp Schneidemann stole his thunder by throwing open a Reichstag window and declaring a coalition government to replace von Baden's. Not to be outdone, Liebknecht stepped onto a balcony of Frederick the Great's palace and declared his own new government. It was a comic opera without the singing. Rosa obviously found no humor in any of it.

"What were you thinking, Karl?" she demanded after we had run Liebknecht to ground.

We were in the office of the Spartacist Bund, which was a rundown one-room apartment above a tailor shop. It was almost eleven and I was dead tired. Liebknecht proved to be a prim, scholarly looking fellow with long hair, an unkempt mustache, and a pince-nez that made him look a little like Trotsky, which was probably intentional. He did not look happy being subjected to Rosa's grilling.

"You've been away, Rosa. You don't know what is happening here."

"Oh and you've been out of prison, what, two weeks? Enlighten me, Karl. What is happening that led you to declare a government when we have no army, no money, and lack the support of more than a handful of followers?"

Liebknecht sighed deeply.

"We must stay ahead of events, Rosa, and that is difficult. Things are moving so quickly. The labor councils are pushing to overthrow von Baden's government, but the strongest force in Berlin is the Freikorps. The dregs of the gutter form its backbone, but every day more soldiers leave the army and join it. They grow more organized, too. In Berlin, that bastard Waldemar Pabst is now in charge of the Freikorps and they are beginning to act with some logic, something more than random mob violence. They are a dangerous threat, Rosa."

I'd heard of the Free Corps, the random bands of deserters from the German army who had formed together into angry, hardheaded bands of brawlers. If they were being better organized and given a mission, they would be very bad news.

"If we are to be taken seriously in this madness, we must seize the initiative. I convinced the metalworkers' council—"

"Barth, you mean."

"Yes, Rosa. Barth. We need him. He agreed the council will support us if the Spartacists seize the government. So I had to declare. He had to know we are serious."

"And Schneidemann declares on the same day? That is not serious, Karl, that is ridiculous. We look like fools."

Well, it was pretty obvious who ruled this roost. Liebknecht grumbled and pulled at his mustache, but he didn't stand up to Rosa. I felt she was being a little hard on him, since it was true we hadn't been in Berlin until that night, but for two rival politicians to fling open windows on the same day, each to declare a government he didn't have the power to establish, was pretty funny, I had to admit.

Rosa was relentless. "So what is the plan, Karl? What happens tomorrow?"

"We meet with representatives of the labor councils. We plan the new government administration."

"Wonderful. And the Freikorps sweeps us all into prisons as soon as the German army returns." Rosa finally softened for her old comrade. "It's all right, Karl. You are the hope of the revolution. We will do our best."

I went to bed that night with no idea what was coming. At first, I didn't even know where to lie down, but it was made clear by all, including Jogiches, that I was sleeping with Rosa. We didn't make love, though. Aside from a lack of privacy, Rosa was too consumed with the moment. This was her time, what she had worked for since her youth in Poland: an honest-to-God (well, not God) revolution, with her at the center of the whirlwind. Marx help us.

I have never been so flat-out busy as I was during the next six weeks. Revolution is hard work. The next day's meeting with the metalworkers' council, a surly bunch led by the obnoxious and unrealistic Emil Barth, was just the start. We met almost daily with one labor council or another, sometimes with representatives of all of them at once. We passed out leaflets, led discussion groups, Rosa and Liebknecht gave speeches. There were constant crises, with sailors rebelling, Freikorps oppressing, starving townspeople crying for bread. Always Rosa and I were in the middle of it, arguing, marching, inspiring. At least, Rosa did all that and I gave her the support she needed, including the occasional roll in the hay when we could find a moment.

Most demanding, perhaps, was the constant need to provide content for *The Red Flag*, the revolutionary daily journal that Liebknecht had re-established and for which Rosa was principal writer. Every day, all day, she would put out fire after fire, wheedling, debating, proclaiming. Every night, she would work to exhaustion hammering out the next day's piece for *The Red Flag* on her Underwood typewriter. Finally I could stand it no more.

"Rosa, you must rest," I insisted.

Only Rosa, Jogiches, and I were in *The Red Flag*'s office that December night. She was obviously exhausted, nodding off over her typewriter with a cigarette hanging from her mouth.

"Rosa, listen to me. You will be in no shape to eat breakfast, let alone lead a revolution, if you are too tired even to open your eyes. Come, go to bed. I will write the article."

And so it was. While Rosa slept, I banged out a stirring, rabble-rousing piece that Emil Barth would love. It ran in the next *Red Flag* under Rosa's byline. Even Leo approved: he nodded at me with a smile on his face after reading my work. I knew that he especially appreciated that I took care of Rosa. From that night on, we had that in common.

My stock rose with the Spartacists. I must have written half the content of *The Red Flag* over the next two weeks, with Rosa writing the rest. Then, at one of our endless street-corner rallies, Rosa suddenly gestured for me to step up to the podium. She introduced me as an American devoted to the cause, who had been raised on Marx and Engels and came to Germany to throw himself into the revolutionary struggle. Puffed up by this introduction, I made quite a speech, if I say so myself. I cursed the bourgeoisie, damned the military, said a good word for Rosa and for Liebknecht and generally cut quite a swath. For a finish, I swore that America was only waiting for Germany's example to pitch Wilson into a river and establish the rule of the proletariat. That was perhaps an exaggeration, but it all went over tremendously and I was the hero of the day.

The events leading up to the Spartacist Revolution were devilishly complicated and, nowadays, no one much cares anyway. After Germany's surrender, two governments ruled Berlin, each claiming primacy. One was the successor to von Baden's official government, the one proclaimed by Schneidemann, now a coalition group led by Friedrich Ebert of the Socialist Party. The other was the People's Council of Deputies, consisting of representatives of the labor councils including Emil Barth. Amusingly, Ebert was a member of that government, too. He was more flexible than Liebknecht, who refused to participate in the People's Council because it let Ebert in. Rosa knew it was all a great mess, but worked patiently, day after day, to reason with the Left and advance the agenda of the Spartacists over the right-wingers and Ebert's milk-and-water socialists.

The next major event of relevance occurred at Christmas. It was a cold winter, not good for the downtrodden poor who filled Berlin's streets. Among those poor were veterans of the Kaiser's armed forces, whom the government had dropped like bricks and who had no food, wages, or jobs. For some reason, the sailors were always the most aggressive. Just before Christmas, an angry group of sailors who hadn't been paid for their service took over the old Imperial Palace in protest. Rosa was certain these sailors would join the Spartacist movement when the time came for true revolt, armed or not. Two days before Christmas, she wrote in *The Red Flag* that revolt against the Ebert coalition government was inevitable, but it shouldn't start until a clear majority of the people joined it. After the paper hit the streets that day, we Spartacists marched down to the palace where the sailors were holed up. Army troops surrounded the building. We stood outside the line, cheering the sailors. I looked up to the second floor where sailors were looking out of the windows and waving to us. I blinked hard. I couldn't believe what I was seeing. One of those sailors looked just like Riley.

32

Bloody Christmas

Riley

It was me, all right. Here's what happened.

Slipping out of the hospital was not a problem. I took my pistol and some ammo, plus what money I had left. My first challenge was to get some civilian clothes to replace the hospital garb I was wearing. I still had most of my poker winnings, so I went to a Frenchman's house and bought two suits of clothes from him. The poor fellow's little house was pocked with bulletholes and his family looked like they hadn't eaten in a week, so the money I paid him was welcome.

The fact was, northern France was a wreck. The Great War took place in that country more than anywhere else, for four hellish years, and the people paid a terrible price. Farm fields were burned or blown to hell or just trampled on. Towns were brought to rubble. People starved and stole. Some of the soldiers, released from service and impoverished, roamed the countryside in little bands, preying on whoever passed by. If Clemenceau was full of fury when he insisted on a harsh peace at Versailles, he had cause.

I started walking. Miles of walking, through blackened country, deep snow, passing folks who looked like ghosts. The hospital was in the dense and almost black Argonne Forest, where so many Americans had died. I walked east, figuring I'd hit Germany sooner or later. I remember one fellow, still in his French uniform, who I passed on an open road in flat country. I must have seen him from two miles away and I watched him the whole time we approached each other. It was cold, gray. I noticed increasing details about him as he got closer. He was a corporal. He had about four days' growth of black beard. He was missing his right arm, from the elbow, and his sleeve was sewn shut. He was skinny and he stumbled a little with each step, like he was dragging his feet instead of picking them up. His eyes were foggy and looked right through me. He didn't react to me at all and I didn't acknowledge him. He looked about nineteen years old.

I never knew the names of the villages I passed through. In one, a woman sat smoking on the ruins of her house. The ruins were smoking too. She called to me, asking if I wanted to sleep with her. When I shook my head and kept walking, she offered her daughter. I tossed her a cigarette and kept walking.

Everywhere, I approached the people who didn't look utterly desperate and destitute to ask about trains. I knew that one French word, *train*. At first, people looked at me strangely, like I must be feeble-minded to be asking for something as normal as a train in the midst of such desolation. Eventually, I found a shopkeeper who spoke a little English. He said that with a bit more walking I would come to Nancy, a large town, and from there I might be able to hitch a ride to Strasbourg, which was still in Germany though not for long. A train ran from Strasbourg to Berlin, mostly serving the Allied soldiers who were now stationed in Berlin and other parts of Germany. I didn't much like the idea of sharing a train car with any American soldiers, lest they become too curious about me, but I had no other options. I walked to Nancy and, after much inquiry, found a fat Alsatian wine salesman who would drive me to Strasbourg. After the ruin I had seen, I was astonished that such commercial activity still existed in Alsace, but mankind will always find a way.

The salesman's English was poor and he babbled in French to me all the way from Nancy to Strasbourg. I alternated between nodding like I understood, shrugging like I was angry, and simply ignoring him. He did give me a bottle of wine when we pulled to a stop at the railway station in Strasbourg and he said goodbye.

Strasbourg had been ravaged and almost destroyed back in the German–French war in 1870, but it held up pretty well in the Great

War. In fact, I saw no signs of damage and didn't even know that there had been a dust-up in the city after the Armistice in November, when a labor group tried unsuccessfully to establish a revolutionary soviet council to rule the town, as was done in Munich. I just saw a peaceful, pretty city, the little bit I could see from the steps of the train station. Trying to read the train schedule posted on the station wall, which was in German, I noticed it was only two days before Christmas. I wondered what the babies back home would be getting for presents.

As I tried to decipher the tiny entries on the schedule, the stationmaster came plodding by. I wished Cornelius was with me, as I didn't speak German any more than I spoke French. Spanish is the only foreign language I've ever managed to learn, even now, and that's because I grew up speaking it with the migrants. I stopped the stationmaster, a heavyset man whose uniform cap sat high up on his bald head like someone had tossed it from across the room and made a ringer. By saying "Berlin" over and over, accompanied by grunts and gestures, I was able to figure out that there was a train for Berlin that was supposed to be leaving in ten minutes, but it was always late and no doubt would be late again today. I bought a ticket from him and sat on a hard bench to wait.

Other than the shabby French farmer clothes I was wearing, all my worldly possessions were in a small cloth bag at my feet. They included one spare change of clothes, the little amount of remaining money in my money bag, which had been nearly emptied buying food as I trekked across Alsace, and a Luger I had taken from a dead German at Cantigny, with a couple boxes of ammunition. Although more money would have been welcome, all in all I felt I was pretty well fixed.

There was a big round clock in front of me, as you often find in railway stations. A cold wind blew through the station, making me shiver in the light jacket the French farmer had sold me. The time for the Berlin train came and went with no sign of it. I wondered what in the hell I was doing. I was AWOL, on the run into what was recently an enemy country, when I should be doing everything I could to get back to Marta and our little daughter I still hadn't seen. I remembered writing to Marta how I couldn't stand to be away from her and would be back as soon as I could. I was a liar. When I heard about Cornelius in Berlin, something just snapped in me, I don't know what. I couldn't go back without him.

I pulled a letter from Marta out of my pocket. It had caught up with me in the hospital. She had just learned of my mustard gas sickness when she wrote it and she was full of concern. There was much news of our little daughter, Fern Arlys Riley. Ma had never liked her name and told Marta she was crazy to stick her daughter with it, but Marta insisted. I left the name issue up to Marta, what with Fern being a girl and all, but Cornelius picked his boy's name: Walter Hal. The Hal, he said, was after some prince in a Shakespeare play. The Walter was after me. Seemed funny, since Cornelius hated the name Walter and always called me Riley, but that's how it was. Marta loved the baby boy and talked in her letter about how the two children were inseparable, took baths together and everything.

Marta included a poem about Fern:

> Behold this child
> With raven eyes
> And brow so mild.
> Behold this child
> Whose radiant smile
> Reveals no guile.
> Behold this child
> With raven eyes.

I thought it was just beautiful. It made me cry, sitting on that hard bench in the Strasbourg train station, even though I had read it a thousand times before. Marta had a gift. It hurts me to hear Cornelius make fun of her poems.

The end of her letter was the worst. Walter Hal's mother, Fay, was gone. She'd gone to high school with us and Cornelius had gotten her pregnant just before we left for the war. She was a nice girl, not real smart. Ma and Marta tried to take care of her and the baby there at the farm and I know they were kind as could be. But Marta said Fay was troubled and flighty and never really bonded with the baby like mothers do. Anyway, one day when Hal was a month or so old, Fay just up and left. No note, no nothing. She knew the baby would be cared for, and of course he was. Marta knew that Cornelius had been captured and probably killed, so she figured Walter Hal was our baby now. But I felt that if Cornelius was alive, I had to bring him back to his son.

I had just finished reading the letter again when a bunch of laughing, cocky men came into the station. They were American soldiers in uniform and they gathered in a little group not ten feet away from me. I decided I'd better be some kind of Spaniard, a ruse I've used many times in my life since then. I didn't need to worry, for the Americans were focused on their assignment in Berlin and the chances they'd go home soon, so they paid me little attention. One fellow asked if the Berlin train was expected soon. I responded with a string of Spanish and he lost all interest in me, the way Americans do with someone who doesn't speak English.

The train finally pulled into the station two hours late. Few people got off, as there wasn't a lot of reason to go to Strasbourg at that point in history and no one had the money for train tickets. I chose a car as far from the Americans as I could and sank into a window seat. As we rattled through the German countryside, the contrast with France and Alsace was startling. The actual fighting hadn't touched Germany. In contrast to what I saw in the Argonne and in Alsace, German farmland was intact and German cities still functioned. I saw no shell craters, no bombed-out buildings, no beggars in the street, although the German economy was in shambles and unemployment was rampant. The German generals made sure to surrender before the war encroached significantly on German territory, with consequences darker and more terrible than could have been imagined at the time.

We pulled into Berlin the afternoon of December 23, 1918. Even in this immense and important city, there were few travelers in the train station. The shadow of the war still pervaded and so did the menace of an uncertain political situation, with a socialist coalition government and revolutionary labor councils and communist ideologues who called themselves Spartacists after the slave who challenged the Roman Empire. If Cornelius was really alive, what kind of mess had he gotten himself into?

I didn't have the least idea where to go next. I walked out of the train station and heard strange noises, like animals growling and howling. It turns out the Berlin Zoo is right in the middle of town, next to the train station and at the west end of the Tiergarten, the massive city park that I hear was the model for New York's Central

Park. I walked the streets, looking for a cheap rooming house. The cold pierced me to the bone, so I sought shelter in a bar even though it wasn't yet three o'clock in the afternoon. There were naked women dancing on a stage at the end of the narrow, smoky confines of the establishment. Berlin has been like this forever, and still is, based on my last visit. I sat at the bar and ordered a whiskey with my dwindling funds. What they brought me wasn't bourbon, but I made it do.

Down the bar from me were four or five German swabbies. They weren't in uniform and I'm not sure how I knew they were navy, I just did. If you've been in the military, even for a short time, you get a sense for such things. For one thing, I couldn't understand what they were saying, but I knew it was foul-mouthed. Nobody swears like a swabbie.

The swabbies had obviously been there awhile and were well-oiled. They shouted to the dancers on the stage. They drank, quickly and deeply. One of them staggered over to me, put his arm around my shoulders and said something in German into my face, breathing a dangerous concentration of alcoholic fumes. Deciding there was no harm in being American with him, I said in English that I didn't understand what he was saying. He seemed delighted to learn I was an American and called over one of his buddies, who spoke English pretty well.

"You are American?" he asked.

He was a little guy, like me, and tough-looking. He didn't seem as drunk as the rest.

When I acknowledged my nationality, he laughed and toasted me.

"We love Americans. We fought French and English for four years and we hate them, but you Americans are okay. We are friends now, so let's drink to that."

We raised our glasses in salute and drank.

The sharp-eyed, tough-looking little sailor wasn't done with me.

"Why are you here in Berlin?" he wanted to know.

"I came to see a friend," I said.

The sailor laughed and twisted around to spew some German at his friends. I think he was telling them I had come to Berlin for a woman. I asked him why he was in Berlin. His eyes narrowed and his voice grew soft.

"Surely even you have heard of the sailors' revolt?"

I shrugged and shook my head.

"Just before the war ended, our asshole admirals ordered a naval assault that would have slaughtered hundreds of good men for no purpose. The sons of bitches. But the sailors revolted and wouldn't carry out the orders! Since then, navy men have been the toughest fighters for justice in this crazy country of ours. Sailors are revolting everywhere in Germany. We came to Berlin to join the cause."

This sounded promising, like the sort of movement Cornelius would be involved in. I took a swig of whiskey while I considered my next move.

"My friend," I said. "We have much in common. I am a deserter from my country's military. I have heard about the labor councils here and I think they are the hope of the world. I came to join them. Can you help me?"

The little sailor looked at me dubiously.

"You came just for that, American? What do you offer that would make us want you to fight for the cause?"

Fortunately, I had moved my Luger from my bag to my belt, anticipating that Berlin might prove a lively city. I nodded toward the stage, where a nearly naked girl was holding up a bottle of schnapps in her outstretched hand and singing loudly, to the delight of the crowd. The sailor acknowledged that he saw the bottle. I drew my handgun as fast and smoothly as I could and got off a shot that broke the bottle and spilled schnapps all over the stage. The hall got very quiet.

The little sailor held out his hand.

"My name is Berger. Come with me."

Where he brought me was not where I hoped to go. After a brief parley with his friends, who obviously saw him as their leader, the little sailor led us out of the bar and through the streets until we eventually came upon a large institutional building of imposing size and gravity. Steep concrete steps led to massive doors. Great pillars surrounded the front wall. Berger told me it was the former Imperial Palace, now the headquarters of the German navy. Stationed at the front of the Palace was a squad of German soldiers, looking nervous.

"Now you will see something," said my friend, who seemed to be getting drunker as we walked along the streets.

No one tried to stop us or question us as he led us to a nondescript door at street level below the steps. He knocked. In a few moments, the door opened and a sailor appeared. He embraced our little leader and we entered. We walked down a long bureaucratic hallway, up a narrow set of stairs, and into a great room on the second floor occupied by revolutionary sailors who had seized it to protest the fact that they hadn't been paid their wages. Men, most but not all of them in naval uniform, sprawled around the floor or paced around the perimeter smoking cigarettes. Some stared grimly out the windows at the soldiers; those men were armed. I was fed up and grabbed the little sailor by the shoulder, spinning him around to face me.

"What's going on?" I demanded. "Where are we and what is this?"

He shrugged in a European sort of way.

"We are what remains of the German navy. We have taken the palace and if we don't achieve our demands we will take Berlin." Then he smiled and clapped my arm. "You said you wanted to join the revolution. Here you are."

There I was. A large band of naval deserters, outraged at not receiving their back pay, had taken over the palace. They seemed to have no plan for any next steps. They must have thought that either the government would quickly agree to their demands or the Spartacists and other revolutionary groups would flock to their aid. Or perhaps they didn't think at all. I expect that's the more likely option, but because I didn't speak German, what did I know?

I came clean to some extent with Berger. I told him I was looking for an American friend who was a communist and in Berlin. I told him everything I knew, which was just that Cornelius had been seen on a podium with a woman, both of them speaking for the Marxist cause. Berger just nodded, stone-faced, and walked away from me. I was left surrounded by sailors I couldn't speak with other than to say "Cornelius?" and be met with blank stares. I stood at a window and watched the crowd. That must be when Cornelius saw me, as he said in the notebook. I didn't notice him, there being a lot of people watching in curiosity as the sailors and soldiers stared at each other. As darkness came, I curled up in a corner and tried to sleep. I hoped to slip out the next morning and look for Cornelius.

But the next morning, all hell broke loose. I was awakened at dawn by excited shouting from the windows. I looked out and saw a much larger contingent of soldiers hustling into formation, creating long ranks of heavily-armed men that extended along the entire front of the palace. Worse, artillery troops were rolling heavy guns into position and pointing them right at us. The atmosphere on both sides changed quickly—there was going to be a fight, a hard one.

A man whom I gathered commanded the sailors marched through the room, disposing the forces. I later learned that this man's name was Dorrenbach. Under his direction, a group of his men ran to a balcony and set up a line of machine guns, each with a gunner at the trigger and another man to feed him the cartridge belts. Men with rifles lined the windows, ready to fire down at the soldiers. Suddenly, Berger appeared, a revolver in each hand, and he gestured for me to follow him. I didn't think I could slip out with the building surrounded and everyone hyper-alert, and I would probably be shot at by both sides if I tried, so I decided to stick with the sailors and followed Berger, gun drawn. We went back down the stairs and down the hallway through which we had entered the day before, up to the small pedestrian door. Before we got to the door, the hallway narrowed, creating small niches in which a man could hide from anyone who came through the door. Berger hugged the wall on the left niche and motioned for me to do the same on the right.

"This is our one job, assigned by Comrade Dorrenbach," Berger said. "Soldiers may try to come at us through this little back door. If they do, my friend, we are to kill them."

This was a little more than I had planned on. I didn't give a damn about any German revolution, I just wanted to get my friend back to his son where he belonged. But if I had to kill a few more Germans to do it, well, nothing I had seen up to that point in my young life had given me much reason to be fond of those folks. As with so much I have done, I seemed to have fallen into this job and it was just the next thing I had to do in order to keep on going.

I noticed that Berger would be able to flatten himself against the wall of his niche and reach his right arm around the corner to shoot, leaving his body protected. On my side, if I reached my right arm around the corner to shoot, I would be exposed.

"I don't suppose you want to change sides?" I called over. "I'm right-handed."

Berger just laughed and pulled a flask from his pocket. He was still a little drunk.

"Ah, but I am right-handed, too. And you are an American and I a German. I think we stay where we are."

He drank and threw me the flask. Schnapps is vile, but welcome at some moments in life. Inspired by our exchange, Berger explained to me that castle towers in Europe were built so their staircases spiral down counter-clockwise, meaning that right-handed swordsmen could hug the wall as they dueled with attackers from below. Interesting, I suppose.

Sporadic cracks of rifles sounded from the front of the palace. We couldn't tell which side initiated them, but it sounded like both sides fired. Then more silence.

"What's the end game here, Berger? What do the sailors want?"

Berger drank more schnapps and thought about my question.

"All men are different. Some want to get their pay and go home. Some want to keep fighting the war. Some want a people's government, throwing out the old aristocracy. I think if you had to say one thing, it would be that Germans want their lives back. They want to start over, before the war, without the politics, just be left alone. You know, I don't really give a shit who runs Germany. I just want my life back."

I tossed him a cigarette and he gave me another pull at the flask.

"You're a good fellow, American. I'll tell you what you want to know, but you have to promise you'll stay, you'll help me fight. I'm scared, you know."

I promised.

He smiled.

"It's easy. I only didn't tell you last night so you would stay and fight. The woman who you described, who gives speeches on Marxist doctrine, can only be Rosa Luxemburg, the one they call Red Rosa. She leads the Spartacists and writes for their newspaper, *The Red Flag*. Everyone in Berlin knows her. Just ask anyone, they'll tell you where to find Red Rosa. I think if you find her, you'll find your friend."

I chewed on this a moment. Figures that Cornelius would be with a woman. I wished he could have stayed with Fay. It would be just like him to take up with some communist firebrand when he needed to come home to his son.

An enormous, almost simultaneous series of artillery blasts

overwhelmed us. Ebert had pulled the trigger on his firepower and ordered his troops to blow the palace to kingdom come. The sailors responded gamely, mowing down the troops with coordinated machine gun fire. After the first blast, the soldiers charged and were quickly turned away by the machine guns. It was a fast, bloody exchange that left a dozen or more dead on each side.

We could only guess at this in our little basement corridor. I began to fear that soldiers would come, not through the door we were defending, but from down the hallway behind us. Then we would be truly fucked. From the noise, I guessed there was hand-to-hand fighting taking place. There's a certain noise a man makes when he is skewered on a bayonet that isn't quite like anything else. I didn't remember any of our sailors having bayonets.

Berger was sweating.

"What do you think?"

"Hard to say. Lot of fighting up there. Can't tell what's happening."

Berger nodded, sweating more.

"Fuck this," he said finally. "I need to see what's happening."

"Berger, don't! Stay where you are."

But Berger wasn't listening. It's always the way in a fight: acting out of fear gets somebody killed. It happened to Sid Crew, when it was me who was scared and it should have been me who was killed. This time, it was Berger. For no good reason, he crept up to the door, opened it, and stuck his head outside. I could have written the script. There was a volley of gunfire and Berger fell through the doorway, dead on the spot, jamming the door open. Damn.

I felt released from my promise and from everything except getting out of that building alive. I pounded back up the hallway and up the stairs, bullets flying at me from behind as Berger's killers poured through the open door. In the great room at the top of the stairs, the battle was in full swing. Sailors poured volleys out the windows. The room was dense with acrid powder smoke, cutting visibility to near zero. I took an exit to the right, followed by shouts but no guns fired at me. It seemed like I ran a mile down a fancy imperial corridor, flanked on both sides by paintings of dour-looking German emperors. I flat-out ran, fast as I could, with no thought but to find a way out. Finally, I reached the end of the endless hall, but there was no window, no door to the outside. I kicked open a locked door into some sort of office, maybe for navy clerks since the palace was being used for a naval office before the sailors took it over. I broke a window and looked out. The battle was joined hot and heavy to my left, but I thought I might just slip away unnoticed. I opened the sash and straddled the window, then dropped down one flight onto the pavement below.

But I didn't go unnoticed. As I hit the ground, a volley of gunfire speckled the palace wall behind me. I was able to hold onto my pistol. I rolled and returned fire from a prone position. I picked off one, two, three German soldiers. Then there was another blast from Ebert's artillery. There is always a moment, after a blast like that, when men are frozen in confusion. I took that moment to run, disappearing down an alley with no one in pursuit.

So far, I didn't care much for Berlin.

Once I caught my breath, I started asking passersby where I could find Rosa Luxemburg and the Spartacists.

33

Cornelius Visits the Zoo

Cornelius

Bloody Christmas, we called it. My phrase, actually, as Rosa wanted to call it Ebert's Massacre. She agreed my phrase had more punch, although she didn't like the religious overtone. It would have been more accurate to say Bloody Christmas Eve, but that definitely would not have had the same zip.

Christmas Eve morning, I awoke naked in bed with Rosa. After abstaining for days from sheer exhaustion, Rosa had thrown Leo and the others out of the room, stripped down to nothing and pushed me onto the bed. I like a woman who knows what she wants. We made love all night. I awoke the next morning with Red Rosa draped over my chest, my hand cupped on her bare behind. There is something soothing about lying quietly in bed with your hand cupping your lover's bottom. I recommend it.

I looked into Rosa's face until she opened her eyes and smiled at me.

"Hello, American boy."

"Hello, Red Rosa. You look beautiful this morning."

Drowsily, she pushed her hair away from her face.

"You are a liar, American. But I love you and I love your lies. What time is it?"

"Late, by your standards. Leo must be fuming."

"Oh, Leo can stuff himself. I am playing with my little American and I won't be rushed. Are you jealous of Leo? You know he was my lover?"

Seems to me like she didn't need to have mentioned that.

"I know. Long ago?"

"Yes, long ago. I met Leo in Poland and fell in love with him on sight. You should have seen him then: so tall, so strong, so passionate in his fight for the people. We were in bed an hour after we met. I was married to a good man, a truly good man, but Leo was my love." She nibbled my neck. "Does that bother you?"

It did, actually, but I answered her question with a question.

"What happened?"

She shrugged.

"Time. We fought so long together, the fighting began to outweigh our love. We still have the same cause. He would die for me and I for him. It is enough. And now I have my beautiful American boy who is going to pleasure me all over again…"

And she rolled her leg over me as her hand prodded me to action. Which was nice until Leo came bursting into the room.

"Out, out, hussy!" he shouted. "Ebert is making his move! The sailors are being slaughtered!"

Rosa sprang to action, no thought for her nakedness. We both threw on our clothes as Leo filled us in. At dawn, Ebert had ordered a combination of Freikorps and regular army to charge the palace. The sailors were fighting bravely and were holding their own. As far as Leo could tell, the fight was still raging. We had to get there to see for ourselves.

We raced through crowded streets, as word of the battle had gotten out and all sorts of people wanted to watch for all sorts of reasons. Street-corner bullies shoved against office workers and beggars, all anxious for the show. As always, Rosa was recognized and drew cheers from supporters and cries of "Jew" and "whore" from right-wingers. While Leo crunched the occasional skull as we passed by, Rosa looked straight ahead, elbowing her way through the throngs with a fiery determination. We heard sporadic gunfire as we approached the palace, but no artillery. When we pushed to the front of the crowd and saw the battlefield, we realized the fighting was over. The ones cheering were the sailors.

We learned that Ebert's forces had been repulsed, though it was a near thing. Corpses from both sides lay on the ground under a cold December sun. Through the smoke of battle, we could see sailors in the windows and on the balconies, pumping fists, cheering, mocking the soldiers who were re-grouping in front of the palace. One look at those soldiers and I knew the battle was over for the day. Clearly, they could have mounted another charge, but their heads were downcast, they weren't smiling, and they were shuffling aimlessly. They were beaten.

Rosa and I exchanged glances. We knew this was the moment. If we could put the spirit of the sailors into words and spread those words to every worker in Berlin, we would win. I knew it, Rosa knew it. This was the time. Leo barged forward, eager to speak to the sailors, but Rosa shouted him down.

"Where are you going, you oaf? You will get yourself killed! Come, get me to my typewriter. That work is more important than anything we can do here!"

So back we went, Leo again leading the way. Soon, we were back in the office, Rosa was typing away, and I was shouting encouragement and phrases like "Bloody Christmas." Liebknecht came in to say that the People's Council wanted to meet with us. Rosa shrugged him off until her article was finished. She ripped it from the typewriter and gave it to the printer's boy, ordering that it be run off in a tear sheet that could be distributed throughout the city. Then and only then did she allow Liebknecht to lead us to the People's Council.

The council was in a state of pandemonium. Everyone in the German capital seemed to sense that things were coming rapidly to a head and that the swirling conflicts and crises would soon erupt in a history-defining battle. Although in fact the winner would not be known for many years, and then he would wear a swastika, at the time we were all convinced that our moment was at hand. At a long table in the front of the labor hall, every person was screaming at someone else or at no one. I saw Barth standing at one end, spittle flying, practically gibbering in his effort to command attention. Fists waved in the air, oaths were shouted out. Faced with all this heat, I felt Rosa turn to ice.

She stepped to the table, flanked by Leo and me. Leo pulled out a chair and turned it sideways, dumping its occupant on the floor. Rosa stepped up onto the chair and Leo pounded the table incessantly until the noise subsided.

Rosa let her eyes slowly circle the room, a mischievous smile on her lips. Finally, she spoke.

"You seem excited, comrades. You shout, you curse, you go on like old women. Is it the sailors who have you so excited? Yes, it is the sailors. They stood up to Ebert and made Ebert show his true colors! He has shown the world that he is no socialist, no friend of the workers. He is no different than Ludendorff or Kaiser Willie or any other ruler of this country! It is time to be rid of them all!"

Bloodthirsty cheers, Barth bellowing out the loudest of them all. But Rosa held up her hands, palms out.

"Calm yourselves, comrades. Now is our time, but we must be clever. If we are clever, if we go slowly and carefully, we cannot fail. It is the time of the proletariat and we must prevail."

Barth stood up.

"Slowly? Carefully? This is no time to go slowly and carefully, comrade. Now is the time to pounce!"

Rosa waited for the rumble to subside. Her smile, that killer smile, slowly spread across her face.

"You wish to pounce, Comrade Barth? I remember when you pounced on that barmaid you thought was so taken with you. She rejected your pounce, did she not?"

The crowd howled. Barth was known for his awkward and unsuccessful advances on female comrades.

"We will pounce, comrade, but only when we are ready. We will pounce when the people are behind us and the labor councils are behind us and the sailors are behind us. We will pounce when we will win and that day is soon, Comrade Barth. Who will be with us?"

The room cheered madly, of course. No one could resist Rosa. Even Barth knew better than to try. He skulked back to his chair and sat quietly, staring daggers at her. The hall was Rosa's to command.

"Here is what we must do, comrades."

Rosa looked around the room and took a deep breath. I sensed she had made a decision on the spot.

"We will call a congress of all true defenders of the proletariat: the workers, the labor council, the sailors. Even the socialists, those who want to join us. We will organize into a great party, a party worthy of joining hands with our Russian comrades and fellow workers all over the world! We will form the Communist Party of Germany, an inspiration to followers of Marx in every nation. Inspired by our comrades from the German navy, we will seize the moment by creating the party that will trigger the worldwide revolution!"

They absolutely adored her. Rosa stood transfixed, waving her fists in the air, willing the crowd to feel her passion. There was no question whatsoever that the first Congress of the Communist Party of Germany was going to happen and happen soon. And of course, with their energies poured into organizing such a congress, the labor council wasn't going to be starting up the half-baked revolution that Rosa feared. Clever lady.

We spent perhaps two more hours with the council, agreeing on the tasks necessary to organize the congress. Rosa was a wonder, meeting all objections, answering all questions. She made us believe. In the end, we had a plan. Leo and Barth would approach the sailors on the next day, Christmas—Leo because he would relate well to the sailors, Barth because he was a prick who would withdraw all support if he didn't play a major role. Liebknecht, meanwhile, would try to stall Ebert from ordering any further attacks on the sailors in the palace. Rosa and I would pump out articles for *The Red Flag* and speak at every street corner we could command. Members of the labor council agreed to arrange the hall for the congress. It was a good plan, on paper.

Rosa and I felt well satisfied when we made our way back to headquarters. Waiting for us there was Riley.

I was astonished and delighted to see him. We hugged, which I can tell you was not a custom of ours. Rosa was mystified and suspicious, but melted when I told her that Riley was my best and oldest friend. Slowly, I teased from Riley his story: mustard gas, an escape from a hospital, a long trudge across Alsace, the battle of Bloody Christmas. It was good to see him. I translated everything to Rosa, who found it amazing.

"Tell your friend he is my friend, too."

She walked up to Riley and kissed him on the cheek. Rosa had a way about her, even with a tough guy like Riley.

Late that night, Riley and I were alone in the room I shared with Rosa. Rosa had moved out her things without a word from me, not to hide our relationship but to give Riley and me time alone. Besides, she might have felt so caught up with the cause that she needed a rest from our love-making. It was all right with me. Rosa was a demanding lover and a rest would do me good as well.

"You haven't asked about Fay or the baby," Riley said as soon as we were alone.

Fay was a girl from our high school that unfortunately I'd gotten pregnant just before Riley and I left for the army. I didn't find out about it until we were in France. She'd had a baby boy and I'd told her to name him Walter, after Riley, with a middle name of Hal, after Prince Hal. He would grow into a fine fellow and have children of his own. In fact, he would marry the girl born to Marta and Riley.

"So how are they? What's the news?" I asked.

"They're fine, far as I know from the last letter. Cornelius, I have to tell you, Fay's run off. Nobody knows where she went, no note or nothing. I'm sorry."

Well, this took a moment to digest. To be honest, with all the excitement, I'd almost forgotten about Fay and Hal. Perhaps it's for the best, I thought. A baby would be too much for me right then, maybe ever.

"Hal's fine," Riley continued. "You know Ma and Marta are taking good care of him and three of my sisters are still home, too. He's got Fern to play with and he'll be fine until you get home."

"Until I get home?" I asked tentatively.

"Yes. It's time, Cornelius. The war's over, we've got babies to see. There's nothing here for us. Time to go home."

"You mean she left Hal at the farm? She didn't take him?"

"That's right."

I felt angry, which I think was understandable under the circumstances.

"She just left? And she left her baby? What the hell kind of mother does that?"

"Fay's a troubled girl, Cornelius. Maybe she'll change her mind and come back, but from what Marta says, I'm afraid it doesn't sound likely."

I pounded the bed with my fist.

"Dammit! She can't just run off. She's got responsibilities! She's a mother!"

"Cornelius, we've got responsibilities too. Our responsibility now is to get home."

Something steely in Riley's voice told me not to argue with him. Besides, I truly didn't know what I was going to do. So I got Riley talking about what had happened since Paris and I brought him current on my own adventures. He was the first human being that I told of von Kleist's meeting with me in Berlin and my assignment to spy on Rosa. I was more determined than ever not to do any such thing, of course, and since no one had bothered me from that quarter since leaving prison, I felt it was a resolved issue.

I decided to tell Riley about my relationship with Rosa. He'd have found out soon enough, anyway. He looked a little sour, but didn't comment. Riley looked a little sour most of the time, of course.

I was pleased that first thing the next morning, Leo told us that the date of the congress was set for December 31, just a few days away, because we didn't want to lose the momentum of Bloody Christmas. This gave me a natural way to explain to Riley that I couldn't really leave for home with the congress taking place so soon. That made him more sour, but he didn't balk at it. Who knew what might happen in the meanwhile?

As you can imagine, with the congress to be organized on such short notice, there was an immense amount of work to do. Rosa and I were writing and speaking. Leo and Liebknecht were meeting with the sailors, the labor councils, and other sympathetic groups. The sailors, by the way, were a no-go. They just wanted to get paid, not to be communists, which made Ebert a double idiot for attacking them. After a few days, they walked out of the palace on their own, believing they had made their point. I don't know if they ever got paid.

I dispatched Riley with some of the lesser comrades to put up posters all over town, announcing the congress. I explained to him the risk of the Freikorps to anyone caught posting communist literature in Berlin. I figured that if anyone could handle an encounter with the

Freikorps, it would be Riley. I believe he ended up knocking some of them around, but I was too busy to keep up.

The days passed quickly. I grew accustomed to leading impromptu rallies in the streets, damning the government, and promising *braunschweiger* in every pot. By now, Leo was my fan and he led the cheering like a champion while intimidating any right-wingers who happened to pass by. Rosa and I only managed one bout in bed that whole week, but the work on the outside was really quite satisfying. Looking back, I might have had a long and successful career rousing rabble.

I woke on the morning of the congress, eager for the event. I had not been assigned a speaking role, because there was much competition for the podium and Liebknecht feared there might be some anti-American prejudice among certain members of the audience. Leo spoke up for me, I'm pleased to say, but he was voted down. The organizers all had the brains to recognize that Rosa was the star of the show and she was given the prime evening slot. The night before, Rosa had kissed me and said I could sleep late and take the day off, as she needed to be at the congress early to make sure all went well. She wanted me there no later than six in the evening, so I could be sure to see her big moment at the podium.

I took her up on the offer and slept until nearly noon. Not only had Rosa already left for the congress with Leo and Liebknecht, but Riley had gone off with some comrades to post a flurry of last-minute announcements. I was quite alone.

I lay in bed, taking stock of the situation. Here I was, James Cornelius O'Neal from Independence, in Berlin in the bed of my lover, the world's most famous female communist, who was decades older than me. We were on the leading edge of a revolution which I truly felt could change history. Power and control would at long last be given to the working class instead of the old bastards who had always run things and whose moral bankruptcy and incompetence had nearly destroyed the world in the horrific war just concluded. It was great fun. Against that background was the fact that we might be killed at any moment by the forces of reaction, plus I had a baby back home to think about, plus I didn't know how I was going to handle Riley's clear determination to take me home to a life that seemed dreary, flat, and unpromising compared to my current situation. On the whole, though, I was very happy. I was twenty years old, remember.

I finally rolled out of bed and shuffled into the main room, which was filthy and littered with unwashed dishes. Communists were as messy as teenage boys and as preoccupied with thoughts of revolution and sex. As I opened drawers, vainly trying to find some coffee to brew, I noticed out of the corner of my eye a pile of flyers that Riley and the boys had left. I picked one off the top of the pile and looked it over, with a certain pride of authorship since I had written it. The translation would be:

WORKERS OF BERLIN!
BREAK YOUR CHAINS!
NEVER AGAIN WAR!
BE PRESENT FOR HISTORY! MAKE HISTORY!

**Attend the first-ever Congress of the
Communist Party of Germany!
Baby-sitting available.**

I was especially proud of the last touch. Now a parent myself, I figured that we could lose a lot of potential party members if they had nowhere to park their children. Plus, it made us seem more caring, more human.

It seemed a shame to me that we would leave copies of such a well-crafted poster to sit on the kitchen table, so I decided to distribute them myself. I would be violating a major rule of the party, which was that no one should post flyers alone. There was always the danger of violent interference by the Freikorps or just your average right-wing bullies. But I was young and thought I'd live forever, so I dressed and off I went. I thought perhaps I would meet up with Riley's party and could join with them. I left our little quarters, bound for the Kurfürstendamm, where I figured more people would see the posters and where I could stop frequently for coffee and pastry.

Ah, the Kurfürstendamm. While I have plenty of reason to dislike Germany and Germans, some of the most pleasant hours of my life were spent at the sidewalk cafés along the broad Berlin boulevard called the Kurfürstendamm, near the Tiergarten. In my opinion, it beats the pants off the Champs d'Élysée. It is the epitome of a relaxed, amusing, urbane European thoroughfare featuring broad sidewalks, outdoor cafés, intriguing passersby, the works. It never failed to lift my spirits, even in the deadly days of Hitler's Berlin. So I took my time that day, posting a flyer, stopping to chat with a housewife or a waiter, posting another flyer, having a cup of coffee. It was cold for New Year's Eve, but the sun was out and the air was crisp and fresh. Just at that moment, I was having a thoroughly enjoyable revolution.

I did not even become unduly concerned near the train station by the zoo when I was pinning a poster to the station bulletin board and three men in Freikorps uniforms came up behind me. I should have been watching for them: Riley would have been. As I finished affixing my poster to the board and turned around, there they were, not three feet from me. These confrontations usually amounted to a few harsh words and nothing more. Still, I was alone and these fellows did not look pleased.

"Hello, comrades," I said. "Are you interested in coming to the congress?"

The man in the middle, who seemed to be the leader of the three, looked to be a hard-bitten war veteran. I was sure that a few months earlier his Freikorps brown had been an army gray, which was typical of the Freikorps. He actually smiled at me, although it was the smile of the witch in Hansel and Gretel as she led them to the cookie oven.

"I can promise you, Cornelius, we will come to the congress."

This was trouble. He knew my name, even the familiar name by which Riley and Rosa knew me. This was deadly danger, coming at me from nowhere.

They saw in my eyes that I was ready to run, so the two flunkies each seized one of my elbows and held me in place. The leader pulled the remaining posters out of my hand, ripped them in half twice and threw the shreds to the wind.

"Shall we go?" he asked. "I have a friend waiting and he is anxious to see you."

They took me to a suite at the Hotel Eden, not far from where they had picked me up. It was a luxury Berlin hotel, second only to the Adlon in the wealth and prestige of its clientele. Unbeknownst to me until that moment, it was also the center of operations for the Freikorps and its peculiar commander, Waldemar Pabst. He was in the living room of the suite when I was pushed through the door. Pabst was a balding, middle-aged man with a mustache and a slight paunch that pushed against his brown Freikorps uniform. He looked like a bookkeeper who would shortly have to hurry home to his domineering nag of a wife, but it didn't matter, for I only had eyes for the immensely tall figure sprawled languidly in the chair across from Pabst. It was von Kleist.

I cannot say I was surprised: it had already occurred to me that my abductors could only have known to call me Cornelius from von Kleist. As always in the presence of that monster, my innards turned to ice and I could hardly speak for the fear that had me by the throat. He looked like he'd been having a hard time of it since we last met. His cheeks were sunken, there were bags under his eyes that hadn't been there before, and there was a brandy bottle at his side that he appeared to be punishing heavily. But he was still Otto von Kleist and I wanted nothing to do with him. He looked at me while petting a little dachshund that was lying contentedly on his lap.

Von Kleist spoke before Pabst could say a word.

"Cornelius! Now, this is truly delightful. I expect you thought I had forgotten you. Believe me, nothing could be further from the truth."

He wore a Freikorps uniform, his aristocratic bearing oddly out of place in the brown dress of a Bavarian bully. Von Kleist and the Freikorps struck me as a dangerous combination. He turned to speak to the Freikorps commander.

"We have an honored guest, my commander. Cornelius escaped me in Mexico and bested me in Paris, yet here he is, alive and healthy. What shall we do with him?"

Pabst scrunched up his lips as though he'd sucked a lemon. His mediocre intelligence and inferior character were instantly apparent, but post-war Germany was a playground for such specimens.

"I am not interested in your stories of the past, Captain von Kleist," he snarled. "The Freikorps fights for the future, for all the Fatherland. You wanted this communist brought here, so you tell me what to do with him."

Von Kleist smiled lazily and appeared to ponder the question. Slowly, he unfolded his long body from the chair, gently placing the dachshund on the floor near a bowl of water. He stepped over to me, violating my space, placing his face within inches of mine. I could smell his breath, which like his sweat had an acrid metallic odor.

"Cornelius," he said softly, "you have done well. You do not know it, but you have done well. You have gotten close to Rosa, you are her lover. She absolutely trusts you. You are perfectly positioned now to fulfill your destiny."

What do you say to a six-five sadistic maniac who is breathing madness into your face? Generally, I find it best to remain silent.

Von Kleist turned to Pabst, who was nursing a brandy and looking cross.

"You know the plan, Wally. It is what Ludendorff wants and it is brilliant. We made sure the war ended before German soil was violated, so we can quickly rebuild. Ludendorff did that by privately demanding surrender, but publicly demanding that we fight on. All that remains is to hang the blame for the surrender firmly and irrevocably on the Marxist Jews, those who stabbed the heroic German army in the back. The nation is angry, Wally, angry at having bled and died for a lost cause. If they blame the Spartacists and the Jews for the surrender and that fool Ebert takes the blame for the inevitable economic collapse we face for the next decade, then true German blood will take back the nation and Germany will rule the world, as it has always been destined to do. And it is my old friend Cornelius who will see that this happens."

The madman took an envelope from his breast pocket. I saw that it was addressed by a woman's hand, in florid purple writing, to James Cornelius O'Neal. He waved it in my direction.

"This, Cornelius, is your ticket to a place in history. The envelope is sealed, but I am happy to tell you what is inside. It is a heartfelt love letter, to you from your dear Rosa. After some truly passionate language—the strumpet should really be ashamed of herself—it gives the details of the meticulous plot by which Rosa and her Jew friends arranged the surrender of the glorious German army, abetted by the traitor Ebert. And when you repent and bring this letter to the attention of the German people, as you will do before the sun sets at the first Congress of the German Communist Party, then Germany's destiny will be set in stone. Rosa and the Bolsheviks dead, the Freikorps and traditional Germany triumphant."

I stared at the envelope in his hand. Of all the things I could have said at that moment, I said, "But the handwriting isn't anything like Rosa's."

Von Kleist laughed.

"See, Wally, he is on our side already. Don't worry, Cornelius, the masses don't know her handwriting and no one cares anyway. This letter will be all the confirmation that the German people will need to convince them of what they already want to believe. Tomorrow will be a bad day for the Jews in Berlin, I think."

Pabst chuckled and raised his glass in a silent toast.

"Tomorrow?" I asked, startled.

"Yes, Cornelius. Today is your day of glory. We will take advantage of this congress your friends are having and use it to tell the nation how they were stabbed in the back by the Jew communists. Understand, Cornelius, I am not like my friend Wally here. Wally doesn't like Jews. I feel about them just as I feel about all other human beings: they are meant to be my playmates. You remember what I mean by that, don't you, Cornelius?"

I did, by God. My knees were buckling at the memory.

Pabst looked disapprovingly at von Kleist.

"You should learn to watch what you say, Captain von Kleist. Germany will not always be ruled by socialists. You are a captain of the Freikorps and you do not want to sound like a friend of the kikes."

Von Kleist smiled apologetically to me, as though asking pardon for a friend who had passed gas.

"Excuse me," he said politely.

He then grabbed Pabst by the shoulders, kicked over his chair, lifted him high in the air, and threw him, hard, to the floor. Von Kleist placed the sole of his shiny leather boot on Pabst's throat and pressed, cutting off the little man's air.

"You are a peasant and a stupid little shit," von Kleist said. "The Freikorps is a joke, set up by Ludendorff and the Prussian nobility to serve their interests."

He started rubbing his boot up and down Pabst's nose. Christ, he was close to breaking it.

"You speak to an aristocrat, a von Kleist, a member of one of the ancient Prussian houses. You really should be more polite, Wally."

And he kicked him hard in the ribs.

The dachshund whimpered at the violence and von Kleist picked him up solicitously.

"Liebchen, Liebchen," he cooed. "It's all right. Little Wally just needed correcting, that's all."

Pabst rose slowly off the floor and returned to his seat, not saying a word. Von Kleist turned back to me.

"Here is what will happen. You will go to the podium tonight at the congress—"

"But I'm not scheduled to speak."

"It does not matter. You will go to the podium and announce that your conscience compels you to speak. You will tell the hall that Luxemburg, Liebknecht, and the other Spartacists plotted the defeat of Germany with Ebert the socialist and that Ebert surrendered even though the German armed forces were not beaten and would have prevailed in the war."

"They won't believe me," I sputtered. "Christ, they'll gag me before I get half of that out of my mouth!"

"It does not matter. You will say enough to cause a stir and police will be waiting to arrest you as soon as you leave the hall. This letter" —he again waved the envelope—"will be found on your person. We will spread word that you were shot while trying to escape and slip you out of Germany quietly so you can return to your home in... Missouri, was it? In no time, this will all seem like a dream."

Right. A bullet in a Freikorps cell was what awaited me. Or worse.

"So, Cornelius. Will you do it? You know, of course, what awaits if you don't. Will you make history with us?"

Yes, I said. Of course I said yes. Just as I had before.

Von Kleist shook his head sadly.

"Cornelius, I am not sure I believe you. You may think that you will agree to anything and betray us in the end." He petted the dog in his arms. "But I am sure you can be convinced. This is why I asked Wally to bring this little *liebchen* to join us."

The dachshund looked at me quizzically while von Kleist kissed the top of his head.

"Liebchen will convince you."

Of all places, we went to the zoo. Pabst stayed in the suite at the Eden, at once both disgusted and terrified. I was escorted closely by two of the thugs who had lifted me off the Kurfürstendamm. In the lead walked von Kleist, cradling little Liebchen in his arms. I remember sidelong glances from sympathetic faces in the sidewalk crowd, who no doubt reasoned that anyone hustled along by such a trio of Freikorps villains was not headed for a *biergarten*.

We quickly reached the Berlin Zoological Gardens. This was an important section of Berlin: the famous zoo, the main train station, and the principal city boulevard all came together at the southwest corner of the Tiergarten, the massive city park that defined the heart of the city. They still do. I was hurried into the zoo, past the admission gates where the ticket-takers didn't dare impede these brutish-looking Freikorps soldiers. Although it was the middle of the afternoon on a Tuesday, the grounds were crowded with families, bundled up against the cold and enjoying the holidays as a respite from the hunger and uncertainty that pervaded their post-war lives. Vendors hawked hot chestnuts and mulled wine. I wouldn't have minded some, as the combination of the chill in the air and overwhelming terror had me shivering uncontrollably. I was pulled along past cages in which boars, bears, and foxes lay sullenly, laughed and gibed at by Berliners and their children. Understand, this was long before the modern zoo, with its large habitats designed to make it difficult to see the animals. These beasts were in small cages littered with offal, exposed to view.

We reached the largest cage of all, which had also attracted the largest crowd. We pushed our way through the throng until we were up close to the bars of a cage so large it consumed an area almost the size of a city block. It was plainly a special attraction, with a specially designed cage, commanding far more room and attention than any other cage in the zoo. Von Kleist pulled me forward until he had my face pressed directly against the bars. I looked from right to left, taking in the dirt floor, the shoddy-looking pool to my right, the blank wall that bordered the far side of the cage, the bars around the other three sides. There was but a single beast in that huge cage, but what a beast. It was a beautiful, majestic tiger, looking far more dignified and at peace than the grubby humans who surrounded its cage. The tiger was huge, standing nearly as tall as a man, with a sinewy body that rippled as it lifted one enormous paw after another, circling its cage. It was tragic for such a magnificent beast to be enclosed within these bars, for the gawking amusement of *hausfraus*.

"Isn't she a beautiful animal?" von Kleist asked me as he stroked the dachshund in his arms. "The Berliner Zoological Gardens brought her here just before the war. She is their prime attraction. I remember my first sight of her: fantastic! Look how her muscles ripple beneath her shiny fur! Look how she lifts one leg after another, planting her feet, looking from left to right and back again for her prey! If we could only make these bars disappear, then you would see what this tiger is born to do! For she is a Bengal tiger. Do you know what that means, Cornelius?"

I shrugged and shook my head, although I expected it had something to do with being from Bengal.

"Not all tigers are man-eaters. In fact, most are not. But the Bengals, they are the masters of their domain. They eat men. They eat python, they eat elephants, they eat whatever comes before them. They are truly great. And I knew, when the zoo acquired such an animal, that it was a sign. A sign for what, you ask? That is what Liebchen will show you."

Von Kleist gripped the dog more tightly in his arms and bundled off, with me being propelled behind him by the two thugs. We pushed through the crowd watching the tiger, many of whom were children thrilled at beholding such an elegant and deadly beast after an afternoon of tedium. We went behind the cage and von Kleist pulled a key ring from his pocket. He inserted a key into a door on the back of the cage and we entered, with one of the thugs clanging the door shut behind us. We found ourselves in a narrow, dark space that the four of us filled. Von Kleist signed wordlessly to the henchmen, one of whom picked up a bucket from the corner of the little room. The other took the dachshund from von Kleist's arms and held it while the bucket was poured over the poor dog's head. It whimpered, and so would you have done, for the contents of the bucket stank like animal innards left out in the sun. Which, I believe, is what they were. A moment later, the dog's head and upper torso were covered with a bloody, stinky mess of guts. By now the dog was silent and shivering, as though sensing his imminent death. And he was right.

In the wall that formed one side of the tiger's cage was a wooden door, perhaps two feet high and three feet wide, sufficient for a man to crawl through. It had obviously been put there with some effort, for a particular purpose.

"You will notice the door," said von Kleist, as his minions drenched the dog in more animal guts. "It took considerable effort for me to exert my influence and convince the authorities to install that door. But I was determined, from the day I heard the Bengal tiger would arrive, to use this beast for the good of the cause. And, of course, for my own amusement. Is he ready? Yes? Now you will see, Cornelius."

Von Kleist took the dripping, miserable little dog back from his henchmen. From the top of its head to its shoulders, the dachshund dripped the foul-smelling gore of some slaughtered animal. Careful to keep the gore from dripping onto his uniform, von Kleist nodded a command to the Freikorps soldiers. One unlatched the center-opening trap door and slid it open a crack in both directions. Von Kleist kicked the door twice, to get the attention of the tiger. He gave the dog a last kiss and handed it to the Freikorps soldiers, who bent and placed the dog's head and upper body into the opening. There was a moment of silence, broken only by the dog's whimpering. Then came a roar from the tiger. As children watching from around the perimeter of the cage screamed, we heard the tiger bound to the wall, snuffling and grunting as it chewed off the dachshund's little head. I saw the Freikorps men shake in fear as the tiger's jaws tore at the dog they were holding. Finally, they pulled the dog back into the room and I saw the slavering, drooling mouth of the tiger as they slammed the door shut. Von Kleist took the headless corpse of the dog and held it out to me.

"You see, Cornelius? This is you. This will be your fate if you betray me. You understand, Cornelius?"

He waved in my face the bleeding stump of the dachshund. Its head was gone, chewed off down to the neck and below. I remembered Miguel's head, waved in front of me. My throat choked with bile. I nodded.

Von Kleist smiled.

"Good. It is enough."

He stuck the envelope in my breast pocket.

"Give a good speech, Cornelius. You will be observed."

And they let me go.

34

Revolution

Cornelius

I did what anyone would do if a maniac like von Kleist waved a decapitated dog in his face and ordered him to betray his greatest love. I got drunk.

It was not an act of conscious volition. Released from the zoo, I walked in a daze down the Kurfürstendamm and into the nearest bar, where I proceeded to pour schnapps and beer down my throat as quickly as I could. As best I recall, my thinking went something along the following lines:

1. If I made the slightest effort to seize the podium at the congress to indulge in some half-baked confession, my friends would hoot me down and Rosa would never speak to me again.
2. If anyone found me with the letter that was currently burning a hole in my breast pocket, Rosa and I would both be assassinated, along with anyone associated with us.
3. If I bolted and ran, and von Kleist caught me, I would die from slow torture that made what happened to Liebchen seem a kindly act.
4. If I bolted and ran, and von Kleist didn't catch me, Riley would condemn me to a life in the prairie that would stifle me and chain me to an infant I had no desire to meet.

5. If I successfully followed von Kleist's instructions, not only would I betray the woman I loved, but I would certainly be "shot while trying to escape" and thrown into a pauper's grave in Berlin.

All in all, it seemed a far less attractive menu than I'd conjured up in bed that morning. So I threw back three schnapps while nursing the first beer. Then I nursed another schnapps while throwing back three more beers and fiddling with a box of bar matches. Then the reverse. After much thought, I stopped thinking. I reached into my pocket, took out the envelope, and opened it. The letter was really quite an impressive piece of work. Beginning "Dear Corny" of all things, the writer expressed undying love for yours truly and then outlined a wholly believable account of working with Ebert to stab the German military in the back and bring Germany to its knees, so the communist revolution could triumph. It was signed, "Your darling Rosa."

My darling Rosa. I suddenly had to get to her and to Riley. They were the two best people in a crisis I had ever seen and I loved them both. I stuffed the letter in my pocket, threw money on the bar, and leapt to my feet, a motion that caused the room to spin for a moment. I was surprised at how drunk I was, but no matter. I had to get to the hall to be with my best friend and the woman I loved and admired more than anyone. What I was going to do when I got there, I still didn't know.

I staggered down the Berlin streets, reached the hall and flung open the doors, suddenly feeling high, wide, and handsome. The joint was packed with the usual factory workers and intellectuals, but even in my intoxicated state it struck me that the audience was more diverse than usual. I saw what looked like shopkeepers, *hausfraus*, even country folk. This bucked me up tremendously. For once, we weren't just preaching to the red choir. This was truly the proletariat and they had come to a communist organizational meeting, of all things. Hot damn! We were on our way! Even von Kleist couldn't stop this revolution!

My timing was perfect, for Rosa was just stepping up to the podium to tumultuous applause. She was the star attraction and I suspected the *hausfraus* came just to see her. Her head barely topped the podium and Leo made a humorous show of bringing over a step for her to stand on, a bit of theater that both Leo and I had perfected for many an audience. Properly positioned, Rosa gripped the sides of the podium and allowed her good-humored gaze to roam the auditorium. Gradually the crowd quieted down.

"Comrades!" she began. "Our task today is to discuss and adopt a program."

Good start! I liked the way she hit the emphasis on "Comrades!" so firmly. But then she started quoting the *Communist Manifesto*, which I have to admit is always a snoozer. She went on for a while about how Marx and Engels originally urged cautious first steps, but later realized that a truly revolutionary movement would be required if capitalism was to be overthrown. She actually started reading off a shopping list from the Manifesto:

> 1) Abolition of landed property and application of all land rents to public purposes. 2) Heavy progressive taxes. 3) Abolition of the right of inheritance. 4) Confiscation of the property of all emigrants and rebels. 5) Centralization of credit in the hands of the state by means of a national bank with state capital and an exclusive monopoly. 6) Centralization of the means of communication and transport in the hands of the state...

And on and on. Come on, old girl, I thought, this isn't stirring the hearts of the masses. You can't inspire a revolution on cold gruel, the folks want red meat! When she kept droning on, laying out the intellectual stuff with no real pep to it, I figured she needed my help and I should get to the podium immediately. Plainly a touch of Dear Corny was required here. I ignored the fact that I was having considerable difficulty focusing on anyone or anything and started elbowing my way through the crowd. It took me some time to get to the front and I can't say that Rosa's speech got any better. She must have been nervous and nerves made her go all intellectual. She'd been a much more effective rabble-rouser in any number of street-corner speeches, but tonight she was coming off like wet wallpaper. I brushed by one old fellow who was actually snoring on his feet, propped up by the proximity on each side of muscle-bound factory workers who were grousing about the length of the speech. Finally, I reached the edge of the stage and waved gaily at Rosa, who paused just enough for a sharp intake of breath before droning on with the next lesson in communist theory. I remember tripping over peoples' feet in the front row and laughing about it. Liebknecht left his seat next to the podium and came over to hiss at me.

"What are you doing? Rosa is speaking. Sit down!"

I guffawed, perhaps a bit louder than I intended. Liebknecht had a little cowlick hanging over his bald head, which I found hilarious.

"Calm down, Karl. We need a calm Karl, calm Karl. I know Rosa is speaking, that's the problem. She's stinking up there."

I boosted myself onto the stage, with Liebknecht shaking in outrage and Rosa sticking to her script. I started falling backward and Leo grabbed my arm to hold me up.

"Thank you, Leo, my man," I managed. "Have you seen Riley anywhere? No matter."

Rosa was approaching what was apparently her big finish, the poor girl. Her last line was thusly recorded:

> It is only important that we know clearly and precisely what is to be done; and I hope that my feeble powers have shown you to some extent the broad outlines of that which is to be done.

Well, didn't that get the heart pounding? I knew I had to help her. I led some polite applause as I stood beside her and gently nudged her away from the podium. I never felt so full of beans. That was damn good schnapps, I must say.

"Comrades!" I exclaimed, mimicking Rosa's tagline.

All eyes were on me, as you might imagine. Take this, von Kleist.

"First, let's have one more hand for the little lady. Isn't she the smart one, though?"

I clapped but no one followed my example. Rosa badly messed up, clearly. Down to business.

"I have news! I have documentary proof right here!" I pulled von Kleist's letter from my pocket and waved it over my head. "Documentary proof that Ebert is a shit! That Waldemar Pabst is a shit! That all the Freikorps are shits, shits, shits!"

That was the stuff! I felt a surge of energy in the hall. People were gasping, nodding, some even stood up to applaud.

I unfolded the paper in my hand.

"This purports to be a letter from the lady you just heard, from the good and noble lady, Rosa Luxemburg. It is signed with her name, it is in a woman's hand, it is addressed to me, who has the great honor to be her lover."

That got their attention. Rosa reached over to put her hand on my arm, no doubt wanting to thank me.

"In this letter, Rosa supposedly outlines how she and the other comrades, especially the comrades who happen to be Jewish, plotted for Germany to lose the war. Do you believe that?"

"No!" Leo shouted behind me.

"This letter claims the Spartacists are the cause of Germany's problems! Do you believe that?"

"No!" A handful in the crowd joined Leo now.

"If you believe this letter, you believe the Kaiser, Ludendorff, Ebert: all of them, they're the proper leaders of Germany. Do you believe that?"

"No!" The crowd roared as one, with me now.

"Do you believe they're shits?"

"Yes!" they all cried. Well, a few stuck with no, but that was just an error.

"Of course they're shits! We are the people! Spartacists, farmers, workers, soldiers, sailors, it doesn't matter. We are the people! We are Germany!"

Wild, wild cheering. I scanned the stage. Rosa, Leo, and Liebknecht were all staring at me, open-mouthed. It was my moment. I did, though, feel a rumbling in my belly that concerned me.

"Now is our moment! Now is the time! This letter is a lie and we consign it to the hell from which it came."

Inspired, I pulled out a match from the bar, struck it with an unsteady hand, and set the cursed letter aflame. The crowd went wild, raising the roof of the hall with their huzzahs as the pages burned in my hand. As I watched the flames dance, the rumbling below intensified and the room began to spin. The schnapps and the beer would no longer be denied. I bent over and retched, the flood from my stomach quenching the fire and spattering the people in the front row.

There was a moment of stunned silence before the crowd roared louder than ever. The sight of fire and vomit apparently stirred their Teutonic souls. They were standing, shouting, stomping their feet.

I seized the podium and managed to cry out "We take Berlin!" before collapsing, oblivious, onto a chair.

The crowd screamed through a five-minute standing ovation, then spontaneously marched from the hall singing "The Internationale." Rosa stared daggers at me and said I had ruined everything, but I was in no shape to be bothered.

Although I didn't know it, I had just lit the fuse that set off the Spartacist Revolution of January 1919.

35

The Day of Reckoning

Cornelius

New Year's Day, 1919. I knew right away it was going to be a bugger. The sugar from the schnapps kicked in and woke me around three in the morning. I had somehow gotten back to my bed at *The Red Flag* headquarters. I was alone in the dark, which didn't surprise me as I doubted Rosa wanted to risk being next to me if I threw up again.

You know that a hangover will be bad if the room is spinning when you wake up. The room was spinning now. My mouth was dry, a sharp pain cut through my brain, and my stomach felt jumpy, as though it was trying to decide from which end to discharge its contents. I prayed to the god of atheists that I would be left alone, that I could just lie quietly in a dark room with my eyes shut for however long it took for this abomination to pass.

I must have dozed off, for I suddenly became aware that sunlight was brightening the room and Riley was sitting in a chair staring at me. He didn't look happy, but when does he? He stared darkly and intensely at me, which doesn't mean anything with Riley. He's just a dark and intense guy.

"You getting up?"

I swallowed to hold down a surge from my stomach.

"Never. I'm never getting up again."

Silence. After a few minutes, I opened my eyes again. Riley still sat there, staring at me. I noticed that in his belt, under the rough worker's jacket that he had picked up in Berlin, he had tucked away his Luger.

"Where's Rosa?" I asked.

"Out. Everybody's out, working. Not speaking the language, I don't exactly know what's going on, but I'd say from the look of it that you stirred things up pretty good last night. The party folks stayed up all night yelling at each other and they left at first light. Got the sense they think some sort of revolution might actually happen now and they're maybe in two minds about that."

This was a bit too much for my poor brain to handle at that moment. I closed my eyes and we were silent a long time. Riley has always been comfortable with silence. I never have, but that morning it was all I wanted. I slipped back into a troubled sleep. When I again awoke, I was alone. I felt a little better, so I stumbled into the main office and found Riley there, cleaning his pistol.

"You really are expecting trouble, aren't you?"

Riley considered it.

"It sort of smells like it. Always good to keep your gun clean, of course."

I decided I had to tell him about von Kleist. Before yesterday, it seemed unimportant, like von Kleist was a shadow from the past and no one I needed to worry about anymore. Now, after the Hotel Eden and the dachshund without a head and my public defiance of von Kleist's plot in my speech, we were all in serious danger and Riley and Rosa both needed to know that. Riley already knew about my mission to spy on Rosa in prison, but now I told him of the "stab in the back" letter and the man-eating tiger in the Berlin Zoo that was licking his chops at the thought of me. Riley chewed silently on his lower lip, as was his way. At length, his only comment was "We better get you a gun."

We didn't leave the headquarters that day. Riley smoked his cigarettes and I nursed my hangover. Leo stopped by to pick up some literature and I asked him what was happening.

"You roused the people last night, Comrade O'Neal," Leo informed me, looking grimly pleased. "After your speech, the workers paraded into the streets, smashing street lamps and brawling with the

Freikorps. Today three different strikes have been announced that we know of. The whirlwind is coming, it would seem."

"That's good, isn't it? Isn't that what we wanted?"

Leo grinned.

"Some of us, comrade, some of us. Not Rosa. You are in for a rough time tonight when Rosa returns. She is furious. She doesn't think the time is right. She thinks we need more organization and more popular support before the revolution can succeed. She's out there now, trying to calm everyone down and get them to rescind the strike announcements. She and Barth almost came to blows. I wish they had. She'd have murdered that little pimp."

Leo headed for the door but I stopped him.

"What do you think, Leo?"

The big man clapped a hand on my shoulder.

"Comrade, I've been fighting the revolution my whole life. I've fought with words, with passion, with my hands, with clubs, with guns. Whatever comes, I am ready."

And he left, before I could gather the nerve to mention that he should watch out for a certain tall sadistic maniac in a Freikorps uniform.

Rosa didn't make it back until late in the evening. She came bursting into the office, with Liebknecht trailing behind her. She and Liebknecht were in the midst of an argument that seemed to have been going on all day and that was far from finished.

"Rosa, I tell you, Barth has a point." Liebknecht was remarkably worked up for such a cold-blooded little fellow. "I've never seen the workers so stirred as they've been since the congress. This is an opportunity for real action, for real revolution, and it may never come again. Ebert is shitting his pants right now."

Rosa favored me with an icy glare, but confined her remarks to Liebknecht.

"The state of Herr Ebert's pants is of no relevance. Ebert is nothing, I keep telling you. He is a puppet who holds a title while the ancient masters of Germany still rule! Wilhelm, Ludendorff, all of them! They use Ebert and they use the Freikorps to get what they want, but it is the old autocrats who still rule the roost here."

Liebknecht shook his head.

"No one is ruling the roost, Rosa. The war ended all that. There is a vacuum of power in Germany and it is time for the workers to fill it."

"With what? With words and Marxist doctrine? Where are your guns, Karl? How will you seize the communications network in the town? If you give commands, will you be obeyed? This is not a revolution, this is a child's game and it plays right into the hands of the Freikorps and their masters. They will say the Spartacists made Germany surrender, the Spartacists are now rebelling, and they will crush us with the Freikorps and what remains of the army. It is too soon for this, Karl. You can't start a revolution just because some drunken fool makes a speech."

Well, that seemed harsh. Something was dawning on me. She'd said you can't fight a revolution with words and Marxist doctrine, but that dry stuff had been exactly what she was feeding the crowd from the podium the night before. Was she being intentionally boring and pedantic, to cool the temper of the crowd? She was certainly capable of it. I wondered if, perhaps, my speech might have been a trifle ill-advised.

Riley startled us all by speaking. He almost never spoke in front of the comrades; some thought he was a mute.

"Cornelius," he said, "you must tell them about von Kleist. They need to know."

Rosa and Karl looked at me for the translation. It was a hard moment, having to tell the woman I loved not only that she was in danger from a monster like von Kleist, but that I had hidden from her the fact that he existed and had set me to spy on her. But I knew Riley was right and I asked both of them to sit down, then I spilled it.

They were pros, I'll say that for them. They had both been through a lot in their long careers as revolutionaries and the news of yet another enemy, even von Kleist, didn't shake them at all. Rosa's lip curled a little when I described what happened to Liebchen, but otherwise they were silent and impassive.

Liebknecht spoke first.

"Comrade, what have you told them?"

Rosa snorted.

"What is there to tell them, Karl? That we favor a revolution? Every child in the streets of Berlin knows that about Red Rosa. We have no plans, no organization, not even thoughts that are not in *The Red*

Flag for all to see. And we know that Cornelius denounced the plot and burned the letter publicly last night. Don't be foolish."

Rosa could certainly silence Liebknecht when she wanted to: there were no further aspersions on my loyalty. Then Rosa asked me something that surprised me.

"What does your friend think we should do?"

Here were two battle-hardened revolutionaries, veterans of jails in Poland and Germany, turning for advice to a twenty-year-old stranger from Missouri who didn't speak their language. There is simply something about Riley that people turn to in a tight spot. I know I have since the day we met.

Riley didn't blink.

"They should keep on doing whatever it was they were going to do," he said to me, to translate for him. "Only difference is, I'm staying next to you and the lady, everywhere you go, every day. If we see von Kleist, I'll kill him."

When I translated what he said, Rosa and Karl nodded and went back to arguing about strategy, the von Kleist subject disposed of. As I say, there is something about Riley.

The next few days were a blur of meetings, street fights, arguing, chanting, all the hubbub of a bubbling revolution. I didn't get much sleep. Leo was able to get me the gun that Riley had recommended, a neat little handgun that he said had good stopping power, and I carried it everywhere, including to bed. Leo, Riley, and I took turns standing guard over Rosa and Karl at the office of *The Red Flag* during the few hours they slept. Rosa would spend an hour or two at dawn typing out copy for the publication, after which she and Karl would begin the endless rounds of the Revolutionary Stewards, the labor councils, and the other constituencies that Rosa was trying to placate and organize. Riley and I always accompanied them, Riley's hand always ready to draw the pistol in his belt. But there was no sign of von Kleist and there were no attempts to harm Rosa, bar the usual vituperative abuse from roughnecks on the streets.

Riley did an odd thing. He left Leo and me to guard Rosa one day as she made her rounds. That night, when we were alone at *The Red Flag* with Rosa in bed and Leo outside on guard duty, Riley handed me a small leather bag, hanging from a string.

"Put that around your neck," he said.

Inside the bag was something round and a little squishy, like a rubber ball.

"Don't squeeze it and don't open it. Just put it around your neck. Like this."

He opened the top of his shirt to show me that he was wearing a similar bag, hung from a cord around his neck.

Well, I wasn't about to wear that thing without an explanation. When Riley explained what it was for, I thought he was crazy. But I wore the bag.

Three days passed. Then Ebert, the fool, made the mistake of dismissing Berlin's chief constable, who was a favorite of the masses because he had refused to obey Ebert's order to charge the sailors during Bloody Christmas. Led by Barth, as always, the Revolutionary Stewards called for a mass protest demonstration the next day. Liebknecht joined in the call: each day, he was becoming more estranged from Rosa and more in tune with Barth's demand for immediate revolutionary action.

This time, they got more than they bargained for. Hundreds of thousands of people poured into Berlin to protest Ebert's dismissal of the chief constable, the ongoing economic crises, and just the generally crappy quality of life in Germany. Many were armed and looking for trouble and plenty of scraps broke out all over the city. Rosa was worn out trying to preach restraint and, in any event, once this occurred, there was no reasoning with either Barth or Karl. Barth and his Revolutionary Stewards took over the old police headquarters and elected themselves, and Karl, members of what they called the Interim Revolutionary Committee. That announcement drew Rosa's scorn.

"Who do you think you are leading, comrades?" she flung at them in a heated meeting at police headquarters. "You think you lead that crowd out there? That is like a bobber floating on the ocean, thinking it leads the waves."

Barth was livid. He sat at the head of a long table, very full of himself. The members of the committee sat around the table, looking red-faced and determined, Liebknecht included. Riley and I protected Rosa's flanks, while she stood at the foot of the table reading the riot act. We both had our hands on our guns.

"We have heard enough from you, Comrade Luxemburg," Barth stated. "We understand your views and we reject them."

Rosa stamped her foot in frustration.

"Ebert has thousands of well-trained and fully armed soldiers ready to march into the city. All this rioting does is give him an excuse to come."

Barth jumped to his feet, bringing Riley's Luger an inch out of its holster.

"Let them come! Thousands of soldiers, you say? We have hundreds of thousands out there, the working people of Berlin! No one can deny us! No one can stand in our way!"

What a blockhead. But the die was cast and Rosa led us back to *The Red Flag,* discouraged. That night she lay in my arms, crying and shaking. I'd never seen her so vulnerable.

"You don't understand, you don't understand," she sobbed as I tried to comfort her. "My whole life. This is what I've worked for my whole life. If only we keep our heads, we can make Germany a workers' paradise, a paradise far better and purer than what Lenin has achieved in Moscow. There could be a statue of Karl Marx in the Reichstag in two years."

"And there will be a statue of Rosa Luxemburg right next to him," I teased.

She wasn't buying it and tossed her head impatiently.

"No more, no more. We are undone. This will never happen in my lifetime. The window has closed. Our chance is gone."

And she snuggled into my chest and closed her eyes. I knew she was right. I'd been in the trenches and seen the power of weapons and military discipline. If Ebert brought even the tattered remnants of the German army against this disorganized crowd of factory workers and shopkeepers, it would be a slaughter.

And so, of course, it was. While the workers kept demonstrating and orating, Ebert quietly moved troops into the city. A rumor circulated that the army's commander, a long-nosed old thug named Gustav Noske, had proclaimed himself the bloodhound for the government. I remember watching a company of armed men marching through the Brandenburg Gate, surrounded by protestors waving placards. The Revolutionary Committee had distributed many that bore the same slogan. Riley asked me what it said.

"It says, 'The Day of Reckoning Is Near.'"

"Reckoning?" said Riley, casting his eyes over the troops and the shouting demonstrators. "Whose?"

Ebert made his move on a Thursday. It was cold, but after days of a gray gloom, the sun shone brightly. People swamped the cafés on the Kurfürstendamm, eager for a respite from the shouting rioters, the grim-faced soldiers, the swaggering Freikorps. I was sitting at a window table in one of the coffee shops with Rosa, Riley, and Leo. Even with the glorious sun in our faces, we did not share the simple happiness of the people around us. Rosa's despair at the course of events, coupled with the tension and danger surrounding us, kept us silent. And our mood suddenly spread from table to table, in response to what was approaching.

We heard them before we saw them. In what had become a customary sight since the congress, a mob of angry men pounded down the Kurfürstendamm, waving signs and shouting slogans. They called for the overthrow of Ebert, the power of the Revolutionary Stewards, the rise of the workers. Some sang "The Internationale." Some took random swipes at unsympathetic gawkers as they passed by. There was no organization, no leadership, just another street demonstration like dozens before.

But this time, the sound of marching boots echoed from the opposite direction. Turning a corner around the street to our left was a troop of soldiers led by one crisply-uniformed officer. He showed no emotion as he strode along, in step with the troops behind him. Given the starving, demoralized German soldiers I had seen all over Berlin, I was awed at the seeming spark and discipline of these men. Where had Ebert recruited them?

Leo stood, intent on joining the imminent conflict. Rosa took him by the arm and implored him to stay.

"Leo, you will make no difference. This time, this one time, please stay with me and see me through. I cannot lose you now."

He sat back down unhappily. The young officer didn't halt or shout commands to the demonstrators. He didn't even break stride as he raised one hand to beckon forward his troops, pulled out his pistol with the other, and began to run forward. The troops lowered their rifles and charged. A few of the demonstrators threw rocks or brandished clubs. Most turned and ran for their lives, but they were not fast enough.

The soldiers piled into the fleeing demonstrators like a storm wave crashing against a rocky shore. Using both ends of their rifles, they clubbed down the workers, one after another. Workers tried to fight back, but I only saw a handful of their blows land. They were simply overwhelmed. The officer didn't hesitate to shoot men where they stood; he must have taken down six as we watched. Bullies on the sidewalks, some in Freikorps uniform, cheered the soldiers on. It was, as Rosa had predicted, a slaughter.

The restaurant had a back door and we took it. We returned to *The Red Flag* and checked in with comrades throughout the city. It soon became clear that similar kinds of confrontations were happening all over Berlin. Ebert was cleaning house.

We holed up at *The Red Flag* for three days, taking our news as we could get it. On the third day, Liebknecht stopped by. He was a beaten man. He plopped down heavily in a chair by the table where Rosa and I had written so many articles for the *Flag*.

"It is over, Rosa. You are right. They have won."

Rosa poured him a cup of coffee and put her hand on his.

"No, Karl. They will never win. The dialectic cannot be stopped, you know that. The triumph of the working class is inevitable and you and I will never stop fighting for it, even if we never see it in our lifetimes. The fight will go on."

It seemed gracious of her, considering.

Riley had been outside, keeping watch. At that moment he entered and said, "Time to go."

A crowd of the Freikorps was walking down the street in our direction. In the wake of the army's victory, the Freikorps had become increasingly aggressive, smashing in synagogues, molesting women, beating anyone who protested. Riley told us there was a large bunch of them heading for *The Red Flag*. Leo drew his gun and stepped to the window.

"Cornelius, tell him there's too many of them. We need to protect Rosa."

Riley had figured out that Rosa was Leo's weak spot, as she was mine. The Freikorps were too dumb or too cocky to block the back exit, so the five of us were able to make our escape. Leo, the old campaigner, had a safehouse already in wait in the Wilmersdorf neighborhood where a friend of the cause lived and there we went. I never saw what the Freikorps did to *The Red Flag* offices when they found us gone and I never wanted to see.

We arrived at our destination, a house at 53 Mannheimer Strasse, well after midnight. It was a little two-bedroom bungalow that fit in well with its quiet suburban surroundings. There was no telephone in the house and our arrival was a surprise to the comrade who was staying there. We had to pound on the door to roust him from bed to let us in. The man's name was Paul and he lived there alone, paying rent to a ferret-faced little greaser named Mehring whom we met the next day. Apparently, Mehring lived nearby and had an unpleasant habit of showing up unannounced whenever he felt like it, using his key to the place without hesitation or embarrassment. Paul was a good, stolid sort of fellow, but I disliked the little weasel Mehring instantly.

Paul actually seemed rather excited to have the great Rosa Luxemburg as a houseguest. He set aside one of the bedrooms just for her. Liebknecht and Leo took the other, while Paul bunked with Riley and me in the living room. The next morning, while Paul was making us *weissworst* and eggs for breakfast, no doubt expending his supply for the month, Mehring scared the bejesus out of me by suddenly opening the front door and walking in. In the excitement of the move, we had neglected to post our usual guard, so we had no warning that Mehring was paying us a visit. When he walked in, he found himself facing the barrels of both Riley's pistol and mine before Paul called us off and introduced us to his landlord.

Given his reception, it was perhaps not surprising that Mehring regarded us suspiciously. I got the sense, though, that he was just suspicious and creepy by nature. His ratty face was perpetually wrinkled in an unpleasant sneer and he peered at the world over metal-frame glasses perched on the tip of his nose. He was one of those people who play constantly with his own hands, pinching and picking at them and leaving red and white marks in his pale flesh. After he recovered from the fear of seeing our drawn pistols, he spoke to Paul in a querulous tone.

"Herr Paul, I come to get your monthly rent and I find you sleeping in your own living room with two men with guns. How can this be?"

"I don't see how this is any of your business, Herr Mehring," Paul stated as a matter of fact. "And the rent isn't due until Monday."

Mehring made a clucking sound with his tongue. His eyes darted toward the closed bedroom doors. From one of them came the sound of Leo's snoring, which was legendary among the Spartacists.

"When tenants have a history of late payments, I try to remind them in advance."

"You old goat," Paul said, glowering at him, "I was two days late once because I was out of town! Be off with you and I'll pay you on Monday!"

I felt it was fortunate that Rosa was still safely in her bedroom. She had, however, left her shoes on the floor in front of the sofa. Mehring shot a glance at the obviously feminine shoes and gave us all a final sneer before he marched out of the house, banging the door behind him.

"Sweet fellow," I commented to no one in particular.

We kept ourselves shut up in that house on Mannheimer Strasse for a few tense days. Comrades brought us word of developments in the city. Ebert, or whoever was pulling the strings of the German army, had Berlin in a tight lockdown. Freikorps members were still raging through the streets, terrorizing the citizenry with the complicit assistance of the government. Topping the wanted list was Rosa, for whom a substantial reward was offered. Liebknecht or Barth should really have been their prize targets, but because of her tart tongue and popularity, and because she was a woman, Rosa was hated with a special fire by her enemies. We heard of one poor lady who was badly beaten and abused because the Freikorps mistook her for Rosa.

Every comrade who dared to visit us urged Rosa to flee the city, but she refused. Even Leo tried to convince her to fight another day and it certainly would have been the logical move. My impression, even though she never said as much, was that Rosa had reached the end of her line: either the revolution would reassert itself in the chaos of post-war Germany or she was done with it.

Riley chafed and muttered, knowing the longer we stayed, the more likely we would be discovered. To my surprise, though, he didn't press me to abandon Rosa and leave. I think he knew the depth of my feelings for her, plus he wanted to see how things played out. Or maybe he just felt he had committed himself to protecting Rosa from von Kleist and he had a job to do.

Regardless, we were still in that house on Mannheimer Strasse on January 15, 1919, a day infamous on the calendar of communist history. The morning passed as had the preceding two or three. I woke on the floor of the living room, stretched the kinks out, and had breakfast with Riley and Paul. Everyone else tended to be late sleepers, if nothing was scheduled for the day. When Leo awoke, he announced that he needed to check in with the comrades at the steelworkers' union and he left. We were not happy with such a conspicuous Spartacist being out on the streets, but Rosa was still in bed and without her, there was no arguing with Leo.

The day passed. Liebknecht and Riley played cribbage, despite the language barrier, and Riley won. Rosa wrote. Paul went for groceries, if he could find any, as his houseguests were playing havoc with his supplies. I sat and read one of Rosa's books I found in Paul's Marxist library. Her writing was at once heavy going, but also rewarding and stimulating. If only life worked the way economic theory says it does, communism might have been a great idea.

Shortly before the dinner hour, as I was wondering when Paul and Leo would be getting back, the lock suddenly turned and the door opened. It was Mehring. I assumed he was back for the rent.

"It's not Monday yet and Paul isn't here," I said. "Come back later."

"I don't think so," said Mehring.

Something in his tone caused me to look up from my book and Riley to jump to his feet, gun drawn. Mehring was flung aside from behind and in rushed a knot of burly Freikorps, armed to the teeth and looking ready to kill. Riley considered, thought better of it, and lowered his weapon. I had left mine on my bedside table, so I had nothing to consider.

One of the intruders stepped forward and glared down at Rosa, who had coolly returned to her writing.

"You are Rosa Luxemburg?"

"You know I am," said Rosa, not looking up.

The bastard smashed her across the face, knocking her off the chair. Riley and I and even Liebknecht made for our guns, but we were stopped by a battery of small arms aimed at us and at Rosa.

"I am Lieutenant Lindner of the Freikorps," said the brute. "You will all come with us."

So we did.

36

The Tiger and the Lady

Cornelius

Our guns were taken away, of course, and the four of us—Rosa, Liebknecht, Riley, and me—were bundled into two cars for a swift ride to the Hotel Eden, the luxurious center of torture and murder for Waldemar Pabst and his Freikorps killers. I knew that Riley was on full alert, constantly looking for an opening, and I was ready to back his play, but Lindner and his thugs were competent at their work and gave us no chance to make a move. At least Leo was still at large.

We were dropped off at the main entrance of the Eden as though we were guests. I remember clearly that as we were pushed roughly through the lobby and were waiting for an elevator, not a single one of the well-garbed clientele in the lobby spared us a glance. Here we were, clearly prisoners, a group that included the most famous Marxist in the world next to Lenin and Trotsky, and we might as well have been invisible. Well, not quite invisible, for a couple of guests who were heading for the elevators turned in the opposite direction when they saw us. People get used to anything and it was obvious that the Hotel Eden and its visitors had grown accustomed to seeing the odd Freikorps victim in the lobby, bound for torture and death.

The elevator, a marvel of modern technology, opened and a sweet elderly couple emerged. In what seemed like theatre of the absurd, the woman smiled and nodded politely at Rosa as she walked by her, even though Rosa was still in Lindner's firm grasp and blood was dripping from her lip. Four Freikorps soldiers, including Lindner, joined the four of us in the elevator car. I thought perhaps that this was where Riley would make his move, but since all of us had gun barrels aimed point-blank at our bellies, he didn't chance it. We let ourselves be escorted down the hallway to Pabst's suite, where I had previously met with the Freikorps commander and von Kleist. This time, the door opened to reveal only Waldemar Pabst, surrounded by three of his flunkies. We were pushed inside and the door was slammed shut behind us.

Pabst looked more sleek and confident than he had before, although I admit that most men would find it easier to be confident if Otto von Kleist were not in the room. As he glared insolently at Rosa and gave her the once-over, I wanted to smash his pudgy face.

"So this is the Jew whore Rosa Luxemburg," he said.

"So this is the fat little man Waldemar Pabst," said dear Rosa.

Pabst nodded to his minions.

"Hold them."

Riley, Liebknecht, and I were held firmly while Pabst proceeded to beat Rosa mercilessly with his fists. When she fell to the floor, he kicked her ribs. I thought he might kill her, but abruptly he stopped, took out a handkerchief, and wiped his sweaty face.

"You should not anger me, Mrs. Luxemburg," he sneered down at her. "I am far from the worst you will face tonight."

I knew what that meant, so I took a shot.

"Listen to me, Herr Pabst. You make a mistake if you kill us. We can make you the ruler of all Germany."

I had no idea what I was talking about.

"Oh, really?" he said, smiling incredulously. "Listen, you men. This young Bolshevik shit will make Waldemar Pabst the ruler of all Germany!"

They laughed, on cue.

"Tell me, shit-face, just how do you plan to do that?"

I was still pondering that one when the door opened behind me. Von Kleist loomed into view, looked us over, and sighed in a pleased sort of way.

"So, it is true. You are all here. Good."

I gave up any pretense of talking my way out of this fix. Not with von Kleist in the room. He still wore his brown Freikorps uniform topped by a brown naval-looking captain's hat with a hard brim.

Karl suddenly decided to make his presence known. He stepped forward and looked up into von Kleist's face.

"You are an officer in what they call the Freikorps," he said calmly. "I appeal to you. We are innocent of any crime. We are held here only for our political beliefs, yet this man"—he pointed at Pabst—"has attacked and beaten a small, helpless woman. If you are a gentleman, you will take us to a court where we can be dealt with according to German law. Even Herr Ebert would not countenance what is happening here."

Von Kleist smiled and the room went quiet.

"I am not a gentleman, Herr Liebknecht," von Kleist said icily, "I am a German. And if you think that whatever has happened here compares in any way to what is about to happen, you are sadly mistaken."

Riley stood stock still as his eyes darted from one side of the room to the other.

"Herr Pabst," said von Kleist. "I take it there is no further requirement for the existence of these prisoners?"

Pabst drew himself up to his full five-foot-five.

"Do with them as you will. I wash my hands of them."

And he strode into the back room of the suite, closing the door behind him.

"What a putz," von Kleist said to the amusement of the Freikorps in the room.

Even in my extreme jeopardy, I noted the peculiar use of a Yiddish word. Yiddish is such an expressive language it can't be resisted, even by virulent anti-Semites.

The anti-Semite in question stepped over to Riley and shifted to English.

"It is truly good to see you again, Mr. Riley. I swore that I would have my revenge when I learned what happened to my Yaquis. I know it was you who did it, but I don't know how. Can you share it with me?"

Riley just stared up at von Kleist, measuring distances, weighing odds.

"It doesn't really matter," von Kleist said with a shrug. "We will be sure to be very careful with you tonight." He turned to me and

305

said, also in English, "And you, Cornelius. Perhaps you thought you disappointed me with that rather remarkable speech at the Communist Party meeting. Not at all! I was there, you know, dressed in worker's garb and hunched over to conceal my height. Believe me, good fellow, no one applauded more heartily than I."

He rubbed his hand on my back, causing bile to rise in my stomach.

"You see, while our little stab-in-the-back story would have been good to promote, you did something even more important. You pushed the workers into open revolution at a time when they were unprepared to deal with the consequences. Nothing could have been better for us! For now Ebert's army controls Berlin and we control Ebert. When Ludendorff returns to rule Germany, he should really build a statue of you in Potsdamer Platz. But I'm afraid he won't."

Von Kleist barked instructions to his men in German. We were to be taken in two cars, Riley with Rosa and me with Liebknecht. We were to be accompanied by five members of the Freikorps, plus von Kleist. Extreme care was to be taken in watching us, especially Riley.

He turned to me and spoke, still in German.

"And now, Cornelius. We are going to the zoo."

You need to understand the geography. The huge urban park called the Tiergarten is essentially a rectangle, running east and west along its long axis. It takes up a significant section of land in the center of Berlin. At the east end lies the Reichstag, the Brandenburg Gate, and a cosmopolitan boulevard lined with trees, called Unter den Linden for "under the linden trees." At the west end is one of Berlin's principal railway stations, plus the Berlin Zoological Gardens, one of the leading zoos in the world. Dividing the zoo from the western end of the Tiergarten is the Landwehr Canal, in whose surprisingly deep and turgid waters bodies have been disappearing for generations. A series of footbridges cross the Landwehr.

We were whisked to the Tiergarten in no time. After we were dropped off on the northwest edge of the two-square-mile urban park, von Kleist started marching us off toward the zoo. We were pushed and prodded and Rosa had an especially difficult time with her limp. She fell to the ground and one of the three Freikorps escorts in von Kleist's command clubbed her ribs with his rifle butt. Riley and I lunged to protect her, but to his credit, Liebknecht beat us to it. Disregarding the gun aimed at his breast, he broke away and shoved the beast who had struck Rosa.

"Animal," he exclaimed.

It was his last word. Von Kleist drew his pistol and shot a bullet into his brain. Karl Liebknecht collapsed onto the ground. He didn't have much of a sense of humor and he made a critical mistake in supporting a revolution before its time, but he had devoted his life to a greater cause than himself. Not many people can make that claim.

We left Liebknecht in the park like a dead dog. He wound up in a pauper's unmarked grave, but he is still remembered by the faithful. Without a word, von Kleist pushed us forward to the gate of the zoo. He reached into his pocket and pulled out a large key, which he used to open the metal gate and hurry us in.

"You know the way, Cornelius," he said. "Your tiger awaits. Rosa here is in for quite a treat and so is the tiger."

A zoo is a strange place in the nighttime, when no people are present. You hear animals more intensely: rustles and growls, shuffles and bumps. We were shoved past cage after cage. The moon was full and imparted an eerie yellow light to the proceedings. Rosa seemed dead on her feet, dragging her weaker leg, clinging for support to the Freikorps soldier guarding her. A black bear stared at us, seeming to wonder at our plight. A leopard snapped, a wild boar growled. In short order we reached the tiger cage.

Remember, this was long before the modern zoo with simulations of natural habitats. Back then, cages were cages. At least the man-eating Bengal tiger, as a rare and beautiful beast, was accorded the largest cage at the zoo. Inside were a few bales of hay and a water dish. When feeding time came, zookeepers would toss red meat between the bars. Of course, when von Kleist brought along a victim, rather more exotic fare was provided.

When we arrived at the tiger cage, von Kleist clutched Rosa closely to him. She seemed on the verge of unconsciousness.

"Now, dear Rosa," he cooed in her ear, "your Cornelius will meet his fate. Not the lady or the tiger this time, but the tiger watched by the lady. And Cornelius, know that when your time is done and your head is safely in the tiger's belly, your Rosa will be mine, just like Miguel. I will see you in hell."

He nodded and Riley and I were dragged off by the three Freikorps ruffians. I saw von Kleist press Rosa up to the bars of the tiger cage to give her a clear view of my decapitation. I was shaking so badly I could not walk. I nearly wet myself. We were soon to die. In my mind's eye, all I could see was the little dachshund's dismembered corpse.

The three Freikorps men opened the locked door behind the tiger cage and pushed us in. One of the three was Lindner, the ugly son of a bitch who had struck Rosa at Paul's house. If there was any way to kill these bastards, I meant to do it.

One Freikorps soldier pushed Riley against the back wall of the room behind the tiger cage and stuck his pistol in Riley's ribs. The other two grabbed my arms and forced me to the floor on my knees. Lindner lifted a bucket of slops from a corner of the room and poured it, laughing, over my head. I coughed and choked and almost gagged at the rancid smell of the animal guts that covered my hair and dripped over my face and into my eyes. Lindner opened the center-opening trap door that led into the cage, this time opening it all the way rather than the crack through which von Kleist had inserted Liebchen's head.

"Say hello to the kitty-cat, Jew-fucker," Lindner whispered in my ear.

Next thing I knew, I was flung headfirst through the slot opening into the cage, landing with my head and torso, down to my waist, exposed to the tiger. My legs were held firmly by my two captors.

I don't know if you've ever had the upper half of your body flung into a tiger cage with foul-smelling guts covering your head. It is disconcerting. I was quaking with terror, almost fainting, but I knew that my very life, and the lives of people I held dear, depended on whether I could keep my head for the next few seconds.

Coughing the slops from my mouth, I wiped my eyes and opened them. As I looked up, I saw von Kleist at the opposite side of the cage, holding Rosa in a headlock up against the bars and forcing her to watch. The sill of the opening in the wall cut into my stomach. I forced my head up from the dirt, straining my neck, and searched for the beast. There it was, lying in the far left corner of the cage. A gigantic, magnificent animal, a wonder of creation. The eyes in the beast's huge head blinked, as though it were irritated at the commotion keeping it from sleep. Then it must have scented the delightful aroma of the innards dripping off my head, for the great golden eyes suddenly focused on me. It rose to its feet, sniffing the breeze. I estimated that in perhaps twenty seconds, I would be a dead man.

The tiger started toward me, carefully placing one great paw before another. I reached for the cord around my neck and yanked at it, then yanked at it again. The bag came loose in my hands. The tiger was picking up speed.

Hands shaking, I emptied the bag of its contents: a meatball. From behind the wall, I heard Lindner shouting some abuse at Riley, or at me, it didn't matter. I almost dropped the meatball, but I held on and gauged my throw. The tiger was about twenty feet from me now, loping, almost at a run. Its great jaws opened and it roared. I could see the slaver and the great wet tongue and the deadly teeth.

Holding my body up off the ground, I tossed the meatball straight in the air. My heart skipped a beat when I saw I'd thrown too far left, but it didn't matter. The Bengal hardly slowed as it stretched its head to take the meatball in its jaws and swallow it down. It kept coming. Twelve feet away, then five feet. It moved into its leap, prepared for the kill. I threw my arms over my head.

In the middle of its jump, the tiger stiffened and dropped. It rolled once, stone dead. The strychnine-laced meatball which Riley had seen fit to provide me had done its job. The tiger lay dead, not three feet from my face.

I heard a struggle behind me, then three quick shots. The grips on my legs disappeared. I saw von Kleist aim his pistol at me and I saw Rosa knock it away just as he fired. Riley gave a heave and pulled me back into the little room behind the cage. The three Freikorps he had dispatched lay dead and the gun he had taken from one of them was still smoking in his hand.

"Rosa!" I exclaimed.

He shoved a gun in my hand and we were out of that room in an instant. Rounding the cage, I saw von Kleist hurrying away with Rosa in his grip, toward the zoo gate that led back to the cars. I tried a shot, but the distance was too great. We both started after them. Von Kleist didn't break stride as he threw lead back at us, more to slow us down than with any expectation of hitting either of us. Rosa's leg was giving out on her and she was slowing them down, so von Kleist used his brute strength and size to pick her up off the ground and carry her like a doll at his side. It kept us from firing any more shots and didn't slow him down a step. He bolted through the gate and down the footpath toward the bridge over the Landwehr, with Riley and me pounding behind. For once, I outran my friend, almost too far, for von Kleist took a better-aimed shot at me and this one whizzed past my ear.

Riley grabbed me from behind. He saw that von Kleist, having reached the footbridge, stopped in the middle of it and was holding his gun barrel to Rosa's head. We were not yet in range for a sure shot and von Kleist was holding Rosa in the line of fire.

"Gentlemen, you have my admiration," he called out to us. "You have met me three times and you have survived." He nuzzled Rosa a moment with his gun barrel and seemed to whisper in her ear. Then he said, "But not your Rosa, I'm sad to say," and he blew her brains out.

I think I screamed. Quick as light, von Kleist bundled her body over the railing into the canal and blazed away at us with his pistol. Riley pulled me to the ground and we returned fire, but to no avail. Von Kleist backed away rapidly, still firing. We followed him, but by the time we reached the crest of the bridge, he was at the waiting car. With a final wave, he ducked into the vehicle and was gone.

I don't remember much after that. I was in shock, I suppose. Riley got me out of there and we found the apartment of a comrade to bunk in. I do remember something Riley said that night, but not where we were when he said it. I just remember him staring at me through his cigarette smoke, those dark eyes boring into me.

"That man needs killing," I remember him saying.

Part Five

Munich

37

Some Very Hard People

Jim

Riley and I were having dinner at a Perkins restaurant near his hotel. "Did you finish it?"

"I got to where von Kleist killed Rosa Luxemburg."

Riley frowned. He'd been cranky lately, anxious to get back to his hacienda.

"I wanted you to finish the whole thing. I'm sick of this weather. It gets in my bones."

"I've got a job, Riley. I can't spend my whole life on this project. There's not much left in the notebook. We can talk about the rest over the phone."

Riley stirred his coffee and considered it, but shook his head.

"Might as well finish what we started."

"Have you seen my parents yet?"

They lived not forty miles from where we sat, but Riley hadn't been to see them the whole time he was in Minnesota and he had sworn me to secrecy about his being there. Strange for someone who claimed to be a family man, compared to Grandpa Jimmy.

"I figure I'll give it a miss this time. I'll be back. There are lots more notebooks in that box."

"Why are you so insistent on keeping the notebooks secret? The whole family would want to read them."

"And that's why," Riley said, as firmly as only Riley could. "There's a lot in those notebooks that might hurt people, might make them think less of us, might draw attention in ways you don't want, maybe from some very hard people. So I figured I'd dump it in your lap, let you decide what's right to do after I'm dead. But you have to read all the notebooks first."

I knew I'd finish the first one. I'd come this far and I wanted to see if the boys killed von Kleist. I wasn't sure I'd go on after that. What I'd read so far just couldn't be true and it sounded like even more crazy stuff was ahead in the other notebooks.

"Riley, don't take this the wrong way, but I gotta say, there's stuff in here that's hard to swallow. I've researched Rosa Luxemburg and Karl Liebknecht and Jogiches and Pabst, but there's no mention of anything about young American soldiers or about von Kleist."

I could see I was angering him a little.

"Not asking you to believe anything, I'm just asking you to read the goddam thing. Just asking you to help me get these goddam notebooks cleaned up and off my plate before I'm dead. Cornelius went before me, so I'm stuck with the job." His tone softened a little. "Look, Cornelius and I saw a lot of things. Things just kept happening to us, we always seemed to fall into the middle of craziness. Think about what you've already read: we saw George Patton get a blowjob from a German maniac and we were there when Churchill watched a famous Frenchman's guts get poured all over a restaurant. Not the sort of shit governments want spread around and it gets worse the more notebooks you read. Lots worse. Edgar Hoover and Bobby Kennedy didn't agree on much, but neither of them wanted Cornelius and me in the history books."

Great, now we were conspiracy theorists. I let it pass and the conversation drifted to other topics.

As we were saying goodbye in the parking lot, Riley put his hand on my shoulder.

"Finish the damn thing," he said.

38

The Trail Leads
to Munich

Cornelius

Leo went mad when we told him. He beat his breast, the first time I've seen anyone actually do that. He tossed over the table, pounded the walls, and cursed endlessly, vowing to start the killing with the Kaiser and Ludendorff and work his way down. He must have spent five minutes on what he was going to do to Ebert alone.

I was utterly miserable, despite knowing deep down that Rosa and I couldn't have lasted. What was I going to do, spend the rest of my young life in Europe, putting up placards and giving speeches with my middle-aged radical lover? Rosa knew it too, of course, and never kidded herself about it like I would do sometimes. Rosa wasn't the first woman I made love to, but she was my first lover. I still think kindly of her, along with my second wife and Dorothy Parker and the rest of the handful of ladies I've loved over the years. I cried real tears for Rosa and Riley held my head in his lap while I did it.

Assessing the situation with Leo after he calmed down, we realized we were truly fucked. We met in the last of the Spartacist safehouses, where Leo had told us to go if we got separated. It was an abandoned shack in the eastern part of town, with no heat in the midst of a frigid Berlin winter. We were down to the dregs of our money, which fortunately was in U.S. dollars. The city hadn't seen much damage in the war, but the economy was in shambles. Inflation made German money worthless: starving Berliners would light their last cigarette butts with a hundred-thousand-mark note. Those who could afford to eat out insisted on paying for their meal when they ordered, since they knew the price would go up before the meal was done. Endless lines waited for miserable pickings at the food shelves. With Rosa and Karl dead, Leo was number one on the Freikorps hit list, while Riley and I no doubt gave Herr von Kleist an itch he was anxious to scratch.

We meant to kill that bastard, no doubt about it. As for Leo, at first he announced that he would rather double his efforts to fight for Rosa's cause than go on some sort of murder rampage. But when we told him not only what von Kleist had done on the bridge over the Landwehr, but in the Mexican cave, Leo was right there with us in the hunt for von Kleist.

We three became like pack dogs, sniffing the streets for a hint of the beast. Leo had his contacts even among the Freikorps, but none could or would give any information as to the whereabouts of the bastard. I remember once, we were drinking with a Freikorps lug in a gay bar and we'd had quite a few. The connection of the Freikorps with a gay bar was not as unusual as it might seem: I could tell you stories about Freikorps chief Ernst Roehm, for example. Anyway, this particular Fritz was well-oiled with our liquor and was eager to help until we told him who we were after. He froze up and said he couldn't help us.

"What do you mean you can't help?" Leo barked. "You know this man. It shows on your face!"

Riley was staring impassively at the floorshow, where colored lights flicked over the shiny bodies of two men rubbing their hands over each other to throbbing, rather creepy music. He asked me to translate the last remarks and I did. Riley pulled his Luger and pointed it, under the table, at the crotch of the Freikorps queer. I relayed Riley's graphic description of what would happen in thirty seconds if the German didn't spill his guts.

He just laughed. He was drunk, all right, but it wasn't drink that made him ignore Riley's threat.

"I don't say the man you seek exists," he explained, "but if he did, I would be much more afraid of him than of anything you could possibly do to me."

Riley put the gun away. Later, I teased him, saying I thought he always followed through on what he promised.

"I do," he said. "Except when I'm lying."

Since Leo was too well-known and Riley couldn't speak the language, I drew the perilous task of casing the Hotel Eden lobby, trying to ferret out our prey. I borrowed various clothes from comrades and tried out different hairstyles, hats, and eyeglasses to keep from being recognized. I saw Pabst pass by numerous times, but never von Kleist.

Meanwhile, the reaction to the deaths of Rosa and Karl was stupendous. People took to the streets, posted placards on walls, and scuffled with the Freikorps. The usual Bolshevik bustle, none of it very meaningful, as Rosa would have been first to point out. Leo was in the thick of it, fearlessly leading the protests with his great shaggy mug sticking out for his enemies to chop off at will. So it happened, but after Riley and I left Berlin.

We got word of von Kleist's whereabouts from an unexpected source. A prominent Bavarian communist named Schneider had come to Berlin to visit his mother. Clearly, the surviving leaders of the Bolshevik cause in Berlin had to take him to dinner. Riley was sick of being surrounded by jabbering he didn't understand, so he stayed home. I nearly did too, for truth be told, without my dear Rosa, I no longer gave a damn who ruled Germany. But I hadn't had a decent meal in weeks and some of the comrades still had enough to pony up for a feast to honor a visiting brother-in-arms. So off I went.

The dinner was a snooze, as I expected. Lots of political theory and bombast, mostly from that blasted Barth at whom I wanted to throw my dinner roll. Schneider painted a bleak picture of Bavaria, which had been the first German state to be ruled by a socialist premier, a fellow named Eisner. A recent election had gone against this Eisner, but in late January he was still holding on. Schneider didn't like him, but he had to admit it was remarkable to see any form of socialism, much less a Jewish premier, in a German state such as Bavaria.

"Truth is, it does my heart good to be here in Berlin," he confessed to us. "I'm sure you have your troubles, but what I see in Munich passes all understanding. An evil is about to spread over Germany and it will start in Bavaria."

Barth scoffed.

"Evil spreading? Comrade, where have you been? Germany is

overflowing with evil and has been for years, for centuries! Did you miss the war? Do you not know of the assassination of Rosa Luxemburg and Karl Liebknecht?"

Like you gave them any support while they lived, you little pimp, I thought.

Schneider slumped in his chair. He was a pleasant sort of young fellow, looking like a college professor somewhat down at the heels, but he seemed shaken by recent events.

"I know, I know. I do not minimize the tragedies, here and everywhere. It's just that in Munich there is something happening that I cannot explain. I think there are deep chambers in the human heart, deeper and dirtier than I ever imagined, and they are only now beginning to surface. The war has opened doors that should have remained forever closed. I've never seen or heard of what I now see and hear in Munich every day."

I asked him to explain. He bolted down his drink, and he did not look like a heavy-drinking man. Even Barth became silent, waiting for Schneider to go on.

"There have always been Jew-haters in Bavaria," he said. "But now the talk is open, hateful, everywhere you go. The Jews and the communists stabbed Germany in the back, it is said, before Germany could win the war. The Jews drink the blood of Christian babies. A Jew can hardly walk the streets without being spit on and even beaten. And it's not just Jews. There is hate everywhere: hate for foreigners, hate for the crippled, hate for gypsies, hate for anyone in any way different from so-called Aryan Germans. I don't understand it."

Leo looked grim.

"You exaggerate, comrade."

"I do not," Schneider replied pugnaciously. "Walk the streets of Munich, Comrade Leo. Go to the beer halls, the political rallies, even the churches! Then tell me there is no evil growing in Germany."

The mood was now irretrievably somber. Schneider finished his drink.

"I am sorry not to be better company," he apologized. "Let me tell you of just one incident, one among many, to give you an idea of what I am talking about. A few days ago, I was walking down a street in Munich on my way to the grocery store. It was a good day for February, not too cold and the sun was out. I was feeling good. I turn a corner and what do I see? I see the backs of three Freikorps thugs who are bent over, punching and kicking some poor bastard lying on the sidewalk. They beat him mercilessly, using sticks and their fists and their boots. A few feet away, a young woman is held captive by more Freikorps. A very tall Freikorps officer, a monster of a man, is watching the scene while calmly smoking a cigarette."

At the word "monster," I looked up from my plate.

"Finally," Schneider went on, "the tall man called a halt to the beating. It looked like it might be too late, since the victim was a bleeding mass on the sidewalk. The tall man took the woman by the arm and walked her into the middle of the street. He spoke loudly to the crowd that had gathered.

"'This is just a lesson, my good Germans,' he said. 'Just a lesson. That pile of dung lying there on the sidewalk is one of the Jew communists who stabbed Germany in the back and caused the surrender that now leaves you to starve and your families to suffer. And this girl I am holding is not a Jew but she was seen eating with him, walking arm in arm with this filthy Jew scum! So she needs to be taught a lesson, too.'" Schneider was shivering as he continued. "He ripped off the girl's blouse so her breasts were exposed and he stood there grinning at the crowd. He held out his hand and one of the Freikorps gave him a pair of shears. He proceeded to cut the girl's lovely long brown hair until almost none was left. Then the bastard put the shears against one of her bare breasts, as if to cut off a nipple. 'Remember, Germans!' he shouted to the crowd. 'Remember what happens to those bitches who mix races and consort with Jews.'

"What is happening? What can make a man do something like that? I do not believe in God, but what I am witnessing these days in Bavaria convinces me there is a devil."

Schneider fell silent. I leaned forward and spoke very softly.

"This tall Freikorps captain. Tell me about him. What did he look like?"

Schneider shrugged.

"Mainly, I remember his eyes. His eyes were unholy, glowing. It was as though he was getting sexual pleasure from cutting that woman's hair and making to cut at her breasts. How can a man like that exist?"

I didn't know. But I thought I knew who he was.

Schneider returned to Munich two days later and Riley and I

accompanied him. Leo didn't try to stop us, nor did he try to go with us.

"Good hunting, my comrades," he said as he hugged us goodbye at the train station. "Put an extra bullet in that bastard's brain for me. For my part, I swear to you I will never give up. I will fight for Rosa's cause with every fiber of my being and I will bring justice to whoever was complicit in her murder. I swear it!"

There were tears in my eyes as we leaned out the train window and waved goodbye to him. There would have been more tears if I had known Leo would be dead in a few weeks, murdered by the Freikorps.

Germany was indeed a dangerous place.

39

Lunch at the Hofbräuhaus

Cornelius

We pulled into the Munich station on a cold afternoon in mid-February. Schneider's family was waiting for him and I was quite touched when Schneider hugged a little boy and a little girl to his bosom and kissed his wife warmly. I thought of doing the same, for Schneider's wife was a fetching, buxom little frau with blonde hair pulled back and breasts that pushed out against her bodice in a most distracting way. Not that I was over Rosa yet, of course.

Schneider was the sort of trusting fellow to open his home to two American strangers, just because we professed to be Marxists and Leo vouched for us. Without blinking, his wife accepted the news that she was now responsible for two unannounced guests, one of whom didn't speak German, the other of whom was eyeing her chest in a most discreet manner.

The Schneider abode wasn't far from the train station and, as we walked toward it, it was easy to dismiss Schneider's accounts of the evils in Bavaria. Munich is a lovely and clean city that seems much more friendly and family-oriented than cold Berlin. But the world was soon to know just how accurate Herr Schneider's remarks had been. There was indeed an evil growing in Munich and when we were there, it was just starting to take root.

For a treat, we went to the Hofbräuhaus for lunch. Schneider took pleasure in telling me that Lenin, when he lived in Munich, regularly frequented this establishment. We chose seats at one of the many long tables in the enormous hall and sat down to listen to the oompah band and drink beer. This was part of the good Germany so beloved by Jack O'Neal, with all its philosophers, its science, its artistic tradition personified by Beethoven and Goethe and Schiller, and its beer and brass music. The twentieth century also witnessed too much of the bad Germany. And like the girl in the rhyme, when Germany was bad, she was horrid.

We told Schneider in the train all about von Kleist and why we were traveling to Munich. He took it well.

"Gentlemen," he said. "I will help you all that I can. I am a family man. I believe with all my heart in the integrity of the working man and in the struggle to overturn the capitalist system and replace it with one that will serve all classes. And I sympathize with you, Comrade O'Neal, for your loss and the loss to the cause that Comrade Luxemburg's death represents. But I am not a killer. I will help you, but I cannot kill for you."

That was all right. Put Riley next to von Kleist, I figured, and the killing part was all set. We just needed to find the bastard.

Schneider gave us a quick summary of what he knew of the Freikorps in Munich. Even more than in Berlin, the line was thin between a genuine member of the organization and simply a mean drunk who carried a lot of hate within him. There were some who wore the Freikorps uniform, but this group could always count on help from any number of Bavarian men, most of them discharged soldiers, for any devil's brew that was fermenting. The beer halls were their gathering places, including the Hofbräuhaus. Some of the smaller halls catered only to this element and an outsider risked his life just by entering. Jews, of course, placed themselves at high risk simply by breathing Munich air.

"I don't see how it could be worse than Berlin, Comrade Schneider," I protested. "Look at Rosa and Karl, murdered with impunity. The Freikorps run a torture chamber right in the Hotel Eden and everyone knows it. I know I just got here, but it seems very peaceful on the streets and it's a very pretty place."

Schneider laughed and his wife shook her head as she attended to one of the children.

"Munich is a wonderful city!" he said. "People take their ease in the Englischer Garten, they watch the Glockenspiel figures turn round and round, they drink the best German beer and eat the best German sausages. But listen to the talk of the Bavarians as they do these things. I grew up here, a Jew. I cannot count the times I was beaten, the times I was humiliated. There has always been an underlying hatred here, an underlying conviction that Germans are a superior race with all others inferior to them. The charming surroundings, the good life here, never diminished that attitude. Perhaps it made it worse. Then the war came. Bavarians went mad with the fever. They volunteered their sons and contributed their fortunes, not for the Kaiser, but to show the world that Germany is best, that Germans are the master race. Then it came crashing down on them. Germany surrendered unconditionally, without citizens of Munich or Berlin hearing a shot fired. What then? The Kaiser fled into exile with Ludendorff close on his heels. The German economy was destroyed along with their fortunes, but what was far worse was the assault on their conviction that Germans are a superior people and cannot be beaten by any other nation. Since that certainty cannot be challenged, they seek scapegoats, people to hate and blame, and it is easiest to choose those they already hate. Look in the eyes of these Bavarians, comrades. You will quake for our children's futures."

Mrs. Schneider cast her husband the universal glare of wifely disapproval.

"Enough doom and gloom," he said, "and on to business. You gentlemen want to find a particular member of the Freikorps. He is conspicuous, so one method would be simply to walk the streets until you find him. This seems inefficient, so let me suggest another way."

I wasn't bothering to translate for Riley as it would have bogged us down. He occupied himself by smiling quietly at the little Schneider girl, but she seemed mildly frightened of him.

I'll say this for Schneider, he knew how to get down to cases.

"I have been thinking about this man you seek, von Kleist," he said. "Why would he come to Munich? He seems the sort of man who might be best employed as an assassin if there were someone important here that the Freikorps wanted to kill. Is that right?"

"Absolutely," I said. "We saw him used that way in Paris during the war."

Schneider nodded, pleased with himself.

"So is there someone in Munich the Freikorps would want to assassinate, but who might prove especially difficult to kill? I believe there is. The head of the so-called socialist government, Kurt Eisner. He is not as malleable as your Herr Ebert. He speaks out against the Kaiser and the aristocracy for starting the war and, most of all, he is a Jew. It could well be that the Freikorps wants him killed and has sent for an outside assassin to do it."

This seemed speculative and pretty much irrelevant to me.

"If that were so," I asked, "why would he draw attention to himself with incidents like the one you told us about?"

Schneider shrugged.

"Perhaps he wants to win the respect of the Freikorps in Munich. Or perhaps he just couldn't help himself, for he seems to be that kind of man. Anyway, this got me thinking of how we might draw von Kleist out. I know a man who is connected with the right-wing element here in Munich, including the Freikorps. We are not friends, of course, but my wife used to work for him and he was kind to her. Sometimes we have coffee together and he tries to get information from me about our movement while I try to get the same sort of information from him."

I waited while Schneider swigged his beer. He was thinking.

"This man, whose name is Hummel," he went on, "is very highly placed in this town. I think that if there were truly a plot to assassinate Eisner, Hummel would know about it and would know how to contact the man who has come here to carry it out."

This grew more interesting.

"So what if I let slip to Hummel that according to our intelligence, two men have arrived in Munich to kill Kurt Eisner? I could demand to know if this were true. What would he do? He would deny all knowledge, of course, but he might pass word on to the man you seek. Assuming he does, wouldn't this man, and all the Freikorps, want to know the identity of these two men and their plan? Might they not suspect that others in the Freikorps are playing a double game? Tell me, Comrade O'Neal. If your man thought that competitors were in town, would he not seek them out?"

"In a heartbeat," I agreed.

Schneider was on a roll.

"Just so. And if I also gave Hummel some idea of how he might contact these two assassins for the Freikorps, might your man not come knocking on your door?"

"Absolutely."

Schneider nodded.

"So that is what I will do for you, Comrade O'Neal. But understand, if this monster takes the bait, it will be for you and your friend to deal with him. It sounds to me like he is a very big and nasty fish."

40

"Just Talk to Herr Linz"

Cornelius

It took several days for Schneider to set a date and time to meet with Herr Hummel, who owned one of the larger banks in Bavaria. He was not the biggest fat cat in Munich—that honor fell to Gustav Krupp of the great munitions firm that for centuries had supplied the arms for Germany's war machine. But Hummel was definitely a player and as right-wing as a Bavarian could be, which is saying something. I suspect he was playing Schneider for his own purposes and also that he had a soft spot for Frau Schneider. I was developing one, too.

While we waited, Schneider took us to a meeting of the Munich Communist Party. After he introduced me as a close friend and colleague of the martyred Rosa Luxemburg, I received a very warm welcome. I even gave a short speech about Rosa's vision and about the need for all Germany's communists to come together and make Germany a workers' paradise that would eclipse even that of Russia. By the end of the evening, I had a roomful of loyal friends. Riley looked bored to tears.

Shortly thereafter, Schneider had coffee with Hummel and reported that all went as planned. Three days passed, then four. We passed time by walking along the streets of Munich. We saw no sign of von Kleist, but we did see numerous examples of the race-hatred and paranoia that Schneider so ably described. It sat strangely in the fairytale setting of old Munich, like a slug crawling across a wedding cake.

By pre-arrangement, Schneider told Hummel that the two mysterious assassins could be seen every afternoon at four taking coffee at a pastry shop on the Marienplatz. So each day, Riley and I had coffee at the specified shop. I must have gained a pound or two just sampling their wares, for the cakes were really quite good, especially considering the post-war challenges. Riley stuck to black coffee.

On the fourth day, as I was eating an especially tasty pastry with chocolate cream filling, a nasty-looking fellow suddenly sat down at our table. He smelled of old sweat and booze. He looked like a tramp, wearing an old ratty overcoat and army boots with the sole flapping loosely from the toe. His hair was greasy and hung down the sides of his head unclipped. His breath was foul and I counted three missing teeth.

"Order me something," he said.

Riley had his hand in the pocket of his jacket and I knew it was wrapped around his pistol.

"How about if we order you to leave?" I offered.

The cretin smiled, revealing gaps in his teeth.

"I am here because I have been sent here by the most powerful people in Bavaria. Why are you here?"

"Perhaps we were sent here by the most powerful people in Germany," I said. "Or perhaps we were sent by no one. Perhaps we are tourists here to see the Glockenspiel. In any event, what business is it of yours?"

A waitress stopped at our table. I gestured to our guest, who pointed to a marzipan tart in the display case. When she left, he responded.

"You need not tell me anything. I am simply an agent for people who are curious about you. Word has reached them that you may work for people who have similar interests to their own. Word has it that you may be engaged on an errand similar to an errand they wish to undertake. My principals simply wish to ensure that such efforts are coordinated."

The marzipan tart arrived and our guest wolfed it down, spraying frosting from the gaps in his teeth.

I leaned over the table and spoke very softly to him.

"Perhaps we don't care about your principals. Perhaps we think you should get the fuck out of this bakery before my friend erases your miserable existence."

He finished his tart.

"Perhaps. I will go and I thank you for the tart. Let me just add that if you have any interest in pursuing this conversation, come tonight to the Weissbräukeller and talk to Herr Linz. He will be able to answer your questions. Nine o'clock."

He pushed back from the table and made to walk away.

"Wait a blasted minute," I said. "Who is this Herr Linz? How will we know him?"

The tramp smiled.

"Herr Linz is easy to identify. He has a little mustache under his nose, like Charlie Chaplin. He had to shave it to fit under a gas mask during the war. He will answer all your questions. Just talk to Herr Linz."

41
Naked Boxing

Cornelius

That afternoon, we gathered at Schneider's house with a large group of comrades, a sure sign that my relationship with Rosa had earned us their trust and brought some degree of trust from us in return. Well, at least from me. Riley didn't trust anyone, but he knew we needed help in some form.

"Congratulations," Schneider said. "You have drawn the fly to the flypaper. We wish you luck."

"Very kind of you, Herr Schneider," I said, "but we need a bit more than just luck. We need backup."

Schneider's eyes narrowed.

"Backup? *Was ist das?*"

So I told him *was das ist*. He agreed. The comrades gave us a rousing cheer.

Night found Riley and me sitting in a café across from the Weissbräukeller. I'd never seen a building that stood so ominously and made my spirits sink so deeply. For a hostelry supposedly dedicated to good cheer and fellowship, the Weissbräukeller turned out to be a gloomy castle of darkness, twisting halls, windows that loomed like sightless eyes, and gargoyles perched on windowsills seemingly daring passersby to enter. It looked the perfect Gothic setting for the racist Bavarian killers we knew lurked inside.

The Weissbräukeller, we learned from our comrades, was one of the worst fascist beer halls in the city. No Jew dared enter. This was where the Freikorps recruited the brutes of the city and made contact with recently discharged and thoroughly disillusioned German soldiers. This was where they plotted their Jew-baiting adventures, their attacks on left-wing partisans. It sat on the very edge of the Isar River, leading me to wonder how many bodies had disappeared off the dock that I could see extending off the back of the property. It looked to be the ideal place to settle old scores with Otto von Kleist and the ideal place to die while doing so.

"Nine o'clock," Riley said, checking his railroad watch. "Let's go finish this thing."

I uttered a silent prayer to the Marxist god as we walked across the street. Riley pushed open the door of the tavern. Out came the inevitable oompah music. Inside was a large room filled with round tables instead of the more usual long rectangular beer hall tables. Apparently the patrons at the Weissbräukeller preferred their privacy. The usual buxom waitresses, perhaps a little more down at the heel than most, circulated with trays bearing large mugs of heady German beer. The band played their polkas and waltzes from a raised platform that projected out into the center of the hall, unlike the proscenium stage at the Hofbräuhaus. Seated at virtually every table were beefy Bavarians, many wearing Freikorps uniforms, wolfing sausages and wild boar and swilling beer.

Except at one table, off in the corner. Riley gestured to it, bringing it to my attention. Seated alone at the table was another tramp, looking even more disheveled than the man at the bakery. He looked dirty, unwashed. As we had been told, a little toothbrush mustache decorated his upper lip, closely trimmed at the sides so it looked like Charlie Chaplin's, just as the man in the bakery had said. He wore a uniform I didn't recognize. He was slumped in his chair, picking at his pale white hands. In front of him was a glass of clear water, no beer.

Riley nodded to me and I led the way over to the table. The man continued to look down at his hands.

"Herr Linz, I believe," I said.

Linz carefully finished picking a piece of skin from his thumb. When he lifted his head and looked into my eyes, I swayed on my feet.

I've seen memorable eyes in my time. Those of von Kleist, of course, and those of Winston Churchill bubbling with merriment and shrewdness. Rosa, Einstein, Edgar Hoover, Martin Luther King, all had eyes that let you know you were in the presence of some sort of greatness, for better or worse. But no eyes ever had such an effect on me as the eyes that now glared up from that rather ridiculous face on that undistinguished body in that dismal bar on the River Isar.

Their color, for one thing. They were an odd shade of blue-gray, a color I've never seen on any other human eyes. Cold, empty, doll-like eyes banked by fires that burned with hate. It took me a moment to think of where I'd seen those eyes before: on wolves.

The corners of his mouth lifted in what I supposed was meant to be a smile.

"I am, as you say, Herr Linz. Sit down, gentlemen. I've been waiting for you."

As we did as bidden, I noticed that Riley had his hand on his pistol. I ordered two beers from a blonde-haired barmaid.

"Are you in the army, Herr Linz?" I asked, by way of conversation.

"I *was* in the army," he answered stiffly. "Now, I guard prisoners out in the country. The army is no more. It was stabbed in the back and it is gone, but we will return."

Well, then.

"What prisoners do you guard, Herr Linz?" I asked curiously. "The war is over."

Linz looked up at the ceiling, then down at his feet. There was something uncanny about the man.

"There are always prisoners. Armies may be betrayed, navies may disappear, but there are always prisoners to guard. It is a fact of life."

"You sent for us, Herr Linz. What do you want?"

Again, Linz pierced me with those demonic eyes.

"What do I want?" he mimicked me. "What I want is for the clock to go back. I want the mustard gas expelled from my lungs. I want Germany where it belongs, at the peak of the world, with the Jews and the Bolsheviks and other human scum in the dust beneath our feet. That is what 'Herr Linz' wants." Suddenly his glare darted over to Riley. "And you? You are silent. Don't you speak, man?"

333

Riley said nothing, of course, not comprehending Linz's German, which seemed to me to bear a slight Austrian accent, consistent with his last name, as Linz is a city in Austria.

"My friend doesn't speak German," I explained. "We are Americans."

Linz nodded, as though a last puzzle piece had slid into place. I felt, more than saw, some large individuals drifting over to our table.

"We do not get many Americans in this place," Linz said. "They are not welcome here."

I tried to smile.

"The war is over, Herr Linz."

"Is it? If you think so, I congratulate you on your ignorance, Herr O'Neal."

It took a moment for it to register that he knew my name. Riley was much faster. His hand went for his pistol the instant he heard my name pass Linz's lips, but before it cleared his belt, we were seized from behind and held firm. The big Bavarians who'd surrounded us stuck guns in our faces and we were helpless.

Linz rose to his feet. The hall fell silent, as though every patron were aware of what was happening in our corner of the room. Even the band stopped playing. The musicians quickly gathered up their instruments and exited the stage. Linz addressed the crowd, his voice carrying surprisingly well in the drafty tavern.

"Friends! Germans! Again the forces of Bolshevism are in our midst! These two are Americans, soldiers of the bastards who came across the sea to fight against the Fatherland! Worse, they are Bolsheviks, supporters of the Jews and the liars who stabbed our glorious troops in the back and brought us down into the dust when we should be up among the gods!"

I've had friendlier introductions. Our handlers lifted the guns from our belts and held us fast.

"We have a special welcome for these boys tonight," Linz went on. "A very special German welcome indeed. You see, this one here," indicating Riley, "this boy is a boxer. He fights with his fists in the American sport of pugilism." Linz spoke the word "pugilism" in broken English, sputtering over each syllable. "We do not want to take advantage of these boys, do we? No, we want to give them every chance. We even want to challenge them on their own grounds, on the grounds of pugilism, with a German ready to face them in the ring of honor! And to ensure that the match is conducted fairly and with the utmost respect for the rules of decorum"—Linz was grinning broadly—"I myself will referee!"

There was pandemonium from the crowd, who were all for it. I glanced over at Riley, who winked at me gamely. Linz bustled about, clearing the raised platform, directing the oompah band to the corner where they could play accompaniment to the match. When everything was arranged to his satisfaction, Linz waved his arm at the stairway in the corner behind our table, which led upward to a second floor that likely contained the living quarters of the proprietors.

"Representing the Aryan race!" he shouted. "Entering the arena, please give your warmest welcome to Herr Otto von Kleist!"

And there he was, at the top of the stairs. Von Kleist wore a loose salmon-colored robe that hung from his massive shoulders down to just below his knees. His hair was cropped close and his face had a feminine cast, as though he were wearing some sort of makeup. His feet and hands were bare. In one hand, he carried a small cloth bag. He stood a moment and peered over the crowd. He looked every inch like the monster he was.

After a swift simultaneous intake of breath, the crowd began to stomp their feet, whistle, and applaud. Von Kleist marched ceremoniously down the stairs, one step at a time, his bare feet slapping on the wood. He raised his hands above his head, as if to encompass the entire hall in his embrace. The noise of the crowd grew louder as the hands gripping Riley and me grew tighter. Von Kleist reached the bottom of the stairs and headed for the stage, Bavarians sober and drunk giving way before him. He did not spare us a glance. When he reached the stage, Linz raised his hands to silence the crowd.

"Bring the Americans!" he intoned.

Riley and I were manhandled to the edge of the stage. Von Kleist put his bag on the floor and pointed to Riley, who was pushed up two steps onto the platform with von Kleist and Linz. Von Kleist looked coolly down at him from a height advantage of nearly a foot. He said something in English to Riley, but I couldn't make it out. Then von Kleist strutted about the stage, enjoying the adulation. Suddenly he let the robe fall to his feet and he stood there, naked as a babe, with his arms raised over his head.

Linz looked uncomfortable, but the crowd went wild. I shrank from the screaming, the stomping, the sheer visceral hatred unleashed by von Kleist's astonishing nudity. It was as if some primeval German hero, a Siegfried from ancient times, had landed in their midst and released the Teutonic beast that dwelled in each of them. The band drew in its collective breath, then launched into a hearty rendition of "Deutschland Über Alles."

Unable to be heard over the bloodlust of the crowd, Linz gestured for minions to strip the clothes from Riley. In moments, he, too, stood naked on the stage. As von Kleist continued to strut around like a peacock, Riley shuffled his feet and punched the air to warm himself up as best he could. In doing this, he maneuvered his way over to me and took my arm.

"I can't beat him," he said to me in English. "He's too big. Find a way out of here while I fight him."

I nodded as Linz clapped his hands, silencing the crowd. He gave a chop of his hand that had only one meaning. The fight was on.

The two naked men circled each other, fists clenched, arms protecting themselves. I stood at the edge of the stage, with a big Bavarian holding each arm. Von Kleist was so tall, with so long a reach advantage over Riley, that the outcome of the fight seemed inevitable. As Riley told me, he didn't stand a chance.

Von Kleist threw some jabs, which Riley easily ducked. Riley's footwork was as good as ever: he danced around the stage with ease, one foot sliding across another, unhampered by his nakedness. I saw a waitress in the crowd running her eyes lustily over both fighters. Riley ducked one more jab and suddenly he was under the big man's guard, hammering blows into his belly with the speed of lightning. Von Kleist recovered and threw haymakers, but Riley danced away unharmed. Plainly, von Kleist had never been tutored by Skelly. But no boxer can give away a foot in height and sixty pounds in weight. The outcome of this fight remained inevitable.

Still, Riley's burst had drawn the attention of the crowd. I felt the grips on my arms loosen as my handlers leaned forward, intent on the fight. Riley danced and ducked and landed a blow on the German's kidney. I backed up slowly as my guardians inched forward. In moments, with no real effort, I had disappeared into the heart of the crowd with no one seeming to notice.

Riley was looking good, backpedaling around the platform, avoiding von Kleist's roundhouses. Linz must have thought so, too, for suddenly, as Riley skipped by him, Linz pulled a sap from his coat pocket and slapped Riley's kidneys with it. The surprise more than the blow stopped Riley in his tracks and von Kleist unleashed a left hook that blew Riley off his feet and into the first rows of the crowd, which added blows and kicks of their own before throwing him back on the stage. Linz waved the sap in the air and hooted in triumph.

Von Kleist had recovered his wind and his attitude. He stepped over to the little cloth bag, picked it up, and drew from it what first looked like two large brass bracelets. Then I realized what they were: brass knuckles with wicked spikes that looked capable of impaling a man's face with a single blow. Later, I heard from Susan Moore that von Kleist had given one of the knuckles to her husband and had still beaten him to death with the other. Von Kleist didn't offer one of the knuckles to Riley, who was too good a boxer.

I'd been watching the fight in a sort of trance, but now I realized I had to do something and do it now, otherwise Riley would be dead in seconds. He put up his hands, but I saw him look in vain from left to right for a place to run. I looked as well, but was hemmed in tightly by the crowd of drunken bloodthirsty Bavarians intent on seeing Riley's brains spilled by the deadly brass knuckles.

As Riley began circling for his life, feinting away from blows that von Kleist wasn't yet throwing, I suddenly knew what I needed. I looked around the walls for it and thankfully saw one, hanging on the wall near the main entrance: an old-fashioned kerosene lamp, burning its smoky light. Between me and the lamp were about two tons of beefy Teutonic flesh, not the sort of folk likely to make way easily. I stole a glance at the stage. Von Kleist threw a right cross that Riley just managed to avoid. His chest was heaving: he was expending a lot more energy by his circling and ducking than was his opponent, who was calmly picking his moment to throw the lethal blow. Linz laughed loudly. This couldn't continue more than another moment or two.

I picked out the most Jewish-looking fellow I could find among the people around me.

"*Juden!*" I shouted and I cold-cocked him, knocking him to the floor. "*Juden! Juden!*" I shouted over and over, and I started kicking the fellow.

Others nearby were drunk enough to join in and start kicking too, while the fellow's friends tried to fend them off. In seconds, a jolly little brawl was underway. It didn't take much with the clientele of that establishment, I will say.

Linz and von Kleist looked over, distracted by the fracas. Riley, bless him, kept his head and struck von Kleist another series of blows in the midsection, but instant and potentially lethal retaliation drove him back. Seeing a path open in the melee, I ran to the lamp, pulled it from the wall and crashed it with all my strength into the draperies that covered one of the front windows.

Now, if you ever find yourself needing to distract a vicious crowd of fascists and call for the attention of friendly communists hiding nearby, I fear you will have to devise a different strategy. You are unlikely in this modern age to have any kerosene lamps handy, and any draperies nearby would probably be flame retardant. I was luckier, for like many buildings in the Europe of 1919, the Weissbräukeller was a fire trap. The lamp exploded on contact with the wall and flames immediately leapt up the draperies in a most satisfactory fashion. It wasn't even necessary for me to yell "Fire!" for the cry was taken up immediately by all around me. Part of the crowd started fighting and trampling over each other to get outside, while the rest of the crowd was already fighting. Best of all, Schneider and his fifty faithful comrades finally sensed that something was up and came charging from the alley across the street waving their blackjacks and billy clubs. As they laid into the bullies emerging from the tavern, I became occupied in the brawl myself and lost all track of Riley.

42

Into the Isar

Riley

I was pretty much a goner. I was young and in good shape, but nobody can dance and duck like that for very long. It was only a matter of time before I stumbled and one punch with those knuckles von Kleist was wearing was all it would take.

When the fight started in the crowd, I knew I'd be dead if I took my eyes off von Kleist. I kept darting glances around, looking for a path to open up so I could run like hell out of there, but there were just too damn many Germans all around. Plus I'd seen that Linz carried a gun under his coat and would likely plug me if I made a break.

Then I got lucky. There were three men in a little knot at the end of the stage, wrestling and punching at each other furiously, and they fell onto the stage and knocked into von Kleist. Linz, meanwhile, was looking into the crowd and screaming for order. I threw my arm around his neck from behind, pulled his gun from his belt and kicked his sorry ass into the crowd. I spun on von Kleist to shoot him dead, but he was too quick. He saw what was coming and took off, leaping from table to table and onto the staircase he'd come down just a few minutes before. I got off two shots, but now more of the crowd was on the stage and I couldn't get a clear aim. So I followed him, table to table, then running up the stairs after the beast. Both of us naked as jaybirds, you understand.

I reached the top of the stairs. The tavern was filling with smoke, billowing in white and gray clouds as the timbers burned rapidly. I was faced with a short hallway with four closed doors, two to my left and two to my right. I had no training then, not in this kind of fighting, so I simply sprang to one of the doors and flung it open, holding Linz's pistol in front of me like a talisman. I found no one in there, just an empty, seedy bedroom.

I started to turn, but von Kleist flung open the door behind me and was on me. His massive arms wrapped around my body, lifted me off the floor and flung me down. The gun went flying. I rolled. Von Kleist stomped his foot down where my head had just been and I bowled into his knees, driving him back. He was still naked, but he must have been starting to dress, as he had taken off those damn brass knuckles. I looked around and saw that the gun had landed on the first step down from the landing. I jumped for it, landing belly down on the floor with my right hand grasping for it and coming just short. With my left hand, I grabbed the newel post at the top of the banister. Von Kleist was back on me, clutching my legs and pulling me backward, away from the gun, almost breaking my grip on the post. I pulled forward as hard as I could and, for an instant, we were in stalemate, two naked men, von Kleist pulling me backwards and me pulling forward. A few more inches and I'd have the gun.

Von Kleist pulled himself forward and placed his big right hand on my ass. I knew he'd pull himself forward again so when I felt his left hand pull up, I shoved myself forward the last inch and grabbed the gun. I swung my elbow backward and felt it smash into von Kleist's face. His reaction gave me just enough slack to spin onto my back and blow the son of a bitch to hell. But the son of a bitch didn't cooperate. He clocked me in the face and was off, disappearing through the open door he'd come from. I got off one wild shot.

I ran into the room just in time to see the bottom of the bastard's feet as he leaped out an open window. I got off another shot and stepped to the window.

Below me was the River Isar, which passed within two feet of the Weissbräukeller's walls. I was searching the dark water for von Kleist when, abruptly, he surfaced and began gulping air. He had dived in and then swum as far as he could to my left, toward where the street ran into the river. I thought to try a couple of potshots, but I wanted to conserve my ammo. Besides, I didn't think I could hit him when he emerged from the water as the distance and the angle were against me. So I jumped in after him. Feet first: I'm no diver.

With my arms and legs windmilling, I willed myself to hold onto the Luger. I hit the water and sank like a stone into the dark, cold depths.

43

Von Kleist's Ass

Cornelius

I fought my way out of that damn bar and I put my back against the outside wall, swinging a club I'd taken off a fallen comrade. Schneider was next to me, doing the same thing. He wasn't a big man, but he was game. He must have crippled or knocked unconscious a dozen of the bastards while we fought together side-by-side.

The fire grew worse, the heat driving all the brawlers farther into the street. No sign of cops or Freikorps or law of any sort. We heard an interior wall collapse. At the same moment, I was struck by a vision: a naked von Kleist running pell-mell away from the river and up the street in front of the Weissbräukeller. Before I could react, a fist crashed into my jaw. I recovered and cracked my assailant across the knees and then across his face, driving him back. A second naked man came running from the river after von Kleist. It was Riley, of course, and he held a Luger in his hand. I ran after him.

Von Kleist had a significant start and was well up the slope of the road, nearly at an intersection where he could turn off and drop out of sight. Riley sank onto one knee, extended the hand gripping the gun, and took careful aim. Von Kleist was still in range and he wouldn't miss. He pulled the trigger.

Click.

The gun was empty.

Von Kleist reached the crest of the slope. He turned for an instant to glance back at us.

"*Au revoir*, Riley!" he shouted.

He turned his back on us, bent at the waist and showed us his naked ass. Then he disappeared.

Riley dropped the gun and covered his face with his hands. I took off my jacket and draped it over him. Then I knelt beside him and put my arm over his shoulders.

"Let's go home," I said.

And that was how the Great War finally ended for Riley and me: kneeling in the flickering firelight from a fascist bar, watching von Kleist show us his ass cheeks. At least, the world thought the Great War was over. We were to learn that what we were living in then was only the intermission.

44

Going Home

Jim

"Well, I finished the first notebook."

"Christ, I should hope so. You only had a few pages left. Don't know why I had to sit for a week in this damn cold waiting for you."

Nice mood, Daddo.

Riley poured us each a glass of bourbon. His bags were packed and he was ready to ride. This would be our last night together for a while. I'd already decided I wasn't going to ask him about Herr Linz: he wouldn't tell me and I didn't want to give him the satisfaction. Instead, I asked why he and Cornelius decided to go home then, after chasing von Kleist all the way from Berlin.

"It's hard to say," Riley said. "We were hot to kill him, for good reason, but after what happened at that bar, we lost the will. Sometimes you can be all set on something one minute and then it just doesn't seem worth it. Don't know why. After all that work, listening to Germans jabbering and not knowing what was going on, getting the crap beat out of me by von Kleist, lying naked in the dirt, I just didn't have the energy any more. I wanted to go home. I wanted Marta."

I nodded.

"So how'd you get home?"

"Well, we were out of money and out of ideas. So we went back to Berlin and up to the first American army officer we saw and turned ourselves in. We were both AWOL by now. We sat in the cooler for a couple of days, not sure what they were going to do with us, and all of a sudden the clouds parted. They brought us drinks and slapped our backs and put us on the first boat back to the States."

"How did that happen?"

"We never knew. Somebody high up must have decided the less said about us the better, but whether that was Patton, or Pershing, or even Winston, we never knew. Anyway, we were on a liner with a bunch of other soldiers, hardly believing we were heading home. But Cornelius didn't make it back to the farm. Just like that song, 'How You Gonna Keep 'Em Down on the Farm?' That was Cornelius."

"Tell me."

Riley sighed. He poured another bourbon for himself.

"We hardly talked the whole crossing. We were tired, but something was eating at Cornelius. Being tired never stopped Cornelius from talking. He was thinking. And when we were almost in New York, he told me he wasn't going home. He was going to stay in New York City and seek his fortune. When we docked, Cornelius couldn't get down that gangplank fast enough. New York City caught him like a magnet and it never let him go, not to the day he died there. City wasn't for me, but there it is."

We sat and drank bourbon while Riley smoked.

"So he didn't go home to see my father?"

"No, he didn't." Riley looked uncomfortable. "Cornelius wasn't a family man. Maybe neither of us were."

There was a long pause. We had lots of those. Finally, Riley turned to the subject of the remaining notebooks.

"The next one to read is yellow. It's about the twenties and the death of Arnold Rothstein. Lots of trouble we had with gangsters back then. Will you read it?"

I'd been thinking about that very question. The first notebook was fantastic, even bizarre in parts, but I still wanted to read the rest of them. What worried me was the time spent with Riley, breathing his smoke, absorbing his negative attitude. Still, there was something about all this...

"I'll read it. And I'll talk to you about your version, just like we did for the first one. But I want something from you."

Riley's eyes narrowed. He wasn't really a giving sort of fellow.

"What would that be?"

"I want you to tell me what you and Cornelius were doing in Berlin when the wall fell. The whole family's been wondering. What could have dragged the two of you over there at your age?"

For once, I'd surprised him. But he agreed, as long as I promised not to tell anyone until he was dead.

This is what he told me.

45

Back to Berlin

Riley

We went because we were invited. The invite came from an old fighting buddy of ours, Stanislav Kirov, called Stan. He was a big gun at the KGB for a long, long time. He near killed us during the whole Klaus Fuchs business, but he wasn't a bad guy, considering.

We got letters from Stan now and again in the seventies, after he retired. The letters petered out in the eighties, maybe because we stopped responding. Cornelius was failing and I was never much for writing. Anyway, one day in 1989, I got a phone call from Stan.

"Comrade! Riley! You old bugger, how are your nuts?"

"Is this my pastor? I'm sorry I haven't been to church for a while."

Stan gave a throaty, raspy laugh that turned into a minute and a half of coughing phlegm.

"Riley, you old bastard. You okay? How's Cornelius?"

"You know how it is, Stan. We're both fucking old. How do you think he is?"

"Too bad. That Cornelius, he always made me laugh. Anyway, you boys need to come to Berlin. I want to see you."

"What the hell for, after all these years? We're not much to look at."

Stan's voice dropped.

"Listen to me, Riley. Things are happening. Berlin will soon not be the same as we knew it. I want to see it when it happens and I want you and Cornelius there with me. It is fitting."

We went back and forth, but I agreed. Cornelius was failing, more mentally than physically. He was forgetting basic things and it broke my heart to see it. But damn it, I wanted to go and I wanted Cornelius to go with me. If it killed us, what the hell? We were both more than ninety fucking years old.

So I flew to New York, signed Cornelius out of the home, and we went to Berlin. It was good to see him again. He was hard to talk to on the phone and I never liked telephones anyway. Together, we could be almost like always. It was tough in airports, though. Herding an old fart through an airport is tough, especially if you're an old fart yourself. But we made it and the cab took us to a hotel on the old Kurfürstendamm. Many memories there.

It's not like we were ignorant of what was happening. The Soviet Union was going down the crapper, at long last. That Gorbachev fellow with the birthmark had one foot in the free world and one in Soviet Russia and, in that position, he would inevitably take it in the crotch. Berlin, the eternal hot spot of the twentieth century, was afire, almost reminiscent of 1919. We sensed it, even driving in. Or I did. Cornelius dozed.

Our cab took us by the Tiergarten. In my mind, I saw the tiger, von Kleist, Rosa. Gradually, I became aware that the people on the street seemed different, as though the night were special. They walked quickly, they smiled, they shouted happily. It was early evening on November 9, 1989.

We'd been told to meet Stan at the bar of the Adlon Hotel, just on the eastern side of the Brandenburg Gate. He promised me we'd have no trouble at the checkpoint and he kept his word. Stan still had weight in East Berlin, I thought, for we were waved through in an instant. It was heartening to stroll under the lindens over to the old Adlon. Cornelius knew right away where we were.

Stan was at the bar, telling God knows what stories to the barman and a waitress who hung on his every word.

"Comrades! Victor, Heidi, look! These are the most murderous secret agents the United States ever had! And look at them now."

Stan ordered some poor guests away from one of the tables and I settled Cornelius gently into a chair.

"I don't suppose they have bourbon in this joint."

Stan grinned devilishly. He held out his hand and the bartender placed in it a bottle of Jim Beam.

"I know you, Riley. I know everything about you. It's why you could never beat me."

"Bullshit," I said. "I'd say over the years, we came out about even."

Stan slapped Heidi on the bottom and pushed her away.

"You are entitled to your opinion, even when it is wrong."

He pushed himself precariously to his feet and dropped into a chair at our table. He'd obviously been there awhile.

"I do not know why I am so kind to you. You were both so much trouble to me over the years. But when I knew what would happen here, in old Berlin where we battled so well, I knew there was no one to share this with but you and Cornelius." He poked Cornelius in the ribs. "How are you, old man? How are you?"

Cornelius opened his eyes and gazed at the old spy.

"Fuck you, Stan."

He closed his eyes again, provoking a great Russian laugh.

"So what's going on that's so special?" I asked. "Is Gorbachev tearing down the wall? We both know that's not happening."

Stan put a finger against his nose.

"There are more things in Heaven and Earth, Riley, than are dreamt of in your philosophy. Look out that window."

I did. The crowds were growing in size and intensity. Everyone was heading westward, toward the Gate. If the people on the Kurfürstendamm were giddy, these East Berliners were euphoric. Something was up, I had to admit.

Stan explained it.

"Moscow decided days ago they just didn't care anymore, the wall is coming down. But the fools couldn't bring themselves to manage the message, so word is spreading quickly all over the city. One day soon, that wall will open up and the people will pour through, no stopping them. I thought you'd want to see that."

It was a lot to take in. For Cornelius and me, the Berlin Wall had become a symbol of the whole damn century. We'd seen the trenches,

351

the ideologies, the Nazis and their horror, the Cold War, the atom bomb. It was a crazy time, our lifetime, and somehow the Berlin Wall neatly summarized the way things were. For it to go? Things would be different afterward, that's all.

Suddenly, for no reason we could see, the pace of the passersby quickened. They began to run. Without the need for a word, all of us in the Adlon bar ran to the street to see. The Brandenburg Gate was only about two blocks away, the street jammed with singing, chanting, happy people, mostly young people. They held hands, swayed. Then, unbelievably, a head popped over the top of the wall. It was just a kid, looked to be about twenty. He pushed himself up, jumped on the top of the wall, raised his arms and shouted joyfully. The resulting roar from both sides of the wall might have been heard from Washington to Beijing. It was the sound of the twentieth century ending, a bit early, just as it started a bit late with the march of the Germans in August 1914 and the foolish Punitive Expedition in the Mexican desert two years later.

As we stood and watched, more bodies popped up on top of the wall and then they all started dancing on it, from both sides. American rock music blared from God knows where. Cornelius waved at the young girls passing by. I don't know what exactly he understood, but the joy of the night could not be denied. I owe Stan a debt. It was something to see.

We stood as long as we could, watching the party. I'd have stood there all night, but Cornelius was fading and Stan was drunk. Finally, by mutual unspoken consent, we wandered off in the opposite direction from the crowd, down the broad boulevard in front of the Adlon. At the first corner, Stan left us, off to whatever woman, whatever apartment he could find.

And so, once again as so often during our many years, we found ourselves alone. I felt Cornelius shiver and I wrapped his scarf more tightly around his neck. We made eye contact and smiled at each other. We'd had quite a century, quite a time. Then Cornelius and I strolled on, arm in arm Unter den Linden, surrounded by youth excited for the future, two old men remembering the past.

THE RILEY SERIES
James Anderson O'Neal

riley.threeoceanpress.com

" Riley was my grandfather on my mother's side.
He was born on May 6, 1898.
He died on October 18, 1993.
Every day in between, he was a tough son of a bitch. "

Riley produces a box of memoirs written by the late Cornelius. The memoirs, spiced with Riley's salty comments, recount wild adventures the two friends supposedly engaged in. The old men claim that, in their younger days, they battled Lucky Luciano and Chairman Mao, spied for Winston Churchill, traded barbs with Dorothy Parker, marched with Martin Luther King, enraged J. Edgar Hoover and Roy Cohn...

Who can believe these guys?

Believe them or not, you'll have a great time following Riley and Cornelius as they barge through history from Pancho Villa to the Berlin Wall, roaming around the world and across the 20th Century.

Next in the Riley series:

RILEY AND THE ROARING TWENTIES

No wonder crime reporter Cornelius loves the lights of Broadway. He spends his days and nights with Dorothy Parker, Damon Runyon, Harpo Marx, and J.P. Morgan, while tracking the exploits of gangsters from Lucky Luciano to Al Capone. But when criminal mastermind Arnold Rothstein gets Cornelius in his clutches and squeezes hard, can even Riley save the day?

threeoceanpress.com

CPSIA information can be obtained
at www.ICGtesting.com
Printed in the USA
FSHW04n0519200418
47180FS

9 781988 915036